A SWIFT AND SUDDEN EXIT

NICO VINCENTY

CONTENTS

AUTHOR'S NOTE

A Swift and Sudden Exit contains sensitive material including, but not limited to: medical procedures, alcohol consumption, domestic violence (off page), violence (on page), sexual content (on page), queerphobia, misogyny, police brutality, injury, and death.

For Liz, who loved both time travel and bisexuals.

2058

THE MOON WAS FULL, and burned with the fire of a dying sun.

Zera drew the short straw that night and donned the ill-fitting protective suit before venturing into the barren wasteland she used to call home. Gravel crunched beneath the thick soles of her reflective boots, the sound muffled by her helmet but resonating in her teeth. Sweat dripped into her eyes. Her helmet, set at full opacity, restricted her vision even further. But the darkness was better than a wild case of moonburn on her face.

"I hate this," she muttered into her comms.

"Everyone hates it, you're not special," Kissi said. "Keep going north."

"You should come down here, Kissi." In the distance, she spotted the tell-tale darkness of the Pit. "Instead of hiding in that cushy computer room."

"Lose a limb and you can join me—not that you could hang in here. This requires finesse, which no one has ever accused you of having."

"What can I say? All brawn, no brains," Zera huffed out. The heat surrounded her chest and compressed it, more like diving into the ocean than walking across the Earth's surface. Loose ground shifted as she climbed over a short rise; whatever building this used to be, it was long gone, crumbled to dust in the unrelenting fire of the days.

"Please tell me they just need surface minerals tonight," Zera said.

Kissi was silent. Zera could picture her analyst rearranging her locs, ignoring the question.

"Kissi?"

"I don't wanna say it," she replied.

Zera let out a prolonged groan.

"You could've warned me before I left."

"There wasn't time! I promise I'll make it up to you when you get back."

"I'll put it on your tab." She checked her wrist band, analyzing her oxygen and heat levels, as well as the charge in the tank she carried on her back. Did she want to use the energy to cool herself off now, or later?

She eyed the Pit in the distance. Later. Definitely later.

"I've got you clocked at a kilometer out," Kissi said. "Accurate?"

"Unfortunately," Zera grumbled. "Need anything while I'm out?"

Kissi hummed. "We're out of milk. And bread."

"I'll add it to the list."

"Oh! And apples."

"Oh, no, those are way too expensive."

"I'll pay you back."

"I know your salary, you can't afford it."

The moon was halfway through its ascent, so Zera picked up her pace. It was a particularly boiling night, and the sooner she reached her destination, the better. Another fifteen grueling minutes passed before she reached the lip of the Pit, its depths cool and inviting and just a little deadly.

"There you are," Kissi said. The comms crackled as another line opened. "Okay, set your scanner for copper, nickel, and anomalies. You've got Lieb on standby."

"If anything goes wrong, just count me dead then," Zera said.

"Try not to do anything stupid, I'm really comfortable here," Lieb said, his voice as deep and gravelly as the earth below her. He added a groan akin to a grandfather in a rocking chair, just for good measure.

"Ah, the sounds of an angel. You know, you could always make a comeback out here. I get lonely sometimes." She sighed wistfully.

"We're not supposed to waste resources. Don't mess up so I can get a raise for conserving energy."

"You're certainly very good at that," Kissi said, which earned another fatherly scoff.

Metal clanks reverberated through the suit as Zera unhooked the two-meter anchor pole from her back, the drill bit hitting the ground with a muted thud. She dragged it in a cursive spelling of her full name until it beeped for a solid spot, then pushed the drill lever and grabbed the wire from her thigh holster. Leaning into the pole, she used her weight to hold it while it drilled into the ground.

"Sounds extra hard tonight," Kissi said.

"That's what he said," Lieb chimed.

"Not to you," Zera grunted, losing her balance as the post hit its mark.

"Says who?"

"I'll keep my sources secret, thanks." With the anchor in place, Zera was able to hook the wire to her harness. The Pit lurked at her back now, an ominous gap threatening to swallow her. It was creepy as hell, but at least it wasn't as hot as the other dig sites.

"Anchor set?" Kissi said.

"Yep. Stability?"

"Reading one hundred percent. Carry on."

"Alright, going in." She held the wire and leaned back, letting it take her weight while she was still within reach of the edge. When the anchor held, she loosened the wire and started her descent, ignoring the sensation of forgetting something.

"Did you change your scanner settings?" Kissi asked.

"Of course I did." Zera dug her boots into the brittle earth, her stance wide enough to keep stable while fumbling with the machine on her wrist band. The picks hanging at her belt clanked as she shifted, and the thin wire groaned.

"Jesus, did you forget your knife, too?"

"Shut up, Lieb, no I didn't." She reached down to check her ankle just in case. Yep, still there. "Okay, back on the roll."

"Finally," Lieb grunted.

"Didn't you dig up rocks in your past life? Where's your patience?" Zera asked.

"Burnt up with everything else."

"Moon's rising quick and Theta team is beating us, let's go," Kissi said.

Zera didn't need to be told twice—if the other team beat them back to the hatch, she'd rather stay outside and die with the sunrise instead of facing the endless harassment.

She kept one hand on the wire and the other on the wall while the blue lights of her scanner danced like stars on the gray dirt. The temperature in her boots dropped dramatically as she dipped below the moon's sight, a welcome but limited reprieve from the heat. Inch by inch she descended, hoping and praying the scanner wouldn't ding until she fully submerged.

At least one deity listened, and she got below the shadow line without the scanner sounding for the desired minerals or anything weird in the dirt. Her relieved sigh bordered on inappropriate, but she didn't care, too busy sending some gratitude out into the universe. A tap to the top of her helmet reduced the opacity to zero, which made her search much easier.

"Kissi?"

"All clear," she said. "No dust storms in sight, nothing on the Richter. Anything interesting?"

"Nope."

"Good," Lieb said. "Maybe I can take my boots off."

"Don't jinx me."

Zera continued down, eyes and wristband both scanning the area. Once the initial adrenaline rush settled, the job got terribly boring, a slow race between the moon and the scanner.

After an hour of scanning, stopping, and scraping, Zera sighed and said, "Tell me a story." She had one mineral canister full after a lucky find, but a dry spell kept her second one pitifully empty.

"Absolutely not," Lieb said.

"She was talking to me," Kissi said. "I'm the best storyteller around."

"Oh, here we go." Even though Zera couldn't see Lieb, she could *feel* him roll his eyes.

"Once upon a time, in a land far, far away, there was a place with two moons."

"Oh, shit," Zera said. The blue lights stopped on a pocket of rocks, and she planted her feet and brought out the canister. "Was everything on fire?"

"No, these were normal moons," Kissi said as Zera scraped into the canister.

"Technically it would mean a normal sun."

"Do you wanna tell the story?"

"You know higher-ups listen to these comms, right?" Lieb said.

"Yes, and later they'll commend me for keeping up morale with our digger," Kissi said. "Now, where was I?"

"Two moons."

Zera plucked the last bit of the deposit from the wall. Her underalls stuck with her sweat, the stretchy fabric sending puffs of warm air through the suit.

"Right, two moons," Kissi said. "And the two moons were also goddesses."

"Didn't see that coming," Zera said. A few feet further, she found another deposit. "Jackpot."

"Right? Not just one, but *two* goddesses," Kissi said.

"No, I—never mind. What about these goddesses?" She excavated, racing against the fast approaching shadow line above her.

"Oh, well they were the embodiment of good and evil, of course."

"Of course."

"This is the most boring story I've ever heard," Lieb said.

"Maybe if you stopped interrupting me—"

Something sparkled in Zera's headlamp as she visually scanned the area, nearly making her drop the pick and the canister. Nothing ever sparkled down here.

An anomaly? Anomalies were worth their weight in gold. If she could bring one back to the bunker...

She finished mining while Kissi and Lieb squabbled like geriatric siblings, the sparkly object winking in her periphery. The scanner didn't pick it up, even when she pointed right at it, but it was probably because the angle was off. If she hurried, she could grab it and get out before they'd even finished their argument.

With the full canister lidded and firmly attached to her belt, she turned her attention to whatever had the audacity to shine in this barren waste-land. It was only ten meters to her right, she could side step over to it, no problem.

Kissi and Lieb were now discussing years of service, the story long forgotten. Zera moved, carefully crawling sideways using the handholds of diggers gone by. The wire groaned in protest as the angle steepened, but the anchor held fast. As she got closer, she saw something smooth and silver stuck in the rock. Oh, this would be good.

The anchor shifted slightly. Her body dropped a few inches, and her stomach dropped to her boots.

"You good?" Kissi asked, coming out of the conversation at Zera's strangled gasp.

"Yeah, yeah I'm good," she said. "Anchor just shifted a little."

"Get out of there," Kissi said, voice sharp. "You're at ninety percent."

"It's okay, it'll hold."

"Kissi's right, any sign of trouble means get the fuck out," Lieb said.

"It's fine," Zera insisted. She shifted her weight, and the anchor held. "I think I found something."

"Whatever it is, it ain't worth it, kid. Don't make me come drag your ass back here."

"First of all, you're only like, fifteen years older than me." Zera made a solid base with her feet and tried to keep the pressure on the wire even. If she reached just right, she could grab whatever the thing was. "Second, I've almost got it."

"I'm serious, Zera. Get out."

The wire groaned again, but she reached the object, a shock going through the suit as she made contact. Now she just had to pry it out. She wiggled it and some of the dirt gave way around it, but the thing stubbornly held its position.

"I've got it, I just need to..." She put a little more muscle into the wiggle, and the earth spat it out. "Neat."

The round, silver thing was extra shiny in her headlights, and heavy in her pocket when she dropped it in. Then the ground creaked, and a shiver traveled down the line.

"Oh, no."

"Zera?"

"You weren't supposed to hear that."

Another shake of the line. A squeal down the metal. The cord gave, just a little. Problem was, it wasn't supposed to give at all.

"Oh, shit!" The anchor pitched forward. Zera stabbed her picks into the wall and jammed her feet into the dirt as the line slackened.

"Zera!" Alarms from Kissi's computer screamed through the comms. "Hang tight."

"I'm on the way," Lieb said, and Zera could barely hear the sound of him donning his gear over the rushing in her ears.

"Okay, I'll just hang out," she said, her voice an octave higher than usual.

"The anchor stability is at fifty percent," Kissi said. "It'll hold as long as you don't move."

Zera nodded, though they couldn't see it, and changed the helmet shield opacity to one hundred percent again as the heat slowly rose in her suit. The moon was nearly overhead now, and soon the edge of the Pit wouldn't protect her.

"Lieb, what's the ETA?" she asked.

"Eight. Shit." The sound of a vehicle choking and backfiring made her wince. "Engine's too hot. Gotta toss some water on it, so maybe fifteen. Hold tight."

An awfully long time to hang on a wall. The anchor lurched again, dropping more of her weight into her already tired limbs.

"I think I can climb." It was a better alternative than waiting for her muscles to give out. "Kissi, can the roller work at fifty percent?"

"What? No."

"You said that too fast."

"I mean, it technically can, but you would have to take *at least* fifty percent of the weight. One wrong move and you're gonna find out what's at the bottom."

"I can handle it." She had no choice. She heard the car sputter and die again, earning a few more creative expletives from Lieb. "I can do it, just keep an eye on me."

"Always," Kissi said. "I'm gonna manually override the roller, so when you give some slack, I'll take it up."

Zera smacked the button for her coolant. Cold spread through the tubes of her suit, chilling the sweat and making her shiver, which the already-loose dirt did not appreciate. With no choice but to proceed, she extended her arm as high as she could and swung the pick into the rock.

Gravel rained down, and she instinctively ducked despite the helmet. An experimental tug found her hold better than expected, and gave her the confidence to sink the second pick in. The next step was finding a good enough hold with her foot to push up.

"I think I got it," she said, just as the first pick stripped all the dirt from its place. She just managed to adjust her stance before the second pick took too much weight and sent her plummeting to her death.

"That sounded so confident," Kissi said.

"Shut up and take up some slack," Zera said through gritted teeth. The wire vibrated as the roller pulled at quarter-speed. Once it reached the maximum tolerance, it stopped, holding just enough of her weight so her arms didn't struggle.

Another two picks—this time with firmer test tugs—and she hauled herself up again, her muscles burning as she took her full weight. She called for Kissi to pull again and held her breath until it reached its end, as if that would help keep her buoyant against the gravity threatening to drag her down.

The sound of an engine sputtering to life came through the comms.

"We're up," Lieb said. "Hang tight."

"Doing my best," she groaned, and heaved herself up again.

It was slow going, but any progress was better than waiting for her arms to collapse. She could drown in her own sweat at this point. Even the outer suit stuck to her now, the weight of it making each movement harder.

"ETA three minutes," Lieb said, and Zera exhaled sharply.

"Take your time," she said, because she *had* to be a little shit about it.

"I mean, I can if you want me to—"

"Stop it, we're working here," Kissi interrupted. "Not to freak everyone out, but I'm starting to get some seismic readings, so if we could focus—"

"Let's go!" Zera said. She was close enough to hear the gears turning the reel. It felt like bad luck to think she'd almost made it, so she shut the thought out and focused on the next move instead.

With the lip of the Pit in sight, she started climbing faster, as if she could climb out before the earth noticed and gave way. The sound of Lieb's rescue vehicle carried past the scorched earth and tumbled over the edge into the Pit. She was so close to the top she could feel the vibrations in the ground.

Vibrations. The car wouldn't cause vibrations. She was well and truly fucked.

"Hurry, we're nearing failure and the Richter scale is climbing," Kissi said.

Zera could no longer waste her breath on a reply, and instead drove the picks into the shuddering wall to propel herself upward. It was more of a mad scramble than a climb, a race against the Richter. The reel turned and the wire squealed. The top of the pole appeared over the edge of the Pit. If she could just reach the edge before the quake hit...

Another centimeter appeared.

Then another.

The vehicle's rumbling stopped, but the ground's trembling continued. Suddenly the top of the anchor moved down faster than Zera was moving up. Kissi swore loudly in her ears. The vehicle door slammed.

The anchor broke free.

Zera's weight dropped and her exhausted arms screamed. Time slowed as the wire slackened. Would the anchor hit her? Or just pull her down with it?

The anchor weighed fifty kilograms. She weighed approximately seventy kilograms. If she estimated the distance to the top of the Pit to be ten meters and the anchor fell at the velocity of—

"Zera! Jesus Christ, climb!"

Lieb's voice, now in the same space instead of over the comms, broke her panic-induced physics reverie. He hung over the edge with two picks of his own, the blades sunk into the ground and holding her original anchor like chains on a swing. He actually *caught her*.

"Any day now!"

"Right! Kissi, let's go!"

She resumed her climb. Though the wire shifted and shook, Lieb managed to keep it just stable enough for her ascent. Each swing of her picks made her back ache, and her sweaty hands slipped in her too-large gloves. Everything from her shoulders to her fingertips was cramping, and she still had five meters to go.

"Zera!"

Right, focus.

"C'mon, kid, you've got this."

It was probably the nicest thing Lieb had ever said to her, and she was too tired to point it out. Dammit.

Her breath came in deep, gulping gasps as her muscles screamed for oxygen. The impending quake made her hands go numb. But she climbed and climbed, never entertaining the alternative.

"Grab my hand!"

Zera pushed up as far as she could and slung her hand up, crying out as she missed. Black surrounded the edge of her vision as her panic skyrocketed.

"Again!" Lieb interrupted her before she could spiral. Using the near-last of her energy, she climbed one foot higher. Then, with the absolute last of it, she reached again for his forearm.

An embarrassing sound of relief exited her mouth as her hand made contact and the rubber of her gloves stuck to his sleeve. He dropped the pick and grabbed her so hard she'd likely bruise through the suit.

"Unbuckle!"

She unhooked her harness and reached for his other hand. For one second, Lieb was the only thing keeping her from falling. The thought made her already-shaken head swim.

"Push!"

Zera somehow found enough energy to push with her legs as he hauled her toward the edge. She bumped both picks and the anchor as she rose, and she didn't even have enough time to hope they didn't grab her before Lieb rolled and pulled with his entire body.

"You've gained weight," he grunted as they tumbled onto the hot ground. The anchor, now free from its hold, clattered and clanged as it tumbled into the Pit.

Silence. Stillness.

Zera rolled onto her hands and knees, truly intent on standing. But then the quake hit, knocking her flat on her stomach and forcing the air from her lungs. She'd forgotten about it, with the drama of the last few minutes.

The ground rolled, and large chunks broke off the edge of the Pit. Zera grabbed Lieb's arm and shoved him away from the encroaching edge. Every time they tried to stand, the quake knocked them down, like it wanted the to Pit to catch them.

"Almost over!" Kissi's voice broke through the melee. Did she mean the quake, or Zera's survival?

Just as the new edge of the Pit reached their boots, the quake slowed and stalled. Zera laid on the quiet ground, the aftershocks shaking her brain as adrenaline slowly buffered from her blood.

"I've never been so happy to see your face," she said. Lieb's suit had a shadow on it from where he lay on the hot ground; the materials sector would be pissed.

"You can't see my face."

"Exactly."

"You get my girl?" Kissi asked.

"No, I let her drop."

"No need to be an asshole."

"'Thank you, Lieb,'" he mocked. "'Thank you for driving out here in the middle of the night and saving my life. Thank you for pulling me out of the abyss.' Oh, you're welcome, Zera. Any time. Anything for you."

"Thank you, Lieb." She pushed up and dragged him to his feet and into a hug, which lasted just long enough to make him uncomfortable.

"Yeah, yeah, you're getting soft." He gave her shoulder a rough pat before weaseling out of her grip. "What did you grab that was so important?"

"I don't know." She dug into her pocket. Turned out, it was an old-fashioned pocket watch, half the silver tarnished black. Grime and dirt cemented the seam shut, and her gloves were too thick to pry it open. Never mind—her knife would work just fine later.

"You're fucking kidding me," Lieb said.

"What is it? It better be good," Kissi said.

"Just some stupid pocket watch."

"Well I didn't know it was stupid before I grabbed it," Zera said. "We're told to grab anomalies. I spotted an anomaly, so I grabbed it."

"The scanner picked it up?"

Zera paused.

"Sure, let's go with that."

"Zera." The admonishment made Zera flinch.

Lieb's air left him in a slow, frustrated wave. "I hate you sometimes."

"Thank you for saving my life."

"You're not welcome. Get in the truck."

The rescue vehicles had no air conditioning, but they could at least roll the windows down to get some semblance of a breeze through the stuffy cabin. Protocol dictated the helmets had to stay on if the windows were open, but protocol didn't specify they couldn't crack the faceshield, just a little. The moving air, though scorching, was monumentally better than baking alive in the suit.

Kissi cleared her throat. "Just so you know, Theta *and* Epsilon both made it back already."

"Did any of them nearly die?" Zera asked.

"No, but—"

"So we still win."

"You nearly died trying to grab a fucking pocket watch, we won exactly zero things," Lieb said.

"I didn't just *try* to grab it, I *successfully* grabbed it."

"Both of you shut up." Kissi's sharp words snapped their jaws shut, and they bowed their heads as if she were physically there. They spent the rest of the trip in silence save for the shifting of the gears, though Zera felt Kissi's disappointment through the comms and dreaded the lecture waiting for her.

The moon was on her descent now, glaring angrily at their backs as they pulled into the hatch. Squeaks and squeals sounded entirely too loud in the enclosed space as the doors shut behind them, and Zera unbuckled and pulled off her helmet as soon as the light faded.

The first breath was so good it made her believe in love again. Relatively cool, sterile air soothed her roasted innards and settled quickly into her sweat-soaked uniform, sending chills slithering down her spine. Before she could stop herself, a satisfied groan escaped.

"Ew, stop that," Lieb said, glaring from the corner of his eye. She gave him a bright smile, then promptly raised a finger.

His retort was cut short as the door slammed open. Kissi leaned against the frame, her hand over her heart as she took them in.

"You scared me half to death. Don't be stupid like that again."

"I wasn't stupid, I was doing my job." Zera tugged off her gloves and hooked them to her belt, an excuse to move her hands and avoid eye contact.

"You did it stupidly."

"See, I told you," Lieb said.

Zera turned to find Kissi in her personal space, and in the blink of an eye she wrapped Zera in a tight hug.

"I'm disgusting right now," Zera reminded her. Sweat dripped from her short, dark hair, and with every movement warm air puffed up from her suit and into the cooler environment.

"I don't care." Kissi pulled back, the corner of her uniform damp from the contact, and smacked Zera with the back of her tablet. Her dark eyes shone in the low light. "You realize if you die out there, I have to sit and listen to the whole thing, right?"

Zera had forgotten that.

"Sorry, I'll be better next time." From now on, she was triple checking her anchor, and avoiding any anomalies the scanner missed, no matter how shiny they looked.

"Fuckin' better," Lieb muttered. "Did you at least get what you went for?"

"Huh? Oh, yeah, I did." She unhooked the canisters from her belt. "Our little adventure wasn't a total wash."

"Debatable." He put his helmet in the locker, then reached for Zera's and shut them both in. "I'm heading to medical. Kissi?"

He held out his wrist, and Kissi took the small, circular device from her belt and laid it on top of his band. When the light turned green, he stomped through the open door. Kissi gestured for Zera's hand and scanned her in also.

"I guess I should drop these and head that way too." Zera shook the canisters so the insides sounded like the rain recordings that played through the speakers some nights.

"Yes. Tell them to check your head." Kissi spun on her left leg, swinging the prosthetic one around before setting off. Zera followed, the aches and exhaustion settling in with every step deeper into the compound. The low light made her brain buzz, and made each step off-kilter no matter how solid the ground.

Perhaps getting a head check wasn't a bad idea.

2058

DEPOSITORY WAS the first stop following her near-death experience. Zera's two canisters were weighed and tested by an exhausted orderly in wrinkled fatigues. He cross-referenced the results with the assignments for the night, then packed the canisters into the fourth cubby behind him. Two of the twelve cubbies were full, the worst arrival time they'd gotten in six months.

"Anything else to declare?" he asked. Zera rested a hand on her pocket, the outline of the watch barely tangible through the thick fabric. It couldn't be important, right? Kissi and Lieb both agreed it was stupid.

Kissi elbowed her sharply in the spine. Well, there was her answer.

"Found this." She begrudgingly slid the pocket watch over. Now, in the light of the compound, she could see the tarnish over most of the silver. Noticing the one shiny spot must've been a miracle—or an omen.

The orderly picked it up, his thick, gray brows nearly meeting in the middle as he analyzed the watch through his bifocals. Zera resisted the urge to tap her foot as a dehydration headache settled behind her eyes.

"Probably nothing, but I'll pass it on." He tossed it unceremoniously into another bucket. Zera could feel Kissi's eyes boring into the back of her skull, but she chose to smile at the orderly and turn toward medical.

"'Probably nothing'," Kissi said.

"I heard him."

"You almost died for *probably nothing*."

"I was there, thank you." The headache now extended into her neck.

Kissi huffed and fell into step beside her. Her locs swayed as they walked down the hall, and her dark skin held an unusual pallor in the fluorescent lights. Guilt settled into Zera's gut at causing her friend such distress.

More diggers than usual filled the main medical bay. When Zera finished first, they got to enjoy an easy, quiet check up. Finishing later meant longer wait times, and a higher chance of landing the extra terrible bed in the far corner.

The blood analysis machine waited at the front, by far the worst part of the encounter. Zera put her hand in and looked up at the ceiling as the machine poked her finger with a needle. It was a tiny needle and a tiny sample, one she should have been used to giving, but idea of the stick still made her sweat. Protocol, they said. She might have too much radiation in her blood to survive one day, they said. But it wasn't today. Probably.

As she stepped behind a partition, she spotted Lieb lounging on one of the beds, chatting with his nurse and wearing his "charming" grin. The nurse—some new guy—apparently enjoyed the attention, as he kept reaching up to nervously fix a curl falling into his face. Zera moved quickly once she saw Lieb reaching to fix the curl for him.

"Every time," she whispered, unhooking her gloves from her belt and depositing them in the bin. Her sweaty boots squelched as she pulled her feet out before dumping them in the designated box. Her suit zipper caught every few inches, and goosebumps rippled across her pale skin as the cooler medbay air cut through her soaked underalls. The stretchy fabric stuck and fought as she wrestled it into the bin with an extra flourish.

When she was free from the clutches of her clothing, she hit the button to seal the chamber and closed her eyes. The room filled with a mix of steam and mist, the temperate water just present enough for her to scrub the sweat from her skin and hair. The edges of the droplets sparkled on the lines of her geometric tattoos now, which meant she was about fifteen minutes away from passing out if she didn't get to a bed.

She shut the water off and held onto the sides as warm air blew the remaining moisture from her skin. The heat and the exercise of the excursions were never her issue—it was the conversion from super hot to relative cold and all over again which made her feel sick.

Fresh fatigues and her lanyard and key card waited outside the shower walls, and she pulled them on with shaky hands and spotty vision. It was all she could do to stumble to the nearest bed, the stiff mattress reluctantly accepting her weight. It felt like heaven.

"Well, you look like shit."

Zera cracked her eye open to see a fuzzy, human-shaped being in black scrubs. She blinked a few times until the blob turned into a man of small stature, his red hair slicked back and his blue eyes glaring.

"Thanks, Martin. I feel like shit," she replied.

"Because," Kissi sang, rolling on a stool and crashing into the side of the bed, "she nearly died for *probably nothing*."

"How long are you planning to hold onto that?" Zera asked. Martin grabbed her hand and ran a scanner along the length of her forearm.

"You have to give me at least twenty-four hours."

"Ugh, fine." Zera looked at Martin. "How bad is it, Doc?"

"Not a doctor," he muttered. "You're hella dehydrated."

"Is that the true medical diagnosis?"

"Absolutely."

"Can you also diagnose her with dumbassery?" Kissi tapped her fingertips against the back of her tablet. "It's a deadly condition. She needs help for it."

"Pretty sure that's incurable," Martin said. "Let me get you a hydration pack and a protein pack."

"No, no, we don't need all that," Zera said, pushing herself off the bed. "You're supposed to just tell me to drink some water, then Kissi offers to give me hers for the day, and then we're golden."

She stumbled as her blood pressure tanked, the world going a few shades darker for a second.

"Sit your ass back down." Martin caught her by the arm, and even if she had a good four inches and thirty pounds on him, he somehow got her back on the bed.

"Martin, we haven't seen you in weeks, and the first thing you do is bully me and come for my pockets. You know I don't get paid enough for a hydration pack *and* a protein pack," she said, embarrassingly short of breath. She'd had to get two hydration packs last month after a bout of food poisoning, which took up most of her medical budget for the quarter.

"Charge it to me," Lieb said. Oh, good, he'd joined the crew around her bed too.

"Shut up, Lieb," Zera said.

"Just take it," he said. "I didn't need one tonight. Just give her mine, Martin."

"Will do."

"Hey, no, I don't need—"

"Maybe if you're hydrated, you won't make dumb decisions, hmm?" Lieb rested his hand on her shoulder. The back of his arm sported a purple bruise from the night's events.

Zera tried to glare at him, but the bright lights made it feel like her eyeballs were fracturing, so instead she glared at the ground.

"Thanks," she mumbled.

Lieb patted her shoulder a little too hard.

"Don't mention it."

"I won't." She settled back against the mattress while Martin procured the goods. With expert precision he stabbed her arm with an IV needle, too fast for her stomach to turn. She hated to admit it, but after a few minutes her headache receded, and her limbs felt less like they were made of concrete. Now she owed Lieb for saving her life *and* giving her water. How annoying.

Delta team's digger and their back up limped in a few minutes later, so Martin and Lieb's soon-to-be bunkmate both scrambled to get him to a bed. Kissi muttered that the guy's leg was definitely sitting at the wrong angle, and Zera decided that was *not* something she needed to see. Instead she closed her eyes and let the IV do its work.

If she did her math right, she had thirty-four more missions to run before she could retire. She was, officially, more than halfway done. And who knew, maybe the pocket watch she found would be a decent enough anomaly to knock off a whole mission.

"Huh," Kissi said, more to herself than to Zera.

"What is it?" she asked, keeping her eyes closed.

"Did you notice anything weird about the minerals you got?"

"...Why?"

"'Cause now they've got a different signature than when you first scanned them."

"Fuck," Zera said. "Is that bad? It sounds bad. Sounds like I'll have to go back out too soon."

"I don't think it's bad." Kissi didn't sound convinced. "It's just weird."

"What kind of weird?"

"I don't know, just weird." She shifted on the stool, tapping the tablet with renewed vigor. "Maybe it's just 'cause you had to go so far down for it. Different radiations at different elevations or something."

"It wasn't that far."

"You had eight more meters of cable."

"No shit?" Zera opened her eyes at that. "You didn't warn me?"

"It wasn't necessary, you had eight more meters," she said. "Look."

She showed her the tablet screen, where a bunch of numbers ran like ants.

"I have no idea what this means," Zera said, earning a groan. "Tell me, my beautiful friend."

"Fine, only 'cause you said I'm beautiful. The stuff around it is older, so my running hypothesis is that with its exposure to our air, it's trying to change its properties."

"Like it's been buried since before the 2040 Storm?"

"Possibly. It would explain the radiation differences, as well as the surface readings for electromagnetism."

"Oh," Zera said. At one point she probably knew why that was scientifically important, but she'd purged that knowledge and replaced it with survival skills.

"Are you listening?"

"Intently. I'm just not understanding," she admitted. "Took you a couple years, but you've gone full on analyst on me."

"Yeah, well, didn't have much of a choice." Kissi knocked her right heel on the floor. The prosthetic made a dull thunk against the linoleum.

"Stop that, you'll break it."

"It's fine." She waved Zera off. "I'm gonna flag the data and send it, see what they want me to do with it."

Zera leaned her head back and closed her eyes again. She didn't want to admit it, but her whole body ached from the effort of holding onto the wall, and the skin of her palms was shredded and tender despite her thick gloves. Her dehydration headache was gone, replaced by an aura in her vision and numbness through her ribs. Kissi could chase her mystery all she wanted—Zera was going to sleep.

"Hey, time to go." Martin's voice startled her. "I need this bed, we've got three serious injuries coming in."

"Got it," Zera said. Martin removed the needle from her arm, the bag next to her now sadly empty. Another one wouldn't hurt, but she had neither time nor funds available.

"Thanks, Martin," Kissi said with a smile. His cheeks turned a shade of pink made more obvious in the bright hospital lights.

"Always a pleasure," he said, voiced pitched a little higher. Before they could say anything else, he cleared his throat and walked away.

This time when Zera got up, the world stayed in one place, and she followed Kissi and Lieb out of medical and into the hall. It was the calm before the storm, the hallways eerie and empty except for the ghosts of diggers past. At a few minutes past four o'clock, they had just enough time to grab food from the mess, finishing their meals of potatoes and beans just in time for the morning bell to ring.

The sounds of cadets in the barracks rumbled before they got the main door open. Sergeants shouted as the initiates ran through the hallways, eyes barely open and fatigues nearly on. The air was so thick with nervous sweat Zera practically had to swim through it to get to the lieutenant doors.

"Ever miss it?" Kissi asked.

"Never," Zera replied. A cadet was on collision course with her, but she didn't move, holding her position and forcing the young man to dodge. He was bigger, but she was stronger, and the clip knocked him off course and into the wall. The part of her raised with manners wanted to apologize, but after spending years dodging officers herself, she knew it was best to keep walking. They all had to learn eventually.

"This is all my fault. Next time, I'm taking you out sooner," Kissi said. "Then we can avoid all this."

"This isn't your fault." She had the feeling Kissi wasn't just talking about the annoying cadets.

"I'm your watcher, it's my job to override if the situation is dangerous."

"You couldn't have known the danger."

"I should've."

Zera opened her mouth, but let the argument drop. Kissi had moved on from blaming her and was instead blaming herself. Eventually she'd realize it was just another accident. They happened all the time—it wasn't worth it to perseverate.

They reached the lieutenant doors, and blessed silence greeted them as they passed through. It wasn't much of a promotion, going from cadet to ground crew, but it was enough to get them a quiet barrack.

Day shift was up and at it, moving without any of the zeal or fear the cadets had. The two women in their bunk were already gone, the beds made and area spotless. This was one of Zera's favorite moments, coming home to a clean room.

"Are you gonna shower?" Zera asked. She leaned against the bunk ladder while untying her boots, ignoring the groan from the metal structure.

Kissi sat on the bottom bed and unbuttoned her fatigues. "Nope. Probably should since you had me sweating bullets, but I'm too tired now."

Zera certainly understood. Iron joists squeaked as she climbed to the top bunk and dropped onto it. The unyielding mattress protested her weight and her lumpy pillow gasped a dying breath, but it was the most comfortable thing she'd ever laid on.

It was easily five degrees warmer on the top bunk, but just as Zera thought to complain, she heard the hiss of Kissi releasing the seal on her prosthesis. She put the device next to her bed and pulled off the sleeve stuck to her residual limb. The scent of cleanser reached Zera's nose as Kissi wiped everything down and performed the daily maintenance needed for it with the same expert precision she used everywhere else.

Zera could handle the top bunk.

"'Night, Kissi," she mumbled. "Thanks for saving my ass."

"Hate you. Goodnight," Kissi replied.

<hr />

It was never possible to get enough rest in the barracks, even the lieutenant ones, but Zera had perfected the art of dropping into a deep sleep and staying there until the alarm sounded. They got to move at a leisurely pace, relatively speaking, and even had time to sit down for breakfast before training, though the meal was defined by awkward dinner portions and the standard allotment of burnt, stale coffee.

Zera didn't think her adventure the night before was that dramatic, but her body disagreed. Despite daily training, her forearms and shoulders ached every time she moved them, and the blood pounded behind her eyes as her body screamed for hydration. But when it came time to choose between a cup of plain water or a cup of coffee, she grabbed the latter.

"Training is gonna be a bitch today," Lieb grumbled. "Heard we're doing dead hangs."

"Don't speak that evil into existence," Zera said. Kissi rubbed her eyes, trying to work some life back into them. "What kinda numbers you got today, Kissi?"

"Probably figure out whatever you did wrong last night."

"That's a long list," Lieb told his coffee.

"Just hope you really didn't find anything," Kissi said. "I don't need you going AWOL."

"I won't go AWOL just 'cause I picked something up," Zera said, rolling her eyes.

"You don't know that!"

"It's just gossip," Lieb said.

"Exactly," Zera agreed. "They don't kidnap diggers, our numbers are already too low."

"Promises, promises," Kissi said.

"If anything, *you'll* go AWOL after finding the weird numbers," Zera said. "Remind me why they didn't tap you for an analyst role earlier? You're damn good at it."

"You're just saying that to make me forget about your stupidity," Kissi said. "But also, I figured I could do analysis as a retirement job. Something easy."

"Right." Zera didn't think the analyst position was easy at all, but it was another reminder of how smart Kissi was.

They cleared their dishes and weaved through incoming dayshifters. This was always the precarious time where the nightshift was still half asleep and the dayshift was exhausted. One wrong move would have her trapped in a pocket of slow movers and make her late to training.

"Kissinger! Zazzera!"

The call was so sharp Zera's body pulled an about-face before her mind caught up. Colonel Vylek, armed with her sleek officer's fatigues and a cold, gray stare, strode toward them like an oncoming train. All three of them snapped to, saluting her.

"At ease, Jesus," she said with a look of vague disgust. She nodded to Lieb. "You keep going, Liebowitz. I didn't call you."

"Yes, Colonel." He saluted and visibly relaxed, continuing his march to the training hall. Zera had the distinct feeling he wanted to make an obnoxious face at them, but couldn't risk being seen by Vylek.

"You two," Vylek started.

"Yes, Colonel," they said in unison. Beside her, Kissi gulped. Zera frantically tried to think of why they would be in trouble, with the pocket watch the only thing coming to mind.

"Come with me."

She didn't wait for acknowledgement. Zera chanced a look at Kissi, but her dark eyes stayed trained ahead as she moved to follow. Thanks to the adrenaline, Zera's muscles were no longer sore, enabling her to catch up without much issue. Any hunger she felt disappeared.

"Colonel, is this about—"

"I'll tell you when we get there."

"Yes, ma'am." Zera clamped her mouth shut. Excuses raced through her head. Sure, maybe the anomaly wasn't picked up by the scanners, but that's why they still used human diggers, because technology wasn't perfect. And maybe it was just a watch, but what if it was something important? She had to do her job. That was it, she was just doing her job.

Vylek said nothing as she led them through doors and halls well above their pay grade, eventually landing them in a command section.

The first thing to hit Zera was the temperature. Most places in the bunker were warm, and if they weren't warm, they were hot. On a rare day, they might find a nearly comfortable place, bordering on temperate. But this room? This room was *cold*.

How much energy did they use keeping the room this cold?

A large platform sat in the middle of the room, its surface raised to waist height. It didn't have any lights, but it made the whole room vibrate as if a swarm of bees was trapped inside. Wires tied together in bundles trailed away from it like dark tentacles in a gunmetal ocean, disappearing into pockets on the walls. Screens the size of Zera's bunk covered almost every vertical surface, displaying maps and waves and pictures of people she'd never seen around base.

"What in the holy hell..." She didn't have to be an analyst like Kissi to know they were doing something top-secret in this room, probably something dangerous.

"You two are being reassigned," Vylek said. Shivers went down Zera's spine, and they didn't come from the cool air.

"Reassigned to what, exactly?" she asked. Scrambling for some decorum, she added, "Ma'am?"

"Zazzera, you found an anomaly last night, correct?" Vylek didn't seem to think an answer was important.

"Yes, ma'am," she said. "I was told it was probably nothing."

"Oh, absolutely, it's worthless," she said. "But every once in a while, an anomaly has some residual radiation that activates something the 2040 Storm made dormant."

Zera's heart thumped so heavily she nearly choked.

"Am I radioactive now? Wait, am I dying?" Zera turned to Kissi, who took a wide step away from her.

"Why do they always think they're dying?" Vylek muttered, pinching the bridge of her nose. "No, it just changes the way your body interacts with the world."

"Then what's Kissi doing here? Or did I infect her too?"

"Have you always had a habit of questioning your superiors?"

Zera clamped her mouth shut, her cheeks burning despite the frigid air. She was just seeking clarification, but apparently Vylek wanted an audience, not a conversation. Kissi moved beside her and reached out just enough to hook a finger on one of her pant pockets, a small comfort.

"Since the 2040 Storm, each hub around the world has been trying to figure out a way to make the surface more survivable, or to reverse whatever happened eighteen years ago," Vylek said. She grabbed a tablet from a nearby desk, and the closest wall screen fizzled and changed to a map, the old state lines drawn over it. In the middle, an orange dot blinked.

"Here is the epicenter of the event. There was a shift in the magnetic fields, and light bent in ways previously only theorized. Gravity changed. Within moments, we went from this"—she put up a picture of a grassy field—"to this." The grassy field turned into the barren wasteland Zera crossed every few weeks.

Kissi stepped toward the screen, the light making her dark brown skin turn a midnight blue. "Like the curtain dropped," she said. That was how all the radio newscasters described it, back when they first retreated into the bunkers.

"The curtain didn't drop," Vylek said. "It tore."

Zera wished she'd paid more attention in science class. "I'm sorry, ma'am, but I'm having trouble following." Something tickled at the back of her brain, just out of reach.

"Something tore between space and time, changing the entire Earth in a few seconds," Vylek explained. "We've been able to lock onto that moment, and send people back to collect data in an effort to reverse the effects of the Storm in our current time."

Kissi's gaze snapped to Vylek, but the Colonel was staring at Zera. Despite the chill, a bead of sweat slid down Zera's spine.

"Time travel," she said. "You invented...time travel."

"Well, I didn't do it," Vylek said. She gestured at the desks around her. "People a lot smarter than me were in charge of that. I just wrangle the crew."

"How does it work?" Kissi asked. Before Vylek could answer, Zera added, "Do the people come back?"

A beat of silence. "Usually."

"'Usually?'"

Zera spoke before Vylek noticed Kissi's disrespect. "Ma'am, I'm still having trouble grasping the concept of time travel."

Vylek shrugged. "A cosmic catastrophe changed the world, and we figured out how to harness it for our own uses."

"I have a lot of questions," Zera said.

"And they'll be answered in due time."

"So you're serious? This is our reassignment?"

"Yes. Your post-dig tests confirmed you're eligible for the program." Vylek turned to Kissi. "You, Kissinger, just happened to show the right aptitude at the right time. I need another traveler and another anchor, and here you two are."

"Wait, I'll be stuck here?" Kissi said, straightening. She was trying to stay calm, but Zera knew her well enough to spot the way her eyes widened slightly and her chest rose. She was pissed.

Vylek rose to meet her.

"You mean, will your analytical skills possibly be instrumental in discovering the key to returning the world to a habitable environment? Maybe even before the earthquakes take us all out?" she said, her voice as cold as the air around them. "I hope that is what you mean, Lieutenant Kissinger."

Kissi's shoulders sagged slightly, but to her credit, she didn't look away. "Yes, ma'am," she said through clenched teeth. "That's exactly what I mean."

"That's what I thought," Vylek said. "Today, you are formally moved from ground crew to Tempus. Future dig missions are cancelled. You'll be moved to the barracks on this side of the base. And your training starts today."

A knock sounded from across the room, but not from the door they'd entered through. Vylek glanced at her watch. "Hmm, right on time. Come in, Dr. Doyle."

A middle-aged man entered, one wheel of his wheelchair squeaking with every turn. Though he wasn't particularly built, Zera could see the muscles and veins of his forearms bulging under the rolled up sleeves of his white lab coat. On his lap he carried a black box not unlike the ones diggers used to transport explosives.

Zera felt a drop similar to the one she almost had in the Pit the night before. How many missions would she need now until retirement? Did the count start over?

"These the new recruits, then?" Dr. Doyle asked in a thick Irish accent.

Vylek nodded, but Zera balked. "Wait, we're not recruits if we don't have time to think about it."

Apparently, that was the wrong thing to say. Vylek rounded on her with fire in her eyes.

"There is no *thinking about it*," she hissed. "You two are soldiers. This is your new mission. You can take it, or you can be dishonorably discharged and moved to the labor sector. Do you want to spend the rest of your days digging up root vegetables?"

"What?" Zera and Kissi said at the same time. Vylek sneered, and Dr. Doyle looked very much like he wanted to be anywhere else.

"I can come back," he said, gesturing toward the door, but Vylek gave a sharp shake of her head.

"Zazzera? Kissinger?" She raised her eyebrows. So this was it: either they were going to accept this change without a fight, or be terminated. Zera glanced at Kissi out of the corner of her eye and found her face resolute, the muscle in her jaw clenched as if she were holding back what she really wanted to say.

"Yes, Colonel," Zera said. Vylek didn't smile. When the silence stretched, Zera elbowed Kissi in the ribs, making no attempt to be subtle.

"Yes, Colonel," she said through gritted teeth.

"Very good. Have a seat."

Time travel. After years of digging in a dead, radioactive wasteland, now they wanted her to *time travel*.

2058

Zera sank into a chair as a rock settled in the pit of her stomach. Dr. Doyle gave her an encouraging smile, but it didn't do much to calm the rolling in Zera's gut.

"Sleeves, if you please," the doctor said. Zera rolled up her fatigues, exposing her forearms. The room was so cold goosebumps raced across her arms, and her nails turned an odd shade of blue.

Dr. Doyle popped open the case, revealing thick syringes with needles as long as her middle finger and big enough around for an ant to crawl through. Zera immediately looked to the ceiling. She wished they were explosives, then she wouldn't be on the brink of passing out.

"He's implanting a new tracker," Vylek said. "The ones you already have mark your location, but we need more power than that."

Something touched her arm and she jumped. Dr. Doyle looked at her, the alcohol swab suspended over her skin as he waited for her go-ahead.

"Sorry," Zera said, and looked away.

Zera kept her arm out and counted the ceiling tiles. Dr. Doyle lied that the needle would be a little pinch; it felt like a full on bite right in the middle of the sword tattoo on her forearm. The tracker slid into her arm with all the grace of a grain of rice down the windpipe. Her stomach clenched and black dots danced at the edges of her vision, but she kept her face neutral. At least, she hoped it was neutral—she couldn't really feel it.

Tattoo needles didn't count as real needles to her. After all, they technically didn't go below the skin. Injections felt different, felt *invasive*, and no matter how many immunizations or trackers she received, she never got over it.

"Good, Zera?" Kissi said. Her far-away voice broke the spell, and Zera's body stopped protesting so hard. The syringe was long gone, replaced with a piece of gauze and tape.

"You'll be a bit sore and have a bruise," Dr. Doyle warned. "But if—"

"Thank you, Doctor," Vylek said.

Dr. Doyle paused, then nodded and closed the case. His wheelchair squeaked as he exited the room.

Zera took a deep breath. "Yeah, I'm good."

"I'm glad." Vylek sounded neither glad nor concerned. "Training starts now, and you deploy in three hours."

"Three—three hours of training, and then she deploys to a different *time*?" Kissi said. Anger flashed across Vylek's face, and Zera jumped in to cover.

"What she means is, we may need a little more time. We're just trying to make sure we do our new jobs correctly."

"The job is the same as it's always been," Vylek said, her glare still on Kissi. "You'll go out to collect samples, and Kissinger keeps you tethered. Do a good enough job, and you'll need significantly less than seventy missions until retirement."

Early retirement? "And we'll be able to talk the whole time?" If she could talk to Kissi, she might just make it through.

"Of course not. She'll just anchor you here, and pull you back if necessary."

Zera gulped and attempted to control her breathing. Somehow, she would do this without any means of communication. This wasn't just any dig she was going on, and she had the distinct feeling Vylek was holding back major details.

"Any other questions?" Vylek asked.

"Tons," Kissi said, and Zera elbowed her again. She was already on thin ice, and Zera didn't need Vylek deciding Kissi wasn't suitable for the job. If she could trust anyone to bring her back through space and time, it was Camila Kissinger.

"Good. Go through those doors, there's another recruit in there waiting. Dismissed."

Zera snapped into a salute and Kissi followed, though her movements weren't quite as enthusiastic. When Vylek saluted and left, they relaxed, and Zera turned to the other door hiding in the dark corner of the room.

"You can't be serious," Kissi hissed.

"We don't have a choice," Zera said. "You heard Vylek, these are our orders."

"But this is insane, she can't honestly think they can send you to another time."

"Is it any different from sending me out into that wasteland we call a planet?"

"Of course it is!" Kissi made a frustrated noise before lowering her voice. "Environmental danger is one thing. This...this is a suicide mission."

"Do you wanna go back to the labor sector? 'Cause I sure as hell don't," Zera said, her hand on the door handle. "Now come on."

Kissi looked like she had no desire to follow. Zera understood her trepidation, but what choice did they have? They were soldiers, it was their job to follow orders—even if those orders were batshit crazy.

As promised, a lone figure waited for them in the small conference room next door. He was a couple of years older than her, maybe early thirties, and the classic kind of handsome reminiscent of times way before the 2040 Storm. A thin scar on his cheekbone marred his chiseled face.

He stood from his rickety, mismatched chair as they entered, holding out his hand. "Edward Byrd, nice to meet you," he said. He smiled a lot and held onto her hand for too long, as if they'd known each other for ages. And his grip was incredibly strong, which was a more admirable quality than the smile or the handsomeness.

"I'm Zazzera, this is Kissinger," Zera said. He wasn't privy to their nicknames, at least not yet. They had to almost die together at least once for that.

"No first names? Okay." He kept his tone light. Zera eyed the patches on his uniform. He had the same four-pointed star she'd received upon initiation into ground crew, as well as the blue sword and snake of the medical crew. Perhaps he was older than he looked; it wasn't easy to get multiple distinctions in a timely manner.

The door opened and another lab coat came in. Her hair was more gray than black, and pulled into a puff on top of her head. Zera could see a pen resting behind each ear, and a third in her hand. She squinted at them, ignoring the glasses perched on top of her head.

"Two travelers and an anchor, right?" She gestured between them with her pen.

Byrd put on that smile again and extended his hand. "Edward Byrd, nice to—"

"I know who y'all are." She batted him away. Now that she was closer, Zera could see *Dr. Laura Phillips* on her name tag. Phillips pushed up her sleeves, exposing medium brown skin, and said, "Sit down, sit down, we're running behind."

"We just got here," Kissi said.

Dr. Phillips made an indignant noise. "We're always behind! That's why we have to go back." She threw her arm behind her in a wide gesture, moving so fast the pen flew from her grasp. Without missing a beat she grabbed another one from her lab coat pocket. "Sit down and listen up."

Zera pulled out the nearest chair and dropped into it, reaching for the tablet waiting on the cracked table top. Kissi and Byrd moved slower, but Dr. Phillips didn't notice. She was at the screen in front, and hung her pen on her collar so she could trade it for a stylus.

"There are three basic rules you need to remember," she said. Zera leaned forward, her eyes on the screen instead of the tablet, even though they probably said the same thing. "Oh, wait! Your mission."

Zera was very focused on the rules, but she figured learning the mission was probably a good move too.

"The first ride," Dr. Phillips said, writing the numbers on the corner of the board, "is back to 2040. To the day of the Storm."

"We have to relive the Storm?" Zera had already survived it once, thanks to some quick thinking on her mother's part. She had no intention of attempting it again.

"No, no, no." Dr. Phillips sounded frustrated. Every new traveler probably asked that question, but Zera thought it was fair. "You're going back to the *day of* the Storm. The Storm starts at forty-three minutes past six. You hit your return call before that, and you're golden."

She attempted to scribble on the screen some more, but Byrd raised his hand. When she didn't turn around, he spoke.

"What are we supposed to do there, exactly? How many days do we get?"

"We'll get to that." Dr. Phillips waved the question away. "It's time to go over the rules. First off, you can't change anything, so don't even try. You try to change stuff, and things go bad."

"Then why are we bothering?" Kissi asked. Zera blinked and refused to look at her friend. Why did she ask so many damn questions?

"Good question, anchor," Dr. Phillips said without turning around. "We know we can't change anything, 'cause everything already happened. No one knows what caused the Storm, so we're just trying to reverse the effects here and now. And to do that, we need data."

"See? Just like our other job," Zera whispered. Kissi glared from the corner of her eye.

"Rule two! Don't try to find yourself," Dr. Phillips said.

"Find ourselves? People do that?" Byrd asked.

"Yes, and it's stupid. We don't have time for that! You only have time for data, data, data." She actually wrote the word three times on the board. "We need any sort of samples you can find. Air, dirt, grass, human blood, whatever you can scrounge up. But you have to be careful and mindful of the time. You have one return syringe. It gets broken, you're at the mercy of your anchor noticing and pulling you back."

Zera glanced at Kissi, and she nodded in return. There was no doubt about it—Kissi would take care of her.

"That feels inadequate," Byrd said. "After all, what if we get separated from the syringe in an emergency situation? We should have a back-up."

"You got the funds for that?" Dr. Phillips turned to squint at him. "Didn't think so. Rule three, don't talk to anyone. It's not worth it. There's no last-time flings, or confessions, or apologies. Everyone is already dead, so don't waste your time."

"I feel like that should be rule one," Kissi muttered. Zera knocked Kissi's ankle with her foot. Now wasn't the time for quips, it was time for learning so she didn't die somewhere between time and space.

"Just 'cause you can't change anything doesn't mean you should try for mass chaos or any of that nonsense. The amount of trouble you cause is indirectly proportional to your likelihood of survival. Trust me, we've got the data to match it."

Don't change things, don't find yourself, don't talk to anyone. Three simple rules, not unlike the ones for digs. She was just mining in a different time period.

"Everyone keeping up?" Dr. Phillips nodded. "Good. Let's discuss data collection."

Zera wondered if Dr. Phillips knew she hadn't technically introduced herself yet. The doctor went through an entire lecture on how to collect samples and transport them back to their time. All in all, it wasn't that different than Zera's initial assignment. She could do this. She just had to bury her deep fear of the situation in the recesses of her mind.

"How dangerous is this?" Kissi asked when Dr. Phillips paused for breath.

"Oh, tremendously," she said, as if that were obvious.

"Have people died before?"

"Many times."

"How many?"

Zera really, *really* wished Kissi would stop asking questions.

"Yeah, that's not my department," Dr. Phillips said. "Look, I can get you there, and I can give you a way back. What you do in between those two moments is on you."

Silence pressed on them, and the dread that had been threatening Zera this whole time expanded in her stomach and chest. The digs didn't seem so bad now. Hells, even the labor sector didn't sound like a bad idea.

"Alright, let's go for final checks." Dr. Phillips waved both arms to shepherd them out of the room.

"That's it? That's the whole training?" Kissi sounded alarmed. Zera's heart jumped too. It felt like there was a page missing in the manual, a very important page. "I haven't seen the equipment, or the program, I'll have to configure my settings—"

"All that will be done while your traveler is getting final checks," Dr. Phillips said, exasperated. "Now come on. We're short on time."

Byrd hopped up and opened the door, holding it open for them to pass through to the next room, where three soldiers waited. Two directed Zera and Byrd to another door on the right, while the third took Kissi back to the first room. Zera's heart squeezed painfully as Kissi moved further away. How would it feel when they were literal years apart?

"Just the travelers then, hmm?" Byrd said. Zera kept her head forward. If she made any attempt at a friendly conversation, she might throw up. "Ah, I see. You're psyching yourself up."

"Something like that," she said. It was mission time, and she had significantly less time to prepare and considerably more distractions. She ran down the list of gods in her head, praying to Jesus and Allah and throwing a Hail Mary in for good measure as she changed into underalls and new black fatigues. She used both the Greek and Roman names for Ares and Hermes and Artemis just in case they were feeling some type of way today as she loaded her pockets with sample containers. She even reached out to Vishnu and Freya as she strapped a pistol to her ankle and knives to the back of her belt. Surely *someone* was listening.

Byrd looked entirely too excited about the situation. Sharing a changing room wasn't a new occurrence, and Zera rarely, if ever, glanced anyone's way, but scars crossed Byrd's torso like he'd been beaten or whipped or both. She looked away before he could notice her staring, and she wondered how a person could get hurt so many times and still be alive. But it seemed Byrd's scars didn't bother him, as he had an actual pep in his step when the soldiers led them back to the main room.

Zera's adrenaline pushed heat through her veins. Her body, despite being accustomed to the current climate, started sweating. Perhaps, she thought, it wouldn't be so hot in the past.

There were more people sitting at the desks in the first room now, and it took a second for Zera to find Kissi in the group. She was bent over the screen, her fingers flying as she set everything the way she wanted.

"What do you think?" Zera asked, showing off her new fatigues instead of vomiting like she really wanted.

"About the same as my old software, really," Kissi said, her eyes on the screen instead of Zera's outfit. "I can track your time placement and your relative location, and the tracker even gives me some of your vitals. Your heart rate is one-oh-seven, by the way."

"Sounds about right." She dropped her arms. "This is insane, yeah?"

"Absolutely."

"I can't wait to tell Lieb about it."

"If you survive."

"Way to be encouraging, Kissi." Zera ran her hand through her short hair, keeping the movement casual instead of nervous. "Just what I need to hear before this crazy mission."

"Just being realistic," Kissi said. "I had a second to check through the drives. There's been a lot of deaths. Like, a *lot*."

"Please don't tell me. How long have they been doing this?" Zera casually looked over her shoulder to make sure no one was within earshot. Byrd was at a different desk, chatting with the person Zera assumed was his anchor.

"A long time. Like, a weirdly long time," Kissi said. "Phillips wasn't kidding, they have a lot of data. Things are improving with time, but it's still not great odds."

"I'll be careful."

"Damn right you will be." Kissi shifted in her chair, almost like she was going to stand, but instead just reached out and took Zera by the hand. "They said I can bring you back early, so try not to do anything stupid."

"I never actually *try* to do stupid things," Zera said. *Just another dig.* As long as she thought that, maybe she wouldn't devolve into an existential crisis.

"Ready, Zazzera?" Byrd said, clapping her hard on the shoulder. Zera locked eyes with Kissi, who was doing her best not to laugh.

"Keen and green," she replied. Kissi turned a snort into a cough. If Byrd caught on to the jab, he didn't show it.

"We're making history here," he said, moving toward the platform. He sounded like he actually believed it.

"Just like all those who went before us," Zera muttered. Vylek and Phillips entered the room, and the doctor made a beeline for Zera. She waved some sort of sensor over her, the green light reflecting in the lenses of the glasses she'd finally found on her head.

"Yes, yes, these are good readings," she said, though Zera wasn't entirely sure she was talking to her. "Yes, you've got good potential. Okay."

She flitted over to Byrd and repeated the process while two soldiers beckoned Zera toward the center of the room, right next to the massive platform. They pushed her arms out and her legs apart and patted down her body, checking and double-checking the carabiners holding her supplies to her belt.

Dr. Phillips handed each of them an autosyringe. "You've got ninety minutes once you get there. Make sure you punch these into your leg before then, and it'll bring you back here."

"Should we synchronize watches?" Byrd's grin was entirely too big. Zera tried to smile back, but nerves tightened her jaw.

"I'll just count on you to keep time," she said.

"Let's go!" Dr. Phillips shoved them toward the platform, and Zera nearly tripped over the mass of cables. Byrd grabbed her by the back of her uniform, steadying her. She sent back a more genuine smile, and turned to the machine that would send them back in time.

"Ladies first," one of the soldiers said. When she passed the inspection, they pushed her up. The black material was dense, and the vibration of the machinery beneath was so powerful it muffled her steps.

Vylek stood at the back of the room, leaning against the wall with her arms crossed. Her face was blank except for the grim set of her mouth, and when Zera made eye contact, the Colonel held it. Locked in her gaze, Zera wondered if the Colonel was committing her to memory, just in case she lost another soldier.

Zera broke first, the surface of the platform suddenly becoming very interesting. Two Xs dictated where her feet belonged, and the buzzing of the machine drowned out her thoughts and numbed her legs. She could see Byrd out of the corner of her eye, practically bouncing like a kid. Kissi focused on the screen in front of her, another lieutenant in black scanning her work. He gave a thumbs up to Phillips, who passed the gesture on to Zera.

"Systems are ready, Zazzera. You should get there at thirteen minutes past five."

Zera nodded and moved her head side to side, the cracks from her neck the only thing loud enough for her to hear.

"I'm ready," she said, uncertain if they could hear her. Kissi looked like she wanted to say something—maybe goodbye, maybe *stop*—but pressed her lips together and returned to the screen. This was her part of the game.

Kissi gave the computer a command, and the idling machine kicked into gear. The hum was now a roar, threatening to deafen Zera. It felt like her bones were breaking, like her blood was bubbling, like every molecule was threatening to tear apart from the rest. Her teeth chattered so hard she thought one might chip, and her muscles spasmed as she clenched her jaw against it.

"Wait, I don't have a scanner!" she called.

"Don't know what to scan for!" Phillips yelled back.

The lights cut in the room as the machine stole the energy. The air, previously so cold, now inched toward boiling. Lights appeared around the ring of the platform. They moved toward Zera, and every sensation intensified. Another step in, and she thought her lungs and heart would burst from her chest. Another step, and she could no longer hold in the scream.

Blackness spiderwebbed her vision. The lights were one step away now, and her body was numb. There was no air, no feeling of gravity, not even any pain. She could no longer see the others in the room—they were all hidden behind the stars exploding in her eyes.

Her body ripped apart.

It wasn't painful, not really. One minute, she knew where every limb was, how every joint was positioned. The next, it all disappeared.

She saw stars again, but these were real stars, watching from the cold, dark sky as she floated. Waves of green and blue and purple rose around her, carrying her and drowning her in their light. The stars blinked out one by one as the river overtook them, and its energy pushed and pulled Zera in every direction, tearing her body apart and putting it back together with each movement.

There was no time to be afraid. Her mind wasn't present enough to formulate fear. Something in her blood told her not to fight it—the current of time would win, no matter how hard she tried.

She closed her eyes against the bright light, but it barely dimmed the flashes. She was moving faster now, or was it slower? The current raised her and dragged her down, a weight tied to her chest as she sank further and further. The deeper she got, the more the colors changed, from green and blue to orange and red. The red got darker and darker, fading through each shade of blood until the inky black swallowed her whole.

IT TOOK a moment for Zera to realize the river had spat her out. Ringing stabbed her ears, and her bones felt denser than lead. Her first gasp proved painful, like shards of glass sat in her lungs, but the next one was a little easier, and the one after that almost painless. Lights danced in her eyes though they were closed, and she wondered if she was still in the room, lying like a fool on the platform.

Except it was warm.

It wasn't the stuffy sort of warm of the bunker, nor was it the blistering heat of the surface. The temperature was gentle, and as the stars faded she saw flickers of light and shadow. The ringing faded too, replaced by the soft rustle of leaves as a cool breeze kissed her.

Zera opened her eyes and saw real, green leaves attached to a real, live tree, one that reached for the sun instead of red and blue lamps. Grass tickled her neck—grass growing from the actual ground. Birds sang, insects buzzed, and when she took another deep breath, she didn't smell burning. For the first time in eighteen years, she smelled the sweet, rich earth of Central Park

She was twelve years old when the 2040 Storm happened; old enough to remember the way the world was, but too young for the details. She remembered kicking a ball around a field with grass just like this, and rows of kids with backpacks walking single file, and tan skin as she waved goodbye to summer camp friends. Life was so bright, so open. So different from how she lived now.

She didn't cry, though nostalgia and longing swirled in her chest. The view was perfect and beautiful, even if the trees were unkempt and rocks poked her backside. Free air, *outside* air, blessed her lungs. It was liberating, intoxicating. She wondered why she'd hesitated to accept this mission, or how she was supposed to return to the dark and heat. Her heart pulsed at the thought and brought her closer to crying than the memories ever could.

Her watch beeped, alerting her fifteen minutes had passed. The glow of the moment dulled as she remembered the world was ending in a little over an hour, and she'd wasted valuable time just staring at the park.

She ran her hand through her short hair, ignoring the grass and dirt stuck in it. If anything, they would be a trophy, though Phillips would probably count it all as samples and make her sit there until someone collected every last bit. Or maybe they'd make Byrd do it.

Byrd. Where the hell was he?

Nature was loud. Where she came from, the world was quiet except for the wind making dust rattle across the dead and barren land. Beautiful music surrounded her as she searched for Byrd, pausing to fill her sample canisters one at a time. Here, birds sang and insects buzzed and leaves ran all over each other. If she strained her ears, she could hear the city humming and murmuring, and chatter from people on the hidden trails.

She could also hear someone retching, much closer than the path.

Zera ducked behind a tree and tried to pinpoint the person's location, but it got lost amidst the rest of the noise. If she remembered right, there wasn't a trail nearby. What was the likelihood of the person being a patron of the park?

"Zazzera!"

Well, that answered her question.

Relief flooded through her and she stepped out from her meager hiding place. Hearing his voice quieted the fear in the back of her mind that Byrd hadn't made it.

"Byrd!" she called.

"Zazzera! I'm here!" He sounded close, and now she could hear his steps in the brush. She climbed over a small ridge and found him wandering below, his head on a swivel as he searched for her.

"You must have a great analyst," Zera said, leaning against a tree. Byrd spun and his hand went to his pistol, but relaxed when he saw her. "You can't track for shit."

"Well it's harder to track when there's actual foliage," he said, smacking a tree branch aside. Predictably, the branch swung back in his face.

"How the hell did you get chosen for this?" she asked, though she couldn't hold back a grin. She usually didn't get to have anyone out with her on a mission. It was kind of fun.

"Dumb luck, of course." When he and the tree reached an agreement, he stood tall and put his hands on his hips. "Now, we're here to explore, right?"

Zera hoped he was kidding. "We're here to get data. Did you not hear Phillips?"

"I heard most of it," he said, waving her off. A pain went through Zera's stomach and she swallowed it down. He was probably just showing off, doing the same dance most of the other people in the unit did. Everyone was tough until they got caught in the trenches.

"Well, I'm gonna get samples." She gestured to her belt and pointed to the north side of the park. "Should we head that way?"

"I'll go the opposite, cover more ground," Byrd said. Zera didn't like the idea of splitting up, but he was already walking away with his chest puffed. She could be annoyed at his antics, but she chose to smile and hoped the fake expression might form some real joy. After all, they were back in the real world, with the way things were supposed to be. People could go outside, meat was readily available, hell, she could even have ice cream or watch a movie without spending half her paycheck. And if they found the right thing to fix it...

"Meet back here," Zera called after him as the great explorer picked his way through some thorny bushes. "Ten minutes before the Storm."

"Yes, mother!" He didn't turn around to acknowledge her, only threw a wave over his shoulder.

"Ten minutes!" she reiterated, because she had a feeling Byrd was the type of guy who showed up fashionably late. He waved again and continued his trek, a man on a mission.

The world, so loud before, now seemed oddly quiet with Byrd's conversation gone. Something tingled between Zera's shoulder blades, like someone was watching, but when she looked back there was nothing but trees and grass and rocks. It was probably the impending Storm weighing on her. She needed to focus.

The land, while green and lush and nothing like what she was used to back home, had a vague sense of familiarity. The location here didn't match where the machine was in the other time—that would be somewhere deep underground—but she couldn't shake the feeling she was close. The future sat in the corner of her eye, watching her every move while she kept getting distracted by the present.

A lizard scuttled on a tree trunk, the movement nearly leveling Zera. She hadn't seen a lizard since...she couldn't remember when, but it was long enough for her to forget their stealth. It cocked its head and looked at her. When it decided she was a threat, it leapt from the tree and escaped beneath a nearby bush, the leaves barely whispering in its wake.

It was afraid of her, when it had so much more to be afraid of that day.

Zera checked her watch. Approximately sixty minutes remained. The sun was on her face, the air didn't singe her lungs, and she could go anywhere she wanted within a sixty-minute radius.

Her blood chilled. Could she find her mother in sixty minutes? It would be against the rules, one of only three rules she had to follow. Rules made to prevent her from harming herself or others. Very important rules made by very important people.

But if there was a chance...

She moved again, this time with a purpose. If the machine transported her to roughly the same place as the base, then she needed to head south, toward Broadway. She didn't remember the name of the bookstore, but she remembered the red awning and the stairs into the basement, her mom holding her hand the whole way down.

Twigs snapped under her boots as she ran, the sun on her right. The last rays of light danced through the trees and hit her with little pockets of warmth, the heat an echo of what she was used to.

Yellow tape interrupted her trek. The corded area ran as far as she could see in either direction, blocking her progress. She was already tight for time. How much would she lose going around?

The blue of the sky was fading into orange and pink and red, and she was still so deep in the park that the city lights felt far away. She ducked under the tape and kept running. The sun dropped below the treeline and the temperature dropped with it, the chill settling quickly into Zera's unacclimated bones. Instead of slowing her, the cooler air spurred her on, lightening her steps and her breath.

A break in the trees ahead was supposed to be the path, but instead she found herself in the middle of a clearing. That in itself was not unusual, but the woman standing there alone certainly was.

She wore fitted jeans and a loose, white blouse, the sleeves rolled just below her elbows. As she turned to face Zera, her long braid tumbled over her shoulder and swayed, the dying light turning the light brown to the color of wet sand. Though her smile was beautiful, it was the way she looked at Zera that stopped her in her tracks.

The woman *recognized* her.

"You came back," she said. Zera's eyes widened and her heart raced in a way that had nothing to do with the pretty woman in front of her. This woman knew her. *How* did she know her?

"What?" Zera asked, her years of training fleeing her in an instant. Not that there were many details about interacting with outsiders. A sharp sound came from her left, but when she looked, there was nothing but trees. The woman's jaw dropped.

"Oh, my God," she said, then let out a laugh that could only be described as *musical*. Zera wondered if this was how everyone used to be, and she just forgot. The woman stepped closer to her. Zera could see her freckles and thin, silvery scars on her cheeks and collarbones.

"What?" Zera took a step back. The woman stopped her advance and took her hands out of her pockets, holding them up as a display of innocence. Zera's eyes roamed for weapons, but the only silver she found was the woman's rings and bracelet, and unless she was hiding it under her bust, there was little chance she had a gun.

"Oh, no. This is it, huh?" The woman searched Zera's face. "The first time."

"The first time for what?" Zera was good at staying calm in emergency situations, as long as she could muscle her way out of it. The woman looked harmless, but now that she was closer, Zera could see the lines in her forearms, and the way the muscles of her legs stood out even in her jeans. Zera pulled her weapon and aimed it. "First time for *what*?"

"Jesus, I forgot how jumpy you were," she said, holding her hands up higher. "I'm just here to look at the aurora. There's going to be another storm tonight, just like the one in 1944."

"How do you know about the Storm?" Panic seeped into her veins and coated her words. No one was supposed to know about the 2040 Storm—that was the whole point.

"It's been twelve years. The aurora is supposed to reach here tonight." She still spoke so casually, so easily, as if they'd known each other forever. But Zera would remember meeting someone like her. "And here I thought you came to see me...it. See it."

"Just tell me who you are and how you know about the Storm." Zera flipped the safety off. The woman kept her hands up, but seemed utterly unfazed by the action. Zera was bluffing, yes, but she didn't need her to know that, so she let off a warning shot into the trees. "Tell me!"

The woman took her much more seriously now.

"I'm not going to hurt you," she said. "You need to know about 1944. And our night together."

"Our what? Wait, no, don't change the subject." Zera pointed the gun back at her. Her legs shook, but at least her hands were steady. She hoped Byrd heard the shot and would come to help. "You mentioned the Storm. Tell me how you know about it."

The woman paused. "The geomagnetic storms, like all those times before. Like at the college, you need to remember the college."

"What times? What *college*?" Zera took another step forward, but the woman stood her ground. The approaching night leeched color from the sky and the stars sparked into existence one at a time. The Storm would happen soon, and Zera needed to be gone before it hit.

Another shot rang out, and for a second she feared her nervous hands accidentally pulled the trigger. The woman's face went blank and her eyes widened. Slowly, her hands dropped to her side. When a second shot echoed, the woman pitched forward, and something whizzed past Zera and landed in a tree somewhere in her periphery.

Blood marred the woman's white shirt, and each second stained more of it red. She looked surprised, putting her hands to her abdomen and blinking rapidly when they came back wet. Her eyes met Zera's, and then she fell.

It took Zera too long to realize the shooter might aim for her too. She dropped to her knees and put her hands on the woman's wound, the flesh underneath too soft and giving. Red seeped through her fingers, coloring her pale skin.

"Help!" She knew she should run, but her heart seized at the thought of leaving the woman here to die alone. Where the fuck was Byrd? "Stay with me," she said. The woman's chest heaved and she wrapped a hand around Zera's wrist, her grip weak and fingers slick with her own blood.

"I even..." The woman paused and took a wet breath. "Even made you cake."

How could she be thinking about cake at a time like this?

"What's your name?" Zera asked. She had to keep her talking, keep her conscious. Maybe she would survive until real help came. Her only answer was a cough and a gurgle as blood ran from the corners of her mouth. "Fuck, no, you're okay—help!"

Someone crashed through the underbrush behind her, and Byrd emerged, sweating and gasping.

"Zazzera? Are you alright? I heard the..." He spotted the woman on the ground and flinched, taking one step back. "What the hell?"

"There's a shooter somewhere, they hit her twice—where's the med kit?" she asked. Byrd moved next to her and fumbled through the pack at his waist.

"I have it here somewhere," Byrd said. The woman's eyes went wide and her grip turned to iron as she struggled, blood pumping faster from her wound.

"Hey, hey, it's okay, he's with me." Zera released her pressure on the abdomen to cover the woman's hand with her own. Her mouth worked but no words came out, the color of her skin fading with the last rays of light. "She was talking about the Storm, and the times it happened before. You know anything about that?"

"No." Byrd's hands paused. The woman was shaking now, and he couldn't tear his eyes away. "That's a lot of blood."

"Byrd!" Zera barked, making him jump.

"Right, here it is." Byrd dropped the med kit onto the woman's lap and pulled out his pistol. "There's anticoagulant and gauze. I'm going after the shooter."

"We don't have time for that," Zera said. "The Storm—"

"I'm not risking them getting one of us. You focus on her." He let his gaze linger on the woman for a second longer before taking off.

"No, Byrd—dammit." It was a struggle to hold the woman and tear open the med kit. Wasn't he the one medic trained? He needed to be here, and Zera could go after the shooter. His stupid idea of chivalry might get them all killed.

The contents of the med kit spilled over the woman's legs and the ground next to her, and Zera tossed one thing after the other until she found the wound coagulant. She leaned forward to rest her forearms on the wound, her wet fingers sliding over the packaging as she tried to open it.

A bloody hand rested on hers. The woman was pale now, deathly pale. Above them, an aurora started to flicker, a barely visible line painting her skin green.

"We can still do something," Zera whispered. The woman shook her head. "No, no you can't give up."

Why was Zera fighting? The woman was dead before Zera even got there.

She smiled, and though her teeth were coated in red and her eyes were glassy, she was still beautiful. With trembling fingers she pulled one of her rings off and pushed it into Zera's palm.

"What—"

Light and fire exploded, knocking Zera back into the river. The waves tossed her in every direction until she didn't know up from down. Colors spun into one blinding wave. She rocketed through, and her muscles clenched and her lungs squeezed as she braced for impact. Surely this was it, she would be crushed, or she would splatter all over the floor of some random time.

She landed with a halfhearted thud onto the platform. A groan from her left told her Byrd made it back too. Alarms blared and people yelled, but Zera barely heard them over the ringing in her ears. She forced a breath, then another, this new air stale and heavy compared to moments before.

The Storm was over, and she was back home.

2058

CONSCIOUSNESS WAS LESS than compliant for the next few hours.

Zera vaguely recognized medical personnel, their white coats blinding her. She tried to tell them the blood wasn't hers, she wasn't injured, but she wasn't completely sure the machine hadn't ripped out her insides and left them in 2040. Somewhere in the maelstrom she heard Kissi, her voice high and frantic as she attempted to push past the line of nurses and doctors.

The river clung to her, nauseating her with something akin to seasickness. The flow of time was trying to pull her back in; it didn't want to give her up quite yet. She was at the line now. Either she could cross it and give in, fall back into the river, or fight to stay in the present.

Though the air was terrible, she dragged it into her lungs, inhaling so deep her ribs and spine cracked with the pressure. Someone attached a monitor to her chest, and she focused on the rapid beeping. Her heartbeat was steady, but entirely too fast.

"There's blood all over her," a nurse said. "We'll have to cut away her uniform."

"Where's she hurt?" That was Kissi. "Was she shot? Stabbed?"

"We don't know, Lieutenant Kissinger." The medic sounded annoyed. Zera was ready to get annoyed right back, except her voice eluded her.

Someone tugged the collar of her shirt, and something cool and flat touched her skin. The blood rushing in her ears had reduced enough for her to hear the cut of the scissors through her uniform. The person repeated the gesture on the other side, and then simply lifted her shirt away.

Good, now they could see she wasn't bleeding and move onto more important things.

"See any wounds?"

"No, ma'am. We may have to turn her over."

"No," Zera croaked. She was surprised dust didn't spout from her lips for how dry her throat felt. "Not mine."

"Not yours? Whose is it?" Kissi asked. Zera still couldn't see her, or answer her.

"Heart rate is coming down, oxygen saturation improving," said someone above her head.

"Good, she's recovering," said the nurse to her left. He checked his watch. "Faster than usual."

"That's my girl."

"Lieutenant Kissinger, I won't tell you again—"

"And I won't tell *you* again, I'll stay out of your way, but I'm staying."

Zera loved Kissi very much.

"Fine," the nurse growled. He ran scanners over Zera's chest and head, the green lights reminding her too much of the space between times. The machine beeped faster as her heart rate elevated again.

"What's happening?" Kissi said. Zera's lungs felt full of water, choking and drowning her. She couldn't *breathe*.

"Lieutenant Zazzera, you have to calm down." The nurse sounded far away. The imaginary water left her lungs to go to her ears now, and flooded her brain.

"She's coding—"

"Zera, hold on!"

The water overtook her, and the world went black.

Her mind returned to her body in bits and pieces, but eventually confirmed she had, in fact, survived. After all, no religion mentioned screaming machines and itchy sheets as a part of their afterlife package.

The first breath sent her into a coughing fit, and the machines voiced their dismay. Two nurses ran into the room, and while one shut down the alarms, the other placed his hands over her chest and back, holding her together. The action, while odd, helped control the pain lancing through her body.

Dark spots marred the white blanket over her lap, and at first she thought it was blood. That would be her luck, to get to see the world as it used to be and come back coughing up blood. But upon further inspection she saw it was just spittle and phlegm, which was both comforting and disgusting.

"Breathe, Lieutenant," the nurse said. Zera looked up to see Martin, his blue eyes fixed on her. "Really deep."

She did as she was told, her vision clearing with each breath. The hospital room was small, but clean, and she didn't have to share it with anyone. There was, however, one notable absence.

"Kissi," she said, the name scratching her tonsils. "Where's Kissinger?"

"Lieutenant Kissinger is outside," Martin said. His counterpart, a severe-looking woman with silver hair pulled into a tight braid, wiped Zera's shoulder with an alcohol swab and jabbed her with a needle.

"Hey!" She tried to flinch away, but the woman's grip was strong, and she held Zera's arm in place as she emptied the syringe. Warmth flooded her, making it easier to breathe.

"That was for the pain," Martin said with a glare toward his partner. His presence finally reached Zera's consciousness.

"Wait, is this where you go when you disappear?"

Martin shifted uncomfortably. "This is technically the full-time gig. What's the last thing you remember?"

Zera thought back, and winced as green lights flashed in her mind's eye.

"Scanners, I think. But it felt like the in-between again."

"You remember the space in between?"

She looked up and caught the tail end of Martin's expression, but it was gone before she could define it, a friendly smile back on his face.

"Not many remember it," he added. Zera had a sneaking suspicion *no one* remembered it.

"Am I gonna be okay?" The shards of glass in her lungs had softened to sand, and her limbs started to feel like her own again. She felt sore all over, like she'd lost a terrible fight.

"You made it past the first hour," the other nurse said. Her nametag read Polina Androva, and while she had a thick Russian accent, her voice was high and clear. "You'll be fine."

"Past the first—how long was I out?" Zera looked for a clock, but the walls were bare.

Martin checked his watch. "About six hours. You need to eat."

Zera wanted to say she wasn't hungry, because she'd just traveled through time and nearly drowned in its river, but at the mention of food her stomach rumbled to life.

"Let me grab something for you. Doc should be here in a second," Martin said. Androva placed her stethoscope around her neck and gave Zera a curt nod.

"You're good," she said, and her confidence gave Zera a little more to match. They swept out of the room before she could ask about Kissi again. It sounded like she was supposed to wait for Dr. Phillips, but the room was stifling after spending an hour outdoors.

Her body protested as she tried to move, coughs racking through her, but she took a play from Martin and held her pillow to her chest so it didn't feel like her sternum was cracking in half. When she could breathe again, she slid off the edge of the bed and grabbed the IV pole to use as a cane.

A wheel squeaked as she shuffled across the room. Diffuse pain in her chest and abdomen kept her hunched over, and by the time she reached the door, sweat beaded her forehead and her breath came in gasps. She leaned against the frame and got herself together. A day ago she'd climbed out of the Pit, and now she could barely walk to the door. Pathetic.

Once more oxygen reached her system and the dark spots receded, she reached for the handle. It twisted before she had a firm grasp on it and the door swung open. She pitched forward, balance gone, straight into a surprised Dr. Phillips.

The doctor held her hands up and backed away instead of reaching to catch her. Zera tried to get her feet underneath her and stumbled into the wall opposite, the IV pole crashing to the ground behind her. The world spun, but a pair of strong hands grabbed her by the armpits and pulled her back.

"Steady," Kissi said. She didn't let go until she was sure Zera would stay upright. "Trying to make a break for it?"

"Got bored," Zera said. She leaned against the wall so no one would notice her legs shaking.

Dr. Phillips straightened her lab coat and glasses. "Lieutenant Zazzera, glad to see you're awake."

"Yeah, glad to be here," Zera said. Kissi pulled her arm over her shoulders and took most of her weight. The trip back to bed was much faster than the voyage out.

"Yes, well, that was quite the entrance you had," Dr. Phillips said, giving them space as Kissi helped her back into the bed. Zera decided she would stay there a little while before her next adventure.

"What do you mean?" she asked. Whatever it was, it didn't sound good.

"Well..." Dr. Phillips blinked and looked between the two of them. "Your anchor didn't pull you back."

"Of course she did, I'm here," Zera said. "Kissi got me back, just like I knew she would."

"No, that's the problem," Dr. Phillips pressed. "Kissinger didn't pull you back."

"She—what?" Zera looked to Kissi so fast it made her vision swim.

"I didn't get the signal." Kissi crossed her arms over her chest, the universal sign she was stumped and pissed about it. "I checked everything a thousand times, but there was nothing, you just *appeared*."

"And that's not normal?" Zera asked.

"Not at all," Dr. Phillips said. "If we pull without a call, it's usually to bring back a body."

Zera didn't like that explanation.

"We stayed too late," she said. "Wait, Byrd. Is he alive? Is he okay?"

"Yes, Lieutenant Byrd is fine." Dr. Phillips waved the question away. "Probably. He's not awake yet. But I need to know what happened."

Zera thought back. The memories of the green lights still made her stomach turn, so she focused instead on what happened before, in the meadow.

"I think we went through the Storm again," she said.

Phillips threw her hands up. "I told you the time. I told you *specifically* to avoid the Storm."

"I know! It wasn't on purpose." Zera rubbed her eyes with the heels of her hands, but the colors reminded her of the place between, so she stopped. "There was a woman. She distracted me."

"There's always a woman." Phillips groaned. "When will you lot learn that the women aren't worth it? They're in their time. You are in yours."

"It wasn't like—she mentioned the Storm," Zera said. Her cheeks burned, and she ignored Kissi's raised eyebrows and curious expression. "I got distracted by *that*. Then she got shot."

"So?"

"'So'? I couldn't just leave her there to die!"

"What did it matter? She was already dead when you got there."

Phillips had a point. Zera knew this. She'd even had the same thought. But Phillips was already moving on.

"It must have been the Storm that thrust you back into this time," she said. She pinched her chin and stared at the floor, and Zera had the feeling she was talking more to herself than to her. "Interesting."

"Why is that interesting?" Kissi shifted to put Zera between her and the doctor, as if that would keep Phillips from throwing her out of the room.

"Any other soldiers that went through the Storm again died," Phillips said, matter-of-fact. "Didn't return and die, *stayed there* and died."

"I did neither of those things," Zera said. She tried to swallow, but her mouth was weirdly dry. How narrowly had she survived?

"Exactly." Phillips rummaged in her pockets and found a capped syringe. "I need another blood sample."

Zera's stomach turned as Phillips stepped closer and uncapped the needle. She reached for Kissi's hand and closed her eyes. Her stomach churned when Phillips rubbed an alcohol swab on her elbow, and bile rose in her throat as the needle punctured her skin. She did her best not to imagine all her life force draining into that one tiny syringe.

"I'll be back," Phillips said as she walked out the door. Zera hadn't noticed she'd moved away. A little drop of blood welled at her elbow, but otherwise the needle left no mark.

"She's a piece of work," Kissi said. A cart beside her held various pieces of medical equipment, and she grabbed a thick square of gauze.

"I think she's one of those 'creative genius' types," Zera said, taking the gauze and putting it over her elbow, the nausea receding.

Kissi dragged a stool over, the wheels squealing and protesting the move. "What was it like?"

"Huh?"

"Being back there," she said with a playful punch. Zera chose not to show how sore she was.

"It was...amazing." Her answer left in a rush. If she closed her eyes and ignored all the negative things about her trip, she could feel the sun on her face and see the green of the trees. "The sky was still blue, and the grass... oh my gods Kissi, do you remember how soft grass was?"

"Not even a little," Kissi said with a sad smile. "And look, you even got a bit of a tan. Did you bring back anything good?"

"Just the normal stuff." Zera shrugged. "I saw birds, though. Oh! And lizards!"

"And what was the deal with that woman?"

"Huh?" Zera blinked. That was a left turn in the conversation, and she wasn't ready for it.

"You mentioned that woman getting shot," Kissi said. "The Doc didn't seem that concerned, but it sounds concerning to me, especially 'cause..."

"'Cause of what?" Zera asked. Kissi looked away for a second, pressing her lips together. "'Cause of *what*, Kissi?"

"I just did what I'm good at. I found something."

Zera's eyes went wide. "What kind of something?"

"I'm not sure yet. Something cropped up in the stream of data whenever you, uh, *landed*. Almost like another signature."

"Well, Byrd found me eventually," she said. "And he came back again when the woman got shot. He dropped off the med pack and went after the shooter."

"Huh. That must've been it, then." Kissi shook her head. "This whole thing is weird."

"Yeah, but it's pretty cool too," Zera said. A knock came at the door, and a second later, Martin opened it. A tray displayed the delectable excuse for food the med bay offered, lukewarmed to perfection.

"Meal time," he said, putting the tray on the bedside table. It was just bread and a bowl of weak soup, but it smelled just good enough to make Zera's stomach growl. He pulled up a stool and sat. "I gotta stay while you eat, make sure you don't choke on your own vomit."

"That's encouraging," Zera said. Martin gave Kissi a lingering look.

"I guess I'll head out," she said, not bothering to hide her irritation. "It's time for my shift anyway. I'll come back in the morning."

"Have fun doing math, loser."

"You rest up, Phillips and Vylek are already talking about another trip."

Zera choked on the dry bread. "Another?"

"See you later!" It probably wasn't her information to share, but Zera was glad for the warning. One trip was bad enough, and a second one so soon might just kill her. The bread vacated her esophagus and she spat it out, remembering too late that Martin was right next to her.

"Sorry," she mumbled, still coughing out the last crumbs.

"Not the worst thing I've seen." He wiped her mouth faster than she could think about it. "Not even the worst today."

"Have you been part of this the whole time?" Zera stared straight at him, and for the first time since she met him, Martin looked flustered. He straightened her bed sheets and adjusted everything on her tray before clearing his throat and looking up.

"You need to eat."

"You didn't answer the question."

He sighed and pushed the bowl toward her. Her resolve crumpled easily and she picked it up, drinking the bland soup like a cup of coffee.

"I've only been here a couple months," Martin said. "I replaced some-one. They act like they're telling you everything but..."

"Always feels like something's missing." Zera shivered and folded her legs under her. There were a lot of things she wanted to warn future trav-elers about, but she doubted Vylek or Phillips would allow it. "Be honest, how bad is the second trip?"

"Don't know." When Zera glared, he added, "I haven't seen anyone take a second trip. The others say it gets easier though."

Her body rejected the idea of another round, but when she thought about the grass, and the air, and the *sun*—

She wouldn't say no, *couldn't* say no.

Martin sighed and held out the other piece of crusty bread, and this time she was able to eat it without choking. Maybe it was just her untrained eye, but all the numbers on the machines looked stable, and none of the alarms were sounding. Even with the meager meal, she felt significantly better.

"How long am I stuck here?" she asked. If her watch was right, she could still make it to mess and grab real food before crashing for a minimum of twelve hours.

"Probably another twenty-four. We have to make sure you don't dissolve into dust or melt into a pile of goo."

"I—has that happened?"

"No, but we're time traveling, so who knows what else can happen?"

"You're a terrible nurse."

"Yesterday you told me I was the best."

"Yeah, well, I changed my mind." Zera sniffed and crossed her arms, willing herself not to think of the potential catastrophic effects that could besiege her. Martin grinned, then agreed to get her more food if she promised to behave.

This time Zera was a good patient and stayed in her bed. Fatigue rocked her all the way to her bones, but her mind buzzed nonstop. When Kissi and Martin were there, it was easy to focus on the good parts of her trip. Alone, she felt the river swallowing her again, and the sticky wet of that woman's blood on her hands. The undersides of her nails still sported red stains where the hospital staff couldn't quite clean them.

Oh, no. This is it, huh? The first time.

The words sent a jolt through her. With everything that happened, she forgot about that small statement. The woman knew her. How?

Zera wished she could draw, if only so she could get the woman's face down on paper. Maybe then Kissi could search the archives for images. She ran a hand through her hair, the buzzed sides soft since she hadn't cut it in a while. The woman might have known her before the Storm, but that would have been when Zera had cherub cheeks and tangled hair down past her ribs. Now, necessity dictated she keep her hair short, and time and circumstance made her face far more angular. The likelihood of recognition was low.

And why would the woman be surprised she came *back?*

Another knock sounded, jolting Zera from her thoughts. She expected

Martin, back with more food, but instead Vylek walked through the door, eyes on the tablet in her hands.

"At ease, at ease," she said when Zera tried to stand. The bed squeaked as Zera settled back. "I'm here for your first debriefing."

"Oh, okay." Panic rose in her chest. There hadn't been time to fill out a report—she didn't even have her first introductory pages done. If there was a tablet hidden somewhere in this hospital room, she hadn't found it. "I, uh, didn't prepare—"

"I know," Vylek interrupted. "This one's verbal."

"Why?"

"Protocol." She didn't look up from her tablet. "Tell me about the trip."

Zera walked through her memories as best she could, starting with the lights and talking until Vylek interrupted again.

"This woman mentioned the Storm?"

"Well, kind of," Zera said. The machine beeped faster, and both of them ignored it. "It seemed like her storm and my Storm weren't the same...storm."

"Huh. What did she say after that?"

"Something about going back to the beginning? To 1944?" Zera offered. "Does that mean anything?"

"Probably." Vylek left it at that, and Zera knew better than to press the issue. "What next?"

"Well, that's when she got shot."

Vylek's face didn't change at that. In fact, she told Zera to keep talking, acting like her heart rate wasn't racing toward a worrisome pace. So Zera talked. She told her everything she could remember up to landing back in the bunker.

"Has any of that happened before? Has anyone met her?" she asked.

To her surprise, Vylek gave her a real answer. "We've had some reports of the gunshots. A few people reported seeing her fall in the distance. But no one's ever gone to check if she's okay."

Somehow, she made it sound like Zera was wrong for trying to save the woman's life. She swallowed any back talk and nodded.

"I'll utilize resources better next time," she said.

"You sure will." Vylek tapped the tablet a few more times, then finally graced her with a look. "You've got one week until your next trip."

"One..." She took a deep breath and reminded herself this was better than digging. "Yes, ma'am."

"Oh, and Zazzera?"

"Yes?"

"This is your one strike. Break the rules again, you'll be back digging."

Zera gulped. "Understood."

Vylek inclined her head and turned on her heel, leaving the room before Zera could salute.

One week. She had one week to get back in fighting shape.

Easy.

She would do it right after she took a nap.

2058

THE STINK of the training room wasn't any better despite Zera's new position, but at least she could visit during day shift now.

The new schedule really messed with her internal clock. Switching to nights hadn't been any trouble, since there were no windows to cue her Circadian rhythm. Now a few years into it, changing back was a challenge.

Sweat splattered on the mat as she blocked another swing from the trainer. He had no shirt and therefore no name tag, and she was too distracted by his absolute brawn to remember how he'd introduced himself. Weapons and rudimentary defensive skills were part of basic training, but with the presence of a shooter in 2040, any traveler who survived the first round received more intense instruction.

"Ah ha! Good one, Zazzera," the trainer said, as if she hadn't almost broken a forearm at the block.

"Can we take a break?" she gasped. It was hot, and fighting was *hard*.

"No!"

The trainer—she thought his name started with a G...Garrett?—kept swinging, and she had no choice but to continue dodging. Gideon seemed to be enjoying himself, if his wide eyes and manic grin were to be believed, but Zera was counting down the minutes.

Gustafson swiped a leg and Zera barely jumped over it, her knees shaking as she landed. After climbing the wall and pushing the sled for hours, her body struggled with the high intensity. She sent a fist out and he slapped her hand away before she even came close.

"Gotta be quicker than that!" Gods, this was just the *introduction*.

Zera forwent strategy and snapped out punch after punch, bobbing and weaving as best she could. She was used to grappling, not fighting, and she leaned into her speed. If she couldn't be skilled, she could at least be fast.

She fell fast, too. And hard.

Gendry grabbed both her wrists, and the next thing she knew, she was staring at the ceiling. That did not go according to plan.

"You're quick!" He leaned down, putting his face over hers. Sweat from his brow dripped onto her neck, which made her squirm. "But I'm quicker."

"Thanks." She rolled away before any more of his disgusting sweat could get on her. He raised an eyebrow at her response, and a chill went through her as she remembered she was speaking to a superior officer. "...Sir?"

"On the mat, we're all equals." Grant—his name was definitely Grant—held out his hand and helped her up. Her muscles screamed, but she pretended not to hear them. "Well, not in skill, but in station."

"That's—yeah, I got that," she said. The clock said she had a few long minutes left. "Are we going another round?"

"No, I think that was good enough for my evaluation. If you come back, we'll *really* get started."

"She better come back!" Byrd called from the bench a few feet away. "That was terrible."

"You think you could do it better?" she replied.

Grant stepped between them. "No teasing on my mat." He leaned closer to Zera. "Especially when you'd probably lose."

"Thanks for the confidence."

Across from them, Byrd pushed himself up with his crutches, wincing as he put pressure through the cast around his lower leg. "Lemme get a shot in."

"Sit back down, you're gonna hurt yourself," Zera said.

He limped to the mat. "I'm already hurt. What's the worst that could happen?"

"Uh, get hurt worse? You're already in time out. Vylek won't like it if you're out for even longer." Zera crossed her arms and inwardly grimaced as her sweaty shirt pressed against her abdomen. She needed a shower, not a verbal—or physical—spar with Byrd.

"I can still take you."

"I don't like this," Grant said.

"Oh, come on, it'll be fun." Byrd moved his crutches and shifted his weight to his uninjured leg. "C'mon, Zazzera, you scared?"

"Of course not. Just don't want to beat up an injured old man," she said.

"Hey! I'm not that old."

He swiped out with his crutch and Zera lifted her leg, moving just fast enough to avoid falling on her face, but not fast enough to avoid the metal connecting with her ankle.

"Ouch! Shit!"

"That was a point to me!" Byrd sang.

"Unfair. You have a weapon," Zera said.

"She has a point! Give her one of your crutches," Grant said.

Byrd shrugged and tossed one to her. "Won't help."

Zera held the crutch like a baseball bat and swung, not really trying to hit him. Byrd somehow flipped his remaining crutch around and, while maintaining balance, smacked hers out of her hand. It clattered onto the floor a few feet away.

"Anyone ever tell you that you telegraph your moves?"

"The hell is a telegraph?" Zera knew, but wanted to prey on the few years between them.

Byrd rolled his eyes. "You're just fucking with me now."

"Well, Zazzera, now that you're thoroughly embarrassed, I suggest you hit the showers." Grant sighed, pinching the bridge of his nose.

"It's really not that embarrassing. I can climb stuff, I've never had to fight people."

"Don't remind me. Just go."

She shared a cheeky grin with Byrd before hitting the showers and scrubbing the sweat away. After collecting her fancy new key card and lanyard, she went back through the secret hallways to their new barracks.

Zera went to climb into her bunk, but stopped when something shiny glinted from the nightstand, something bigger than the ring the woman from the past had given her. At first she thought it might be a new lotion for Kissi's leg, but it was too compact. She took a step closer.

The watch from the Pit.

Why would Kissi have it? Zera turned it in that night—it should've been processed and locked away like other anomalies.

The door creaked open and Kissi dragged herself in, her dark eyes ringed red from staring at a screen for too long. Day shift hours didn't agree with her either.

"Hey." She moved around Zera to collapse face down on the bottom bunk.

"Hey," Zera replied. "Where did you get this?"

Kissi shifted so she could see the watch on the table. "I didn't get it. Where did you get it?"

"I didn't get it. It wasn't here this morning."

"Oh, shit." Kissi sat up. "Is that the one you found? In the Pit?"

"I think so." Zera was hesitant to pick it up, wondering if it would shock her like last time. When Kissi lifted a hand, Zera made up her mind and grabbed it as casually as she could. Grime coated the underside, and dirt caked and packed the seam. There was no feeling except for the cool metal. "Yeah, this is definitely it."

"Does it open?" Kissi held out a hand, and Zera gave it to her. "I wonder if all the mechanisms are still in place."

"One way to find out," Zera said.

Kissi nodded and dug a fingernail into the crack, swearing as her nail snapped. "Ouch, fuck. It's really stuck."

"Let me try." Zera snatched the watch back. She tried to wedge a nail in too, but it bent back, sending a sharp sting through her thumb. "Shit!"

"I told you." Kissi grabbed it again. She brought it so close to her face her eyes crossed, so Zera took it once more.

"You're gonna give yourself a migraine," she said, holding the watch at a normal distance. "I thought this was just dirt."

"It probably is. Just really old dirt compacted by the 2040 Storm," Kissi said. Zera pulled out her pocket knife and flipped it open, digging the point into the watch. Whatever sealed its lips together was so dense the blade glanced off the edge.

"Lost cause," Kissi said, laying back on her bunk. Zera considered bringing the watch and knife into her own bunk, but her muscles still ached from training, and her grip was not as strong as she wanted to handle a blade. She tossed the watch back on the nightstand and instead grabbed the ring the woman gave her. Most of the blood came off, but it still coated the inside inscription.

"Lost cause? No, a problem for later," Zera said, crawling into her bed. The recovery from the trip versus a dig was definitely harsher, but it felt more important. It felt like she was actually *doing* something.

"Oh, I found what that woman mentioned, with 1944," Kissi said, as if discussing the weather. Zera shot up, her vision floating for a second as her brain caught up with the movement.

"What?" The ring tumbled from her hands and bounced under the desk. "Why didn't you lead with that?"

"'Cause you threw a watch in my face. Do you want to know or not?"

"Of course I do." She climbed down to retrieve her ever-expanding jewelry collection.

"It was a precursor to the 2040 Storm," Kissi said, pulling her tablet from her bag. She swiped the screen and handed it to Zera. "Very similar signatures, but on a much smaller scale."

"A precursor?" Zera scrolled through, looking at a graphical analysis of energy waves from the two dates. She didn't understand the science behind it, but the picture explained it perfectly.

"Yeah. That was the first recorded storm, in 1944. I guess she was a weirdly big fan of the stuff."

The woman's knowledge of a geomagnetic event wasn't necessarily the strange part. Scientists could mark those things, the data made that clear. But the woman recognized Zera. That was the part that confused her.

"So she knew about 1944 'cause of this article?" Zera asked.

Kissi thought for a moment. "I'm not sure. This wasn't in any article, I just traced it. I couldn't even find it in the data from all the previous trips."

It wasn't recorded?

"Did you show this to Vylek?"

"I sent it to her. Never got a response. Hell, she probably got someone else to look into it."

"And that's the only other signature that matches 2040?" Zera asked.

"Yeah...wait. No."

Kissi plucked the tablet from Zera's hands and tapped away. A few breaths later she straightened and smiled like a maniac.

"Zera, you genius." She flipped the screen around. "Look. Every twelve years it pops back up, the epicenter at different places. The signature grows each time."

"What does that mean?"

Kissi pursed her lips. "My guess is, if they could program the machine right, they'd send you there instead of 2040."

Zera's insides squirmed at the thought. "There's no way they could send me back that far, right?"

Kissi shook her head. "Probably not. It was hard enough to get to 2040. There's way too much uncertainty going back further."

"Thank the gods." Zera cleared her throat. "Hey, uh, how much do you remember? From before?"

Kissi tapped her chin. "I mean, the usual stuff. I remember starting junior high. I'd just gotten braces, so my mom let me get my hair braided in this awesome pattern to make up for it. That's probably the clearest thing. Why?"

"How about people? Do you think you'd still know them today?"

"If I saw someone I hadn't seen in eighteen years? No, probably not."

The answer was obvious, but it still gave Zera a little bit of relief. Maybe she wasn't an asshole for not remembering this woman. Maybe she was just too young.

Kissi glanced at her. "What about you?"

"Nah, not really," Zera said. Most people had trouble remembering things before the age of twelve, even without living in a post-apocalyptic world. "I remember my mom, and my dad. Not much about school besides movie days."

"Oh! Those were the *best*! The teacher never could get the screen to work right."

"Never! How hard is it to work a wall screen?"

"Apparently, really difficult. Especially for the old folk." Kissi laughed and tumbled onto her bunk, returning to her numbers.

⌁

Before Zera knew it, Kissi was shaking her awake from a weird dream and they went stumbling out of the barracks. She was lucky Kissi was so punctual; without her, she would've been kicked out of the academy two weeks in.

As early as Kissi tended to be, they were still the last ones to the prebriefing, sinking into two chairs in the back. Kissi's tablet dinged as a document dropped, and Zera grabbed one of the older, more beat up tablets from the table. Nothing was on it except the twenty-eight page brief.

Most of the others gave them a cursory glance and nothing more, but Byrd smiled from the front and waved. He wore his new fatigues, but Zera doubted they'd let him travel with the massive cast on his leg.

"Alright, everyone here?" Vylek said. The room quieted, and she tapped her handheld to wake up the screen on the wall. "Let's start with page three."

Zera hoped the meeting would be a little more exciting, like the one before her first trip, but it was the same boring shit all the other prebriefings held. For most of it, Zera played with her new ring, twirling it around her right ring finger. When they reached page twenty-one, a murmur rippled through the room. Apparently, this meeting *was* more interesting than previous ones—they just had to wait until the right time.

"There's gonna be some changes this next go-round." Vylek tapped the handheld again, and large, black numbers appeared on the screen.

1944.

"During the last run, Zazzera encountered a civilian who mentioned *a* storm, but from 1944. Dr. Phillips and I agree that, while samples from 2040 are valuable, we need to get further samples from other sources. If we can figure out why we survived in 1944 and didn't in 2040, perhaps we can make a difference here."

Before, Zera thought the room was quiet. Now it was dead silent.

"We've never attempted to go this far back before," Vylek said.

Oh. Oh, no.

Her gaze landed on Zera. "Zazzera, you're the only traveler we've got right now. So get ready."

Everyone turned to look at her, and Zera reached up to run her hand through her hair. This was unprecedented, untested, and with Byrd in a cast, she would have to go alone.

"Yes, ma'am," she said, her voice cracking. What else could she say? No? Vylek made it clear the first day that she followed orders. None of this was up to her. But they were doing this *because* of her.

Dammit, she should've never talked to that woman. She should've just kept her head down and done her job, and then she wouldn't have to do the extra-experimental thing in this already experimental project. The current nearly got her the first time. This was so, so bad.

"Zazzera, Dr. Doyle is finishing his work on your vaccines, and engineering has developed a new tracker that will hopefully keep you anchored here, despite the distance."

"Hopefully." She clamped her mouth shut. The word was supposed to stay in her head.

"Hopefully." Vylek's face didn't change. "So stay after the meeting."

And with that, she moved on, as if she wasn't asking Zera to do the unthinkable.

Zera didn't listen for the last half hour. Instead, she focused on the simple things, like breathing and blinking and not bolting out of that room and the hutch and taking whatever heat the sun gave her.

When Vylek dismissed the meeting, Zera stood, hoping the table hid her trembling legs. The rest of the room filed out, but Byrd stopped, swaying slightly on his crutches.

"Sorry I'm a lame horse," he said, sticking out his leg. "I tried to get Vylek to push the whole thing back, or at least recruit another traveler, but she won't budge."

"It's fine. Guess I'll just have to save the world without you." Bile rose in the back of her throat, and she swallowed it down. "Would be a hell of a lot easier with you there, though."

"Throw the game then, Zazzera. So we can team up again."

She raised an eyebrow. "I'm not really a sports metaphor kind of girl."

"But you know what I mean."

"Zazzera, with me," Vylek called. Zera nodded to Byrd and weaved through the tables, following Vylek out the back and down a different hallway to Dr. Doyle's office.

"Hello again, Lieutenant Zazzera," he said with a genuine smile. The desk in front of him was covered in trays of test tubes and titration sets, but it was the box of syringes that made her blood go cold. Vylek's silent departure didn't help the situation.

"Dr. Doyle." She made sure her voice was steady. After all, she'd survived field training and trips to the surface. Hell, she traveled back in time. A soldier that tough wouldn't be afraid of something silly like needles.

"I've had to do a lot of digging and, ah, a bit of reverse engineering," he said, pulling out three syringes. "But I managed to recreate the inoculations you'll need for your trip."

He said it so casually, like she was just taking the underground to the next bunker over and not traveling back over a hundred years.

"Right, okay. And Vylek mentioned a new tracker?"

"Yeah, I'm gonna have to give you some light sedation for that one," he said with a grimace. "Unless engineering develops some brilliant new technology in the next few minutes, it's gonna be a little bigger than the first one."

"So you'll remove the first one?" It had taken her a minute to get used to the first tracker they gave her, and while the second one was easier, she didn't want to keep it any longer than necessary.

Dr. Doyle gave her another apologetic look. "Sorry, orders say leave it." Dammit. "Have a seat."

Zera eased into the creaky plastic chair next to the desk. The armrest was wide and cold, and goose bumps sprung across her skin as she laid her forearm on it. Though she willed her muscles to stay relaxed, her opposite hand gripped the edge of the seat until the plastic dug into her skin. It was an effort to look anywhere except the desk, but her gaze kept finding the needles shining in the bright white light.

"So," Dr. Doyle said, startling her. If he noticed, he didn't say anything. "How was the first trip?"

That was the question of the week. Nearly everyone asked, but they didn't want to hear about the woman's blood on her hands, or the feeling of time compressing her body. There was a specific answer they were looking for, and she gave it every time.

"It was awesome. Crazy to see things the way they were before, you know?" Even she could hear how flat her voice was.

Dr. Doyle nodded. "I'm sure it was a grand old time," he said, and Zera thought she detected a hint of sarcasm. He combined some of the test tubes and took the three syringes, filling them with a cloudy concoction. The plastic clicked when he set the tray down next to her, and when he moved his wheelchair toward her, she instinctively moved away.

"Sorry," she said when she saw the look on his face.

He shook his head. "No worries, I know it startles people sometimes," he said, gesturing to the chair.

Heat crawled up the back of her neck. "Oh, no, that wasn't..." She took a breath. "The needles. I'm just not the biggest fan."

"Oh, I see." He didn't sound completely convinced as his eyes traced the geometric tattoos on her forearm.

"Those are little, they don't count. I can't see them—" Her stomach clenched as she pictured the syringe puncturing her skin deep enough to hit bone. She shifted uncomfortably, which knocked the tray and sent the syringes rattling again. Blood evacuated her head, leaving her vision swimming.

"Wow, you really do have an issue with needles," Dr. Doyle said.

"Yeah. So if we could just—just get it done," she said through gritted teeth. "Please."

"On it." Dr. Doyle snapped on his gloves and tore open the antiseptic towel, the smell somehow helping Zera's nausea.

"And Doc?"

"Yes?"

"Don't tell Vylek."

"Your secret's safe with me." The cool towel soothed the hot skin of her shoulder, the sharp alcohol scent cutting through the lightheadedness. As long as she didn't look down, she would be fine.

"Time for the pinches. I'll be quick." True to his word, he delivered the shots in rapid succession, his strong fingers pinching her deltoid and holding her steady. Each poke sent another wave of nausea over her, but she grit her teeth and bore it. She wasn't going to survive time travel just to die from some preventable, ancient disease.

"Done."

"Thank gods." She dropped her head between her knees and breathed, begging herself not to vomit all over the tiny room. The only consolation was the sedation she'd get for the new tracker.

"When you're ready, I can give you another shot to relax you before you get the sedation."

Zera groaned. "Why couldn't you give me that before?"

"Huh, you're right." He didn't sound very sorry, but physicians rarely did. "I'll remember that for next time."

Next time.

Zera didn't want to think about next time. Hells, she didn't want to think about *this* time. Her entire career she followed orders without question, and she tried to keep that same philosophy here, but it was getting more and more difficult to go along with it all.

Eventually she let Dr. Doyle sedate her. When she awoke, she had four stitches in her side and not nearly enough pain medicine, though Doyle assured her that he'd pumped her full of other stuff to counteract the after-effects of the vaccines.

Zera got one blissful rest day from training, and one more long, *long* pre-briefing to tell her everything she heard before. The job would be the same: go back, get some readings, data, and samples, and when she was ready, send the call home. Hopefully she would return, and hopefully it would be in one piece. Nevermind she was traveling over a hundred years into the past.

Byrd was there the day of the trip, wearing an odd expression. Zera gave up trying to interpret it, instead focusing on Kissi, who in turn focused on the screen in front of her. If something went wrong, Zera wouldn't blame Kissi. But if everything went right, she would attribute it all to her anchor.

The machine warmed up, the clock counted down, and with neither pomp nor circumstance they flung her into the river once again.

1944

ZERA TOOK a page from Byrd's book and threw up as soon as she landed.

She was still in Central Park, but the trees were younger and the grounds wilder. Though no one appeared in the immediate vicinity, voices weaved through the leaves and the grass, and in the distance she could hear traffic sounds.

The air almost had the same crisp scent she remembered from her childhood, but the wind carried the hint of something sour, the smell just strong enough to make her vomit again. Waves from the river of time lapped at her arms and legs, and she grabbed at the nearest tree—a sapling, really—and forced herself to stand. The bark bit into her hands, the pain giving her something to focus on besides the overwhelming nausea.

But she was here. She fucking *made it*. Not only was she back in the past, but in an era no living person remembered. The reality hit her almost as hard as the next stomach cramp. She was a godsdamned pioneer. A lightheaded, nearly unconscious and flirting with death pioneer, but a pioneer nonetheless.

Rule number two said not to talk to anyone. But she could still see the city, right?

Sweat poured from her as the summer sun beat down, and she picked her way toward the bustling streets. The trails were small, and any open areas held people of all types with tents and lean-tos. A police officer in a dark uniform and tall hat blew his whistle, but Zera kept her head down and picked up her pace.

The racket of the city grew as she neared, and all at once the park ended and she toppled onto a sidewalk. Tall buildings lined the packed streets, clean and new compared to the New York she remembered. The stench of car oil and unwashed bodies threatened to choke her, and the pedestrians themselves tried to knock her into the walls.

Zera ducked in and out of alleys until she found an empty one, giving her a minute to breathe and gather herself. Women with victory rolls pinned in their hair and patterned dresses passed by, chattering like...like normal people. It felt like the world should be in black and white, and the colors and liveliness threw Zera for a loop. This wasn't some movie—she was really and truly here.

In 1944.

It was becoming increasingly obvious she was in deep shit and zero percent prepared for this excursion. Though her fatigues could pass for a factory uniform, her tattoos and short hair made her stick out. Attention was the last thing she needed, and there were *so* many people around. The return syringe sat heavy in her pocket, tempting her to escape this world and go back to her own.

Zera reminded herself of her job, an incredibly important one. As the side effects from the trip abated, the initial panic did too, and soon her curiosity overtook her fear. This was the very definition of a once-in-a-life-time opportunity. Even if she'd been forced into this mission, she could take full advantage of it.

Every person who passed spoke a different language, dressed in every-thing from burnt and oiled factory uniforms to high-end tailored suits and dresses. Everything was so different, so *alive* compared to what she was accustomed to.

Two men paused outside the shop to her right, one of them setting his hat down on the bench before reaching in his pocket. He retrieved a cigarette, and his friend offered a lighter. With them distracted, Zera grabbed the hat and plopped it on her head, immediately walking away and disappearing into the crowd. She rolled her sleeves down, covering the ink on her skin.

At first she worried her hip bag was out of place, but most people were carrying them. She watched the crowd go by from underneath the brim of her hat, clocking each pedestrian and car as it passed. The entire walk was surreal, like she was living in an alternate reality.

That's when she saw her.

At first, the glistening brown hair was another shade of the tapestry, but then she turned and Zera saw the heart-shaped face and honey brown eyes. Her brows were thicker and her face less scarred, but there was no denying it.

The woman from the park.

The woman from her first trip.

In 2040.

"You." She didn't mean to lock eyes with the woman, and she didn't mean to speak out loud either. The woman's eyes widened and her perfect pink lips parted.

Then she ran.

"Shit." Zera took off after her, trying not to get too close. While she wasn't well-versed in the social standings of the era, she hoped if someone noticed an apparent man chasing a woman down the street, they would try to stop them. But no one gave them a second glance, unless it was to shout at them for getting in their way.

"'Scuse me, sorry," she said, wedging her way between pedestrians. The woman's dress and shoes slowed her down as much as the crowd. All Zera had to do was outlast her, not necessarily catch her.

The woman cut onto another street and Zera jogged to catch up, barely glimpsing the disappearing hem of her dress as she rounded another corner. There was more space on these streets, giving the woman room to run, but also giving Zera plenty of opportunity to catch her. She slipped into a nondescript building devoid of passerby, utilizing a side door blended into the dirty brick wall. No name, not even an address number, distinguished it from the surrounding buildings. Zera attempted to open the door.

Locked.

She didn't have a lock picking set or lock picking skills, but she did know how to throw her weight around, and the door didn't look particularly robust. Adrenaline lent her extra strength as she slammed her shoulder into the door, the wood splintering and cracking so easily she nearly tumbled down the narrow stairs behind it. The woman stood at the bottom of the stairs—waiting for her? Teasing her? Leading her into a trap?

"Just—wait!" Zera called. The woman kept going.

Zera flew down the stairs. There was no door to the basement, it just opened into a dirty room packed with boxes and barrels. Slits of windows let in just enough light for her to avoid running into things, and to dodge the fist flying toward her.

"What the hell?" She stepped back. The woman, who'd looked at her so sweetly back in 2040, now glared and bared her teeth as she swung again. Zera caught her fist like Grant had earlier, but the woman wrenched it from her grip with ease.

"Stop it!" Zera barely dodged as the woman punched again. Grant said she was decent enough at grappling, and this woman seemed to fight the same way. Unfortunately, she also seemed to have more experience.

"Ouch, shit!" The woman landed a blow to Zera's ribs with surprising force. Zera stopped trying to dodge, and instead lowered her shoulder and plowed into her. The woman may have been able to throw a better punch, but Zera was very dense after years in the training room and had a much lower center of gravity.

They collapsed onto the floor, dust kicking up and assaulting Zera's eyes and nose. The woman struggled too, coughing into her elbow as she scrambled away. Zera wiped her streaming eyes with her sleeves, blinking away the grit to find the woman pulling up her skirt. There was a joke on the tip of her tongue, but it died as the woman retrieved a long knife from its sheath.

"Whoa, whoa, whoa," Zera said, holding her hands out. She slowly climbed to her feet, and the woman mirrored the motion. "I'm not here to hurt you. I just want to talk."

"How do you know me?" she asked, brandishing the knife like a sword. Zera took a step back, and the woman took a step forward.

"I don't know you! How do you know *me*?" Zera countered. The woman paused, her brows pinching ever so slightly.

"I think it's rather clear that I don't know you," she said. "Who sent you?"

"What the fuck is that accent?" Zera asked. The woman spoke with something that sounded not quite British, but not quite American. *Posh* was the best word for it. It was a stupid question now that she thought about it, but it was too late to take it back.

"Why, I'd ask you the same myself!" The woman actually turned up her nose at Zera.

"Well excuse me, princess."

"Tell me who sent you, or I'll cut your throat." She said it with stoic confidence, and it occurred to Zera she probably *had* cut a few throats. Using awkward humor to diffuse the situation was no longer a viable option.

"No one sent me," she said, then amended, "At least, no one sent me to find you. I'm just passing through the city, seeing the sights. That's all."

"Liar." The woman took a quick step and Zera leapt away, crashing into boxes and knocking an empty barrel onto its side. She moved it between them, hoping the woman's skirt would keep her from jumping over it.

"I'm telling the truth," Zera said. She opened her bag and showed the contents, which mainly consisted of empty canisters. "Look, I have no weapons, no money, nothing. I don't even know your name."

"Then how do you know me?"

"I…" Zera tried to come up with an excuse. She couldn't tell her where she was really from. But then, how did this woman exist now *and* in 2040?

There were other bunkers, back in the future. Perhaps Zera wasn't the only traveler.

"You're one of us!" she said. "You're time traveling too!"

The look of confusion that passed over the woman's face was both funny and terrifying. "I beg your pardon? Time travel? Are you daft?"

"Apparently," Zera replied, because what kind of idiot would ask what she did and expect an honest answer? "But then…how old are you?"

"It's impolite to ask a lady her age."

"It's also impolite to pull a knife on someone you don't know. Especially when she's not here to get you."

"William didn't send you?"

"Who the fuck is William?"

The woman lowered her knife. "No one."

"Liar."

Her eyes flashed and she gripped the knife harder, but in the end she lifted her skirt to return it to its home.

"What's your name?" the woman asked.

"My name?" Zera snapped her attention away from the long leg on display. "Uh, Zera. Zazzera."

"Zera Zazzera?"

"No, just Zazzera." Stupid. Now she had to hope this other time traveler thought she was lying.

"Well, Miss Zazzera, it's been a pleasure," she said, making sure once more that her skirt was properly aligned. "I'll take my leave now."

"No, wait, I mean..." Zera tried to compose herself and carefully moved to the same side of the room. She wasn't even supposed to *talk* to anyone. But here they'd had a full on brawl—which she'd prepared for—and a conversation—which she had not. And nothing had gone awry, which meant she *had to be another time traveler*.

The woman looked at her with a carefully blank face. "What is it?"

"I just...I have nothing, I'm passing through." She scrambled for anything to keep her talking. "Is there any way you can point me to a soup kitchen? Or tell me which way Baltimore is?"

The woman blinked. "There's a convent a few miles south of here. They will give you a bed and a meal for the night, and would probably have better directions than I."

"Thank you." The woman moved again to leave, and Zera moved in front of her. There was no way this woman was a different person than the one she saw in 2040. Sure, her hair was shorter and she wasn't as muscled, but she couldn't forget those cheekbones and rosebud lips. Something was off about her, and Zera needed to figure out what.

Luckily, the universe was on her side.

A popping sound, much louder than the clicks of whatever was going on upstairs, interrupted their conversation. Screams followed the pops, as well as scrapes of chairs and the hissing of some machine Zera couldn't name. Dust shook from the rafters as people ran across the floor above them, and a second later the dust turned to smoke. The building was on *fire*.

"We gotta go," she said, but the woman was way ahead of her, weaving through the carnage of their fight toward the exit. Zera followed, easily catching up this time, and kept a stable hand on the woman's back as they ran up the stairs. Smoke made her eyes sting and her lungs burn.

A groan from the wood above was the only warning they got. On instinct, Zera grabbed the woman by her skirt and pulled her back, tucking her body underneath her own as the ceiling crumbled onto the stairs. The woman sank her fist into Zera's stomach, but her eyes went wide as she saw the reason for her grab.

"I am so terribly sorry—"

"Just run!" Zera coughed, shoving her toward the cellar doors. The woman obeyed, and they continued their ascent until they tumbled out onto the street. Flames spat from the windows above them, the shattered glass sparkling on the dirt road like diamonds.

"What was this place?" Zera asked. The workers in the building stared at the blaze, the men gesturing wildly as they called for the fire brigade.

"The telegraph center," the woman answered. Oh, the irony. She looked back toward the busy city center, and Zera followed her gaze.

The streets were in turmoil. The buildings were too close and made of flammable materials; it was only a matter of time before the flames spread. Sirens screeched as firetrucks mobilized, pedestrians hurrying out of their way.

"We should—" Zera turned around, but the woman was already striding away. "Hey, wait up!"

The woman kept walking. She had long legs, but Zera was quick and had much more practical footwear. Catching up wasn't a challenge.

"We should help them back there," she said, falling into step next to her.

"I believe that is a job for the professionals, Miss Zazzera," the woman replied. Zera looked over her shoulder again at the fire, and was surprised to find things shifting toward control. Perhaps she was right.

"Okay, good point," she conceded. "Now that we escaped death together, wanna tell me your name?"

"No."

A man with a large, black suitcase and some sort of stand ran toward the fire, and the woman made a sharp turn to get out of his way and go down a different street.

"I apologize, Miss Zazzera, I believe you have mistaken me for someone else. The convent you seek is outside the city. If you walk along the main road a taxi might offer you a ride."

"I may be a little lost, but I know for a fact I know you." It was decades from now, but for Zera, it had only been a week. She grabbed the woman's arm, forcing her to stop. "Just from another time."

Red colored the woman's pale cheeks, and her hand drifted to the hilt of her knife, hidden beneath her skirt. "Be careful what accusations you make, Miss Zazzera. I am not as gentle a lady as you might think."

"What the—gods, you talk like a video game character."

"I beg your pardon?" She straightened her perfect posture even further. "Though I'm not the most educated woman, I still understand an insult when I hear one."

"That wasn't an insult." Zera pinched the bridge of her nose. Looked like people lived a little differently in the other bunkers compared to her own. "Never mind. Look, if I tell you my secret, will you tell me yours?"

It was a gamble, and a stupid one at that. Zera palmed her pocket, feeling the emergency return syringe nestled safe inside. The thought of the needle made sweat prickle along the back of her neck.

"While you make a sound offer, I find I'm rather too attached to my own safety to agree to your request." The woman gave an honest-to-gods curtsy and tried to leave again. "Good day, Miss Zazzera."

"It was in the future," Zera blurted. The woman stopped, her back to her. Zera pulled out the syringe, just in case. The woman could take her name back to her superiors, but if Zera got back first, she'd have a head start. "I spotted you in the future. Decades from now."

Slowly, the woman turned, and Zera figured she had her cornered. The shadow of the setting sun and the rising lamp light made her brown eyes dark and molten. Above them, an aurora started, a weaker version of the one Zera saw in 2040. "That's preposterous. No one can live that long."

"Okay, see, you know how I know you're lying?" She didn't give her time to answer. "Because a normal person would say 'you're crazy' or 'what were you doing decades in the future,' but you didn't care about that part. You think the weirdest thing about that statement is that *you* were there."

The woman's eyes flicked to hers, then to the area around them. Sirens drifted from one street over, but their side was empty. She then looked to the dancing green lights in the sky, but not in excitement, like she had in 2040, and not in awe, as anyone else would. She looked at the cosmic brush strokes like they were a bad omen.

"They'll claim it's a geomagnetic storm," Zera said. The colors flashed on the woman's eyes. "You told me that, right before..."

Her voice pitched low. "Before what, may I ask?"

Zera gulped. It was one thing to admit to her—*their*—current occupation, it was another to tell this woman about her impending death.

"Before another storm kind of like this." Every lie held a bit of truth.

"They keep happening? Interesting," she said in the same tone of voice Kissi had when she found an outlier in her data. "Is that why you're here? Because of this storm?"

"Yeah, they want me to collect samples."

"Samples?" Now Zera had her full attention. "Of what?"

"Everything. Anything that could tell us why these storms happen. Isn't that why they sent you here?"

"No one has discovered an answer, then?"

Zera paused. Her answer didn't match the question. "Look, if we're gonna figure this out, I'll need your help. And before this is over, I think you'll need mine too."

The woman didn't seem to completely trust her, but she nodded. "You might be right."

"Are you gonna tell me your name now?" Zera asked, because it felt important. The woman *herself* felt important. She had some sort of stake in these events, and if Zera was careful enough, she could get more information than Dr. Phillips or Vylek thought possible.

"Hmm," she tapped her chin thoughtfully, "No."

"What?"

"Good night, Miss Zazzera, and good luck."

The woman fled to the busy main street, moving with more agility than Zera thought possible in those shoes. With her eyes down, she melted into the bodies crowding the street. Zera took off after her, but this New York was different than hers, and the woman had home field advantage. Given her seamless assimilation, the traveler must have been here a long time.

Perhaps that's why Dr. Phillips and Vylek never sent anyone back this far—because someone from another bunker got stuck.

1944

ZERA RETURNED to Central Park and spent a fitful night on a bench, never fully falling asleep thanks to the bright aurora bouncing through the treetops. The gold of daybreak drowned out the greens and blues, and once the sun fully took over, she rose and performed her task of sample collection, though it seemed stupid with her new information. The presence of the woman was more important, at least in her opinion, but she risked the wrath of Dr. Phillips and Vylek if she came back empty-handed, especially since she technically broke the rules. Again.

Searching for her today would be a mistake. In her head, Zera knew that. Over and over she told herself the meeting in 2040 was a fluke, that she just ran into the woman's descendant with an uncanny resemblance. Her mind was playing tricks. They couldn't be the same person.

But what if they were? If another bunker was using the same tactic of time travel...

Once her tiny sample containers were full and holstered, Zera went back into the city and found the same streets. Smoke lingered in the air, an acrid addition to the rest of the city smells. In the light of day she easily found the telegraph building. From there, she backtracked to the spot where their eyes met.

Midday foot traffic made it difficult to scan the area from her perch against a streetlamp, but now Zera knew what to look for. Any flicker of honey brown caught her eye, and any woman with ramrod posture and a certain arrogance drew her attention. For hours she waited, ignoring duty and hunger, until the work day ended and people flooded the sidewalk again.

There she was.

The woman's expression didn't change as she met Zera's eyes, but Zera gave her a smirk and a challenging raise of an eyebrow. She willed the woman to run again, now that she was feeling less battered by time's river and had the lay of the land. The woman came to a stop in front of her, and Zera wondered if the knife hid under *this* skirt too.

"You're still here," she said.

"And that accent is still ridiculous," Zera replied.

"What do you want, Miss Zazzera?"

"You know something about what's going on, and I want to know it too," Zera said. "Perhaps we were brought together by fate or something."

The woman snorted. "Fate is a cruel mistress, and she doesn't hand out gifts."

"Not often, no," Zera said. "But not *never*. Ah, fuck, now you've got *me* talking like a video game character."

"Miss Zazzera! Your language!"

"What'd I say? Fuck? Ah, shit—"

"Stars and garters—" She actually clutched her pearls, the small string peeking out from her blouse.

Zera grinned, and recalled their previous meeting. "Oh right, I forgot to say yesterday—you told me to find you here, something about spending the night together?"

"Miss Zazzera!" Pink turned to red, spreading across her neck and ears.

"Sorry, miss, uh..." She let the sentence hang, hoping the woman would finally introduce herself. When she didn't, Zera added, "You also said something about the night being at the college?"

The woman paused for a moment. "Ms. Katherine Scott," she finally choked out. Probably a fake name, since she had more time to think than Zera did. "But you may call me Katherine."

"Nice to meet you, Katherine. You can call me Zera, all my friends do." She held out her hand for a shake. Katherine elegantly extended her own, palm down, as if expecting a kiss to her fingers or something. Zera, confused by the gesture, just awkwardly grasped her hand for a second and let it go, ignoring the shock as their skin touched.

"You said 'Zera' wasn't your first name."

"It's not."

"And you don't wish to tell me your first name?"

"Not even a little."

"Then I'll continue calling you by your given name, thank you."

"Does this mean you'll talk to me?"

Katherine didn't answer. Instead, she walked away, weaving into the throng of people. Traffic was a nightmare thanks to shift change, packing the sidewalks and drowning out every sound except for honks and variations of *the fuck outta here!*

Once Zera proved she could—and would—keep up with her, Katherine gave her a devilish grin and tucked her hand into Zera's elbow. Her slender fingers were bare save for two rings, no signs of the layers silver and gold decorating them like the first time. Perhaps the rings were trinkets she picked up along the way? Was she meeting the most past version of this other time traveler?

This was bad. This was definitely not what Zera was supposed to be doing, not the mystery she was supposed to solve. And yet, as the sun set and the aurora rose once again, she let Katherine pull her toward the city without any resistance.

Zera kept her head down as they walked, but her fear of discovery was unnecessary; everyone was looking up at the sky, pointing out the swirls in the lights. Katherine strode with her head held high and purpose in her steps, and only the nails digging into Zera's arm betrayed the other woman's distrust.

She'd never broken a rule so hard and fast in her entire life. But the rules didn't count if it was another person from the future, right? She hoped so, considering she'd found another traveler and was currently making friends.

A few deep breaths were in order. If her vitals got too crazy, the anchor might pull her back, and she couldn't run that risk. Not when there was still so much to find out about Katherine and whichever bunker she hailed from.

"So, what's your deal?" Zera was under the impression that polite conversation was important during the first tense minutes of a shaky truce, but Katherine shushed her sharply.

"Not here." She cleared her throat, then added, "I apologize—"

"Oh my days, Katherine Scott, is that you?"

Katherine stopped dead in her tracks and Zera's veins froze over. The voice sounded way too friendly. This could be bad. Would she have to fight a third time traveler? She didn't particularly want her ass handed to her a second time.

"Keep your head down," Katherine hissed, then planted a massive, false smile on her face. "Why, Dahlia Wiles, it *has* been entirely too long, hasn't it?"

Zera ducked her head and pulled her stolen hat low over her eyes. She couldn't see Dahlia Wiles' face, but her body and dress suggested great wealth and prosperity. Or someone who knew how to rob the rich when they arrived in a new time. Perhaps Dahlia could be more of an asset than she thought?

"Who is this, erm, *charming* gentleman on your arm?" Dahlia's voice dripped with gossip and judgment, and Zera had a mind to show her exactly how charming she could be.

"I'm afraid it's my poor cousin, just in from the war," Katherine lied. "He's got a firm bout of sea sickness and land legs, I'm afraid. I was just taking him home from the docks so he could have some tea and rest."

"Those docks are a dangerous place, and that's the bottom fact," Dahlia said. Zera had the distinct impression she'd never actually seen the docks. And that she might not be another traveler. So then how did Katherine know her? "Was it terrible on the lines, young man? Did you see anything horrible?"

Zera cleared her throat, unsure how to answer the direct and inappropriate question.

"Yes, ma'am," she said, doing her best to lower her voice and copy their accent. This conversation needed to end, or her hand was going to go numb and fall off from the pressure Katherine held on her forearm.

"Oh, like what—"

"Apologies, Dahlia, I'm afraid we must be on our way," Katherine interrupted, pulling Zera away.

"Yes, yes, of course. Do come by the club soon?"

"I shall. Give my best to John and the boys, hmm?"

The whole interaction made Zera so uncomfortable she nearly pulled the syringe and sent herself back to 2058. Unfortunately, Katherine didn't give her the option. She steered her the opposite direction of Dahlia's retreating form, and this time they walked at double the speed.

"Well, that wasn't a complete flummox," Katherine muttered.

"What'd you call me?" The joke landed somewhere on the sidewalk behind them.

"I didn't call you anything, Miss Zazzera—"

"Zera."

"I'm sorry?"

"I told you to call me Zera. The full name usually means I'm in trouble."

"It's a figure of speech, *Miss Zazzera*, it means—"

"I know what flummox means." Zera didn't know what it meant, but she could gather enough information from the context. She chanced a glance at Katherine, and was surprised to find a tinge of pink painting her cheeks.

"We're almost at my home," she said.

"Your home? How long have you been stuck here?"

Katherine didn't answer. They turned another corner to find a street lined with big brownstones. The brick was fresh, the color a pure chocolate instead of the dingy mix of brown and black and gray she remembered.

Katherine's house sat in the middle of the street, stately and grand like the rest of the row. The heavy iron lock opened with a swift twist of the ornate key, everything smooth and new compared to Zera's time.

Light from the streetlamp and the colorful sky seeped through the lace curtains, painting pictures of purple and blue and green over the floral-detailed wallpaper. The wooden slats of the floor were wide and dark, and when they walked inside it didn't have the same echoing creak Zera associated with floors of aged houses. Old-fashioned rugs sat clean and new, and while the house resembled something out of a museum, it smelled like roses.

Katherine stepped sharply away and flipped on the lights before moving into the next room. The bulbs buzzed like flies, which made Zera worry they'd burst any second. Though they burned orange and warm, they did little to stave off the chill of the house. Pictures on the wall told a story of a young couple together for many years, but there were no signs of a man in the house itself. Perhaps he was gone to war?

"Are you hungry? Can I offer something to eat?" Katherine appeared in the hallway again, making Zera jump.

"You don't have to do that," she said. She *was* hungry, and thirsty, but she wasn't sure she trusted Katherine enough to eat her food. Who knew what poisons the other bunker sent with her?

"I haven't the slightest idea what you mean," Katherine replied.

Zera grimaced. "Ew, that. That right there. The whole upper crust polite thing you did with Dahlia. Yesterday you pulled a knife on me and we agreed we're both from a different time. I think we're past the point of propriety."

Katherine blinked and said, "Well, I suppose you're right." Her shoulders relaxed and she stuffed her hands in her pockets as she wandered away from her. "I'm hungry. If you want something, then come on."

Could still be a trap, but at least it didn't feel as weird.

A hatstand stood to her right, and Zera hesitantly hung the stolen cap on it. The rubber of her boots kept her steps quiet as she followed Katherine to the back of the house. Big windows showed off the tiny backyard and bursting garden, and the kitchen island held a massive vase with real fresh flowers. There were no sounds from upstairs, no signs of life other than Katherine's.

"Do you live here alone?" Zera asked. Katherine bent down, reaching into the back of the oven, and Zera could see her shoulder blades pinch together. She was about to retract her question when she got an answer.

"My husband owns the house." Katherine knocked the oven closed with her foot and turned a knob on the stove, sliding a cast iron skillet onto it.

"And where's he?"

"He travels for work, and I keep the house while he's away."

"How long has he been away?" She was curious how many lies Katherine could come up with.

"You are a very curious woman, Miss Zazzera."

Fear lanced through Zera's chest. She didn't need to test her. "Sorry. Just making conversation."

"I'd prefer another topic, if you don't mind." Satisfied with the heat of the skillet, Katherine poured the tiniest drop of oil Zera had ever seen, then retrieved half an onion and a bell pepper from the fridge. There was a knife block on the counter, and Katherine chose to use one of those with expert precision instead of the one strapped to her thigh.

"Well, let's turn back to the problem at hand." Zera nodded toward the aurora. Katherine didn't look, instead focusing on thinly slicing a couple potatoes and adding them to the skillet. "Wanna share what you know about the thing going on outside?"

"I'm afraid it isn't much, just what I've managed to glean from a few specific journals that I, ah, procured from the University." She stirred the vegetables with a wooden spoon and added salt and pepper, a bit more liberally than the oil. "It's a special interest of mine. I've attempted to speak with the gentlemen scholars of natural sciences, but they are...less than inclined to discuss the phenomenon with me."

"'Cause you're a woman." Zera knew things used to be this way, but hearing the truth was different than reading it in a book.

"Precisely." Katherine watched the skillet instead of Zera, and Zera let the silence hang, hoping to get more information. But the vegetables were cooked and a few slices of Spam were added to the skillet before Katherine spoke again. "Perhaps our meeting yesterday will end up fortuitous for both of us."

Katherine split the meal between two plates and carried them to the table, along with silverware. She didn't seem particularly proud of the food, but to Zera it smelled like sweet ambrosia from the gods.

"Technically not the first time we met." Zera dug in immediately, disregarding the heat. War-rationed America wasn't known for its cuisine, but she hadn't eaten all day, and compared to the mix of plain potatoes and cardboard often served in the mess, this was a delicacy. And it was gone much too soon.

"So you say," Katherine said, taking dainty bites from her own food. When she spotted Zera's empty plate, she got up and retrieved a slice of something sweet and chewy, an oat and honey thing that wasn't quite bread or cake. "I would love to hear the story of our first meeting, if you don't mind."

Zera's chewing slowed. She might be the curious one, but Katherine was right in that litter of kittens too.

"I'd rather not." If Katherine could deflect, so could she.

Katherine stared, and Zera wondered if she was waiting for her to shift under her gaze, if she thought prolonged silence would eat at her until she told the whole tale. But Zera was used to people using silence as a weapon, and had long since developed armor against it.

Katherine tapped her chin, and her eyes narrowed in a conspiratory way. "Zera, would you be opposed to a bit of—shall we call it espionage?"

Zera grinned. "I could be convinced."

"There's an event at the University tonight, where the natural scientists will run a demonstration of a magnetometer in an effort to explain these lights in the sky." Katherine paused to take a dramatic bite of potato. "I doubt it'll work, but perhaps this time technology will be good enough."

"That's a weird way to put it."

"Since my husband is away, you'll have to pretend to be my poor, war-stricken cousin again. Come, let's get you dressed up."

She grabbed the plate, and Zera scooped as much into her mouth as she could before Katherine took it away. She lamented the loss of her meal, but a moment later Katherine presented her with a shiny pink apple in consolation. Zera thought of Kissi as she bit into the sweet, crisp flesh of it and wondered if she could sneak one home.

"Let's go, Miss Zazzera. We must find clothes that fit." Katherine grabbed her arm with that strong grip again and hauled Zera to her feet.

"Whoa, whoa, whoa." Zera yanked her arm away. "I thought we were just gonna break in somewhere and get information. I can't attend a demonstration...event...thing."

"I said espionage would be involved." Katherine seemed confused by the outburst.

"Kat, how exactly am I supposed to blend in?" She gestured wildly to her jumpsuit. "Unless it's conveniently a masquerade ball."

Katherine's lip curled, but somehow she made even that look lady-like. "It's *Katherine*. And of course not, the University wouldn't host a masquerade ball. Though I think Emily Birmingham has plans for sometime later in the fall—"

"I can't go to this," Zera interrupted. It would break so many rules that not only would she be kicked out of the program, she'd likely be court martialed. "You need me to break some locks? Bust some heads? I can do that. I'm not a socialite."

"Well, that much is obvious," she said. "You won't have to mingle with the other partygoers. That will be my job. But you will do exactly as you already stated."

Zera swallowed the lump in her throat. "I've got a bad feeling about this."

"Oh, you'll be fine."

"Then why can't I just go as myself? Why do I have to pretend to be your male cousin?"

"I can't very well explain the presence of a strange woman in my house, especially one with such an appearance as you." Katherine led her up the stairs, her cheeks pink in a way that had nothing to do with rouge.

"What's that supposed to mean?" A cold weight settled in Zera's stomach. Her fingers shook as she ran them through her short hair, the same cut every digger had back in her time. She couldn't change her short hair, just like she couldn't help her thicker athletic build.

Katherine's face was back to a mask. "I mean to say, people are very nosy, so we must be careful with whom you chance an interaction."

"Cut the bullshit and speak English," Zera said.

"You stick out in a dangerous way, and we need to limit that or else one or both of us will get hurt."

Well, that was one way to say it.

"Thank you, was that so hard?" Zera asked. "So what, we're just gonna barge into this college and steal some stuff?"

"That's the long and the short of it, yes. Well, you'll do the stealing, I'll be the distraction."

"I don't like the sound of this. Sounds like we don't have a plan."

"We have a plan, it's just a simple one. Simple often works better, I've found." Katherine crossed her arms.

"Okay, you've gone from sounding like a video game character to sounding like an eighty year old."

"Eighty is a very respectable age."

Zera sighed and pinched the bridge of her nose. Fine, for the sake of the mission, she could let Katherine think she was in charge.

"Okay, whatever. Are we gonna go raid a college or what?"

1944

Zera had almost forgotten how big bedrooms used to be. A collection of dresses hung in Katherine's closet, pressed and organized like a showroom. In the opposite closet, suits hung arranged by color with a few empty spots for the suits the alleged husband had on his business trip.

Katherine assessed Zera with narrowed eyes and reached for a navy blue suit, the fabric so heavy it seemed to lag behind as she carried it across the room. "This one should fit, it was too big for him. We might have to bind your breasts further, but we'll see how it looks first." A white linen shirt joined the pile, then she leaned back on her heels and crossed her arms.

"You just want me to put it on?" Zera crossed her arms as well. No one ever accused her of having an ample bosom, but she'd seen corsets in enough movies to know whatever methods Katherine had would not be comfortable, or medically safe.

"That was my plan, yes," Katherine said. Zera shrugged and stripped to her sports bra and underwear, donning the dress shirt with all the efficiency the military trained into her. The pants were loose through the hips and thighs, but she had to suck in her stomach to button the narrow waist.

When she leaned over to pick up the jacket, the waistband pinched her skin.

"Oh, I don't like this," she said, standing and fidgeting. "You said this one was too *big* for him?"

"He's built for business, as they say," Katherine explained, coming to look at the fabric. Zera didn't know that was a thing people said. "I can snip the waistband a little, give you some breathing room."

"Yeah, let's do that," Zera said with a groan.

Katherine went to her vanity and returned with a small pair of scissors from the sewing kit. Up close, Zera could see the little freckles across her nose, hidden almost completely by powder, and the flecks of gold in her brown eyes. Katherine's brow creased as she angled the scissors and cut, giving Zera more breathing room with incremental snips.

"Better?" she asked, looking up.

Zera gulped. "Much." She still couldn't breathe, but that was for other reasons.

"Now for the shirt."

"If I put that on right now, I'm gonna drown in sweat." Heat was already building beneath the heavy wool trousers.

"Fine. I suppose I can put on your beard."

"You can what?"

Katherine returned to the vanity, this time choosing a small box from her arsenal. When she popped the top, Zera caught the smell of charcoal and hoped it was a coincidence, but the container held an inky black powder with suspicious clumps.

"Are you about to rub coal on my face?"

"Of course. How else would we mimic facial hair? You're very pale, it won't take much."

"Thanks, my bunker still lives underground." Katherine made a face, but instead of responding, she grabbed Zera's jaw with her thumb and forefinger and tilted her face toward the light of the window. She pinched a small pouf between her fingertips and gingerly touched it to Zera's chin and upper lip, the coarse powder sticking to the peach fuzz on her face. It took Zera a lot of mental fortitude to keep her eyes up instead of right at her new makeup artist.

"What do you mean by underground?" Katherine had a layer of innocence to her voice, and Zera didn't believe it for a second.

"Oh, that's how we're playing it? Okay, in that case, I just spend most of my time inside."

Katherine's gentle gaze turned sharp, and she added a few extra puffs before stepping away.

"There, a respectable five o'clock shadow." She used a fingertip to wipe away an errant particle, then returned the container to her vanity. "Now for your hair."

"What's wrong with my hair?"

"It's very untidy." She opened another jar, this one black with a transparent cream in it. A sweet, musky scent surrounded Zera as Katherine styled her hair with the pomade.

"What's that smell?"

"A form of cherry pipe tobacco, I believe. Usually I prefer the vanilla, but Alfred is partial to this one."

Satisfied with her work, Katherine returned the pomade to its place and picked up the dress from her bed. "I'm afraid I must ask for your help now."

"Sure, no problem." This was just another day, helping out a friend. It didn't matter that she was pretty and sunkissed and didn't smell like a rank bunker. Or didn't live in one anymore.

Katherine undressed quickly, moving awkwardly to hide some of her body the way Zera used to at the beginning of her career. Did that make Katherine a new recruit? Zera filed it away as another question to ask. When all that was left was granny-style panties and a cone-shaped bra, Zera forgot her questions and instead focused on holding in her laughter.

"What?" Katherine asked, putting her hands on her hips. It didn't help the visual.

"Nothing, I just..." Zera's voice shook, and Katherine raised an eyebrow.

"Just what?" she demanded.

"Just...You ever put an eye out with that thing?"

Katherine glared. "I'll have you know this is very comfortable."

"I'll bet it is."

"Can you please help me with my corset?" It was a surprise she didn't stomp a foot with impatience, though Zera kept a careful eye on the knife still strapped to her thigh. At least, until Katherine brought out a satin-covered lacy thing Zera had dreamed about but never seen in real life.

"Yeah." She paused to clear her throat, which had suddenly gone dry. "C'mon." The corset was much more rigid and heavy than she anticipated, the sharp ends of the boning barely softened by the fabric overlay. With her back to Zera, Katherine swiftly untied and unhooked her bra and replaced it with the corset. It creaked and cracked as Katherine pressed it to her chest, the long ribbons hanging down her side.

"Are you familiar with the garment?" she asked, a little too late.

"No, but I think I can figure it out." Zera threaded the ribbon one eyelet at a time, her eyes almost crossing by the time she made it to the bottom. She patted Katherine on the back. "There you go."

"You still need to tighten it."

Zera thought it looked tight enough, but apparently she was wrong. "Uh, okay."

She started at the top and gave each cross a tug, the ribbons sliding half a centimeter at most with the movements.

"I'm not made of glass, Miss Zazzera. Use those muscles you insist on showing to the world."

Zera thought she was just wearing a sports bra, but apparently she was bragging.

"How tight do I go then?"

"As tight as possible."

"How will you breathe?"

"Hopefully by inhaling and exhaling, but I'm open to other options if you have any."

"Okay, no need to be a dick about it," Zera said.

Katherine let out a very lady like snort, which she quickly smothered. "As you were, please."

Zera could swear she heard the grin in her voice. "Alright, don't say I didn't warn you."

She pulled at the ribbons until the sides nearly touched, and against her better judgement she ignored the creaking of the corset and continued until Katherine's body morphed into a terrible hourglass. Old movies didn't do corsets justice, neither the look nor the discomfort.

"Thank you very much," Katherine said, her voice as nonchalant as a few minutes prior. How she could breathe, Zera didn't know.

"Are you gonna pass out on me?" she asked. There was a difference in the way Katherine moved; her back was somehow even straighter, and her steps were careful. Falling was not an option when she couldn't bend at the waist.

"I'm not an amateur." If Zera really listened, there was just a hint of tension in her voice, but her face remained calm. With an awkward curtsy, she took the dress from her bed and held it out. "Forgive me, but your assistance would expedite the process."

"Gods, just say you need help." It was heavier than expected and she nearly dropped it, but she managed to catch the layers in time to make it look like she was adjusting it. "Why the corset? The dress looks fitted enough."

"Sometimes a lady needs a little help to accentuate her assets," Katherine said, diving into the waist of the dress as Zera held it. As the fabric settled around her hips and Zera went to adjust it, she got an eyeful of Katherine's meaning.

"Right," she said. "Guess that's why I got stuffed into a suit instead of a corset, huh?"

"I said nothing of the sort."

"Ah, but you're not denying it either," Zera teased. Katherine shot her a glare, but Zera just batted her eyelashes. "C'mon, princess, we've got things to do."

It took another hour to get Katherine's hair and makeup situated, during which Zera snuck her weapons, samples, and anchor syringe into the deep pockets of the suit. Soon enough they were walking arm in arm down the sidewalk, headed gods knew where. This was not Zera's New York; she was completely at Katherine's mercy.

"Time to paint the town red," Katherine muttered.

Columbia University made itself known long before it was actually visible, the lawn and entrance decorated with massive oil lanterns that shone like a hundred tiny suns. The aurora, just visible through the shifting clouds, made the place look like some haunted mansion out of a cheap horror movie. Pairs of people promenaded up the front drive and steps, the ladies all sporting the formal gowns like Katherine, though none had chosen to accentuate their *assets* like she did.

Back before the Storm, Zera considered the music her mother listened to with a record player absolutely ancient. Now, as she crossed the threshold into the foyer, a brass band assaulted her ears with tunes she'd only heard in really old TV shows. The brim of her hat hid most of her grimace, but the nails digging into her arm said it didn't hide enough.

"Keep your head down," Katherine chastised through her smile. "Once we get into the main lecture hall, you'll excuse yourself quietly and cross the campus to the natural sciences building."

"Wait, I have to go to a different building? I thought this thing was for a demonstration."

"It is, and you'll be obtaining our parcels while I watch it." She paused to curtsy at a couple walking by, her iron grip pulling Zera down into a bow. Annoyance seeped into her spine, but she held it down.

"So I go to the natural sciences building."

"Yes, northwest of here."

"Northwest—Kat, I haven't seen the sky in a couple decades, I don't know where the fuck northwest is."

Katherine was much better at hiding her feelings, her only break in composure a tiny puff of air from her nose.

"My name is Katherine. Behind this building, move diagonally to the left. Find the journals on magnetism from 1884 in the back room. Then we can discuss your questions." Her fake smile brightened and she waved to someone at the double doors opposite them.

"What if I wanna see the demonstration?"

"Unfortunate for you."

They swept into an open room filled with men and women dressed to the nines, mingling with crystal glasses of champagne in their hands. There was more grandeur than Zera thought necessary, particularly when Central Park, just a few blocks down, housed the city's less fortunate at night.

Next to her, Katherine scanned the faces, humming along quietly to the song. Her expression was guarded now, her fingers flexing on Zera's forearm. At first, Zera thought it was nerves from their spy mission, but then she noticed how she messed with her skirt, and how her dress was a little different than everyone else's. A little more...vintage.

"Wanna dance?"

"Hmm?" Katherine blinked, confused.

"You're humming the song. Wanna dance to it?" Zera gestured to the open space where a few couples twirled and stepped to a dance she definitely didn't know.

Katherine chuckled. "Are you well versed in the waltz, Miss Zazzera?"

"We're about to find out."

Zera pulled her to the dance floor and placed her hand on Katherine's waist. The dance wasn't particularly complicated, and after a few bars of trial and error, she caught the gist of it.

"This is ridiculous."

Zera shushed her. "Have some fun, Kat."

"*Katherine.*"

Zera spun her so she wouldn't have to think of a response. The movement was clumsy at best, but it served its purpose to distract Katherine from her nerves.

"You're incorrigible."

"Thanks, you too."

Another spin, just for good luck.

The song ended and Zera tugged Katherine to her chest, raising her eyebrows and willing the other woman to snap. But Katherine kept her composure, except for the absolute daggers she glared.

"Go. Now."

"Ma'am, yes ma'am," Zera said, making sure to give an extra low bow before she departed.

No one was walking the campus since the main hall held the live attraction. True to Katherine's word, a squat stone building sat a hundred paces from the front hall, *Natural Sciences* stamped oh-so-conveniently above the entrance. Heavy wooden doors with brass handles and locks barred the way. She checked over her left shoulder and her right, but the campus, painted green and blue by the aurora, was empty. Perfect.

She turned the knob and pushed. The lock pushed back.

"Son of a bitch," she muttered. She tried again and got nothing but a deep echo of the door shaking in its frame. "Fuck."

Her pulse raced. She had to get inside and steal those notebooks so Katherine would answer her questions. Then, maybe, she could help Katherine get back to *her* bunker, and the two could collaborate. It was the perfect plan—Vylek would surely be delighted. She'd probably give Zera a Medal of Honor or something.

Zera evaluated the building. The windows in front were very pretty, but they were also slender, and embedded deep in the stone. She jumped into the bushes and rounded the structure. The window size remained the same until the back, where they widened. It hurt to dig her short nails into the area around the glass, especially when her tugging found nothing but more locks.

Then, one gave.

It was just a little, but it was enough to send her adrenaline into overdrive. With more pulling and even more cursing, she made just enough space to grab the edge with her fingertips and yank it all the way open. Residual heat from the day puffed out and the air was more than a little musty, but that didn't matter. She wrestled the window all the way open and climbed inside, the tight cut of her borrowed suit protesting the whole time.

Darkness swallowed her as she fell through the window, and the wooden floors creaked with her rough landing. Training made her confident in her sampling skills, but at no point during basic did they discuss general heist implementation.

Zera pulled out her handheld. It had no intranet service, obviously, but it did have a flashlight.

Wooden cabinets stood in rows like soldiers in the dark, their brass locks glinting as the light passed over them. The placards on the fronts didn't give her many details, and it took a few rounds to find the drawers labeled *Ma-Ma*.

There were three drawers to choose from. When she pulled the first one, it didn't budge, the lock holding fast as she rattled it. The next two stayed adamantly closed as well. *Shit*. Why were they so protective of this stuff? Wasn't the point of a college to share knowledge?

Zera retrieved the knife from her boot and wedged the blade into the middle drawer. It took a little elbow grease and a lot of bodyweight, but with a dull thunk and an echoing clack the lock broke. A rough gouge in the wood opened up where her knife bit into it, the edge splintering and digging into her hand in revenge.

"Oh, you dirty piece of shit," she said through gritted teeth. Blood welled on her skin, dripping when she pried the drawer open and leaving dark splotches on the pristine paper of the journals inside. She put her hand to her lips to stop the bleeding while the other hand rifled through the front of the line. The first book was wedged tightly into the corner and the leather, old and dry, stuck to the varnish of the wood. It cracked loudly when she pried it from the depths.

"Fucking better..." She flipped through the pages at the front, and her blood ran cold as she found the first header.

Material Sciences.

"Gods above and below and sideways." The book protested its return even more than its exit, and Zera shoved it only halfway back before slamming the drawer shut. Every echo sounded like a gunshot in the big, empty room, and she thanked any deity listening for the noise from the party going on in the front building.

It wasn't any easier to break the lock of the drawer above, though she did succeed in opening it without ripping her skin in the process. Something too tall for the drawer kept it from sliding, and she resorted to thrashing the whole thing in an attempt to shake it loose.

"'Ey! You there!"

So maybe *not* everyone was at the party.

A portly man with a policeman's badge on his chest stood at the open window. This time, her adrenaline granted her extra strength, and the drawer burst from its hinges and fell to the ground. Zera danced away just in time to avoid a broken foot, the policeman's yelling accompanying her dance.

"Stop that! Stop where you are!" He fumbled at his breast pocket and found a whistle, the shrill sound stabbing her eardrums. She grabbed journals at random and flipped them open, discarding them if the page had nothing to do with magnetism.

The anchor syringe weighed heavy in her pocket. She was out of time.

Zera grabbed a handful of journals and made a break toward the front door. The policeman, brave as he was, fell for the ruse and left the window. She skidded and turned, running to the window at full tilt and vaulting through it. The landing was neither smooth nor graceful, but it was effective, and she sprinted toward Katherine and the main hall. More whistles screamed and boots pounded the ground behind her. Her lungs burned as she forced her legs to move faster.

Shadows obscured the light of the lecture hall windows, and Zera realized she was on full display for the whole party. Was Katherine there, her nose pressed against the glass? Would she defend her if the policemen took her?

No, she couldn't take that risk. She knew what she had to do—it just sucked.

A hard cut to the left put a copse of trees between Zera and the policemen. She had five seconds, maybe ten, until they caught up. She eyed the journals in her hand, then the windows of the building.

There was no other option.

She pulled the anchor syringe and slammed it into her leg before she could think about the needle, and the river claimed her right as the policemen came into view.

2058

AT LEAST THE second return didn't make her vomit or cough up blood.

Zera's stomach heaved as she lay on the platform, but with a lot of breathing and willpower she kept everything in its place. Pain shot through her as nerves reconnected, and her bones and joints ached like she'd been drawn and quartered and stitched back together.

"She's alive—"

"—that wasn't pretty—"

"Is she wearing—"

"—what's in her hands?"

"Check her blood and get a mask on her. Now."

Voices and lights swirled above her. The main goal was to keep breathing and not pass out, even if blackness threatened the edge of her vision. The poke of a needle was nothing compared to the rest of the pain, and the sterile paper mask placed over her nose and mouth left a metallic taste in the back of her throat.

"Zera, you with me?"

Zera took a deep breath and tried to force a word out, but a groan was all she managed. She tried to nod, but it made stars explode in front of her eyes. Bile rose and she swallowed it down roughly, ignoring the sting of acid.

"You look a lot better this time around." A mask muffled Kissi's voice, and she placed a cool hand on Zera's forehead. "What the hell are you wearing? You look ridiculous."

Zera couldn't exactly laugh, but the sentiment was there. Kissi smoothed her hair, the cold sweat of her forehead rendering the pomade useless. Joints cracked and groaned as someone pulled the journals from her hands and took them to processing.

"Seriously. You'll need a hell of a story this time," she said. The gentle motions soothed her, and fatigue settled into her like sediment at the bottom of a river, caking her muscles and bones until moving was impossible. "Go to sleep. I got you."

"Uh huh," Zera murmured, and let the darkness take her.

Zera awoke to beeping machines and a blood pressure cuff, and while it still felt like all her bones were stretched and all her organs were twisted, she didn't think she'd die just yet. She cracked her eyes open to find dim lights in the hospital room and Kissi asleep in the chair next to her bed. The bedside table held a pitcher of water, condensation dripping down its sides. Suddenly her mouth felt like sandpaper, and the distance between her hand and the water an odyssey.

Zera sat up slowly, letting the world spin and calm before she shifted toward the side. Pain nibbled at the spot where they'd taped her IV, so she tugged the line to give her more room. With the added length, it was easy to lean over the side and grab the pitcher.

Unfortunately, a sensor popped off her chest, the glue too weak to withstand her stretch. Without the input, the machine yelled loudly, startling Zera and Kissi and probably the nurses down the hall. Zera scrambled with the loose fabric of the hospital gown, trying to find the sticker and put it back in its place.

"Zera—"

The door slammed open, and Martin assessed the scene with sharp eyes. Once he found Zera conscious, he turned to the machine, his shoulders visibly relaxing as he read the alarm.

"Jesus, give me a heart attack why don't you," he said, punching the button to make the machine shut up. With deft, professional fingers, he found the missing lead and returned it to its place. Kissi's dark skin was a shade lighter than usual as she took deep breaths to calm down.

"Sorry, I was thirsty." Zera's crackly voice supported her statement. Martin poured her a cup and she took it with grateful hands, guzzling it. A few drops escaped the corners of her mouth, usually a cardinal sin, but no one commented on it.

"Take it easy," Martin said when she reached for a second cup. Instead, he stuffed a bowl of lukewarm broth in her hands. "Your numbers are better this time, but you're still recovering. I really don't wanna clean up your vomit if I can help it."

Zera grimaced and her stomach turned at the thought, even if all she wanted was to grab the pitcher and down the whole thing.

"I'll let Vylek and Dr. Phillips know you're awake." Martin finished his checkup, apparently satisfied Zera had as clean a bill as she was going to get. Zera wasn't ready to talk to Vylek or Dr. Phillips. Maybe if she *did* vomit, she could avoid it for a while longer.

"Are you gonna tell me what was with that outfit?" Kissi asked once Martin left the room. "You looked like you belonged in that old show we always caught Ms. Patricia watching on breaks."

"The one with the whiskey and the British mobsters? Now that you mention it, it did kind of feel like that." She took a breath. "Did the journals make it back?"

"Yeah, they took them for some decontamination protocol." Kissi held up her hands, which looked scrubbed raw. "Locked down the whole wing just in case you brought back something gross."

Zera thought of the street sides and grimaced. "Definitely a chance." The air conditioning kicked on, and she shivered as it whispered across her skin. New York summer heat was more familiar to her than this.

"Something was different about this trip," Kissi said. "Did you do or see anything weird?"

"I...I mean, yes." Zera blinked. "How did you know it got weird?"

"The numbers were different." She said it like it was obvious. Zera decided not to remind her that numbers were her mortal enemy. "There was a match with something from 2040, but that something wasn't you. That should be impossible with a ninety-six year difference."

"The woman was there again," Zera whispered. Kissi would hear it one way or another, and it was more fun to tell the story.

"Which woman?"

"The one from the first trip, the one that died."

Kissi's eyes went wide. "No."

"Yes." Zera ensured her wires were long enough before leaning against the rail of her hospital bed. "But get this, she didn't recognize me at all."

"You're sure it was the same woman?"

"Positive. She looked a little different—hells, she acted *way* different—but it was her. I'd know that face anywhere." That face haunted her night-mares, but that was unnecessary information.

"Did you get a name? I can search in the archives, or maybe I can get clearance—"

The door opened and Kissi's mouth snapped shut. Vylek and Dr. Phillips entered, the former unimpressed and the latter practically vibrating in excitement.

"How do you feel, Zazzera?" Dr. Phillips whipped her stethoscope from around her neck and invaded Zera's space to check vitals.

"Uh, fine." It was mostly the truth.

"Had a dramatic reentry there." Vylek crossed her arms over her chest. "Report. Now."

Zera took a deep breath and prayed.

"I started in Central Park." Technically not a lie. "After the aurora started, I overheard some—some guys talking about a demonstration at Columbia University that night. They were gonna try and chart it or something? Something with the magnetic fields? So I followed them, and —well, it didn't work, the machine thing, but they mentioned past storms so I went and got the journals."

Vylek's sharp glare bore into Zera. "You stole journals from a university?"

"Not quite the low profile," Dr. Phillips commented, returning to her physical assessment.

"You were supposed to get samples, Zazzera. Data."

"And I did! But I also got first hand accounts of other events earlier in the century. They popped up every twelve years." The explanation was not as impressive as she hoped.

"Not helpful—"

"It might be," Dr. Phillips said. She finished her exam and stepped back. "What did the storm look like? Anything like 2040?"

"No, it was just colors in the sky, nothing crazy. Except for the telegraph building catching on fire, I mean."

"Why were you near the telegraph building?" Vylek asked.

"I was following those guys." She decided to test the waters. "It was weird, too. I could've sworn I saw that same woman from my first trip."

"That's impossible. Dr. Phillips, get her a neurology eval."

"Well, I mean," Zera took a deep breath. "Could she be another traveler? She did know about the Storm when I saw her in 2040. Could she be from another bunker?"

"There are no other bunkers with our resources." Vylek sounded like she was trying very hard to contain her anger. "Whatever you think you saw—"

"I know what I saw—"

"As you were, Lieutenant."

Dr. Phillips stopped moving and made eye contact with Kissi, nodding toward the door. Kissi pretended not to see.

"Sorry, ma'am," Zera mumbled, dropping her gaze to her hands.

"Whatever you think you saw, you were mistaken," Vylek continued. Zera shivered again, and it had nothing to do with the air conditioning. "Now. Give me the *relevant* details of your report."

Zera's voice was robotic as she recounted the onset of the event, how the telegraph tower caught fire and the aurora glowed bright, even above the light pollution of New York. She detailed where she took her samples and how she stored them, leaving out Katherine's part. Dr. Phillips tiptoed around her, as if Zera wouldn't notice her taking measurements if she was sneaky enough.

When she finished her initial brief, Vylek nodded. "Good. I'll expect your full report tomorrow evening," she said, her tone icy enough to make Zera fold in on herself.

"Yes, ma'am." It was hard to do things right in this unit, but it was very, very easy to do things wrong.

The dismissal hit Zera in the chest, and the door closing was another slap. Silence weighed on her, pushing her back onto the cardboard mattress and making her heart beat slower.

"I thought it was a good question," Kissi said, shifting her chair closer with an ear-splitting squeak.

"Me too. I just don't know what other explanation there could be, you know?"

"Want me to look her up on the side? I bet I could find something."

"If there is anything, you'll find it. Granted, that's assuming the name she gave me was real."

"Ah, shit, you're right." Kissi rested her chin on her hands. "If I was a time traveler under cover, I'd definitely give a false name. Evie Redenbocker, maybe. Or Dolores Brightwell."

"You just had those in your back pocket, huh?"

"It's a long hour, waiting for you to come back," Kissi said. "What name did you give her?"

Zera didn't want to say. "I, uh, wasn't such a quick thinker."

"What?" Kissi sat up straight. "Zera, no. Tell me you didn't give her your *real* name?"

"I panicked! She was pointing a knife at me, I was confused." Zera threw an arm over her eyes. "Besides, most likely this girl just has some really strong genes or something and I actually met her great-great-great-granddaughter."

"That doesn't explain how the granddaughter knew you."

"Maybe the granddaughter is just friendly like that."

"God, you're so dumb sometimes," Kissi murmured. "Well, what name did she give you? Maybe I can turn something up."

"Katherine. Katherine Scott. Her husband's name was...Alfred? I think?"

"You think or you know?"

"I...think."

Zera didn't want to see the disappointment on Kissi's face at her complete lack of espionage skills. If she was honest, Kissi was the better choice for these types of missions, but she lacked the requisite blood anomalies to tolerate the trips. That's how Dr. Phillips explained it, at least.

"Okay, I'll try to dig up some info on this 'Katherine Scott,' and we're going to have a long talk about keeping our identity and personal information safe," Kissi said.

"At least I didn't tell her my full name." The excuse was weak, but it was all she had. "That has to count for something, right?"

"Well, it's not a complete failure, I'll give you that." Kissi patted her arm once before leaving, turning the light off as she went.

Fragmented thoughts flitted through Zera's head as she lay alone in the room, the steady beep of her vitals machine keeping time with the shifting scenes in her head. Katherine in the park. Katherine in 1944. Katherine crouched and ready to fight. Katherine in the soft clothes before donning her corset.

Something was different about her. Vylek could pretend it was a coincidence, but Zera's current occupation was proof enough that Katherine from the park and Katherine from the past were probably the same person. Statistics weren't her strength, but the likelihood of genetics matching up to that degree seemed significantly smaller than Katherine existing in both times.

It was all too much. Crossing the river took a lot out of her, both body and mind, and after about three thousand beeps from the machine she admitted to herself she couldn't figure anything out tonight. Her body welcomed the decision and dropped her into sleep before she could change her mind.

<hr />

Martin discharged her midday. Zera had fully planned to lumber to her bunk and collapse for the rest of the day, but Kissi had other ideas.

"Good, you're up and moving," she said, falling into step as Zera exited the hospital wing.

"Technically, yeah." After all that had happened these past couple of days, her first real sleep had her feeling worse.

"I got coffee back in the bunk, I've got so much to show you."

"How do you have stuff to show me? I saw you, like, twelve hours ago."

Kissi stopped, and a group of trainees panicked and awkwardly parted around her. She didn't notice.

"Do you really think that lowly of me?"

"Huh?"

"Twelve hours is a long time. Hell, *you* could find archival information in that time."

"First of all, rude." Zera started walking again. Kissi easily caught up with her. "Second, I'm exhausted. I don't know what's going on. I need sleep, like, *real* sleep."

"Well you have to stay up to write your report anyway," Kissi pointed out. "So you might as well listen to me first, it's way more interesting."

Dammit, Zera had forgotten about her report. But she'd rather listen to Kissi repeat the same story for the next six hours than fill out another watered-down account of her trip. Even with the brain fog, Vylek's response to her yesterday still made her insides clench.

Their bunk, which was clean and organized when she left, looked like a tornado made a pit stop in a serial killer's lair before landing in the room. Kissi had two laptops—Zera wasn't sure where the second one came from —and a tablet, but apparently needed even more display space. Papers on a board detailed dates and locations and codes, and a crudely drawn map had matching points with chicken scratch descriptions. At one end hung a full page picture of Katherine and Alfred, the same one from their hallway.

Zera stopped and rubbed her eyes. When she opened them again, the mess was still there, but blurry.

"What the hell happened in here?"

"I told you, I've been busy," Kissi said, going to the nearest laptop. Zera stumbled to her bed and sank onto the edge of it, still trying to make sense of the whole thing. "First, I looked up your friend Katherine Scott."

"I mean, *friend* is maybe a strong word but—"

"I couldn't find a birth certificate, but I did find a marriage certificate, filed in 1939. I tried digging into her maiden name but couldn't find shit." She showed her the picture of said marriage license, but the resolution was grainy and the ink faded.

"Okay, that all checks out."

"Alfred, a self-made man"—Kissi waved dramatically, building to her point—"disappeared under mysterious circumstances."

"What? When?" That shook off some of Zera's fatigue. Was Alfred buried in the backyard and fueling the massive victory garden?

"Well, Katherine reported him missing in 1944, and by 1945 the war was ending, so people kind of stopped caring."

Zera tried to keep up. "Yeah, he wasn't there when I was."

"Doesn't matter. It all started with that weird data point."

"What weird data point?" There were, currently, a lot of weird data points in front of her.

Kissi huffed. "The one I already told you about," she said, throwing her hands up.

"Wait, have you slept since then?"

"That's not important. What's important is the data point." She picked up the second laptop, fumbled with it, then picked up the tablet instead. Her eyes flicked back and forth at dizzying speeds as she scrolled through lines of gibberish.

"This is your little data signature," she said, pointing at a chunk of numbers and letters. "Previously, it was only in 2040. Then, it popped up in 1944, after you left."

"Okay..."

Kissi scrolled again. When she found the thing she wanted, she stopped and shoved the screen in Zera's face.

"There," she said. "Look at it."

"This means nothing to me."

"Oh my God." Kissi groaned. She held the tablet up like a game show host and didn't bother to keep her tone from slipping into well earned condescension. "This is the signature that was present in both 2040 and 1944."

"Interesting." Zera was fading fast. "What about it?"

"Zazzera, focus, for just like, a second," Kissi said. "This *signature* was present during *both* of your trips, *prior* to them."

"So...that thing...represents Katherine?"

Kissi thrust an enthusiastic arm out. "Yes! Exactly!" She threw the tablet onto their end table, nearly upsetting the two laptops, and gestured at the wall. "So I ran a few queries through the archive databases, limiting it to times when we know there were the same type of storms."

"Right, okay, I'm keeping up." Zera was barely holding on.

"The storms pop up every twelve years. It took some digging, but I was able to find Katherine's signature in every one. I'm still working on finding her exactly, but I've got the general area."

"So she's visiting all those times too." Zera stood and moved closer to the wall, trying to make sense of the dates. "We gotta tell Vylek. Maybe she just doesn't know about another program."

"Hell no we can't tell Vylek," Kissi said. "This wasn't exactly sanctioned research, and I've spent a lot of time covering my tracks. We'll get kicked off the team, if not court martialed, and you're already on thin ice—"

"'We'? Why would *we* get kicked off the team? You're the one who did the research!"

"You're the one who found another time traveler!"

"Right, so if anything I should be rewarded."

"You'd accept a reward while I get court martialed?"

Zera stopped, her jaw muscles cramping as she clenched her teeth. Kissi held her gaze with both eyebrows raised, waiting for her response.

Zera let out a breath. "No, I wouldn't," she grumbled. "Damn you."

"That's what I thought. Back to the wall." Kissi found a pencil in her pocket and pointed at the next date on the list: November 1956.

"I really don't wanna go to the 50's. Things were weird then."

"Gonna have to get over it. 'Cause if Katherine's there, we gotta go there."

"How is finding Katherine going to help us reverse the 2040 Storm? She hadn't even heard of it, even when I saw her in 2040." Zera kept trying to figure out the wall, but the more she looked at it, the more confused she felt.

"She's probably jumping around all over the place, so that's how we're going to counteract. We're going to go chronologically," Kissi said, tapping at the dates with the end of her pen. "She knows something we don't. Instead of chasing her through the rabbit holes, we go at it linearly."

"What does all that even do?" Perhaps Zera should have been asking more questions about what they were using for these travels. Trusting the process was her usual route, and it had yet to lead her astray, but Kissi made a couple good points.

"The point is, Katherine hasn't figured out how to undo the 2040 Storm. But if we get all her data, then maybe I can."

Zera opened her mouth, then closed it. Kissi made a very good point indeed.

"And going chronologically is the best way you think?"

"Most efficient, by far. I crunched the numbers." She held up a scrap of paper with a bunch of numbers and letters on it. Zera flashed back to a sweaty classroom with a tired teacher yelling about the importance of algebra. "I have some other data, enough to justify the plan. It'll even give you enough time so you don't have to try and steal anything again."

"To be fair, it was Katherine's idea to steal the journals." Zera paused. "Fuck."

"What?"

"She's gonna be pissed. I was supposed to take those back to her."

Kissi sighed and pinched the bridge of her nose. "Of course you were. Okay, so I'll factor in even *more* time for you to swindle the information from her."

"This feels weird," Zera said. Her stomach twisted like it did anytime she avoided doing homework, or the few times she was late to basic training.

"It's not illegal, and it's technically not going against your orders," Kissi said, which only settled her stomach marginally. "Vylek never said to stop looking for her. You're supposed to look for ways to undo the 2040 Storm, and that's what you're doing. We get what she knows, we fix everything."

"I feel like you're just saying that to make me feel better."

"Of course I am. Is it working?"

Zera took inventory. She no longer wanted to throw up and curl into a ball. "Yeah, I think so."

"Good."

Exhaustion from the last trip lingered in her bones, but the thought of tracking down Katherine, of seeing her again, sent a shot of adrenaline through her veins and a flutter in her stomach. There had to be a way to undo this world.

And maybe the answer lay with Katherine.

2058

THE TUSSLE in 1944 had been an eye-opening experience. Zera had gone in thinking she could force any exit, but she couldn't even beat one woman in a dress. For two weeks she doubled her time in the training room with Grant and Byrd, who loved to drop her with his crutches. They gave her no mercy, even with the gash on her hand.

Next time she saw her, Katherine would be pissed. And Zera had to be ready for more than a knife.

Plenty of pictures of 1950s fashion sat in the archives, but the bunker's provisions were tight enough, with little to no wiggle room for extra wardrobe choices. Once again, Zera would have to improvise, and this time she wouldn't have Katherine's help. She donned the same high-waisted pants from her trip to 1944, plus a long-sleeved paisley button down to match. Ideally, the loud pattern would distract anyone before they noticed she wasn't the classic American gal.

"You look like you're thinking really hard." Byrd grinned at her, leaning heavily on his crutches at the edge of the mat.

"Thinking about tomorrow. Some of us have a job to do," Zera replied. She was still lying on the floor from her final collapse after Grant called it quits and left with a gentle pat on her head. A cast surrounded Byrd's ankle, and she couldn't imagine how hot and uncomfortable the plaster must be. "How's it feeling?"

He looked down at his leg and shrugged. "Could be worse, I guess. Still hurts like the dickens whenever I put weight on it, but that's probably why they told me not to."

"Probably." Zera laughed. "Those docs know some things."

"Yeah, maybe," he said. "I'm just jealous you get to go. I keep trying to tell Vylek I can still be good with a broken wing, but she won't hear it."

"Sounds like a liability." She gave him a wide smile. "But if we got in another fight, at least I could run away and leave you to deal with it."

"That's cold, Zazzera. You'd just abandon me like that?"

"In a heartbeat. So heal up and get back out there. Did they give you a timeline?"

"I get out of the cast next week, but then it's another eight weeks in a boot until I can get in a shoe. In other words, for-fucking-ever."

"Don't fuck it up then." She rose and patted his shoulder. "Any longer, and I just might have to save the world without you."

He narrowed his eyes. "You wouldn't dare."

"I absolutely would." She skipped the shower this time and led him out of the gym and into the hallway traffic, keeping an eye on him as the flow pulled her toward the mess hall. "So you need to get better."

Without warning, the floor vibrated beneath their feet. Everyone in the hallway stopped and shifted to the walls, waiting for the real tremor to hit. More threatening waves shook the corridor, the time between shrinking as the amplitude built. Zera braced against the wall, one arm around Byrd to keep him steady and protect his already broken leg. He tried to shake her off, but a particularly sharp tremble nearly knocked his crutches out, and he stopped pulling away.

The lights flickered, then died completely, thrusting them into darkness. Red emergency lights sparked half heartedly but failed to turn on. Anxious gasps rippled around her. The bunker's inhabitants were accustomed to the tremors, but they usually weren't this bad, or this long, and never had the emergency generators failed.

The bunker tilted hard, sending Zera flying into Byrd, and the person behind her into both of them. The walls were no help once the line of dominoes fell, turning the group into a massive tangle of limbs. Beneath her, Byrd grunted and swore in pain, his ankle knocked around by the movement. Zera did her best to hold onto him and shield him, but there was only so much she could do when fighting gravity.

Slowly, the tremors ebbed away. Heat piled on as the situation settled, the air flow regulators waiting for electricity to kick back on. Everyone did their best to disentangle in the dark, and more than once Zera felt her foot connect with Byrd's cast, earning a painful hiss from him. She kept her apologies to herself, completely planning on blaming everyone around them.

As a group, they found their footing again, but no one made a move. Conversations happened in hushed tones, as if a loud noise might scare the electricity away. Sweat dripped down Zera's temples and back, and gathered on Byrd's arm beneath her hand, but they still didn't move.

"You good?" he whispered.

"Yeah. You?"

"I think everything's still attached."

They waited an eternity until the machinery returned. First came the air regulators, then the red lights, then finally everything else, bathing them all in harsh fluorescents. The hall stank of sweat and fear, and when Zera looked over, she saw a long crack at the junction of the wall and the ceiling.

This. This was why she had to find Katherine. Because if they didn't figure out what she knew and fixed things fast enough, it would spell the end for them all.

Byrd's face was nearly as pale as the white cast around his ankle, and he swayed heavily with the aftershocks of the quake. People parted around them, trying to return to their prior tasks without crashing into the walls again.

"You don't look so good," Zera said.

"I don't feel so good." He swallowed heavily and attempted to straighten on his crutches. Someone clipped his elbow and one crutch slipped out from underneath. Zera grabbed him, unwittingly pulling him onto the casted ankle in an effort to keep him upright.

"Oh fuck!" He gasped, and his pale edges tinged green.

"Oh, no," Zera said, dragging him to the side of the hallway. "Keep it in, Byrd. There's way too many people."

"Trying." He leaned his head against the wall and breathed slow and deep.

"Was it the ankle?" Zera asked. He nodded, and Zera noticed a wet spot on the wall where he left sweat. "Are you, like, going into shock?"

"You don't know what shock looks like?" His words seemed to struggle out of his mouth.

"I'm not the one with a medic patch."

He let out a brief laugh, followed by another difficult swallow. "That's true. But no, I'm not going into shock."

"Do you need me to go get someone?" The flow of people thinned now as everyone returned to their daily tasks, leaving the duo in relative peace. Byrd shook his head.

"No. I think I might need to go to the med bay though," he said.

"C'mon, I'll help you." Zera ignored his protests and slipped an arm around his waist, grabbing onto his belt. He took both crutches under the opposite arm and leaned heavily on her every other step.

"You don't have to do this," he said, though he held onto her with a white-knuckle grip.

"No, I don't," she said. "But if I leave you alone you might pass out in your own sick, and that would really hurt your ankle again."

"I think it's already fucked again." He let out a few choice swear words, his nausea evidently morphing into anger. "Now it's gonna be even longer until I can go back with you."

"You've got time. There's lots of trips lined up." Zera started sweating again. The man was deceptively dense, and despite his outrage, he had little strength to carry himself.

"I don't want the later trips. I want to be there now."

"Take it down a notch, bud. If you went back right now, you'd probably end up a puddle in Central Park."

"I could handle it—"

"Byrd, chill. For real." Zera stopped and pulled away. Without her support, Byrd tilted sharply, and she barely caught him before he hit the floor again. "See? Can't even stand. Going right now isn't important."

"Yes it is."

"You're such an ass," Zera said. "Why do you feel like you have to go right now? I promise, I can handle things just fine on my own until you're back."

"There's just so many things that could help," Byrd said.

"Yeah, I'll get them. Don't worry." Zera was quickly becoming impatient with the argument. "I'm not incompetent."

"I don't think you're incompetent," Byrd said. "I just know two heads are better than one when deciding what resources to bring back."

"'Resources'? We're not there for resources, we're there for data."

"See? That's why I need to go. Data's important, but just think, if there was one thing you could bring back, just one little thing that could make your life easier, wouldn't you grab it?"

"Sounds like you're thinking of something in particular." Zera didn't want to think about it, if she was honest. She already had another time traveler taking up extra space in her brain, she didn't need to worry about anything else.

They rounded a corner and the med bay appeared. Zera thanked the gods; Byrd seemed to get heavier by the second, and she was ready to go back to her bunk, clean up, and pass out.

"I could help myself," Byrd said.

"What? Walking?" Zera already forgot her previous comment.

"No." His eyes, glassy and unfocused, rolled slightly, and Zera no longer cared about his weird rambling.

"Oh, no you don't." She hauled him up again and dragged him the last few feet into the med bay. To her surprise, Martin greeted them.

"What happened?" he asked, taking in Byrd's current status.

"He fell during the quake. I think something happened to his ankle again, 'cause he got super pale and almost threw up."

Martin held up Byrd's head and flashed a light in his eyes. "Byrd? Can you tell me what's going on?"

"Help," he murmured, then promptly lost consciousness.

Zera absorbed most of his weight, and out of the woodwork came nurses who gently pried him away, moving him to a waiting gurney. Like a well-oiled machine, they began taking vitals and assessing Byrd, leaving Zera alone, hot, and sweaty, and more than a little confused. Martin met her eyes over Byrd's unconscious form and nodded toward the door. Looked like her job here was done.

"The fuck was he talking about?" she muttered, replaying the conversation. Byrd had been so adamant about going back, but the reasoning didn't make any sense. They were there for data, and if Zera was going to waste any time, it wouldn't be on some magical item to make her life easier. It would be figuring out where the hell that other time traveler came from.

———

The next morning, Zera woke bright and early with a buzzing in her bones. Sure, she was excited for the time travel—and also nervous for the pain, if she was honest—but she most looked forward to finding that other time traveler.

Unwilling to wake Kissi, Zera grabbed her handheld from its charger and pulled up the intranet. It was easy to find a map detailing the locations of other bases across the continent, but more difficult to find information on them. All the basics were there—how they managed to grow food, what they used to combat diseases, even instruction manuals for any car or truck they could find in order to help as wide a range of mechanics as possible. But nowhere did it have a citizen registry, or any whispers of time travel.

It wouldn't, of course, but Zera hoped she could spot a *little* something.

Kissi, with her skills, could probably hack into the mainframe or whatever and find that stuff, but Zera already relied on her for most of her information, and wanted to do some digging herself. So slowly, methodically, she looked through lists of resources and accesses, trying to find a bunker that matched up with her own. In the end, she decided Alaska was the most likely place.

Armed with an idea, Zera rose and dressed for the morning. Her stomach turned too much to allow any breakfast, but she headed down to the mess anyway and downed the biggest glass of water her credits could buy. For Kissi, she grabbed a cup of coffee and a bowl of tomato soup, the breakfast an odd departure of what Zera had back in 1944. Gods, what she would give to have some fruit again, or the sweet loaf Katherine gave her. She lamented her lack of old cash and the inability to ask for some. If it weren't for Dr. Phillips and her rules, Zera could have an absolute field day and bring back every snack imaginable.

Huh. Maybe Byrd was onto something then.

Kissi was sitting on the edge of her bunk when Zera returned, and joyfully latched onto the caffeinated drink. When she'd chugged half the hot liquid, she asked, "Ready for today?"

"As ready as I'm gonna be." Zera dropped next to her on the bed. "You?"

"Same. It's not easy, watching you go."

Zera winced. "How ugly is it?"

"Oh, horrifying. Limbs flying everywhere." Kissi grinned, and Zera wasn't quite sure if she was serious or not.

"Well, maybe we can get them to use a different traveler next time, after this trip. I don't mind sitting one out." She definitely did mind sitting one out, but if it would take that look off Kissi's face, she could take one for the team.

But Kissi shook her head. "There are no other travelers."

Zera's heart stuttered. "What?"

"I talked to one of the other analysts yesterday. Her traveler made it back, but he passed later in the hospital. He was the last one besides you. And Byrd, I guess."

"Shit." Zera ran a hand through her hair. "*Shit.*"

"I know. So this all really rests on you."

The weight settled onto Zera's shoulders. She knew this was the point to give up on finding Katherine and focus more on the mission parameters as they were given to her. Distractions wouldn't help.

But then she thought of the quake yesterday, her eyes tracing the old cracks in their walls from previous ones. Wouldn't tracking the other time traveler down save her time, in the end? It was easy to compute the math. High risk, high reward.

"We need more than that," Zera said. Kissi nodded.

"You're thinking about Katherine?" she asked.

"If we had double the resources, had any information she or her bunker might have...If we could team up, we could solve this in half the time, I bet."

Kissi sighed. "I think you're right. We need more brains on this."

Zera didn't like the way her words reflected Byrd's earlier sentiment, but shook it off. Unless she could make friends with the other time traveler, all this waffling would be for nothing.

She stood and grabbed her new outfit for the day, a brilliant get up built for the '50s. Kissi followed her lead, though her clothes remained the same subdued jumpsuit.

It was time to go.

1956

PHILADELPHIA SMELLED different than New York. There was still the unmistakable scent of too many humans and cars, but when the wind shifted a metallic tang coated the air. A gust cut through Zera's weak shirt. While she'd prepared to blend in, she hadn't prepared for winter. Gods, when was the last time she'd even *seen* winter?

One of these trips, she'd get it right. In the meantime, she had a heavy coat to steal.

Zera enjoyed the freezing cold and light rain for approximately seventeen seconds before it sank into her bones and stayed there. The weak morning sun tried its best to poke through the clouds, but only succeeded in turning the world an odd shade of gray.

With her bare hands tucked into her armpits and the bill of her cap low enough to keep her face hidden, Zera walked with purpose into the rampant bustle of the city. Foot traffic wasn't as prevalent as before, with more cars packing the streets, but pedestrians held the same attitude: stay out of their way, and they'd stay out of hers.

Normally a group of people like this would make her nervous, and while she still checked her nine, noon, three, and six at steady intervals, she was glad for the warmth the thousand extra bodies lent her. She was afraid her shirt and pants stuck out, but it was an unserved fear. Like her, everyone kept their heads down. Her round face and short haircut was just another in the mix.

Zera had never visited Philadelphia before, and she couldn't help taking in more of the sights between her perimeter checks. Much like New York, businesses crowded the ground floors of the buildings around her, with layers and layers of apartments stacked atop them. At first, it seemed like any other city center, but then she noticed the symptoms of decay, with crumbling bricks and layers of grime seeping into the walls. Reformation would likely come soon.

A map would've been a great addition to her bag, no matter how conspicuous it would be. She was still getting the hang of directions, and a compass wouldn't be reliable with the storms, but logic dictated she would run into one of the crossroads she needed eventually.

A car nearly ran over a few pedestrians in a crosswalk, and curses and fists chased it down its path. Zera, however, was grateful for the interruption because she got to stop and look up. There, in flaking white paint, she could just make the outline of *19th street*.

Perfect. Now, was she supposed to go left, or right?

To the right, factories belched a mix of smoke and steam matching the gunmetal gray of the sky. The air felt thicker in that direction, so Zera ignored the sun and the compass and any advice Kissi gave her before the trip and turned left. Her gut said it was the correct way, and it hadn't led her astray before. Not often, at least.

Left went against the flow, and it required a lot of jostling and apologizing as she headed in the opposite direction. Saplings filled the area as the buildings thinned, their trunks slender compared to the massive sentinels Zera remembered from pictures. They were young and growing, not yet the landmarks they would become.

The Academy of Natural Sciences of Philadelphia was a beautiful building, much bigger than the natural sciences building of Columbia. Students dotted the front steps, waiting for the doors to open for their classes. It was easy to spot, and Zera breathed in the good luck.

"Watch it," a man growled as his shoulder collided with Zera's. He continued on without looking for a fight, but his voice, his aura, his *life*, knocked her sideways. He was so alive now, but these people were dead. Every single one was dead.

The air got too thick, the acrid stench of bodies and cars choking her. Her ears rang as the conversations bubbling under the surface swelled and crashed over her. It was so easy to see them as a conglomerate, but the sudden sense of individuals overwhelmed her. They all had hopes and dreams and plans and goals. And now they were dead—

"*You.*"

Except for Katherine.

Zera usually prided herself on the ability to pull herself out of a panic, but in that moment, Katherine did her the favor.

She'd lost what little weight she could spare, and Zera had the feeling it wasn't on purpose. It turned her cheekbones to razors, accompanying the daggers she glared. Anger flushed her skin red, and the single word was enough to knock Zera right out of her anxious spiral and activate her fight-or-flight response.

The first time, she'd chosen fight. This time, she chose flight.

Her time as a digger gave her extraordinary stamina and faster than average reaction times. Normally she dodged rocks and landslides, but here she dodged people, weaving toward the museum as fast as the crowd permitted. Katherine, held back by skirts and social decorum, couldn't hope to catch her. And Zera needed to keep it that way, at least until she could figure out a plan.

The crowd split and she booked it to the front of the building. Katherine was close enough behind that Zera could hear the leather soles of her heels clacking against the street. Zera skidded to a stop and gently opened the front door, taking a few huge gulps of air to calm her breathing before entering. Puffing like a dragon wouldn't help her fly under the radar.

Inside was barely warmer than outside, but at least the brick walls held back the biting wind and incessant rain. Despite the rubber bottom of her boots, she nearly slipped on the smooth marble tiles, and the squeak echoed louder than any alarm might have. Zera chanced a look out the front windows, and sure enough, Katherine was storming up the drive as fast as her dress and heels would let her.

Zera stepped further into the museum, going to the first glass case and pretending to admire the artifacts inside. Two terrible stuffed monkeys sat on one side of a crumbling tree limb, and a matching skeleton—the most realistic animal of them all—posed on the other side. Black rods held the objects in place, making no attempt at subtlety.

The front door swung open, and there, in all her glory, was Katherine.

Despite her change in health, she was still beautiful, and for half a beat Zera forgot her mission objective. But then Katherine stalked over with the fires of heavens and hells in her eyes, and it came rushing back.

"You," Katherine said again. Zera sidestepped as the woman reached her, putting the glass case between them. Katherine pointed an accusing finger. "You abandoned me."

"Me?" Zera said. Katherine tried to circle to the same side of the display, but Zera sidestepped again. Those two and a half monkeys were the only thing keeping her alive right now. "You kicked me out to do your dirty work for you."

"I was protecting you—"

"You were protecting yourself—"

"Where are the journals? I need those journals—"

"Absolutely not." They moved another circle, and this time Zera kept going, putting two display cases between them. Now she had help from the monkeys and some birds. A massive elephant skeleton stood behind her, but she tried not to look at it. "Look, clearly the past couple of weeks have been tough on you—"

"'Couple of weeks'?" Katherine seethed. "You call twelve years a 'couple of weeks'?"

"—but I can't...Wait, what?"

"Can I help you?"

Zera startled and whirled around to face the new threat. He had white hair and deep wrinkles, and the posture of someone who bent over books all day. Though he wore spectacles—they looked way too ancient for Zera to think of them as glasses—he squinted his cloudy brown eyes and didn't quite focus on her face.

"Oh, uh, I'm sorry." She tried to deepen her voice enough to trick him. A hand took her elbow and she startled again, but Katherine's vice grip held her steady.

"I'm terribly sorry, sir," she said sweetly, as if she hadn't been about to throttle Zera a second before. "We took a moment's reprieve from the rain to admire the curiosities of the museum. I do hope that's alright?"

"What?" Zera hissed.

"Beg your pardon?" The man turned an ear toward them. How could he run an Academy if he could neither see nor hear the patrons?

"I'm sorry, sir," Katherine said, raising her voice. It bounced around the room as she repeated herself.

"Oh, yes, yes, of course." He turned to Zera. "If you like, sir, we have a lecture this afternoon about the use of animal bones as tools during leather tanning. Quite fascinating, really, it has something to do with the composite of the bones. One of our own discovered the technique when he found some members of the...ah...what was the name of their tribe..."

"How can he discover something they used forever?" Zera muttered.

"Shut up and answer."

"Oh, right." Zera cleared her throat. "Uh, no, thank you, sir. I, uh, we're previously engaged for the afternoon." She tried to copy Katherine's dialect and failed miserably.

"You're engaged? Oh, how wonderful!" The man clapped his hands together.

"No, we're not—"

He didn't listen to Katherine, instead coming closer to shake Zera's hand with a weak grip and plant a stiff kiss to both of Katherine's cheeks.

"Every blessing to you both. Have you celebrated? Ah, that must be why you were out in the rain! Well, I won't impose upon you," he said, teetering away toward the back door. "Though, if we're celebrating, perhaps a little tipple is in order..."

Katherine at least had the decency to wait until the man was out of the room before rounding on Zera again.

"Give me those journals!"

"I don't have them!" Zera held her hands up and retreated a few steps. If she didn't make friends with Katherine, then they couldn't get answers. And she couldn't get answers if she got stabbed.

"Well the University doesn't have them, and I don't have them, which means you *must* have them." She stalked Zera like a lion, and Zera did her best to weave through displays without knocking any over.

"I don't have them, I had to turn them in to my superiors," Zera said.

"Where are your superiors? Take me to them." Katherine leaned down and pulled her knife from the same thigh sheath. Relief settled into Zera's chest; at least now she knew where the knife was, and Katherine couldn't surprise her with it.

"I can't just take you to them," she said. "What did you mean by twelve years?"

"Don't play coy with me, Miss Zazzera," Katherine spat. "After your little escape act, everyone dug into my business, and I had to leave New York because *you* didn't have the decency to see our deal through to the end."

"I had to go! They were going to catch me, and what was I supposed to say? 'Oh, sorry, I just got lost. Also no, I'm not a woman in men's clothes, and no I didn't steal these, why do you ask?'" Zera said, waving her hands.

Wisps of hair escaped Katherine's updo, and a few curls turned to limp waves now that the rain had time to soak in. "Give me the journals."

"I told you, I don't have them," Zera said. Katherine stopped her pursuit, her eyes locked on Zera's. Adrenaline buzzed through Zera's veins as she tried to anticipate the next move in this terrible chess game. Then, the worst happened.

Katherine started to cry.

"Damn it! Damn it all to hell!" she whispered, her hands going to her abdomen. Her tears left trails in the powder on her face, cracks in the porcelain facade she maintained. Sobs racked her body, and though she bit back any further noise, Zera could see her ribs straining against the fitted bodice of the dress.

"Oh, shit, fuck, uh—" She took a few cautious steps toward her. When there was an arm's length between them, Zera reached out, her hand flinching three separate times before she finally settled it on Katherine's shoulder. There was a solid chance this was all a ploy, and she was prepared for it. Probably. "Don't cry. It'll be okay, we can figure something out."

"I've tried everything," Katherine whispered. She plucked a handkerchief from the sweetheart neckline of her dress and delicately dabbed away her tears. The mix of powder and rouge left her skin an odd pinkish hue. "I needed those journals."

"Look, I don't have a high clearance or anything, but I can share some information." The words spilled out before her mind could catch up. Katherine's bunker might be different than hers. She acted like execution was in order for her failure. "Just tell me what kind of stuff your CO wants you to get and I can get Kissi to look it up."

"My—I'm sorry, my what?" Confusion was strong enough to momentarily break Katherine's distress.

"Your CO. Or your general, or—or governor or whatever you call your leader." Katherine was smart, Zera didn't know why this would throw her.

"My governor? What does the governor want with me?" She was back to being suspicious, which was pretty much baseline. At least she wasn't crying; crying girls were Zera's weakness.

"Isn't that who you work for?" she asked. Not all bunkers were military, and if Vylek didn't know about Katherine, then she had to be in the civilian sector.

"Me? Work for the governor?" Katherine blinked. Zera blinked back. Next to them, the elephant skeleton waited for their answers. "Miss Zazzera, what is it you think I do?"

"You...don't you do the same thing as me?" Zera asked. "Time travel? That's what you told me back in 1944."

"That's what you've been thinking this whole time?" Katherine tilted her head to the side.

"This whole—Kat, it's been like, two weeks. Three, tops. What does the year we visit actually matter?"

"It's Kate now. And Miss Zazzera, I'm not *visiting* these times." Katherine took a breath. "I *live* through them."

"You..." Zera let the words hang there a second longer. *I live through them.* That explained why she talked differently, why she had a home, and a husband. That was why the signature Kissi found was the same, regardless of the year. "You live through them."

"Yes," Katherine said. The blood drained from her face, and this time her mask completely fell. She was *scared.*

"That's...unexpected." Zera let out a long breath through pursed lips. She turned to the elephant skeleton, the blank eye sockets staring back with solidarity. "Okay, so this changes things a little bit."

If Katherine wasn't a time traveler working for a secret base, then why did she need those journals? Hells, if she'd lived through all this time, then how old was she?

"Hey, how—where the fuck are you going?"

By the time Zera turned back around, Katherine was halfway out the door. How she managed to be so sneaky in that dress and those shoes would be impressive, if she wasn't making a break for it.

"Son of a–"

Not caring about things like etiquette, Zera took off after her. Rain no longer plagued them, but the ground was a slushy mess. Katherine moved carefully, trying to save her shoes. Zera got to run without giving a shit.

"You realize I can outrun you, like, *super* easily, right?" she said, falling into step next to her. Katherine shot a glare from the side of her eye, but kept her lips sealed tight and her feet moving toward the city. Zera rolled her eyes. "Really? You dropped a bomb on me, but now you're gonna give me the silent treatment?"

Katherine said nothing.

"Look, what you said back there"—Katherine's feral glare was almost strong enough to stop her mid sentence—"I'm not gonna, like, tell anyone. Who would I even tell?"

"Your CO." Katherine broke her silence with a hiss. Zera noticed the way her gait shifted, the way her body turned as they entered the busier streets. Before Katherine could melt into the crowd, Zera took her hand and tucked it into her elbow like the gentleman she was.

"You're really overestimating how much power I have. I'm just a soldier. Boots on the ground, trying to get information. And I have a feeling you have some of that information."

"You're a terrible liar, Miss Zazzera," Katherine said.

"You're right, which is why I'm not lying."

"Why are you here?"

"What?"

"Why are you here?" Katherine repeated. "Why did they send you back to find me?"

"It wasn't to find *you*." Zera paused, gathering her words. "It's for data. To try and reverse the effects from one of the storms."

"They keep getting stronger? What happened?"

The blinding light. The heat. Scorched earth greeting her on her first dig, the moon trying to burn her alive. Katherine in that meadow, bleeding from the chest—

"Just some climate change stuff." Sweat dripped down her back despite the cold, and she choked on her next breath. Coughs racked her, and every pedestrian in a ten foot radius stepped back.

"Does it affect your health?" Katherine asked. Something like concern colored her voice, but there was a real chance she was just being polite.

"No, just went down the wrong pipe," Zera gasped. "It, uh, made things super hot. Which isn't optimal."

"No, I suppose it isn't." Katherine delicately bit her lower lip. "Well, Miss Zazzera, perhaps we can help each other after all."

"Oh, thank you for allowing such a thing to occur," she drawled, trying to match the accent. It wasn't perfect.

"Or I could leave you here and alert the authorities there's a woman dressed as a man attempting nefarious acts—"

"Jesus Christ, you'd go straight to nefarious acts? Wouldn't even start with loitering or something?"

"I've learned the hard way not to take chances." Katherine pulled her down a side street. A long row of apartment buildings stood before them. These were not the stately brownstones back in New York, but squat boxes stacked on top of each other like the back of a shoe store.

Katherine led her into one of the boxes and up the stairs to the top floor. The wood creaked and groaned with every step; the whole thing was at best a fire hazard, and at worst a pile of engineering red flags. Zera stepped as lightly as possible, but Katherine strode down the hall with no fear of falling through.

Somehow the apartment managed to be more bland and empty than the brownstone. A double bed sat squashed into the corner, and the previous heavy wooden table was replaced by a smaller, cheaper version. Zera let out a low whistle, noticing too late the pink splotches on Katherine's cheeks.

"It's quite the change from our previous rendezvous, I know." Her voice stayed steady as her hands shook filling a percolator. "Can I make you some coffee?"

"What happened to your husband?" The question shot out before Zera could stop it. Katherine straightened her spine, staring at the wall as if it held the right answer. Finally, she sighed and put the percolator on the stove.

"Which one?" she asked. Zera's stomach dropped to her shoes, and she casually reached her hand to rest on the knife handle on the back of her belt.

"Alfred," Zera said. "What other husband would I be talking about?"

"Perhaps the current one."

"Gods, how many husbands have you *had*?"

"Enough to survive." Zera glanced at Katherine's hands; sure enough, there were four rings now. "As for Alfred, I did not lie to you. He traveled often for business, and he made a trip to Ontario and unfortunately did not return."

"So you got a life insurance check and moved to Philadelphia?"

"Thanks to your shenanigans at Columbia University, I received a portion of his remaining funds and *fled* to Philadelphia." Katherine turned to her, her gaze absolutely withering. Zera gripped the knife handle a little tighter. "The only reason I'm not killing you where you stand is because you may be the only one who can help me."

"You think you could kill me?"

It was a bluff, and Katherine called it, snatching a knife from the block on the counter. "We both know I could. Perhaps you've learned something in the past twelve years, but so have I."

"Okay, okay, you're right." Zera held up her hands. A fight would be the wrong move here, for multiple reasons. "I guess I should tell you it really hasn't been twelve years for me. It's been, like, two or three weeks."

Katherine blinked. "What?"

"Time traveler, remember?" She gestured to herself. "Which brings me to my second question. Exactly how old *are* you?"

A blush coated Katherine's cheeks and neck, and she whirled to use the knife to slice something in a square pan on the counter behind her.

"Come January, I'll be one hundred and five." She spoke to the chunk of coffee cake she was plating rather than to Zera.

"Holy *shit*." A bark of laughter escaped, and Zera barely managed to quell any more from sneaking out. "I mean, wow, you look absolutely *amazing* for your age."

Katherine sighed and turned, leaning against the counter. "I know."

"I mean, I wouldn't put you a day over eighty-five, really."

"Thank you."

"Gods, a hundred and five. So does it really go downhill after thirty?"

"It certainly did for me."

"Holy shit. I mean holy *shit*. That's—a hundred and *five*?"

"Are you finished?" Katherine stared with a bored expression, but there was an unease in the way she held her shoulders.

"Not quite." Zera rested her hands on her hips. "Wait, how many people know about this?"

"Only the few that suffer from the same, ah, affliction," she said stiffly.

"Wait, so I'm the first person you've told?" Zera didn't mean to feel so special, really.

"Well, you shared your secret, it's only fair that I shared mine."

"Bullshit."

"Absolutely. I only told you because I have to."

"That's more like it." Zera's heart and stomach kept switching places, and she was trying hard to keep up with it all. "If we can't be honest with each other, then what's the point?"

"Then let me be perfectly honest with you," Katherine said. "Miss Zazzera, I need your help so that I may finally die."

1956

ZERA HAD NOTHING.

"I'm sorry, you want me to kill you?" Okay, she had *one* thing.

"Kill me? No, not *kill me*." Katherine had her business face back on, as if they were discussing the weather or a recent television episode—was TV even in color yet? "I'm old. Very old. And I'm ready for my body to catch up."

"And how the hell am I supposed to make that happen? I'm not a—a fucking *scientist* or anything. I don't even understand how the hell I got here. I just go where I'm told."

"But you have resources, and if there's one thing I know completely, it's that resources are everything." The percolator pinged and bubbled, and Katherine pulled it from the stove. With the same eerie calm, she poured their coffee and brought it and the cake to the table. "Now that you understand my plight, you can conveniently disappear again. If you're able to come visit me here, then you're more than able to figure out how to fix my predicament."

"I don't have access to *any* of that," Zera said. The thought of Katherine growing old and dying made her heart twist. "I'm military, Kat. And bottom of the barrel at that."

"I assumed your superiors would send their finest for such a sensitive mission."

"Well when you *assume* it just makes an ass out of you and me."

"It may take a bit of conniving—"

"Oh, fuck no! Last time I let you talk me into a 'bit of conniving' I ended up playing dress-up and getting chased across a college campus," Zera said. "Besides, how can you be sure you're not just aging super, super slowly? I mean, your hair grows, you can gain or lose weight…"

"Do I look any different?" Katherine interlaced her fingers in front of her and shifted so the sun hit her through the window. There were no lines at the corner of her pink lips, no wrinkles around her brown and gold eyes, not even a gray hair. A thin, silvery scar marred the otherwise smooth surface of her neck—the only change since 1944.

"No, you don't," Zera said.

"It's very difficult, surviving in this world." Katherine still spoke like a lecturer. "I believe it's time for me to settle down with a husband and actually honor those vows, 'til death do us part."

"As opposed to them disappearing under mysterious circumstances, right?" Zera said. "So let me get this straight: you want me to go back and somehow find a way to stop this whole non-aging thing you've got going on? What's stopping you from just taking matters into your own hands?"

"The one good thing about a long life is there's plenty of time to atone for one's sins." Katherine took the coffees and handed one to Zera, who took a sip. It scalded her mouth, and its strength made her shudder.

"But apparently not enough time to learn how to make a cup of coffee," she said after a painful gulp. She took an angry bite of the cake, and found it much more pleasant, with an odd mixture of orange and cinnamon.

"I am perfectly willing to help you gather any data you need for your actual mission," Katherine continued. "I'm not unreasonable. In fact, I won't even ask for my solution until you've discovered yours."

Zera remembered to pay attention to the conversation and not the cake. "If we figure out a solution for the future, they have no reason to send me back to you," she pointed out. Dr. Phillips said they couldn't change anything, and the image of Katherine bleeding out in her arms was still very vivid.

"You'll find a way, I'm sure." Katherine sipped her coffee with a serene smile.

"I don't like making promises I don't know I can keep," Zera said, putting down her mug. No way in any hell was she touching that shit again. "I don't wanna take advantage of your help and then fuck it up." It was a lame excuse, but the best she could come up with under the circumstances. She'd taken a risk with this interaction, and now it was biting her in the ass.

"I see," Katherine said. She sat down at the dining table with a fluid grace that didn't belong in this shitty apartment, and this time the weak sunlight caught the curves of her neck and her waist. "Well, Miss Zazzera—"

"Seriously, it's Zera. Zazzera makes me feel like I'm in trouble."

"Perhaps you are," she said with a smile. It hinted at something a little wilder underneath the prim and proper. "Well, *Miss Zazzera*, I'm no stranger to broken promises. While I would love to see my end of days, if I can help save the future from ruin instead, then I suppose it would be good of me to assist you, hmm?"

"You're doing that weird fancy talk thing again and I hate it," Zera said, though it wasn't completely true. "Just say what you're thinking."

"If you insist." Katherine looked her dead in the eye. "I'm going to help you, because it's the right thing to do. And all I can do is hope that you help me, because I have no other choice."

"You're getting better at this," Zera said, gesturing between the two of them. "Soon we'll be able to have a real conversation like two consenting adults."

"You're incorrigible."

"I bet you say that to all the girls."

Katherine sat ramrod straight. "And just what do you mean by that?"

Zera swallowed. "Nothing, just a joke." She'd forgotten where she was, *when* she was. She had thoughts about Katherine's reaction, but she shoved them aside.

"Well it was in poor taste."

"I see that now. I'm sorry."

Katherine took a dainty sip from her cup. "You're forgiven. Shall we focus on the task at hand?"

"Only if you promise never to use the word *shall* again." The smile she got from the jab helped ease the tension in the room, and in Zera's shoulders.

"I'm afraid I shan't be promising that."

"Okay I may not be a scholar or whatever the hell you call it, but I know *shan't* is just another form of *shall*."

"Hence why I shan't make any promises."

"Gods have mercy on my soul." Zera ran a hand over her face and took a deep breath. Katherine grinned as if proud of their banter, and Zera had to duck her head a moment longer to quell her own smile. She was supposed to be getting information from Katherine, not finding her cute. Things were not going to plan.

Zera let out a breath. Things *were* going to plan. She just didn't like that the plan was to befriend Katherine and use her.

"Okay, I accept your offer." She didn't know how she would hold up her end of the bargain, but that was for her to figure out in the future—literally. "Help me find a way to reverse the effects from the Storm, and I'll try to find a way to fix your situation."

Katherine didn't need to know the exact date.

"I look forward to our partnership," Katherine said with a smile. It made her look more like herself—or rather, the version of her Zera met in Central Park. "Now, first order of business, we must get you out of those clothes. You're less than covert in that ensemble."

Zera bit back another comment that would certainly get her in trouble. "Yes, ma'am," she said instead. "Hopefully this husband is built a little bigger than your other one."

"I believe you might be in luck." Katherine rose and placed her cup in the sink before going to the wardrobe. Suits hung in a row, just like the last house, but they were obviously older and well used.

"Let's try it," Zera said, stripping off her boots, shirt, and pants. Katherine eyed her, and for a second Zera thought—or hoped—she was checking her out, but then she recognized the look in her eye. It was the same one Kissi got when she found a particularly sexy chunk of data.

"What is this garment you wear?" She stepped into Zera's personal space and slipped a finger beneath the wide strap of her sports bra, pulling it to admire the stretch. Her eyes widened and she let it go, jumping when it snapped back in place.

"Ouch! Shit!" Zera rubbed the offended skin over her collarbone. "It's a bra. I know you've seen a bra before."

"That is unlike any bra I've encountered," Katherine said, looking every which way at it. "Seems very easy to maneuver. And comfortable."

"Uh, yeah, I guess. I'd offer to let you try it, but...I don't think it'd fit."

Katherine paused, as if she just realized the state of their conversation. Pink tinged her cheeks again, but there was no chagrin when she spoke. "I believe you might be correct. Here, try this."

She handed a suit over and stepped away, suddenly concerned with modesty and propriety. A laugh swirled in Zera's chest, but she swallowed it down. It wasn't Katherine's fault spandex wasn't invented yet.

The fabric of the suit scratched against Zera's skin and it was somehow too short at the wrists and ankles, but at least the waist didn't dig into her and the pockets were deep enough for her vials and anchor syringe.

"Well, how do I look?" She held out her arms and did an awkward twirl.

Katherine put her hands on her hips and assessed her with her scientist eyes. "With a cap on, you'll pass for a young man. Though, if we're lucky, no one will spot us during our escapade."

That didn't sound good. "What do you have planned this time, Kat?"

"It's still Kate. During the day, we can gather the same samples you needed previously," she began, turning on her toes and pacing. Her skirt swirled around her legs as she walked. "I assume you're here today because there will be another storm soon?"

"Uh, tonight, yeah." Could she read Zera's mind? They hadn't talked about a storm tonight. Zera considered thinking a dirty thought about Katherine to test the theory, but ultimately decided it would only lead to her own detriment.

"Excellent. The Academy of Natural Sciences has a plethora of magnetometers in the basement, and they will likely use a few to make observations tonight." Katherine adjusted her hair in front of the mirror, pinning the escaped curls back in their assigned seats. "But men tend to be disorganized when the world tilts the slightest bit on its axis, so I don't believe they'll notice if we commandeer one. Perhaps *this time* the technology will be good enough."

"So help me, if I have to break in somewhere again while you wine and dine some rich old guys, I'm gonna pitch a fit." Zera felt no guilt breaking

and entering, but she had limited skills. Going in untrained and unin-
formed—again—sounded like a recipe for disaster.

"You won't have to break in, the door will be wide open," Katherine
assured her. "And, if all goes to plan, we'll return the magnetometer before
they come down from the roof and realize it's gone."

"You have a lot of confidence in this plan, but it seems half-assed
to me."

"I've been thinking about it for a very long time," Katherine reminded
her. "I've had twelve years to make it."

"Guess I'm the half-assed one then." Zera let out a long breath,
running her hand through her hair. "Do you know how to work the
magnet thing?"

"Yes, I do. Thanks to some self-directed study."

"You're a smarty pants, I get it." Zera put her hands on her hips and
began pacing the small apartment too, moving in the opposite direction
from Katherine. "It sounds too easy. What if there's security? And say we
do get the magnet thing, where will we set it up? You already said they'll be
on the roof."

"We don't need the roof, it works perfectly well on the ground,"
Katherine said. "You do the heavy lifting, and I will read the machine."

"I'll be the brawn, you be the brains. Sounds like I'm back home."
Zera nodded and forced herself to stop walking. Her inner thighs burned
where the rough fabric rubbed.

"Brilliant. Meet me at the Academy at eight o'clock and—"

"Whoa, whoa, whoa. Meet you there? What am I supposed to do for
the next"—she checked her watch—"ten hours?"

"I can house you for most of the day, but you must be gone before
Edgar returns home."

"And when is that?"

"Nightfall, or thereabouts." Katherine grabbed her purse. "And I still
have my errands to run before then."

"You're seriously just gonna leave me here?"

"Well I can't very well have you gallivanting about with me, that's
what got us into this predicament in the first place."

"I think my gallivanting was the last thing in a long line of events that
got us into this." Boredom was the least of Zera's worries. She couldn't

lose sight of Katherine, not again. "C'mon, Kat, let me come with you. I'll just carry your stuff or whatever."

"Absolutely not." Katherine exchanged her outer layer for a light overcoat and checked her hair once more.

"Maybe I'll just leave. What'll you do then?"

Katherine saw right through the lie. "Then I'll continue on, as I always have." At the door, she paused, and for a second Zera thought she might give in.

No such luck.

Katherine nodded toward the window. "Perhaps gather some rainwater for your samples. That ought to keep you preoccupied for a while."

"You little—"

Katherine closed the door in her face.

"Goddammit," Zera muttered. The wind howled, and the window creaked and moaned. "Finally go to Philly and all I get is a stupid water sample."

It was easy enough to gather an air sample, and Zera scraped the mud from her boots into another vial to count for earth. Unlike the brownstone, there was limited snooping allotted for the tiny apartment, and nothing interesting to boot. The orange coffee cake called to her from the countertop, and she decided she was allowed one more slice as a reward for her good behavior.

Zera cracked open the window with a sigh and set a sample tube on the sill, resting her head on her hands as condensation slowly gathered and eventually fell as a single drop into the waiting glass.

Katherine had a special interest in the storms.

Drip.

She wanted to live a normal life. Or rather, a life of normal length.

Drip.

And Zera was supposed to pretend like she hadn't seen Katherine, alive and well, eighty-four years from now. The memory hurt worse, twisting Zera's insides, her hands warm and slick as if blood covered them again.

Drip.

Dr. Phillips said they couldn't change the future, no matter what. Everything had already happened. How was Zera supposed to keep coming back and look Katherine in the eye, knowing there was no way to save her?

Drip.

Her job wasn't to save Katherine. It was to help find a way to save the world. Katherine was already dead. Everyone here was already dead.

Drip.

Katherine was willing to help, willing to find information for her. But Zera wasn't used to leaving someone behind. The thought alone made her stomach clench.

Drip.

But Katherine mentioned others with the same "affliction."

Others.

Zera left the water to do its work and resumed pacing. Katherine thought the storms had something to do with her alleged immortality. If there were others with the same problem, maybe Zera could go to them. Katherine could continue on until the 2040 Storm, and Zera could find a way to fix it without looking into those dazzling brown eyes every few weeks and drowning in guilt.

Perfect plan, except there was no way in hell her superiors would go for it. They barely allowed the missions as it was.

Zera was good at many things. Marks from the academy put her intelligence, reasoning, and athleticism above average. But she was terrible at lying.

She collapsed into the dining chair and buried her face in her hands. This was so far above her pay grade she'd need a crane to reach it.

"Fuck me. Fine."

Maybe Dr. Phillips said they couldn't change the future. But maybe Dr. Phillips was wrong.

Philadelphia handled the storm better than New York. Sparks flew in one or two of the buildings, but the fires were manageable and didn't spread. A wave of telephone workers passed, talking animatedly about the reaction of the machines and the loss of some of their work. Behind them, men with toolboxes entered the buildings, prepared for a long night.

The rain stopped an hour after Katherine returned home and kicked Zera out of the apartment, giving her directions to their meeting place and a heavy coat to keep out the chill. After spending eighteen years in a post-apocalyptic firescape, Zera's cold tolerance was next to nonexistent, and as she sat on a bench in historic Logan Circle, she burrowed into the coat and used her nerves to keep warm. At least the coat was thick enough to prevent the rain from seeping through.

Green started poking through the thinning clouds as bells tolled for eight o'clock, casting a ghastly glow over the square. True to Katherine's prediction, a group of scholarly men ran into the Academy, appearing on the roof a few minutes later with clunky devices. The wall was just low enough for Zera to watch as they set up their outdoor lab, complete with telescopes and chemistry sets and flasks full of something to keep them warm.

"Are you ready?"

Zera startled and found Katherine standing next to her, decked out in long black pants and a black blouse.

"Jesus fucking—you're like a goddamn mouse." Zera took a deep breath. "And what is this getup? Are you trying to be James Bond or something?"

"That would be something. But never underestimate a woman in a comfortable outfit," Katherine said, straightening the waist of the pants. "Now, are you ready?"

"I guess so. Wait, you know who James Bond is?" Zera stood, and Katherine slipped her hand into her elbow.

"Of course. I keep up with contemporary literature."

"Literature?"

Katherine grinned and didn't answer, instead leading her to the Academy. Darkness painted the front windows and the door stuck when pushed. While Zera looked for an open window, Katherine pulled something from her pocket. Using the light from the street lamps, she stuck two pins into the lock and opened the door.

"I'm sorry, what was that?" Zera whispered as they entered, her voice carrying despite the volume.

"I married a locksmith in 1902, and he taught me a few things," she explained. The monkeys and elephants stood as shadowy sentinels, their blank eyes judging every echoing step. Zera made sure the door was closed again, being careful to avoid loud noises.

"Would you please hurry?"

Katherine's voice bounced around the room; she was already across, waiting at the back door with hands on hips. The light behind her blurred her features, but Zera felt the sharp edge of her gaze.

"Sorry," she muttered, and caught up.

Katherine led her down the stairs to another locked door, this one dealt with as easily as the first. The men had taken most of the machinery to the roof, leaving blank spaces on the shelves, but one particularly old model remained in place.

"That's the thing?" Zera asked. To her untrained eye, it was just a box with two long rods perpendicular to each other. She told herself not to pick it up by the sticks, no matter how tempting it might be.

"Yes. It appears they aren't particularly fond of this model." Katherine's deft fingers turned and twisted different bolts on the front of the box until it popped open with a loud crack and a squeal from the hinges. A long, flat piece of metal shaped like a nail file drifted back and forth, but if there was a pattern to the numbers it touched, Zera couldn't see it.

"Let's get this bad boy outside," she said. Breaking and entering? Fine. Loitering? That's where she drew the line.

"Right." Katherine closed the box and pulled it to the edge of the shelf. It teetered ominously before sliding from its perch at remarkable speed. Katherine's eyes went wide, and Zera stepped in by reflex, catching the magnetometer in her arms.

Corners and bolts dug into her forearms, but her concern was focused more on how close she was to Katherine. She could smell the faint scent of soap, familiar like a forgotten memory. Up close, the scar on her neck was more obvious, a line of raised silver over the swell of her collarbone. Her hand, trapped between Zera's arm and the machine, radiated warmth strong enough to bypass her layers of clothing.

"It was heavier than I expected," Katherine said, weaseling her hands from their captivity.

"Clearly." Zera shifted the machine so it sat more comfortably in her grasp. It was pretty heavy, probably in the twenty kilo range, but nothing she couldn't handle. "I got it. You lead the way to our super secret science spot."

"Always with the tongue twisters." Katherine sighed. She strode out the door and up the stairs, not caring to slow down for Zera and her cargo. They didn't bother to lock the door behind them, and Zera didn't know if it was as an escape plan or sheer apathy.

More clouds had dissipated during their time inside, giving a better view of the swirling greens and blues and purples of the aurora. The city hummed with voices as tenants left their homes to investigate the phenomenon, but Katherine took her to an empty place behind the Academy with clear views of the sky. If it weren't for the ancient magnet block, Zera would dare to call the setup romantic.

"Put it here," Katherine ordered, and Zera obliged. Outside the safety of the Academy, the box whirred and clicked, something in it shifting enough to make Zera's forearms burn while keeping it steady. She lowered it to the grass and adjusted until it sat on even ground.

Katherine kneeled and opened the box again. The needle swung erratically until she twisted and turned the right knobs, settling its path. She closed the door and retrieved a notebook and pencil from deep in her pocket, handing them over to Zera.

"What, am I your assistant or something?" she asked, but she took them anyway.

"Something of that nature, yes. Write down the numbers I tell you, it will be much more efficient."

The thing about Katherine was, she didn't leave much room for argument, and Zera didn't mind orders so much.

"Ma'am, yes ma'am." Zera sat and rested the notebook on her knee, pencil poised over the page. The machine clicked a hypnotic rhythm barely audible over the sounds of nature and the distant noise of the city. She looked up to find Katherine staring. "Ready when you are, Kat."

Katherine's eye twitched, but she made no comment on the nickname. The grass rustled as she knelt all the way and sat back on her feet, her knee barely brushing against Zera's when she got eye level with the window on the box.

"Very well, here we go."

In her low, melodic voice she called out numbers that made absolutely no sense to Zera, but she dutifully wrote them down anyway.

Once they ran through the pattern a couple times Katherine paused, opened the box and changed some of the settings. They repeated the process multiple times with the new readings, and if Zera hadn't been moving continuously, the gentle ticking and soothing sound of Katherine's voice might have lulled her to dreamworld.

"Miss Zazzera?"

Zera glanced up, fear lancing through her heart. On the page, the steady numbers grew wider and wider until an awkward pencil line ran off the page.

"Sorry, didn't mean to fall asleep there." She uncurled her legs, her joints protesting. With a groan, she said, "Okay, I'm ready again."

"Perhaps we should take a break." Katherine moved so her hip was leaning against the ground. Zera didn't know how that could be comfortable, given how bony she was. "It's been a long night."

"You're telling me." Zera put the pencil in the journal and laid it on the grass. Now that she had permission, she flopped onto her back and stretched out fully, admiring the sky. Katherine's foot pressed into Zera's thigh, and her face tilted up to gaze at the lights.

"You know, I spent a long time being angry with you," she whispered.

"That's fair. I'd be angry with me too. I kinda fucked up our plan."

Katherine let out a ladylike bark of a laugh. "You rather did." With the light of the aurora, Zera could see her smile fade. "I struggle with this life because everyone leaves. And back then, you were someone else who left."

"I didn't want to," Zera said, sitting up. "I wanted to help, I did, but when I got caught...I panicked."

"You don't seem like the type to panic in perilous situations." Katherine looked at her out of the corner of her eye.

"Depends on the situation," Zera said. "Need me to climb out of a pit? I'm your girl. Smooth talk my way out of trouble? Not me. That's your role in this duo."

"I've seen your strength in your fighting skills. It was less than impressive."

"Now you're just being mean."

Katherine turned her head, a smile tugging at the corner of her lips. The light reflected in her honey eyes, and they almost seemed to glow with supernatural radiance. When she looked at her like that, Zera saw the version of her from that day in Central Park.

"I am sorry, Kat," she whispered. "For leaving you then. And I'm sorry I'll have to leave you again."

Katherine's smile turned sad. "Ah, but that's the ticket, Miss Zazzera," she said, mocking her own prim and proper tone. "You will, hopefully, come back."

"You're right. Even if I don't have an answer, I'll at least come and tell you that," Zera promised, as if she had any authority or control over the situation. Katherine nodded.

"I suppose I can always find you again, if I wait long enough," she said lightly, her attention back on the sky. "Unless you can take me with you?"

Zera touched the injection in her pocket. How could she score a second one during her next trip?

Then she remembered Dr. Phillips' surprise when she returned in one piece.

"Well, that would be one way for you to get the sweet release of death. But not a particularly easy way. Or fun."

"I had a feeling you would say that."

The conversation fell into silence, and while Katherine didn't seem bothered by it, every second ticking by kicked Zera's pulse up a notch. She cast her eyes around, looking for something, anything, to say. In the distance, she spotted a bell tower.

"You know, I've never been to Philadelphia. Before today, I mean," she said.

Katherine looked at her and shrugged. "It's not New York, but it'll do. I'm sure it's changed a lot in...When did you say we met the first time?"

Zera almost answered, but her inner voice stopped her. "I didn't. Guess all my historical stuff is currently present, huh? Like the Liberty Bell and all that?"

Katherine scoffed. "*Liberty Bell*. You know they didn't even ring it on Independence Day? My grandfather told me. The more time passes, the more the truth fades away."

"Is your grandfather...like you?"

"No." Katherine leaned forward and unlocked the magnetometer, setting the controls back to their original positions. "My affliction came later. I'm not sure how many of us are left."

"You gonna tell me what happened?" Zera had to try.

"When you tell me from what year you come from," Katherine replied with a wry grin.

"Touché." Zera pushed to her feet and deadlifted the device.

"When will you return to your time?" Katherine asked, straightening her pants and dusting grass from the folds. She spoke purposefully, as always, but there was an undercurrent Zera couldn't quite identify.

"Not sure." She looked at the city again, the buildings dancing blue in the light. The surreal picture took her back to the days of field trips and group projects. "Would you be willing to show a girl the town tomorrow? Don't know if I'll get a chance like this again."

It took a few moments for Katherine to find her answer.

"I suppose that couldn't hurt."

1956

"Sir, you need to wake up and vacate the area, or I'll charge you with loitering."

A baton connected with Zera's forearms hard enough to wake her fully. An officer in a hellaciously old-fashioned police uniform glared at her from beneath the brim of his cap, and she wanted so badly to smack the baton away. However, getting arrested *definitely* broke the rules, so she refrained

"Sorry, officer." The chilly night air made her voice scratchy, which helped her deepen it to a believable level. With the heavy coat high around her throat, she could hide the subtle curve of her jaw. She didn't want to find out what would happen if an officer found a woman alone first thing in the morning.

"Don't let it happen again. There's places for you vagrants to stay, and it's not on these city benches."

Zera grit her teeth. "Yes, sir." Her joints creaked as she rose, but the morning sun and shock of waking made it easier to get going again. Besides, she had a date.

Well, it wasn't a *date* date, not in the romantic sense, but Katherine promised to get her dressed and show her all the sights once she finished work. Zera didn't know what she did for work, but had it on her list of questions for the day.

Edgar, Katherine's husband, left for work at sunup, but Katherine didn't leave until midmorning. If Zera hurried, she could get breakfast—hold the coffee—and a few hours of sleep in the warmth before her field trip.

"You look miserable," Katherine greeted after opening the door.

"Yeah, well, you try sleeping on a park bench and waking up this sexy," Zera said, earning a strangled cry from Katherine.

"Excuse me?" she said, clutching the area where pearls used to be.

"What?"

Katherine's cheeks were red and splotchy, even beneath her powder. "I—you—what you choose to partake in outside of our time together is your prerogative, Miss Zazzera, but I would appreciate it if you refrained from flaunting your escapades like the man you pretend to be," she sputtered.

Zera blinked.

"*What*?" she tried again. What had she said that garnered this reaction? "Oh, fuck, has the word *sexy* not been invented yet?"

"It has, but it's a bit salacious, don't you think?" Katherine said, her voice high and tight.

Zera couldn't help it. She laughed.

If she was red before, Katherine was positively scarlet now.

"Sorry, sorry." Zera found herself apologizing for the second time that day, and the sun was barely up. "I didn't mean to laugh. Your face was just —wow."

"Apology not accepted," Katherine muttered.

"You've been alive a hundred years and married *multiple* men—I assumed talk of sex would be nothing to you by now."

"Sex is natural. Speaking of it so candidly and so early in the morning is less so."

"Should I try again after your coffee?" Zera shook her head, continuing before Katherine could speak. "Doesn't matter. *Sexy* as I use it just means, like, hot."

"I'm gathering that." Katherine furrowed her brows. "Though you are not unattractive, Miss Zazzera, I fear your current state does not live up to your true potential."

Zera took a second to translate.

"I know, Kat. That was the joke."

"Ah, sarcasm. Thought you were more clever than that."

"Wait, you think I have potential?"

"Wasted, yes."

Zera groaned. "Don't you have work to get to or something? You're mean when you're embarrassed. I just want some breakfast and a blanket."

"So very demanding." Katherine moved to the kitchen and gathered what food she could spare.

"Thank you," Zera said, before she forgot her manners.

"You're more than welcome." She forced a formal tone, which was worse than her outrage. Zera kept her comments to herself, instead digging into her food in an effort to keep the peace in this tenuous working relationship.

Katherine laid out a new suit and added a couple of logs to the furnace, stoking it until the flames leapt up, bright and beautiful. A few minutes later, the warmth soaked into Zera like the morning sun.

"I'll be gone for a few hours," Katherine said. "When I return, we'll go on your adventure."

Katherine left, the door clicking shut softly behind her. There was no backyard here, no place for her to lie and feel the sun while she slept. Even the bed, perfectly made with a well-worn quilt on top, didn't feel like the right spot for her nap. It was all so much *less* than the New York house, thanks to Zera and her meddling.

Zera shook her head. She couldn't start thinking like that, couldn't start feeling some type of way about Katherine. She had one goal, one mission.

Memories of turmoil and green flashed. Sometimes she kind of hated the mission.

Without other options, she found a spare blanket and pulled the threadbare sofa close to the furnace. Her body struggled to acclimate to the chill in the air, making her want to hibernate. When she was warm and comfortable enough, she snuggled up and went to sleep.

Zera intended to wake up before Katherine returned, but the creak of the door jolted her awake. She went tumbling to the floor like a rock, the blanket constricting every limb. Getting up sounded too difficult, so she stayed in her new place, her eyes closed as she wished with every part of her for the wood to give way and send her into the depths.

Katherine made an odd, strangled noise, then attempted to cover it with a cough. "Are you alright?" she asked.

"Just laugh. I deserve it." Zera didn't bother to open her eyes. A little giggle escaped, but Katherine once again smothered it. "Go on. It won't hurt my feelings."

"It isn't polite." Her voice wavered.

"Since when have you considered me polite?" Zera said. "I just flopped like a fish onto your dining room floor. Go ahead and get it out while I bask in the moment."

"It was rather graceful," Katherine offered, her facade breaking as she descended into laughter. While it definitely wasn't a belly laugh, it certainly had more depth to it than her usual responses.

"Grace is my middle name," Zera said.

"Is it really?" Katherine sounded some mixture of shocked and appalled.

"No." She detangled herself and rose, folding the blanket with sharp corners. If Katherine was uncomfortable with Zera knowing where the blanket went, she didn't show it.

"What is your middle name? Actually, you have yet to share your first name with me," Katherine said casually.

"Oh, no, I never go by my first name. Nice try though." Really, the last person to call her by her first name regularly was her mother, but she wasn't about to tell Katherine that. "Besides, I can't even break your habit of calling me by my full last name."

"So if I begin calling you Zera, you'll tell me your full name?" Katherine raised her eyebrows.

"If you're lucky," Zera said. "Now come on, weren't we going on a field trip?"

"Right, yes," Katherine said. She traded her logo-embroidered jacket for a cardigan and adjusted the short curls of her hair. "Let's go."

They exited the building, and Zera was proud to say she only flinched a little when the sun hit her. After living in the bunker for eighteen years, she didn't know how anyone could return to normal life again. If or when her mission succeeded, of course.

Or...what if she just stayed here?

A man on the sidewalk spat a wad of chewing tobacco on the ground. Perhaps not.

"Where to first?" she asked, glancing at Katherine from the corner of her eye.

"Well, you mentioned the Bell, so it may be in our best interest to go there first. Just in case things go awry and you need to make a swift and sudden exit again."

"Sounds good to me," Zera replied. "Did they really not ring it on the Fourth of July?"

"It was the eighth, if I remember right."

The Liberty Bell was a bit of a trek from the apartment, but with the cool weather and other-worldly surroundings, Zera didn't mind the walk. Fewer people crowded the sidewalks the closer they got to Independence Hall, giving her a clear view of people gaping at the building.

"Tourists?" Zera asked as a group of well-dressed children ran ahead of a tired-looking woman and a man distracted by his pocket watch.

"Yes. The Bell does wonders for the local economy." Bitterness tinged the edges of Katherine's words.

"Bet it doesn't spread to your side of the tracks."

"Not in the slightest."

They joined the line outside the venue—a deceptively small court-house—and ignored the looks of disdain tossed their way. At first, Zera was afraid they were judging her unusual haircut, but after a quick check of every face in line, she found the reason much more superficial.

"These rich assholes are really pissed we're here, huh?"

"Immeasurably." Katherine's lips quivered as she spoke, as if she were trying to hide a smile.

"That would've been you about twelve years ago," Zera pointed out, earning a scoff.

"I've been rich and poor more times than you'll ever be in your entire life, Miss Zazzera," she said.

"I'll go ahead and take that as a personal challenge."

"Of course you would." They inched a few steps closer. "You know, I've been here a long time, and I've never actually seen the Bell myself."

"Really? Even to tell the curators it didn't ring on the fourth?"

The man in front of them turned around sharply.

"Of course it rang on the fourth, young man." He spat the words out from under his mustache. "To celebrate our independence from those stupid English dogs."

"Right, right, my mistake, sir," Zera said, dropping her voice.

"You'd do best not to spread lies around the fairer sex." His tone was sugary and condescending, and Zera wanted nothing more than to punch him in the throat. "Their minds are weak, and have difficulty sensing differences between fact and fiction."

"Duly noted," Zera said through clenched teeth.

Katherine smiled serenely, her head leaning a few degrees to the left and her eyes wide and piercing. "No worries, sir." Her voice was a solid octave higher than usual. "Naught but crickets and clouds in my mind."

The man opened and closed his mouth a few times, looking between Zera and Katherine with increasing speed and discomfort.

"The line is moving, sir." Zera kept her tone flat, like a character in every creepy movie she wasn't supposed to watch as a kid.

"It's moving," Katherine echoed. They both maintained their gazes, giving him all due respect and attention.

"Keep that woman in line," he eventually grumbled, turning away in a manner so pompous Zera had to roll her eyes. Katherine dropped the act, her expression devolving to her usual vague distaste. With lightning speed, she reached forward. Zera thought she was going to hit the man, but instead she dipped her slender hand into his pocket and retrieved a very nice pocket knife, which she slipped into her purse.

"Hey, I'm supposed to keep you in line here."

"If I had a penny every time I heard that over the past century," she mumbled. "Tell me, will things improve?"

"Oh, for sure," Zera said. "I mean, it won't be perfect, and it takes a hell of a long time, but we're getting there. The global apocalypse helped pick up the pace."

"As is expected." They were at the door now.

"You know, you'll miss out on some cool stuff," Zera said. Why was she trying to convince Katherine to stay alive when she already knew the woman lived until 2040? Perhaps she needed to do some work on self-sabotage.

"I'm sure I will," she sighed. "But I've seen many—what did you say, *cool*?—things already."

"Please, you haven't even seen *Star Wars* or anything."

"A what?"

"A—oh gods, I don't think that's invented yet. Shit."

More heads turned at the swear, but instead of a blank look, Zera made the ugliest sneer possible. It was just as effective, and slightly more efficient.

"You're trying to pique my curiosity in order to change my mind. It won't work."

"Why do you keep tossing out all these challenges for me to pick up?"

They made it to the front of the line, and Katherine retrieved a few of her hard-earned dollars. Though she kept the same face as always, there was a noticeable lack of jingling from other change in the purse.

"I'll pay you back," Zera promised.

"Ah, but when?" Zera was afraid she'd offended her, but Katherine graced her with a small smile. "I've plenty time to earn it."

"And quick hands," Zera said, earning the all-too-familiar glare.

"Watch it, Miss Zazzera."

"Wow, you really don't wanna know my first name, huh?"

The mustached man and his family moved away, leaving them next to the famous Liberty Bell, hung in all its glory by thirteen chain links. The metal was so dark Zera could barely see the defining crack from her angle. Even hanging in the fancy raised dais, the top of it barely passed her eyeline.

"It's smaller than I thought."

"You are not alone in that thinking."

It was big, yes. And the history was impressive. But Zera realized she had no idea how big bells were supposed to be, though apparently her subconscious believed them to be a lot bigger.

"Hmm. Well, we saw it," Zera said, turning on her heel and striding away.

"What, no patriotic revelations at the skirt of the Liberty Bell?"

Zera stopped and turned.

"Was that...a joke?"

"I've got a few left in these old bones."

It was almost like Katherine was softening to the idea of friendship. This was good, Zera thought as they went back across town to the botanical gardens. They needed to be friends so she could extract information from her, for her secondary mission.

The gardens were much more impressive than the Bell, the plants sprawling across the acreage and dancing in the setting sun. Green sprouted as far as the eye could see, putting Kissi's succulent in their room to shame. Though signs warned her not to touch, Zera couldn't help sneaking her hand through the plants, feeling their leaves and petals and branches. Were flower petals always this soft? She didn't remember.

Katherine sent her a sideways glance. "Perhaps we should have started here."

"It's been a minute since I've seen something like this," Zera admitted.

"Are the gardens gone with the heat?"

It was an innocent question, but Zera was getting better at spotting Katherine's more calculating moments. "They're just inside now, and heavily regulated. My ex gave me a succulent, and after she broke up with me, Kissi—Kissinger—wanted to keep it in our room anyway. She was really into plants for a while."

Katherine's steps faltered, and her eyebrows raised just enough to break her careful façade. "After she...and now you share a room with this... Kissinger? Do you not have a husband?" It was a careful question, and Zera knew she messed up.

Zera took a long time to consider the answer. *Lie*, she thought. *Just lie, it's not hard. Act like you misspoke.*

"No, I don't." Truth. "Haven't met anyone worth marrying yet." Oversharing.

"Oh." The single syllable carried its weight in questions.

"Things are a little different in my time. There's a few more freedoms," Zera said, reaching out to touch another leaf. The thick, waxy body bent under the pressure of her fingers, but didn't break. Nature was so strong and durable until something unnatural fucked it up.

"I would imagine so." Katherine's voice was measured, and the mask was back. "What about your family?"

"My father died when I was little from a car accident." Zera shrugged. "And my mom passed from the heat and radiation after."

"I'm so sorry."

Zera turned to find Katherine looking right at her, her hands over her abdomen as if she felt the hollow place created by her parents' deaths. She probably did feel it, just for her own parents.

"Thanks." Zera cleared her throat of the emotion attempting to coalesce there. "Did you keep up with your family? After..."

Any details about Katherine's *affliction* remained a mystery, and she shamelessly wanted to know more. It wasn't so much about the mission now, but her own curiosity. Katherine kept a straight face, but Zera could see the tension in her shoulders, and the way her gait changed just slightly. A hundred years flying below the radar, and Zera wondered how many people missed these little signs, how much Katherine held back.

"I returned home, afterwards." She sounded the same, but she turned to face the plants, hiding her expression. "But once I realized things were different, I left to protect them—and myself."

"You also mentioned others. Did you go find them?" Other immortals weren't the easiest option, but Zera figured they'd make a nice contingency plan.

Katherine nodded. "I tracked one of them down, but William wanted nothing to do with me. Joseph was willing to help me in Boston, but he was killed. He said Bryce was here, but he was killed a long time ago, and the case has gone cold."

"Accidents?"

"No. Murders."

Zera stopped. "Seems weird for so many of them to get murdered."

"Long life leads to plenty of opportunities for violence."

Seemingly without thinking, she touched the scar on her neck. In the bright sunshine, Zera could barely see the end of it poking out from her collar.

"So someone's trying to hunt down you and your friends, and you're just what, playing house in downtown Philly?"

"Nobody is hunting us down, Miss Zazzera." Her face betrayed no sorrow now, only anger. "And so I am trying to survive, until you or I or someone else find a way to let me live out my life in peace."

"So you really don't want to find out who's doing all that? You've got the"—she paused, waiting for a family to pass by before continuing in a loud whisper—"the *time*, that's for sure."

"It is not a serial issue. William, after all, was alive and intact." The breeze changed direction, and Katherine moved with it. "He simply wanted nothing to do with me, and I can't blame him."

"And why's that?"

"I fear I'm rather exhausted of this interview, Miss Zazzera."

There was an air of finality in the statement. Zera bulled right through it. "Yeah, me too, but I'm gonna keep asking questions, because if I get back and I'm missing something, it's gonna be really hard to get back in touch with you." With three long strides, she overtook Katherine and stepped in front of her.

"What do you wish to do, another round of fisticuffs?" Katherine asked.

Zera grimaced. "What the fuck is *fisticuffs*?"

"It's when—"

"Just kidding, I know what it is." She didn't know for sure, but she got the gist. "And you're not gonna fisticuff me out here where it's improper, I know that much."

"Then we are at an impasse." Katherine stuck out her chin, a vision of pompous piety.

Zera groaned. She had to save this. "The more information I take back, the higher the chance I can help you out. And maybe this doesn't look serial to you, but seems weird that people who've hidden as long as you would be randomly murdered."

Katherine lifted her dainty eyebrows and cocked her head, blinking her big doe eyes. Her mouth stayed conspicuously closed.

"Really? That's what we're doing? You're gonna give me the silent treatment? It's like you're five, not a hundred and five."

Technically she was still one hundred and four, and a twitch in Katherine's jaw told Zera she wanted to say just that. Instead, she clasped her hands in front of her and continued her stroll through the gardens, bumping Zera with one bony shoulder as she passed.

"I can't believe this, you're really giving me the silent treatment." She caught up and fell into step beside her. "You know information is the most important thing. I've got literally the whole world at my fingertips when I go back."

Still nothing. A frustrated growl grew in Zera's throat, but she bit it back. Odds were, Katherine wanted her to be so frustrated that she gave up. She needed to change her tactics, but she didn't know how to steer a conversation the way she wanted it to go, not like Katherine. Katherine was all subtlety, but Zera...

Zera was big gestures.

She stopped walking and pulled the syringe from her pocket. Katherine said nothing, but her eyes narrowed.

"If you don't have anything else to share, then I guess I can just head on back," she said, holding it up.

"You wouldn't dare."

"Try me."

Zera could see the wheels turning in Katherine's mind as she weighed pride and privacy against possibility. It was a little mean to trap her between a rock and a hard place like this, but Zera had to know. "You said William wanted nothing to do with you. Sounds to me like you know who killed your friends."

"William *was* my friend." The powder on her face prevented the blush from showing, but Zera could practically feel the anger radiating from her. Katherine started walking again, this time toward the exit.

"Hold up, I'm not done—"

"I am." At least she had the decency to stop walking away. "I've answered enough of your questions, Miss Zazzera. And I believe I've shown enough cracks in my armor to last another twelve years. So thank you in advance for your assistance, and I will see you for the next storm. Good day."

"Kat, you can't possibly—" Surely she was just calling her bluff.

"I said good day."

Those words, used a million times as a punchline, felt like a smack in the face. Sincerity made them taste different. Katherine strode away without looking back, and while Zera couldn't say she knew her well, she knew it was time to accept defeat.

"At least tell me their full names so I can find them for you," she called. Katherine stopped, and Zera pleaded inwardly for her to turn around. "You need your friends, Kat. Something's fishy here."

Katherine looked over her shoulder. "I'll be fine on my own. I have been for a long time." She walked away, her stupid curls and stupid skirt bouncing with each step.

This time, Katherine was the one to leave. This time, Zera got a taste of what it felt like to be left behind.

With a frustrated sigh, she turned away from Katherine's retreating form and sank the anchor syringe into her thigh.

2058

"THEY KNOW. It's over, they know."

After the customary recovery in the hospital wing—Zera now woke up in just over two hours—she got shuffled off to Vylek's office. Her anxiety wanted her to pace the room, but her body only allowed her to collapse in a chair next to Kissi.

"They don't know. I cover my tracks and hide the board any time I hear people in the hall."

"Then why are we here?"

Kissi looked at her hands, picking at the skin around her nails.

"Kissi?"

"There's talks of shutting it all down."

"What?" Zera's lungs constricted, forcing her to cough. No blood, good sign. "No, they can't shut it down yet, we still have so many years to check."

"That's what I tried to say." Kissi left her chair to walk around the tiny room. "I mean, you came back with raw data this time. What the hell were all those numbers?"

"Katherine got them with a..." She squeezed her eyes shut, trying to remember the name, "A magnetometer?"

"Oh, that's spiffy."

"Tell me about it."

Kissi stopped and faced her. "So the next trip, not only do you have to find Katherine again, you gotta find another machine to record the stuff in real time—"

"Kissi."

"—plus then you'll be able to get a little closer to her—"

"*Kissi.*"

"—bada boom, bada bing, we figure out who she's working for and we're heroes. Perfect plan."

"Kissinger!"

"What?"

"Katherine isn't another time traveler."

Kissi paused, then narrowed her dark eyes. "What do you mean she isn't a time traveler?"

"She—"

The door opened behind her, and to her credit, Kissi managed to stay standing despite Vylek and Phillips sweeping into the room.

"Welcome back, Zazzera," Vylek said.

Startled, Zera choked out, "Glad to be here, ma'am."

"What were the measurements? The numbers?" Phillips asked.

Zera glanced at Kissi, but she dropped her eyes to the floor. Right, they still had to follow protocol.

"Uh, they were from a magnetometer," she said. "Taken during the first night of the storm."

"Yes, my hypothesis was correct!" Phillips looked like she wanted a high five, but Vylek refused to look at her. Instead, the Colonel walked around and sank into the chair behind her desk.

"It's not enough information."

"It's—what?"

"It's not enough," Vylek repeated. "You've got one more shot."

"One more? That won't work, there's so many other times where a storm hits, I can get that data for you—"

"We're running out of time, Zazzera." Her blank facade hid most of her emotions, but after a short time with Katherine, Zera could see through the cracks. Vylek was good, but not hiding-for-one-hundred-years good.

"But we're barely getting started," Zera said. Maybe if she explained everything to Vylek, made her see how important these trips were, she'd change her mind.

"No, you are the one just getting started," Vylek said. "I've kept this operation going for the past four years, and our number is coming up."

"So if I take this last trip and don't find what we need, we're supposed to just carry on in this hellscape?" Even with Kissi's warning, the words still hit her in the chest. She was supposed to save Katherine, save the *world*, and now she would do neither of those things.

"You'll get what you're owed, and then funds will be allocated to a more feasible project."

"What could possibly be more feasible than this? You invented fucking *time travel* and they wanna put that money into, what, air conditioning research?"

Vylek glared, and Kissi covered her mouth, her eyes wide as dinner plates. Nausea curled into Zera's gut; she'd never, *ever* spoken to a superior officer like this, and she found herself wishing her final trip could be to undo this moment.

"Are you done, Lieutenant Zazzera?" The cold words slid through Vylek's teeth, grabbing Zera by the throat.

"Sorry, ma'am," she said, choosing to look at her lap rather than stare at those eyes.

"It is possible," Vylek continued, her tone only slightly less icy, "that you can continue the project if the powers at be decide to utilize it in a different fashion. But not if you speak to me like that ever again."

"Yes, ma'am."

"Everyone wants to be the person who fixes everything, Zazzera. But there's only room for one at that table, and sometimes it doesn't fall to you."

"Yes, ma'am."

"You are a soldier. Your job is to carry out the plans we make. Something in your blood makes you more likely to survive the trips, but you are, at most, rare. You're not irreplaceable. Do you understand?"

"Yes, ma'am." Heat built in Zera's cheeks, and a drop of sweat rolled down her spine as the embarrassment threatened to burn her like her last dig. This was why she followed rules, because getting dressed down was so humiliating and angering that it took her right back to school days.

"Colonel—"

Vylek cut Phillips off before she could finish the thought. "Write your report and turn it in to me in the next twenty-four hours."

"Yes, ma'am," Zera mumbled.

"Dismissed."

Kissi and Zera both saluted and received one in return. Phillips looked between them all with her mouth opening and closing, like she couldn't pick the words she wanted. Zera didn't give her time to choose, and instead vacated the office with as much speed as her post-travel body would allow.

"I hate her sometimes," she said once they were far away. "I'm not wrong, am I? That explanation was bullshit."

"It was total bullshit," Kissi agreed. "You okay?"

"Yeah. Just took a good hit to my pride. Did it look as bad as it felt?"

"Worse, probably." Kissi patted Zera's shoulder. "Now, would you care to elaborate on what you said earlier?"

Zera was tired, both from her most recent travels and from the reprimand. She didn't want to talk, or to plan. She wanted to sleep.

"What did I say earlier?" She rubbed her eyes, going back through the last few minutes.

"About Katherine not being another time traveler," Kissi said. "It seems like kind of a big deal."

"Oh, gods, you don't even know," Zera groaned. Not only did she have the fun conversation with Vylek to reflect on, she also got to relive the beautifully terrible time she shared with Katherine. "*I* don't even know."

"But I could know a little more if you told me." Gone was the tender friend, replaced with the analyst.

"You know, you should've gone the academic route. Probably could've solved this whole thing a lot sooner," Zera said. They reached their room, and once the door closed, Kissi whirled on her.

"Too expensive. Quit dodging."

Zera took a deep breath and relayed every detail of Katherine's situation, how she was willing to help Zera in exchange for solving her problem. Though she wanted to hide their little date night under the stars, as well as the trip to the botanical gardens, the stories spilled from her anyway, until most of the explanation was details about their time together.

"Holy shit." Kissi said when she was finished. "That's—she was a hundred and four? Holy shit!"

"I know."

"She looked damn good for a hundred and four."

"That's what I said! But I didn't know how to tell her there was no way for us to fix it."

"You don't know that."

"I do know that. I saw her in 2040, remember? And Phillips said we can't change shit in the past. Multiple times." Zera wasn't sure of many things, but she was sure the woman she met in Central Park was Katherine, and she was very much alive. "I mean, that's probably why she recognized me, right? Why she knew me? 'Cause it's still her. Which means we failed to find a way to fix her."

"Or," Kissi said, holding up a finger, "you convinced her she wanted to keep living."

Ice settled in Zera's chest. "What do you mean?"

"I mean, maybe through the power of friendship, or something a little more...romantic, you convince her to stay alive."

"Are you suggesting I try to seduce the sketchy immortal?"

"I'm saying there's a lot we can learn from Katherine," Kissi said. "If she was there during another storm, a big one, and that's what changed her into whatever she is now, then maybe she's the answer. I mean, she was there the day of the 2040 Storm, right? That can't be coincidence."

"Of course she was there the day of the 2040 Storm, Kissi. She's *immortal*."

"But she was at the epicenter. Don't tell me that's a coincidence."

"I..."

Though Katherine hadn't shared her story, there were enough clues to determine a relative cause. It was more than likely Katherine was the reigning expert on the storms, and could eventually figure out what made the 2040 Storm different.

"Look," Kissi continued. "I think we can agree there's something different about Katherine."

Zera thought about the accent, the dry humor, the casual petty theft. A chuckle nearly broke free, but she managed to swallow it down.

"Yeah, we can agree on that."

"And I think it may be something important. I don't have the data to back it up yet, but I feel it in my gut."

"She has that effect on people."

"I'm gonna buy you some more time."

"You're gonna what?" Zera shook her head, willing the pieces of the conversation to fall where they were supposed to. "How are you gonna buy me more time? You're just as broke as I am."

"No, not—" Kissi groaned loudly, and Zera couldn't help but crack a smile. "Not *literally*, you chucklehead. I mean, I don't have to send you back to the day of the storm. I can send you back earlier, give you a few more hours to get enough information from Katherine so maybe we can do something when you get back."

"And what if it's not enough?" Zera asked. "What if this is the last trip?"

"Then you have a few more hours to hang out with your hot immortal friend," Kissi said with a shrug. "Think you got it?"

Zera thought of Katherine's face when she mentioned an ex-girlfriend. There wasn't disgust, or anger. There was just a wall. Some confusion, at most.

"Not sure, honestly," she said. "The times make it difficult. I mean, I knew things were wild back then, but the history books leave out a lot."

"What's the worst part?" Kissi asked.

"Besides the whole social injustice and rampant misogyny thing?" Zera said. She wondered whether mustache man had ever noticed his missing pocket knife.

"Yeah, besides all that."

"The smell."

Kissi barked out a laugh. "Seriously?"

"Oh my gods, it stinks so bad. No deodorant, and so much tobacco. Ridiculous. I feel like it's stuck to me every time I come back."

"So that's what the stench is," Kissi said. "What's the best thing?"

"The sun." Zera's smile fell, and she looked down at her feet. "I miss being outside."

"Yeah, me too." They were silent for a second, then Kissi said, "Looks like you'll get to head back out there again though."

"Meaning in the past? Or up top?"

"Hopefully just the past, but I guess it depends how much you figure out." She stood and knocked her hand against Zera's knee. "Rest up, you've got a bunch of stuff to learn."

"Learn? What?"

"There wasn't a lot of information about your first couple of time hops." Kissi leaned against the doorway and sent a devilish grin her way. "But the next one is 1968. You're heading for the time of free love, baby, and you'll be ready this time. You won't even have to dress up as a man."

It *would* be nice to not have to disguise herself this time around. "Is there a lesson plan involved?"

"Of course. What do you take me for, an amateur?" Kissi's grin was borderline maniacal, and Zera had to smile back. She could make it through anything as long as she had Kissi.

***

According to Grant, Zera had officially graduated from *utterly hopeless* to *probably won't die* with her fighting skills. In reality, Zera simply stopped trying to force the moves, and instead tried to move like Katherine, letting her body go through space the way it wanted. Turned out, when she didn't try so damn hard, she wasn't that bad of a grappler.

"My turn." Byrd banged his crutches against the ground, the sound blending into the cacophony of the training room.

"Hate to say it, but Zazzera can probably take you now with those limitations," Grant said, rubbing a towel over his bald head.

"Why do you hate to say it?" Zera grabbed her water bottle, gauging its weight before taking a few careful sips. "Shouldn't you be glad I'm getting better at this?"

"Because I'm his favorite," Byrd said with a stupid grin.

"Well you're on thin ice now. Been out of the ring too long," Grant said. The alarm buzzed for the end of their session, and Grant tossed the sweaty towel at Byrd, who batted it away with one crutch.

"I can't help it. I'm healing this damn thing as fast as I can."

"Excuses, excuses. Zazzera, I'll see you tomorrow."

"Yes, sir," she said with a half-assed salute.

"Kiss ass," Byrd commented.

"Can't hear you from the bench."

"See, now that's just disrespectful." Byrd heaved himself up, careful not to put weight through the cast. Thanks to his muscle atrophy, the plaster wiggled a little with each swing through the crutches. "It's not my fault bones take a few weeks to heal."

"Ridiculous, in this day and age?" Zera slicked her hair back. It now tickled the shell of her ears, which was irritating. "We should have the technology to heal broken bones immediately."

"Probably would, if the whole global catastrophe thing didn't happen," he said. They wove through the crowd of the training room, the air thick with perspiration and disinfectant spray. Despite sitting the whole time, beads of sweat dotted his hairline.

"Working on it," Zera said. "Turns out, reversing an apocalypse is kind of difficult."

"Bullshit. You're just having too much fun on your little trips. Be honest, are you sabotaging so you get to keep going?"

"Hells, I'm trying to make it last long enough for your faulty bones to heal up." The words felt forced, struggling through the narrow passages where her throat clogged with panic. Everything rode on this last trip.

"They're not faulty, they're just going for perfection." The smile didn't quite reach his eyes, and his expression sobered. "I heard through the grapevine they might cut funding."

"Yeah, Vylek made it sound like it was a long time coming," Zera said. It wasn't a proper response, and if Vylek found out she let it slip, there would be bigger issues than employment.

"Guess you'll just have to do a little better, huh?" This time, the grin was genuine. "I've got faith, Zazzera. You'll figure it out."

"Zera."

"What?"

"Zera. My friends just call me Zera." Hearing her full last name in a casual capacity brought up images of Katherine, and how it sounded better coming from her.

"Oh?" Byrd cocked his head. "We're friends now?"

"Friends enough. We could be real friends, if you quit faking your injury."

"Well then, I guess we'll never be real friends."

They reached the fork in the hallways between the barracks and the mess. Byrd kept moving forward, hopping awkwardly when he realized Zera hadn't followed.

"What, you don't eat?" he asked.

"Not right now, kinda got some stuff to take care of." She jerked her head toward the barracks.

"Oh, right, ultra double classified stuff," he said, leaning into the crutches so he could make appropriate dramatic gestures with his hands.

"Exactly. You understand."

"Oh, wait, I forgot." He dug into his pocket and retrieved the tarnished pocket watch previously in her room. "I found this in your chair in the pre-briefing room. Where'd you get it? I saw it come through intake, shocked the shit out of me."

Zera tried to look nonchalant. "That? Oh, just a weird thing I found on my last dig. Don't know why it would be in the pre-briefing room, I keep it in my bunk."

"Better handle your stuff better. Don't want Vylek to know how irresponsible you are." He held it out, and Zera took it, stuffing it deep in her pocket.

"Trust me, she knows."

With one last wave with his crutch, Byrd turned and left, leaving Zera to duck into the barracks and meet Kissi.

"There you are—oh my God, you smell disgusting." Kissi pulled the collar of her shirt over her nose as the door closed behind Zera.

"I just got done training, what do you expect?"

"I expect you to shower before you come back home."

"Your message said it was urgent."

"Not urgent enough for you to skip a shower."

"Well you need to specify that next time. Do you want me to go now?"

"Ugh, no, you're already here."

In order to protect the integrity of her bed sheets, Zera took a spot on the floor, Kissi's great mural of research spreading before her. Pictures of Katherine, with varying degrees of clarity and hair length, dotted the wall. Now that Zera knew her face better, she could see the little discontinuities as time wore on.

"Alright, so your beautiful friend Katherine holed up in St. Louis in 1968," Kissi started, kicking her rolling chair back so she could wave a hand at the relevant area of the wall. "Before then, we couldn't find much, but it seems your girl got sick of hiding."

"Don't tell me she, like, inspired Woodstock or something," Zera asked.

"Undetermined as of yet, that doesn't happen until 1969. She did play baseball in South Bend. That was pretty cool." Kissi smacked another piece of paper, the writing too small for Zera to make out. "The moral of the story is she's out and about, so it should be pretty easy to find her."

"And do what, exactly?"

"Get her blood."

"That is, without a doubt, the creepiest thing you've ever said to me."

"Look, Katherine wants us to figure out how to undo whatever got done. Vylek *also* wants us to figure out how to undo whatever got done."

"But the things aren't related."

"But they *are*." Kissi pushed the chair again, spinning to another area. Zera tried to pay attention, but she was close to a picture of Katherine with long, flowing hair covering her bare torso, peace signs thrown above her head. Apparently Zera wasn't subtle, as Kissi tore the picture down. "Zazzera! Pay attention!"

"Okay seriously, you can't blame me for that one."

Kissi waved her off. "Katherine went through an event weird enough to change her DNA—"

"How do you know that?"

"Because aging happens due to decay of protective areas of DNA as well as decreased regenerative properties."

"Bullshit."

"Probably, but it's the best smelling bullshit I've got," Kissi said. "Katherine was in a storm big enough to change her, and then was in another Storm that changed the whole world. She is the answer, so if we want to convince Vylek to keep this going, then we have to get a sample of her blood."

"And how in the hells am I supposed to do that?" She could barely stab herself with the return syringe, let alone find a vein and sink a needle into Katherine.

"Gently, and with permission." Kissi pulled open a drawer. From its depths she pulled a butterfly needle and collection tubes, neatly packaged in a plastic bag.

"Where did you get these?"

"Martin. He asked surprisingly few questions." She held out the bag, and Zera hesitated a breath before taking it. Even though it was covered by a hard shell, the knowledge the needle was so close made the area behind her sternum spasm.

"Kissi, I don't know if I can do this."

"You have to." With as much grace as she could manage, Kissi joined Zera on the floor so they were eye to eye. "I know this sucks, and there's a lot of pressure. But Zera, I've run the numbers. This is our best chance."

Zera swallowed the lump in her throat and made herself look down at the package. The logic made sense, and if she apologized, Katherine could possibly be willing to share a sample. Assuming she still wanted a cure, of course. And if she didn't...

Well then, Zera would just have to ask extra nicely.

1968

ONCE ZERA COULD SEE STRAIGHT, she found St. Louis to be a nice place.

The Mississippi River glittered in the sunset, and as the wind shifted directions, Zera felt a tug deep in her chest. At first she thought it was a remnant of her travel, but then it tugged again in the opposite direction, then again straight forward. She bent over and rested her hands on her knees, waiting for the nauseating spin of her stomach to settle.

In her periphery, the sunset colors shifted from pinks and golds to something deeper and sicker as the storm started. Kissi hadn't been able to get her the few extra hours they needed. Bile rose in the back of her throat and it took multiple swallows and deep breaths before it settled. She'd always been able to see the storms happen, yes, but she'd never *felt* them. They had to be getting stronger.

Once the sun fell below the horizon, the rolling in her stomach settled into something low and steady. She took a few steps and it changed direction again, this time decidedly somewhere around her spleen. When she moved to the left, the sensation dulled. Zera pinched her brows and pulled out her repurposed handheld scanner. It clicked on and whirred cautiously, suspicious of its new role. The light still bounced around, but instead of elements, numbers flashed on the screen. When Zera turned away, the tugging intensified, and the numbers went down.

Well, she probably wanted the numbers to go up, right?

Zera kept her eye on the screen and walked away from the city buildings toward the suburbs. Cute little houses dotted the sides of the street, a perfect picture of the American dream. White fences lined a few of the yards, which Zera thought was overkill, and each yard had big trees and bushes trimmed to different shapes, including a whole pineapple taller than her.

She took every turn the numbers suggested and found herself on a quiet street in the back of the neighborhood where the houses were a little older but no less cared for. Higher and higher the number climbed. The machine got warmer the further she went, reading the waves around them and storing the recordings in its database.

Front doors opened and voices filled the street as the neighborhood came out to see the lights. Zera quickly turned off the reader and stashed it in her jacket, moving her gaze to the ground. No benches dotted the sidewalk, so she sat on the curb, nearly missing a blue car as it flew past.

The tires squealed as it stopped a few meters away. At first, Zera thought the driver was going to reverse to her, but it had stopped for one of the neighbor guys. Zera quickly lowered her head as the guy turned toward the blue car and leaned down to the window, talking to the driver. Their low voices carried just enough for Zera to know when the conversation ended, and she looked up to see the guy jog across the street, his long, wavy hair bouncing. The blue car then pulled into the driveway, almost the same one the guy exited from. When she glanced across the street, the man was already in his own sedan and pulling away from the curb.

The blue car parked and a man stepped out, his eyes following the tan car speeding off. Zera glanced over periodically, waiting for him to say something about their near collision, but he didn't even glance her way. He went inside, then returned without his briefcase and jacket and sat on the front steps. He didn't look at the sky. Instead, he kept his eyes on the road.

The tug in her stomach took root again, and Zera stood to leave this weird guy with his intense stare. Cars moved slowly and people dotted the sidewalks, staring up at the colors. As she passed, she heard parents talking about the same thing happening years ago in other cities. One woman had been there in Philadelphia when it happened and mentioned the power troubles.

As a red car inched by, Zera's nausea settled, only to come back full force when she looked up and spotted Katherine in the driver's seat.

She had her window down, amiably chatting with neighbors as she made her way home. Yes, she'd seen this before, she said. More than once, actually. Her hair, previously coiffed in perfect curls in 1958, was now long and feathery. She was still beautiful, despite her hideous paisley shirt and mauve pants. A smile crept onto Zera's face, and her stomach turned for a completely different reason.

She was supposed to get numbers and samples. She *needed* numbers and samples. But surely they could wait until she'd antagonized Katherine for a little while.

It was easy to follow the car, and easy to hide between the neighbors she passed. She didn't even look that suspicious, she thought. Different lines ran through her head as she tried to decide her best approach. After all, Katherine probably knew the storm was tonight, and anticipated Zera's return. Hopefully.

She was all geared up and ready to say hello when Katherine pulled into the same driveway as the weird guy from before. As soon as she put her car in park he was on his feet to meet her as she opened the car door. Katherine greeted him with a smile, but even in the low light of the aurora, Zera could see the guy was pissed. She stopped following and turned away, pointing her face up and hoping it was a good enough disguise.

Zera strained to hear what they were saying, but between their hushed voices and the number of people around, she couldn't make it out. A sharp cry from Katherine made her turn just in time to see the man drag her into the house, a vice grip on her upper arm. Just before the door closed, Zera saw Katherine rip her arm from his grasp and round on him, fury on her face.

Prying eyes be damned, Zera raced down the sidewalk and up the front steps. Closer, she could hear the shouting, the man's low voice racketing off the walls and Katherine's higher pitch singing back, full of rage. A slap rang out, and everything was silent for a breath before the screaming started again. Zera tried the door; locked and bolted.

"Fuck!" she said, and pounded against the wood. Fixed in their argument, neither Katherine nor her husband seemed to hear. Through the heavy wooden door, Zera could hear crashes, thumps, and swears, as well as shouts of pain. She rammed her shoulder against the door, calling Katherine's name and hoping the door would give up before she did.

Then, silence.

Zera held her breath and waited for signs of life, the quiet from the other side eerie and heavy. Neighbors glanced her way, then shuffled their kids down the road, distracting them with a different spectacle. Footsteps came from inside, and Zera backed up as the locks turned and the door opened.

There Katherine stood, her green blouse ripped and her long, feathery hair mussed and tangled. Dark splotches stained her shirt and there was a splatter across her face, outlining a purple bruise forming underneath her eye. A knife dangled from her fingertips, and from it, blood dripped onto the hardwood floor.

"Miss Zazzera," she said, her voice raspy, "I was rather hoping it was you."

"Are you okay? Shit—"

Zera stepped in quickly and shut the door behind them. Two feet stuck out from the kitchen at the other end of the house, a red pool forming next to them. An odd gurgle echoed all the way to the entrance.

She tore her eyes away from the man and back to Katherine. Up close, she could see more bruises forming, particularly around her neck. Scratches laced her arms, and one of her elbows bled, a white chunk embedded in the skin. Zera prayed to any and all deities it wasn't bone sticking out.

"I'm sorry you walked in on this." Katherine's scratchy voice hurt to listen to, but there were no tears in her eyes, no signs of remorse.

Zera reached up and wiped blood away from Katherine's split lip. "He did this to you?"

"He did."

"Has this happened before?"

"With him? No. And I promised myself a long time ago I wouldn't allow such behavior again." She was trying to stay confident, Zera thought. But her words wavered ever so slightly. Her hands trembled as Zera took the one with the knife and slid the weapon from her grasp.

"He's gone now. He won't hurt you again." Inside, her heart beat a mile a minute, and her mind raced with possibilities. "Are you hurt anywhere else?"

Katherine's hand went to her ribs. "No, I'm fine."

"Liar. Come on, let's get you cleaned up."

"We need to take care of Robert first."

"He can wait."

"We need to wrap him. It'll be easier this way, before rigor mortis sets in."

Katherine went into a bedroom and removed the large comforter from the bed. The whole situation felt like a hallucination as Katherine took the cover and laid it out perfectly next to the body, away from the blood. The gurgling had stopped, and now Robert stared at the ceiling with a blank face.

"Let me help," Zera said, before she realized what she was offering.

"Don't worry, Miss Zazzera. I can handle it." Katherine heaved and rolled him onto the cover, but not before Zera caught sight of the stab wounds on his abdomen and chest. The body landed with a wet squelch, but with each turn and wrap of the cover, the noise softened. Zera watched, dumbfounded, as Katherine rolled it all the way up. She was trying to keep herself together, but Zera could see every hitch in her breath and every wince of pain, as well as the trembling of her lower lip.

"Katherine, come on. That's good enough for now."

Really, Zera didn't want to think about hiding a body, or even helping to hide a body. She just wanted to get Katherine cleaned up and away from this mess. Perhaps if she hadn't seen the injuries she would have been more critical of Katherine's actions, but as she limped toward the bathroom, Zera had trouble finding her in the wrong.

Katherine sat on the closed toilet. With shaking hands she grabbed a pack of cigarettes from the counter, but was unable to get the nearby lighter to catch. Despite hating the smoke, Zera lit the lighter for her before turning on the shower.

"It was him or me." Katherine's voice was barely louder than the water.

Zera felt for the temperature first, then replied, "I know." Many things could change in twelve years, but Zera doubted Katherine could have evolved into a cold-blooded killer.

When the water was an appropriate temperature and the cigarette was snubbed out in an ashtray, Zera moved to help her out of the bloody clothes. Katherine stopped her with a hand on the wrist, her skin sticky with blood.

"Would you do me a favor, Miss Zazzera?"

"Sure." She agreed far too readily.

"Down the hall is the main bedroom. In the closet is a carpet bag—would you mind getting it and emptying the top drawer of the boudoir into it?"

"I can help you here, Kat," Zera said.

She shook her head, a tear spilling onto her cheek. "It's Kitty now. And I'd rather not have you see me like this," she whispered. "You've already seen too much, if I'm honest."

"It was self defense, Kat. No one can fault you for that."

Katherine pressed her lips together and nodded, then pushed herself to her feet with a groan. "You may be right, but still."

"Kat, just let me—"

"*Kitty*, and could you please just go pack the damn bag?"

Zera balked at the harsh retort, fighting to swallow her own anger. "Sure," she said through gritted teeth.

"Thank you." Katherine looked to the bathtub, now filled with warm water, and turned back to the pack of cigarettes. Tremors shook her hands and each breath was short and ragged, but she sucked on the cigarette and refused to meet Zera's eyes.

With no argument left, Zera exited the bathroom and shut the door behind her. It felt wrong to leave Katherine alone, but she reminded herself that she wasn't in the bunker, and Katherine wasn't another soldier. She had to respect her space.

Just as Katherine said, a positively ancient carpet bag sat in the back corner of the closet. Though it was obvious she took good care of it, the pattern was nearly worn off, and the leather parts didn't quite match, as if they'd been replaced at different times. Maybe Katherine wasn't thinking straight and really wanted Zera to grab the nice leather bag on the other side of the closet. Zera batted the idea away as soon as it took hold; Katherine was many things, including deliberate.

She took the carpet bag and pried it open, laying it on the immaculately made bed. Everything was crisp and pristine in the house—except, of course, the kitchen, though that was likely just as spotless prior to the deadly argument. As Zera took the essentials from the top drawer and arranged them in the bag with her own military precision, she waited for the fear and revulsion to set in.

Katherine had just killed a man. In her defense, he tried to kill her first. Zera's version of a military career didn't involve battle or warfare of any kind; they'd learned basic self defense as part of the curriculum, but unless they went into the security sector, they never went beyond that. She didn't understand killing, but she did understand survival, just like Katherine did. While Zera fought against the elements, Katherine had to fight people, and society. Two different wars, just as unwinnable.

Down the hall, the shower curtain rattled and the water changed pitch as Katherine finally stepped into the shower. Now wasn't the time to think, it was the time to act. They had to get Katherine and the house cleaned up, and get her out of town.

Zera resumed her packing. The top drawer consisted mainly of under-garments, a few clothing staples, a wrapped parcel, and an old jewelry box. The parcel, surrounded by a soft, blue cloth, shifted slightly as she held it. Book edges pressed against her palm as she gripped it tighter, keeping it all together. Curiosity poked at her as she arranged the jewelry box. Did it hold all the rings she wore in the future? Why didn't she wear them now?

The water stopped, and Zera put the last of the drawer's contents—an old blue baseball cap with *SB* on the front—into the bag and left it open on the bed. Hinges squeaked as the bathroom door opened, but no foot-steps came down the hall.

Zera gave her to the count of thirty before she went to check on her.

If it wasn't for the wet hair and fresh scent of soap, Zera might've thought Katherine never moved. She sat on the commode, unlit cigarette in hand. She wore a satin bathrobe with a heinous tropical print, and while another night Zera might've paid more attention to the deep V at the front or the way the hem slid up Katherine's legs, tonight she only noticed how pink her skin was from scrubbing beneath the hot water.

Now that Katherine was no longer marred by her husband's blood, Zera could see every last bit of damage he'd inflicted. Bruises blossomed over her arms and neck. The one around her eye swelled with the heat of the shower, though Katherine didn't pay it any mind. Her hair hung long and tangled down her back, another casualty of her aggressive scrubbing.

"I probably look messy," she murmured.

"Oh, you definitely look messy." Zera opened the cabinet under the sink and was happy to find a first aid kit. "But I think I can forgive you, just this once."

"I can't even imagine what you think of me right now."

"I think," Zera said, opening the kit and retrieving some antiseptic and gauze, "you were in an impossible situation, and you did what you had to do."

"Have you ever killed someone, Miss Zazzera?"

The question made her pause. "No, I haven't."

"It's not easy. I think a part of you dies too."

It occurred to Zera this was not the first time Katherine had been forced to kill someone.

"Do you believe in ghosts, Miss Zazzera?"

"Ghosts? Nah." Zera found adhesive bandages and applied them over the deeper cuts still shimmering with blood.

"Why not?"

"Well, haven't seen one, and I'm regularly in places where lots of people have died." She finished her patch job and returned the kit to its place. "Why? Do you?"

"I don't want to," she said. "But sometimes..."

Zera waited. Katherine met her eyes and said, "Sometimes I wonder."

"Wonder what?"

Katherine opened her mouth, then shut it again, shaking her head. "Nothing. Were you able to pack everything?"

She stood and walked with steady steps to the back room, leaving Zera behind.

Zera sighed and followed after her, ignoring the presence of the body in the next room. "Do you have, like, a plan or something?"

Katherine rifled through drawers, grabbing a few last pieces of clothing and tossing them into the bag. "Of course I have a plan. I always have a plan." Her accent dipped all the way back to the New York socialite.

"You have no clue what we're gonna do, huh?"

Katherine paused. "Of course I do."

Zera waited for her to continue. The lights of the aurora played through the lace curtains, dancing on the bed. She could still hear the voices of the neighbors admiring the event.

Finally, Katherine said, "I have to bury him. And then I have to leave."

1968

"I'M SORRY, *bury* him? We're just going to bury him, what, in the backyard? And pretend this didn't happen?"

"Men leave their wives all the time, Miss Zazzera. I'll wait a few months, play the wounded bird, sell the house, and move on. Can you turn around please?" Katherine was all business now, pulling shorts on beneath her robe. Thanks to Zera's big fat mouth back in Philadelphia, gone were the days where Katherine didn't think twice about changing in front of her.

She decided to open her stupid mouth again. "Really? I'm gonna help you hide a body and I know your immortal secret, but changing in front of me is too much?"

"I'd like to keep some sense of modesty, Miss Zazzera."

"*Zera*, Kat. And trust me, the thrill of changing in a room full of people wore off a long time ago." It stung, but she turned her back to her.

"*Kitty*, Miss Zazzera." Katherine huffed, taking an extra moment to choose her next words. "And this has nothing to do with your sexual preferences and everything to do with my own vulnerabilities."

"The fuck is that supposed to mean?"

"It means sometimes the world doesn't revolve around you."

"You got something you wanna say, Kat?" Zera turned around and found her dressed in a white t-shirt and red shorts. Not the ideal body-hiding outfit, but it would do. "You can just come out and say it."

"You said it yourself." Katherine crossed her arms. "I just killed my husband, and you know a large percentage of my dirty little secrets. So excuse me if I'm feeling nervous."

She tried to stand straight during her monologue, but Zera noticed the way she listed to her left. It was a posture she adopted herself once, after a rough tumble with a rock slide.

"Are your ribs broken?"

Katherine's cheeks darkened. "Just bruised."

"Let me—"

"There's nothing to be done. Now, if you'll excuse me."

Katherine brushed by her—extra close, as if to make a point—and went back to the main area of the house.

"Hope you've got two shovels," Zera said as Katherine dipped into the garage.

"We've been through this, Miss Zazzera. I'm not bringing you into this."

"I'm already in it. What are they gonna do, test my DNA? I don't exist yet."

Katherine stopped, startled, and the tools she was rifling through clattered to the ground. "They can test DNA?"

Zera held up her hands. "Uh, clearly not yet." She pulled out her handheld, only to remember there was no intranet here. "Shit, I can't even tell you when it starts. But you've never heard of testing DNA at crime scenes?"

"No!"

"Then we're good." Zera stepped into the garage and rummaged through the tools until she found shovels. Luckily, they owned more than one. "If you haven't heard of it, there's nothing to worry about. Now come on, we gotta do this before it gets too quiet out there."

"Miss Zazzera—"

"I'm helping, Katherine. Get over it."

The sight of Robert's body, even in a comforter, brought bile to the back of her throat, but all it took was one look at Katherine's injuries for the nausea to fade to a tolerable level. Katherine ducked underneath the sink and pulled out multiple pairs of rubber cleaning gloves, tossing a bright blue floral set to Zera.

"This feels ridiculous," Zera said as she pulled them on. The gloves clashed horribly with her tattoos.

"It's not an ideal situation," Katherine agreed. She donned yellow gloves, which would have looked marginally better if they didn't darken her bruises.

Zera grabbed the comforter edge at Robert's feet while Katherine went to his head. The limp body slid and bent awkwardly as they shuffled to the back door, which banged loudly as they ushered the body out.

While the front yards were nice and open, the backyards had tall privacy fences. Luscious green grass coated the area, which was not ideal for hiding a body, but trees, bushes, and flowers spread across the back fence, lined by a nice area of mulch. Once she spotted it, Zera figured out the plan.

"Got extra mulch in the garage?"

"Just one bag. We'll have to spread it rather thin and reuse what we can."

They deposited Robert beneath a young Bradford pear tree, the branches low enough to keep him relatively hidden as they started digging. For all her bravado, Katherine could only move so fast thanks to her injuries. Zera figured the adrenaline was wearing off and the pain was setting in. She'd been there and knew sometimes the crash was worse than the initial pain. She also knew better than to point it out; instead, she simply kept digging, getting the hole as close to the big hydrangea bushes as possible, their perfume cloying in the summer night. The aurora gave plenty of light, and the impromptu block party drowned out their shovels and short breaths.

"You were right," Katherine said at one point. She leaned against the handle of her shovel, and even in the low light Zera could see blood poking through the bandages.

"Can I get that in writing? I don't think I'll ever hear you say that again." Zera kept digging, ignoring the glare from her literal partner in crime. So much for no contact and a low profile. Vylek would throw a fit if she knew. "What exactly was I right about?"

"Someone *is* looking for me, for us."

Zera froze. "Us meaning..."

"Me and the others with my affliction," Katherine said.

The conversation felt so long ago. "What makes you say I'm right? Something happened the past few years?"

"Tonight," Katherine said.

"Tonight?" Zera looked at the corpse in the corner. "Robert?"

"What? No!" Katherine shook her head. "It's what he said before he..."

"Before he tried to kill you?"

"Yes." Katherine took a deep breath. "He said a man was here looking for me. When Robert said I wasn't home, and asked how he knew me...He said we were old friends, that he'd known me as Katherine Longly."

"Okay, I still don't understand why that would set Robert off though."

"Apparently there were mentions of a current intimate relationship, and instead of letting me explain, Robert chose to believe this man."

"Well that's bullshit." Zera resumed digging. "I thought marriage was supposed to be a partnership or something."

Katherine laughed in a slightly manic way. "Ah, Miss Zazzera, your hopes are too high."

That wasn't encouraging at all.

"Things change in the future," Zera said. "You'll have to wait and see."

"Does it change before or after we develop DNA testing?"

Zera grimaced. "After."

"Hmm. Well, I'm still holding out hope you'll find me a way to age gracefully and depart from this earth."

"Oh, right." Zera paused again. "Turns out, for that, I'll need your blood."

Katherine blinked. "Alright. Perhaps after we finish this?"

"Sure, that'll be—"

"Kitty Thomas, what are you doing gardening at a time like this?"

Zera and Katherine startled and spun to the fence line. A middle-aged woman with a questionable dye job peeked over the top. Despite the late hour, her brown and gray hair was curled perfectly, and her makeup was flawless.

"Oh, Dorothy, you scared me." Katherine put an arm around her middle, likely holding her bruised ribs.

"What happened to your eye?" Dorothy must've stood on her toes, because she grew a few inches taller. Something squeaked underneath her, sounding like a step-ladder.

"Nothing, I just fell," Katherine said, too quickly.

Dorothy gave her a pitying look, one that held too much understanding. "Oh, well if you wanted to join the party, Doug has the grill out front. The kids are going crazy, and—oh, I'm sorry, how rude of me. Who's your friend?"

"Zera," Zera said, at the same time Katherine said, "My cousin."

"Oh, um," Dorothy floundered, trying to find the right response. "Well, you're both welcome in front. You can leave Robert behind if he's... gone to bed already."

Surely Dorothy could see the comforter poking out from behind the tree and knew their secret. But she didn't say anything more.

"Thank you, Dorothy, but I think we'll just tend to the garden for right now."

"I understand. Call if you need anything, okay?"

Katherine agreed, and Dorothy hopped out of view, her footsteps muffled by the grass as she hurried toward her front yard.

Zera let out a long breath. "That was close."

"Dorothy didn't see anything," Katherine said. "Even if she did, she won't tell."

"Bold assumption."

"I know my neighbors well."

"And do they know you?"

Katherine didn't reply, she only resumed digging.

It took upwards of six hours, but with Zera's vast digging experience, a deep, Robert-sized hole formed in the shrubs. The body was stiff as they dragged it and dropped it in with a thud. The neighborhood was quiet now, and they had to be more careful as they replaced the dirt on top of the grave.

"What are you gonna do now?"

"I told you, play the—"

"No, I mean about your hunter."

Katherine laid another shovelful of dirt in the hole. "Well, if someone's hunting me, it's only fair I hunt them back, right?"

"Do you have any idea who it could be?"

"There were only seven of us, and at least three of us are dead. So that leaves me three possibilities."

"Do you think it was your friend in New York?"

"William? I don't think so." She exhaled, her sweaty bangs taking flight for a moment before sticking back to her forehead. "But he'll be my first stop."

"Probably a good idea. He might know where the others are."

"Especially if he's the one searching us out."

Another hour and the hole was filled, the excess dirt spread around the garden and a thin layer of mulch applied to the top. All in all, their hiding job was decent, and would improve as the body decomposed. Probably.

Katherine took another shower while Zera paced in the bedroom. How the hells was she going to explain this in her report? Sure, she could shower too, but that wouldn't fix the dirt all over her clothes and the stench of sweat soaked into them. She needed to come up with something before leaving.

The water shut off, but Katherine stayed in the bathroom for much longer. This time she emerged in a nice dress complete with pearls, her hair and makeup styled to perfection. Somehow she managed to hide most of the bruises, though her eye swelled just enough to look wrong.

"What are we doing here?" Zera gestured at the outfit.

Katherine paused to look in the boudoir mirror, changing the way her bangs settled on her forehead. "It's nearly time for me to go to work. Robert and I are usually the first to leave the neighborhood, so no one will notice if my car's gone."

"And what about his?"

Katherine paused and placed her hands on the vanity top. "Shit."

"Such foul language."

A frustrated groan escaped Katherine as she straightened, hands on her hips. She gazed somewhere beyond Zera as the wheels turned.

"I'll have to get rid of it," she said, more to herself than to Zera. "I can take it to the boat ramp by the river and send it in. As long as I keep it in neutral, it'll roll right off the edge. It's a sharp drop."

"How are you gonna send it in? And how are you gonna get back here in time for work?"

"I'm working on that part."

"Let me help, Kat."

"Kitty—"

"No way in any hell am I calling you that." Zera moved so she could meet Katherine's eyes. "Look, you need to get to work, right? I'll just drive his car and dump it while you go."

"I can't ask you to do that for me."

"You're not asking, I'm offering."

"Miss Zazzera—"

"I literally helped you bury the body." Zera's heart squeezed at the idea again; the death was self defense, was *warranted*, but it still didn't sit easy. "I can dump a car with no problem."

Katherine inhaled sharply. "Very well. If you're willing, your help would be invaluable."

"Gods, just say thank you. How long do we have until you have to leave?"

"I usually leave at six o'clock, so these extra fifteen minutes shouldn't be suspicious," Katherine said, checking her watch.

"Fifteen minutes?" Zera hoped to every god she'd heard wrong. "As in, it's fifteen minutes after six right now?"

"Yes?" Katherine pinched her brows. "Why?"

"Fuck!"

Zera ran out of the room to the front door, ignoring Katherine behind her. Surely she hadn't fucked up this bad—she wasn't the brightest sometimes, but she was reliable. Until now.

Outside, the aurora had faded, and she was left with nothing but the navy blue sky, the edges lightening with the impending dawn. She wrenched the scanner out of her pocket and flipped it back on, but instead of the fluctuating numbers, the screen held at zero.

"Shit shit shit *fuck*—"

"Miss Zazzera? Is everything alright?"

Katherine stood at the door. She still leaned slightly to the left, and had her hands clasped at her chest. Zera didn't realize until that moment how slender she was, closer to how she met her in 1956 versus 1944. Despite her obvious displays of strength earlier, now she looked nervous.

"Yeah, yeah it's cool," Zera said. She returned the scanner to her pocket. It was useless now. This was, without a doubt, the worst she'd screwed up in her entire life. But as she noticed the dark spots of bruises on Katherine's face, even beneath the makeup, she couldn't find it in her heart to regret it. At least not yet.

"Where are his keys?" she asked.

It was a good thing all the vehicles at the bunker were stick shifts, though Robert's car was a much smoother ride than the junkers they patchworked in the future. Katherine led her through the sleepy streets, and once they exited the neighborhood, took her to the boat ramp. It wasn't much, just an angled concrete slab leading into the murky waters of the Mississippi, but it would do the job.

Katherine turned around and pulled her car even, rolling the window down. Zera did the same, welcoming the smell of earth and water and Katherine's perfume.

"You're sure about this?" Katherine asked.

"We're already here, Kat. We're golden."

Katherine nodded and dropped her gaze. "Thank you, again," she said. "I don't know how to repay you."

"You'll figure it out in the next twelve years, I'm sure," Zera said. Assuming Zera could come back in twelve years and didn't get discharged and dismembered upon returning to her time.

"Did you get all you needed? From the storm last night? Before…"

"Yeah, got it all right here." She held up the scanner, which lacked a large chunk of data. But Katherine didn't need to know that.

"Right, good." She didn't sound as if she believed it. "Well then I… suppose I'll see you again. In the future."

"Hopefully we'll both have some more answers," Zera said.

Katherine nodded, and with one last smile, rolled up her window and drove away. Zera let out a long sigh and stared at the water. Light spilled from behind the trees on the opposite shoreline as the sun rose, and the river turned liquid gold in the morning light. Maybe she wouldn't deal with the ramifications of this failed mission. Maybe she'd just stay here forever.

She ran her thumb over the lump that marked the tracker in her arm. If she wanted to escape, she'd need to die, and she couldn't do that to Kissi. No, she had to go back and face Vylek and Phillips, and hope they gave her one more chance.

The gear shift protested, as if the car knew its fate. Zera took the anchor syringe from her pocket and held it at the ready. Despite knowing she would survive the sinking car, the idea of the river of time made her insides squirm. Gods, it was going to hurt.

With a start, she remembered Katherine's blood and the empty vial in her pocket.

"Fucking hell!" She hit the back of her head against the headrest and let out a guttural scream. She'd managed to mess up *everything*, and an overwhelming urge rose in her to disappear into the crowd and never face anyone she knew ever again. How mad would they be? For how long would they wait?

It was a stupid idea, and she'd stalled long enough. Any later and someone would see her here in Robert's car. She could wait as long as she wanted, but she'd have to deal with this eventually. Just like the return syringe, it was better to get it over with rather than spending too much time thinking about it.

Zera punched the gas enough to build speed, then rode down the ramp and jerked as the front of the car hit the surface. Water gushed through the open window and she barely held onto the syringe. The needle stung as she sank it into her opposite bicep, away from the rising water, and a second later she no longer felt the pressure on her legs.

Her time was up.

2058

THIS TIME, instead of the hospital room, Zera woke up on the platform, the plastic hot underneath her and the cold air pushing her down.

"Lieutenant Zazzera." Vylek's voice was quiet and controlled, but Zera could feel the fury underneath. She opened her mouth to reply, but couldn't get enough air to speak. Not that it mattered. "Would you like to tell me why you only have half the data we need?"

Fear gripped her, so tight she couldn't force the words out, even if she wanted to. Adrenaline rode so high she didn't hurt to breathe anymore.

"Lieutenant!"

"Problem," she gasped out. "Ran into a problem."

"Obviously." The word was nearly a growl. Zera tried to move, her wet uniform pants pressing cold fabric against her hot skin and startling her. Spots clouded her vision, and she longed to return to unconsciousness to avoid the discomfort. Something poked her shoulder and energy surged through her blood, forcing her awake.

"Zazzera, tell us what happened." Vylek held an empty syringe, the likely source of Zera's sudden clarity. Normally they allowed Zera to wake up on her own. She must have really messed up to earn an interrogation immediately.

"I landed in a bad spot." Every word hurt, but she was glad to come up with a lie in an appropriate time. "Got caught."

"By who?"

The shot was wearing off, the crash worse than the high. In answer to the Colonel's question, Zera rolled just enough so she could vomit on the floor instead of herself. A noise of disgust and a few curses escaped Vylek as she avoided the mess.

"Lieutenant, you have to understand." Phillips stepped in as the good cop. "With the lack of data, we have to close everything down."

"No!" Zera's mind swam; instead of faces, she saw the aurora as it was over St. Louis. "We gotta go again." She couldn't leave Katherine hanging, not when she needed help.

"That depends entirely on what you can tell us," Phillips said. Zera blinked, but it took all her energy to force her eyes open again. Everything felt so weak, so heavy. She wanted nothing more but to succumb to darkness.

"Stay awake, Zazzera—"

"She can't answer right now." Phillips came to her rescue, pulling Vylek away. Zera spotted Kissi in the back of the room, two security guys holding her as she struggled. Zera gave her an encouraging smile, trying to say she was fine, but if Kissi's face matched her feelings, it didn't work. Then, finally, she passed out.

When she woke up later, it was with the distinct sensation of having been unconscious for a very long time. Fog hung over her thoughts, and her mouth felt like sandpaper as she tried to wet her lips. She heard the beeps of the machines, but couldn't make out any features in the dark room as she tried to pull herself awake.

"You talk in your sleep, you know." Something distorted Martin's voice, but whether it was from the room or the effects of the river, Zera couldn't be sure.

"Hmm?"

"Who's Katherine?"

Zera choked, and the subsequent coughing felt like her chest, brain, and stomach all exploded. Pain wracked through her until she was nothing more than a sniffling mess, her face wet with tears. Usually she didn't cry from pain, but the hacking must've forced them out.

Martin's hands were on her a second later, strong despite their smaller size. He held her bones together as the coughs subsided and the pain ebbed down to a manageable level.

"Wow," he said. "You've got it that bad for her, huh? Which sector is she in?"

Zera glared in the direction of his voice, hoping it reached him. She still couldn't see straight, and even the low lights made her eyes hurt.

"Fine, keep your gossip. I'll just ask Kissi later, she knows all the good stuff."

He moved away when she was stable. Next to her, he shifted a bedside table closer, and a second later she felt plastic against her lower lip.

"Drink. It's just some bone broth, but it'll help you feel a little better."

The smell of the drink brought back her nausea, and she dry heaved until her throat burned and her back popped with the exertion. Something felt utterly wrong.

"Okay." Martin put the cup back on the table. "Hold still for a second."

Laying still was no problem. Zera didn't think she could move anything at this point and was lucky enough to keep breathing. She could hear Martin working next to her with clacking plastic syringes, but she kept her eyes closed and focused on not passing out again.

"Here's something for the pain." A burning sensation spread from her elbow, and immediately her joints turned from bone to cotton balls. "And here's one for the nausea." Another burn, and this time her stomach settled. "How do you feel now?"

Zera took an experimental breath. The pain still lingered, but it was dull, hidden beneath layers of fatigue and medication.

"Okay," she said truthfully. She cracked one eye open and scanned the room, disappointed to find them alone. "Where's Kissi?"

"You went into cardiac arrest again with that cocktail Vylek used to wake you up. That was super fun." Martin sounded bitter. He held the broth to her mouth again, and this time she didn't recoil, though she could only tolerate small sips. "I told Kissinger I'd call her when you stabilized."

"Give it to me straight, Martin. How fucked up am I?"

"Only like, forty percent," he said. "If I had to guess, you could make it another three or four jumps. Five if you were willing to die on the job."

"Wouldn't be ideal." She finished the broth and tried to push herself up, but apparently the pain medicine had transformed her muscles to noodles and wet chewing gum. "Fuck. Feels like I got hit by a train."

"Your insides looked like it for a second." Martin took the cup from her. "Trust me when I say you wanna sleep this one off."

"I gotta talk to Kissi."

"I'll get her in here," he said. "But Zera, seriously. Sleep. Now."

Protest hung on her lips, but when she relaxed into the bed, her fight simmered down. He was right; she couldn't do anything, not in this condition.

⌒⌒⌒⌒⌒⌒⌒

It took three days for Zera to improve enough to leave the hospital, and another three after that before she felt normal again. Martin's five-trip estimate seemed rather high given how slow her recovery was this time. She must have looked terrible, because Kissi didn't antagonize her for a whole week.

In proper military terms, Zera was in deep shit. Vylek gave her a proper dressing down once she was healthy enough for it, about how it would be her fault if they failed, and how she was lucky Byrd was still in a boot, otherwise she'd be down in the farming sector with the rest of the inmates. Zera played the good soldier, nodding along and saying nothing except for apologies. When asked about her encounter, she gave a vague answer about a group of people and a fight, and how she had to come back too soon.

The answer to this, of course, was more time in the training room with Grant and Byrd. Byrd wasn't technically her training officer, but he was there more often than not, though his commentary was less than helpful.

"You're still telegraphing your moves."

"I don't know what the fuck that means."

Grant was gone for the day, called away to train more hopeful cases than Zera. Byrd had taken it upon himself to continue the session.

He poked her hip with the end of his crutch. "Your hips tell me where you're going long before you actually strike."

Zera rubbed the forming bruise. "No they don't."

"Yes, they do. 'Cause your core is weak." He flipped the crutch around

181

and shoved her shoulder with the opposite end. The force, stronger than anticipated, shifted her balance to her back foot.

"My core isn't weak, you just waited until I was too tired to fight back," she said as she straightened.

"Look, I'm just trying to help." He held up his hands in innocence.

The gesture sent a lance of irritation through Zera. "I know you are, and I appreciate it, but—"

"But nothing." He limped closer. "You couldn't get what we needed because you couldn't defend yourself. And if you can't get what we need, they're gonna shut down the program, and if they shut down the program, we're not gonna be able to counteract the effects of the Storm."

"Why are you freaking out about this? Kissi told Vylek we got enough data to convince the higher ups of one more trip. We can figure it out." In reality, Zera couldn't muster the energy to argue, especially because he was right. If Vylek ever found out Zera willfully ignored orders, *trouble* wouldn't even begin to describe her situation.

"'Cause I need more than one trip. I can't have you hogging all the glory." The trademark grin was back, his anxious moment forgotten. He stomped his booted foot, this time managing not to grimace. "If I could just get this stupid thing off I'd be fine."

"If you don't quit messing with it, you'll have it on forever," Zera said. She ran a hand through her sweaty hair. The ends reached into her eyes now, but who had time for a haircut when she was jumping through time and trying to fix the world?

"Nah, I'll cut it off myself before that happens," Byrd said. "Come on, let's go again."

Zera's handheld lit up on the bench, and she walked over to find a message from Kissi expressing, in no uncertain terms, that she needed to return to their bunk immediately.

"Can't, I'm done for the day." She tossed the handheld into her bag and picked it up.

Byrd raised an eyebrow. "What, your boyfriend message you or something?"

"Nope." Zera rolled her eyes. "I'll see you tomorrow."

"But I'm bored *now*, Zazzera," he whined.

"Not my problem!"

She walked at max speed to her bunk and slipped through the door so fast her bag caught on the handle and nearly choked her. No sympathy came from Kissi despite the sound Zera made—she only had eyes for the three screens in front of her.

"What's up?" Zera rubbed her sore neck.

Kissi pointed to the wall. "I found them."

A newspaper clipping from an 1884 Boston newspaper hung on the wall at the end of the display. Despite the poor quality of the photo, it was obvious the seven people in it had been through a harrowing ordeal. Six men stood in a line, their cheeks dark and sunken and their clothes hanging loose and heavy on their thin bodies, but it was the seventh person who caught Zera's eye.

Though she was skinnier than ever and her hair was a tangled rat nest atop her head, it was still very clearly Katherine. If Zera needed proof Katherine was exactly as she said, it was here.

"Most of the article is unreadable, but I was able to clean up the image enough to get those guys' faces." Kissi brought up different windows with photos of the men, most of which came from the morgue. "There's a lot of death under mysterious circumstances here."

"Dammit, so Katherine wasn't able to save them."

"Doesn't look like it."

Zera moved Kissi's abandoned prosthesis closer to her and sank into the other chair. "But you know where they died?"

"Where and when." Kissi pulled up names, dates, and locations on another screen. All the things Katherine would need to track down her friends. Only one didn't have a death date.

"William made it all the way?" She scanned the screens until she found his picture. He was a gruff-looking man, probably in his late fifties, with a thick gray beard and dark eyes. No wonder Katherine suspected him—he looked terrifying.

"As far as I can tell. I searched through John Does and every other database I could find, but there's no record of him after 1969. No death certificate, but no proof of life either. It's like he disappeared off the face of the earth."

"Not hard to do in 1969 I bet."

"Not really, no. But harder to do as time went on. If we assume he's like Katherine, then he somehow found a way to stay under the radar until the 2040 Storm."

"Or he's buried in a backyard somewhere."

Kissi paused, then turned. "Do you think Katherine killed him?"

"I don't know," Zera said too quickly. "I mean, she killed Robert. And she implied she's killed people before. But it sounded like it was all in self defense. The last one for sure was."

But just because the most recent death was self defense didn't mean the previous ones—or later ones—were. A sliver of doubt crept into the back of Zera's mind, casting a shadow on her understanding of Katherine. She'd survived through times where women had little power in society. For someone who supposedly wanted to die, what had she done to ensure her survival?

"Guess you'll just have to ask her next time you see her." Kissi showed her a different list with the names and locations of Katherine's companions. Most of them landed in places on their map where Kissi had found spikes in the data.

"Maybe..."

"No."

"You don't even know what I was going to say."

Kissi glared. "So you weren't gonna say, 'maybe I can help her save some of her friends'?"

"No." Zera turned her attention back to the wall so she wouldn't have to look Kissi in the eye.

"Say it, then," Kissi said.

"Say what?"

"Look me in my face and say you're not gonna try and change something in history."

Zera met her gaze and said, "I'm not gonna try and change something in history."

"Thank you, because that would be dumb."

"Katherine will do the changing."

"God dammit, Zazzera." Kissi dropped her head into her hands.

"Okay, you're right," Zera said. "I can't change anything. That's what we've been told this whole time."

"Exactly," Kissi said. "You've already gone way off course. You buried a body, for God's sake."

"Okay, that was one time." And she still had nightmares about it. "Katherine was a fun distraction, but I'll focus this time. For real."

"Thank you."

"Does this mean you don't want me to get Katherine's blood anymore?"

Kissi pursed her lips. The question was a low blow, rooted entirely in Zera's own selfishness. She didn't want to leave Katherine behind after everything. Despite the conversation, she still hoped somehow, someway she could save her from her fate in Central Park.

Zera pulled the ring out from under her shirt collar and slid it back and forth along the chain, if only to keep her hands busy.

"No. You shouldn't," Kissi said eventually. Her voice had no waver, no sign she was trying to talk herself out of it.

"But if I got it anyway, what then?"

"Then you would be a supremely shitty friend."

"Shitty enough that you wouldn't forgive me?" Zera was needling, she knew it. But she couldn't save Katherine without Kissi's help.

Kissi glared. "Zazzera, listen to me. You're a grown woman, I'm not gonna tell you how bad an idea it is. You have to think about *everyone* you're saving, instead of focusing on the one you can't."

Zera's cheeks burned and she started sweating anew. She wanted to fight back, but only because Kissi was entirely right. "Yeah, of course. My bad."

"I get it, it's probably super hard to let people go. But if you come back without data again?" Kissi shook her head. "I don't know, Zera. I don't know if I can get over that."

Zera swallowed and nodded. "Right, you're right."

Kissi tapped one of the tablets. "Katherine's in Chicago, by the way. For your next trip."

Somehow, Zera managed to feel more guilty. "Look, Kissi—"

"I'm telling you this because I trust you'll do things right this time." Kissi looked her full in the face now, deadly serious. "Don't break that trust."

Zera nodded again. Vylek's reprimand was rough, yes, but nothing like Kissi's. It was time she remembered her priorities—and her real mission.

But she could do both. She *had* to do both. She just had to figure out how.

1980

Zera anticipated a lot more colors when hitting the '80s, but she was severely disappointed.

Chicago, at first glance, was just another city. The attire was closer to what Zera was used to seeing back in the modern day, and while the cars looked like they belonged in a museum, they crowded the streets like any other traffic-fueled empire. The hustle and bustle felt more normal than all her previous travels combined.

It took her more than three hours to stand upright after she landed in the back of a massive shipping center that was supposed to be Millennium Park. Only problem was, Millennium Park didn't exist yet. Gravel, dirt, and other questionable oddities stuck to her, but at least her sick and the bit of blood she coughed up would go relatively unnoticed in the area.

There was a pull in her gut like in St. Louis, but it wasn't nearly as strong this time, and Zera either figured it was a figment of her imagination, or her insides were giving up. Men, women, and children stared as she passed them on the busy sidewalk, but whether it was due to her clothes, her hair, or just a sense of *wrong* about her, she didn't know.

As the sun sank, the street lights and store fronts flickered to life. She had one day before the storm would hit, which meant she had one day to find Katherine and get her blood, as well as the data she needed to keep the program running. Next time—if she managed a next time—she and Katherine needed to set up a place and time so there wasn't any disconnect.

Downtown came to life after dark, and with no sign of Katherine, Zera followed the noise until she found the busiest area and set up shop at a bar. Best case scenario, she could garner attention from somebody and get them to pay for her meal, maybe even give her a place to stay. Worst case scenario, she could dine and dash and find a nice park bench to hold her for the night. The women in the bar absolutely sparkled, free from their work days and chattering away, whereas tired men tried to muster the courage to talk to them.

Another night, in another time, Zera would slide right up to one of the vibrant ladies or flirty guys and start a conversation. But she needed to stay focused, not get distracted by the pretty people.

"Why so lonely?" A man sat on the stool next to her, laying his hat on the bar top. His courage wasn't short, though he certainly was.

"'Lonely'?" she asked, raising her eyebrows.

The man grinned, apparently taking her question as a flirtation. "Well, since you're sitting up here all alone," he said, with an honest-to-gods wink thrown her way. It was quickly followed by holding his hands up in an innocent gesture. "Unless you're waiting for your fella. I'm not trying to be a homewrecker or anything."

Zera opened her mouth, closed it, then tried again. "No, no I'm not waiting on a—a *fella*," she said, trying the word out and discovering she hated it. "Just a...friend of mine. But I'm not sure she's coming out tonight."

"Wanna phone her? I got a spare quarter you can borrow." Coins jingled as he rummaged in his pocket, but Zera waved him away.

"No thank you, I don't know her number. She didn't know I was coming to town tonight, it was kind of a surprise?" She didn't mean to end the sentence as a question, but the longer the conversation went, the more nervous it made her.

The man smiled. "From outta town, huh? Whereabouts?"

"Oh, uh, um..."

He mistook her struggle to lie for hesitancy to share personal information, and shook his head quickly, sticking out a hand.

"I apologize, where are my manners? The name's Hank, Hank Rockler."

Hank Rockler was an eager man, either trying to impress Zera and take her on a date, or something a little less formal. Turns out, people were people no matter what decade, and while navigating 1980 Chicago would be a challenge, Zera never had any trouble when it came to chatting with a guy at a bar. Memories of her early twenties reminded her she'd certainly done more for less before. This would be cake.

Following this realization, it was easy to talk to Hank. He carried most of the conversation, and when he graced her with a question, she usually just told him a variation of the truth. After all, what was he going to do, look her up on social media? New York was a distant, imaginary land to Hank, home to rude people and *those damn Yankees*. Baseball was a vague memory from the time before the 2040 Storm, but Zera managed enough bullshit to keep the conversation going long enough for a meal.

"Well, whaddya think, Zera?" Crowds packed the streets now, and music drifted from somewhere a few doors down. Hank carefully wiped his mouth and tossed the napkin onto his plate. His hands were smooth, Zera noticed. No hard labor. "Wanna hoof it?"

"Hoof it where?" she asked. Even if she needed a place to stay for the night, Hank didn't seem like the type of guy to make such a leap so fast, and it made her throw up her guard again.

"I know a little speakeasy just north of here. Plays some great music, and has, uh, a little bit of stronger pop if that's something you're interested in."

Real alcohol? Not crappy, questionable shit from her future?

"Fuck yeah Hank, let's hoof it."

This response startled Hank, who looked about ready to bolt out of the restaurant, potential lay be damned.

"I mean, uh, that sounds great. I'm not the best dancer, though," she said. The archive on base held many videos of the popular dances, but after a disastrous attempt which ended with Zera's wrist nearly broken and Kissi sporting a large bruise on her forehead, they'd decided to forgo any further dance lessons.

"That's alright, I can teach ya," Hank said. He held out a hand and gave her the brightest smile possible. There was an innocence about him that made Zera think he was just a little too young for her, but she was in

Chicago in the '80s, Katherine was nowhere in sight, and she had nothing better to do.

"Alright, but don't say I didn't warn you," she said, taking his hand.

After all the times Katherine had taken Zera's elbow, it felt weird holding onto someone else now. But Zera took it in stride, letting Hank lead her down the busy street. The guy only came up to her eyes, even with the hat, giving her enough clearance to scout the area. Time after time she made eye contact with men scanning, just like she was. She was used to watching a deadly landscape, but this was post-Vietnam, and the war that trained them was much deadlier.

"Lookin' for your friend?" Hank sounded so much like the old timey announcers, and every time he spoke Zera had to remind herself not to laugh.

"Yeah, I know it's a long shot, but..." She shrugged and tried to appear unassuming.

"Hey, if you feel lucky, you get lucky." As the words left his mouth, his smile dropped, and his eyes went wide. "Not that—I mean, I'm not saying anything of the sort about you, Miss Zera, you—you're a respectable and modest lady—"

"Holy shit, Hank, it's cool," Zera said, his chagrin making the muscles of her neck spasm. "I know what you meant."

"Oh. Okay good, thank God." A nervous laugh bubbled from his chest, and Zera very nearly patted him on his awkward head.

"Hank, you don't ask a lot of girls out, huh?"

"What? Of course I do. I mean, well, not a *lot*, I'm not that type of guy, but I get my fair share of dates. Women like me." Red colored his cheeks, and he was so tense her fingers were starting to lose feeling from his arm squeezing. A gentle wiggle reminded him of their placement, and he tried to relax.

"I'm not judging," she said. "I'm just curious." Back in the day, Zera knew what it was like to be so nervous around a pretty woman that words never quite worked right, but something about Hank's nerves was a little different. "What do you do for work?"

"Me? Oh, I'm a lawyer. Just got accepted to the bar and started at McCormick last week." He didn't bother being humble, but at least the brag came across cute.

"Look at you, big lawyer man," she said, easily the dumbest response she had.

Hank ate it up. "Thank you. That law school thing was no joke, but now I'm rolling in the dough. I mean, at least I will be, once my paycheck comes through."

"They like to take their time with those, huh?"

"Oh, this way."

Hank tugged her down an alley, and immediately her hackles raised. Inspired by Katherine, she'd strapped a knife to her thigh and had a few more weeks of combat training, but would that be enough? Hank didn't seem like the type to either start a fight or end one, but looks could be deceiving.

Her sense of alert deflated as they stopped at a green cellar door. Hank made a show of looking this way and that, ensuring the coast was clear before knocking a three-tap pattern. One half of the cellar door opened on silent hinges, the shadow preventing her from seeing the person's face.

"Password?"

Hank lowered his voice. "Easy on the breeze."

This was, without a doubt, the most ridiculous thing Zera had ever been a part of. And she was loving it.

A man opened the cellar door all the way and slid the cover off a lantern, giving them just enough light to navigate the steep, dark stairs into the ground. Hank was very kind and held her hand the whole way, but Zera was used to tougher climbs while also sporting an environment suit. Stairs were easy.

They reached another door with another password—*moon sugar* this time—and the promise of a very lively band on the other side. Music spilled into the hallway as the door cracked open, and the two doorkeepers ushered them in with almost military-like efficiency. While this was all a costume party to her, this was their lives and livelihoods, and they did everything they could to keep it afloat.

Darkness hovered over the speakeasy, the only light coming from a makeshift stage in the corner where four Black men played. A heavy set man kept a steady rhythm on the drums while a short, skinny man slapped at an upright bass twice his size. Two taller men stood toward the front of the stage, one of them crooning with a trumpet and the other crooning into a microphone. When the trumpet player finished his solo he smiled at the singer, who gave him an identical grin.

"I heard this place has the best music and drinks around," Hank said, raising his voice over the hubbub of the club. "Like it really was, back in the '20's."

"I trust your judgment." She had traveled back in time to go to a club mimicking an even earlier time. The irony was not lost on her.

After the uptight demeanor of most people during her first trips, this was a hell of a lot more fun. The dance floor ebbed and flowed like the ocean during a storm as the band kicked up the rhythm, drinks in mismatched glasses held above the crowd. Though she'd heard the term *bathtub hooch* more than once, the musky alcohol smell lingering above the body odor of the dancers was deeper and more sour than whatever mess she'd had in basic. These drinks were going to be different, and she'd love every drop.

The idea of going out and enjoying nightlife was so enthralling and strange it made laughter bubble up in her chest. The noise of the speakeasy swallowed the sound, and Hank didn't notice as he took her hand and serpentined them through the crowd. She hadn't forgotten her mission, but she thought she could get away with a little bit of fun. With three days until the storm, she had some wiggle room.

A squat man with thick brows and a heavy scowl glared from under the brim of his fedora, his hands busy wiping down the row of glasses in front of him. Hank offered a bright smile, but the barkeep remained unamused. Despite his earlier talk, it looked like Hank's first trip to this bar, showing in the nervous twitch of his hand and the line of sweat gathering at his neck. There was a first time for everything, Zera figured, but didn't quite understand why he'd be so freaked out.

"You, uh, Mack?" Hank asked.

The barkeep plucked the toothpick from his teeth—how wonderfully stereotypical—and leaned his hands on the bar. "Who's asking?"

Zera thought this made it obvious the man was, in fact, Mack, but she let the scene play out. Mack glanced over his shoulder for a split second, making no other move except a twitch of the brow. A larger man in a comically small hat stepped from the shadows and crossed his arms over his broad chest, displaying a row of stick-and-poke tattoos of questionable origin.

"I don't want no trouble." Hank held up his hands and let out a nervous laugh. "I just heard through the grapevine that at Mack's place, it didn't matter, ah, who your date was."

What the fuck?

Mack laughed at whatever face Zera was currently making and reached his hand across the bar, rattling Hank's whole body with a firm shake.

"What's your name, kid?" he asked. Voices rose from across the club, and the burly man from the shadows edged his way past Mack toward the noise. He didn't say anything, but Zera noticed the tender touch on his shoulder. She looked back at the dance floor, and while there were plenty of men and women dancing with each other, she also noticed men paired with other men, and women dancing close enough that their skirts mingled together.

"Mine? Hank, Hank Rockler," he squeaked. The noise from the corner quieted, and Zera's attention went to its absence. The big man stood between two men glaring daggers, fists clenched at their sides.

"Nice to meet you Hank," Mack said, bringing her back to the conversation at hand. "And who's your so-called date, hmm?"

"'So-called'? Have you been leading me on here?" she asked. Nerves shot cold and sharp down her spine. Was this some sort of trap?

"Zera, I think it might be the other way around," Hank replied.

"What? No. What? I don't—"

"It's okay," he said, putting his hands on her arms. "I saw you checking out those girls at the counter, I get it. I just figured, if you're new in town, you may wanna get the lay of the land before you get yourself into trouble."

"I'm not..." She stopped, because while he wasn't quite correct about the reason for her lingering looks earlier, he wasn't necessarily wrong about *her*. "Well, in the interest of transparency, I didn't discount you as an option."

"I wish I could say the same." Hank smiled his precious smile and turned back to the barkeep. "Mack, two glasses of your finest, please."

"Comin' right up."

While Mack mixed their drinks, Zera leaned against the sticky bar. "It was that easy to spot me, huh?"

"You weren't very subtle," Hank said sheepishly. "You should probably work on that. I don't know how things are in New York, but we're still working on things here. I didn't want you to get hurt, especially with all the hubbub surrounding the virus and all."

Zera realized she'd mistaken his earlier mannerisms—it wasn't asking her out that made him nervous, it was the risk of outing himself, and getting her someplace safe.

"You were trying to protect me," she said.

Hank shrugged. "Trying my best. Had a friend like you, but uh, she wasn't the best at hiding herself either, so..."

Young Hank, fresh out of law school and at his first job, had somehow managed to contract survivor's guilt without being drafted. She saw it in the dip of his shoulders and the way he gripped the edge of his coat.

"Here you go, kids," Mack said, sliding the drinks in front of them. "Have fun, be safe."

"Thank you much, Mack." Whatever dark thoughts Hank had, they were gone now. He held up his glass. "To your first night in town."

"Cheers," Zera said, and clinked her glass against his. The drink punched her tongue with flavors of lime and mint and the caustic, burning tang of alcohol. If it weren't for her days in basic, she might've dissolved into a coughing fit. Even with her tolerance, it was still a close call. "Wow. Holy shit."

"I know, right?" Apparently Hank enjoyed this acidic explosion. The second sip gave her a little more of the sugar cube dissolving in the bottom, which smoothed out the drink just enough so it didn't send a shiver down her back.

"Any of your friends here in the crowd?" she asked.

"Not yet. Unfortunately I'm chronically early." He drained his drink like someone might take it away. Zera, not wanting to be left behind, did the same. "I'll still teach you to dance in the meantime, if you want."

She eyed the crowd. Though there certainly wasn't the same sparkle and glitter the movies led her to believe, the dance floor was still a swirling vortex of skirts and limbs as people moved together. Prior to the Storm, Zera attended exactly one middle school dance, and never again until going back to 1944. Things were easier then, where the steps were less complicated and she had a different partner.

Fuck it. "Sure, I'll give it a go." She handed her empty glass to Mack. He tipped his head in her direction, his face back to the stoic, blank slate all barkeeps wore. The band changed to a new song with just the upright bass and drums, the twins hanging their feet off the edge of the stage and tapping their heels against it. It must have been a popular song, because the crowd cheered as the beat started.

"Perfect, follow my lead," Hank said. They stayed at the edge of the dance floor where there was more space, and he took both her hands. However athletic Zera thought she was, he quickly proved her wrong. Mirroring his actions by stepping back and forth was easy enough, but once he tried to add a couple hops and a spin, she lost it.

"Shit, sorry," she said as her foot landed hard on Hank's toes. To his credit, he didn't grimace.

"That's the whole point of learning!" He walked her through the steps again, this time at half pace, allowing her to lumber through the moves without accosting his bones. It was laughable how uncoordinated she felt, while Hank breezed through with grace.

"I don't know if I'm any good at this." The words were aimed at her feet instead of him, since she was watching them intently to prevent any further accidents.

The song changed to something a little slower, and the singer and trumpet player stood to rejoin the band. A tug on her hands brought her attention back up, and Hank pulled her into a comfortable embrace. It wasn't strict and formal like the dance with Katherine at the college, but instead familiar and affectionate. Even if she knew how this night with Hank would—or wouldn't, as it were—end, it still felt nice to be held.

"You're very uptight. You need to loosen up," he said. Zera automatically tried to hold onto his waist, like Katherine taught her, and he raised his eyebrows as he relocated her hand to his shoulder. "It's a miracle no one spotted you before I did."

"I just got into town a few hours ago, to be fair," she replied. "And I'm not uptight, just nervous."

"Either way, relax." He showed her different steps now, and she looked down to try and follow. With his knuckle under her chin, he raised her face back up. "Don't worry about where your feet are. And stop trying to lead, you don't know where we're going."

Instead of monitoring every step, she tried to focus on the feel of Hank's hand on her back and the push and pull of his grip. If she stopped micromanaging her body and went along with his cues, dancing became a hell of a lot easier.

"There you go, now you're getting it." He was cute when he smiled, and Zera realized her luck of finding Katherine had perhaps just shifted to finding someone else helpful.

"You could be quite the ladies' man, Hank," she teased.

"Don't worry, Zera, I do just fine." Very gently, he released her and raised their hands up. She didn't fight it, and let him spin her one, two, three times before bringing her back to his chest. He opened his mouth to say something, but instead his gaze shifted over her shoulder and his head cocked to the side. Zera felt a hand that wasn't Hank's on her back, and the touch made her jump.

The first thing she noticed was the woman's dress, all silks and lace and a neckline low enough to remind Zera she was well past the puritanical stage now. Her hair was shorter, and her makeup darker, but there was no mistaking Katherine.

"Well, aren't you a sight for sore eyes?" she asked with a smile that made Zera's heart stutter.

Perhaps Zera's luck hadn't run out after all.

1980

"Is this the first time?"

At first, Zera assumed Katherine had a change of heart about living, that she'd accepted her fate and planned to make the best of it. There was no sign of the harsh, world-weary person she left back in 1968. This Katherine was all smiles.

This Katherine was also very drunk.

"No, not the first time," Zera said.

"Oh. Who's your friend?" Katherine gestured to Hank.

"What are you doing here?" Zera asked, remembering what kind of speakeasy Hank brought her to.

"Hank, Hank Rockler," he said, ignoring her question and taking Katherine's hand.

Zera snapped out of her reverie. "Oh, right, sorry, Hank this is—"

"Kathy," Katherine interrupted, allowing him to kiss her knuckles. "Nice to meet you."

"Pleasure's all mine, Kathy." He turned to Zera. "Is this the friend you were looking for?"

"I...yes?" Zera wasn't sure if she questioned it because of her surprise, or where they were, or because she wasn't certain Katherine would call her a friend. She hoped the heat of the club would cover up the warmth in her cheeks.

"Excellent! Now we won't have to search the city," he said. "Should we get a table? You're more than welcome to join us."

"Wait, you really have friends coming?" Zera thought the friends were a ruse, and was pleasantly surprised to find they existed.

"Of course. I may be a lot of things, but a liar isn't one of 'em," Hank said.

"I'm afraid we're having a girls' night out, Hank, but I appreciate you bringing my friend to me," Katherine said, reaching out to squeeze his hand again.

"Of course, I hope to see you ladies around town sometime." With one last wink, Hank departed for the tables in the corner, leaving Zera in Katherine's clutches. She turned to find her smiling in a way only alcohol allowed.

"You wanna go outside for a second?" Katherine asked.

From anyone else, Zera would assume it was an invitation with a few unspoken offers tacked on, but from Katherine...she wasn't sure.

"Yeah, let's go," she said. Katherine took her elbow, just like old times, and led her back through the cellar door. Outside, the city sparkled and sang, every bit what Zera expected when she first arrived.

"Not gonna lie," Zera said, ignoring how Katherine was hanging on her arm. "You're the last person I expected to see here."

Katherine shrugged. "A few girls from the clinic wanted to show some support. I came along for the ride."

"Kat—"

"Kathy," she corrected.

"Absolutely not." The name felt wrong. "You do realize, uh, the demographic of people here, right?"

"Of course I do." Her eyes wandered over the crowd of dancers, then she dragged her attention back to Zera. "I've been around for a while. Met a lot of people."

"Before you didn't seem so...open to the idea."

"That conversation was twenty-four years ago, Miss Zazzera." The name sent a thrill through Zera's abdomen. "There's a lot to learn in twenty-four years."

She'd been keeping track. Zera tried not to think of the thousand implications of her words, and instead focused on her. The gin from earlier snuck up on her, melting the ice in her core.

"Well, I'm glad to see you." Before she could second guess it, she pulled Katherine into a hug. Her slender arms snaked around Zera's waist and squeezed, telling of the strength she'd rebuilt since their last meeting. Katherine's breathing was oddly slow and controlled, and when she pulled away, she delicately dabbed at the corners of her eyes.

"Sure took you long enough," she said, the alcohol loosening her tongue. Gone was the prim and proper lady with a stick up her ass. "I was beginning to think you forgot all about me."

"How in every hell could I forget about you?" Zera remembered how chatty she got when drinking. Too late now. "You're literally the most interesting person I've ever met."

"You're just saying that because I'm a centenarian."

"That's like, the least impressive thing about you." Whatever was in that drink, Zera never wanted to have it again. Her tolerance was too low, and the gin way too strong.

"Oh? What could possibly be more impressive?" Katherine's eyes were wide and unguarded, the lights of the street glittering in their glassy surface. Despite her age, she looked so very young.

"You dropped the word *centenarian* without fucking up, for one. Two, you have insane knife skills." Zera counted the facts on her fingertips, concentrating on hitting them. Katherine didn't even flinch at her swearing this time. "Also, the way you make coffee is impressively terrible. Have you gotten any better at that, by the way?"

Katherine giggled and shook her head. "Not even a bit. In fact, I might be worse."

"Oh, gods, you really are trying to kill me. My fucking liver enzymes were up, you know." It was supposed to be a joke, but it fell flat on the pavement between them. Tears welled in Katherine's eyes, and her lower lip, painted pink, quivered.

"I'm sorry," she said. One tear escaped and ran a line through the powder on her face. Panicked, Zera reached up and swiped it away with her thumb. An odd ache appeared between her chest and her stomach.

"No, no, no, it's fine, I'm fine," she stammered. When Katherine had cried in the Academy, it was because she thought all was lost. Now she was crying because of Zera's health?

Shit. She was an *emotional* drunk.

"You promise?" Katherine sniffled, and because crying women were Zera's true Achilles heel, she held Katherine's cheeks in her hands and looked right into her eyes.

"I promise, I'm fine, you're fine, everyone's fine," she said. The gin made her vision swim a little as she tried to focus on those honey-gold eyes. "I'm here. I'm back."

"You're back," Katherine echoed. She put her hands over Zera's, leaning into her. "I've been waiting a long time to see you again."

"Think you'll let me hang out for a couple days?"

"Only if you mind your manners, Miss Zazzera."

"What did I say about calling me that?"

"I like your full name. Besides, I'm kind of used to calling you that now." Katherine grinned. "Everyone else calls you Zera, and I like to feel special."

"Duly noted." Zera was glad she hadn't changed her mind. "I have to admit, I'm surprised to see you here tonight."

Katherine shrugged. "Like I said, some of the girls wanted to come for support."

"So the other girls made the choice?" It was supposed to be an innocent question, but Zera was never one for subtlety, and Katherine easily spotted the barb on the end.

"Ask me what you really want to," she said, suddenly sober. Her expression was so fierce Zera nearly cowered. Nearly.

"Hank told me that Mack's is for people who..." She considered her words, then lowered her voice, mindful of their surroundings. "For people who have different romantic interests than what society deems normal, or—"

"Just spit it out, Miss Zazzera."

"It's a speakeasy for gay people," Zera snapped. "Or bisexuals like me. Or queer people. A place where we can feel safe. And after your reaction back in 1968, I'm wondering if your ideas have changed."

"You're wondering if *I've* changed," she said, once again proving her superior social aptitude, even when drunk. "I'm sure the fate of my most recent late husband doesn't help clear the muddy waters."

"Now who's talking around the point?" Zera said. "I've been honest with you this whole time, and I'd appreciate it if you were honest with me."

"To what end?" Tears glistened in Katherine's eyes again, her voice as flat as the floor underneath them. It was an attempt to remove herself from the line of questioning, to distract and deflect until the interrogator lost interest. That was a game Zera had played for a long time until she found a place where she was comfortable with herself.

Honesty would be the best policy. "So I don't take any unnecessary risks."

There. She said it.

At least part of it.

Katherine inhaled sharply, and her eyes widened by a fraction. Even now, she managed to stay in control of her features, keep her guard up, whereas Zera felt like she'd just stripped down and bared her soul to her. Silence pressed into every cell, so heavy she wondered if the river was pulling her back to the future.

"I'll admit," Katherine said, regaining the uptight posture familiar to Zera, "that while I have considered actions of the sort, I have not acted on said considerations, and have little to no intentions to."

"Here's the deal," Zera said. She could feel the grin on her face, no matter how she tried to stop it. Katherine's old accent snuck through her words, which had to mean something. "The girls down the hall may know this shiny eighties version of you, but I know the past versions, and now I can actually tell when you're lying."

"I'm not lying."

"You're sure not telling the truth."

"We are *not* having this conversation." Katherine actually stomped her foot. She likely intended to look like the matriarch of an estate, but Zera thought she looked like a petulant child.

Zera held up her hands. "That's okay. You don't wanna label yourself, especially in these times. Everything's fluid. I get it. I'm not gonna pressure you to say anything." She wanted to—hot damn did she want to—but nothing good would come of it. "I'll just keep my distance."

A muscle in Katherine's jaw twitched, but her shoulders relaxed a few millimeters. When she uncrossed her arms, she flexed her fingers, and it occurred to Zera that she shouldn't antagonize a woman who'd openly admitted to murdering those who had wronged her.

"Hopefully not too far," Katherine said. She reached out and took Zera's hand. "I do miss you when you're gone, Miss Zazzera. I miss you very much."

The alcohol in Zera's system smoothed out her nerves and let forgiveness flow. Of course Katherine wouldn't want to have this conversation, and it was cruel of her to be so stubborn. Their time was short—they needed to enjoy it.

"I miss you too, Kat. Now come on, show me how to party like it's 1999."

"It's 1980, Miss Zazzera."

"I swear, sometimes you willfully ignore my jokes."

"I don't ignore them, they're just not funny." Katherine considered her own joke very funny, and giggled as she dragged Zera back into the bustle of the speakeasy.

"Password?" The doorman asked again.

"Randolph you know it's me, I just treated you yesterday," Katherine said, crossing her arms.

"Yes, Dr. Kathy, sorry," he said, opening the door all the way. Katherine navigated the steps easily despite her state of inebriation, and despite a little wobbling, Zera followed without incident. As they entered the second door, Katherine took her hand, her grip warm and strong. Before, she always held Zera's elbow like a threat, but there was something more tender about this.

"Do you know everyone here or just the guys in front?" The band was back in full swing, and Zera had to yell to be heard.

Katherine shrugged, the muscles of her neck and back moving beneath the silk of her dress. "I work at a very specialized clinic. Tell me, in the future, have they eradicated HIV?"

Zera swallowed. She wasn't well versed on the topic, and now she felt ashamed of her ignorance. "No, not completely. But there's been advances, I know that."

She thought Katherine might cry again, so Zera shook her arm and said, "Your friends?"

A gaggle of girls sat in the corner, their seats all shared and their limbs spilling over one another. Here, in the safety of the speakeasy, they didn't have to worry about someone complaining of their affections, and Zera felt a warmth in her chest that had nothing to do with the alcohol. Not all of them held romantic relationships with each other, she could tell that, but there was something nice about seeing a group of friends together. She had it with Kissi and Lieb back when they were a team, but after the Academy most of her companions disappeared into the ranks.

"Ladies, ladies!" Katherine let go of Zera to clap her hands, the sound only audible because it was offbeat to the song playing. With a pop of her hip and a magician's gesture, she showed off Zera. "This is my dear friend Miss Zazzera, here to join our shenanigans."

"You can call me Zera," she said, sending Katherine a friendly glare.

Katherine leaned over and tapped her on the nose. "I told you once I'm never calling you that, and I stand by it. Now, we need more drinks!"

As more terrible gin concoctions appeared at the table, the night bled and blurred into a sparkling, hazy mess. *Lightweight* was a kind descriptor for Zera, but after years in the Academy she was proud of her ability to find her limit. Normally she stopped well before, and would have that night, if Katherine hadn't handed her another glass and twisted their arms together so they had to move just right to drink.

The women introduced themselves one by one, but their names flew away as soon as they left their mouths. Zera decided to worry about it in the morning, when her mind was sharper. She took turns dancing with Katherine and her friends, allowing them one last attempt at teaching her the complicated steps. When she ended up with remnants of the sticky floor covering her knees and half her forearm, she threw in the towel and returned to the table.

This was not her mission. This was so far away from her mission she might as well request discharge papers when she returned. She sat with her elbow on the table and her head on her hand, watching the shimmers and sparkles of the people dancing and the way sweat dripped on the stage as the performers worked. Back in her time, they were all dead.

This time, the realization didn't hit her like a train. It was expected. Many of them would pass during the epidemic, or in the coming years. There were so many things over the next decades that might take them out.

All of them except Katherine.

The woman of the hour sank into the chair next to Zera and sat another empty glass on the table. Zera lost count of how many glasses Katherine drained, but she seemed to be managing fine.

"Having fun?" Katherine asked.

"I didn't think you knew what fun was," Zera replied, making her smile.

"Turns out, you *can* teach an old dog new tricks." Katherine narrowed her eyes. "But you didn't answer my question."

"I am having fun. So much that I forgot I'm supposed to be working."

Katherine sat up. "Another storm? Tonight? I don't feel it coming."

Zera shook her head, and it took a few seconds for the room to go still again. "No, tomorrow. Kissi gave us extra time."

"She did? How exciting. Now we can be prepared, and we don't have to rush!"

Zera hoped and prayed Katherine would keep her focused on the mission, no matter how pretty she was.

"Come on," Katherine said, standing and dragging Zera to her feet. "It's time to go home."

It was only then Zera noticed the band had stopped playing. The patrons present enough to be aware wandered the tables and collected used glasses, placing them on the bartop with the concentrated care of the drunk. She went to follow suit, but after gathering a few of the delicate glasses, she decided the risk of dropping them was not worth the reward of helping Mack. It was his fault, really, after serving the terribly strong drinks.

The night air didn't sober her up any, but it did make it easier to breathe, and walking with the other women was a nice barrier of protection between her and the unknown. There was no use trying to memorize the route to Katherine's apartment, even if her training dictated the importance of it. She simply let the group carry her away, Katherine's hand still clutching her own.

This building was definitely sturdier than Katherine's Philadelphia apartment; the stairs didn't even creak as they climbed to the top floor. Katherine dug a brass key from her purse, and Zera leaned her head against the doorframe as she wrestled with the lock. It finally clicked and the door swung open with a hearty squeak.

Whereas the previous house was decorated like a sixties fever dream, every corner here had something soft or beautiful, from the gauzy curtains to the mountain of pastel pillows on the couch. Everything had its place—Katherine hadn't lost the intense organization, it seemed—but for the first time, Zera walked into her residence and felt like Katherine actually lived there.

"Wow, I love what you've done with the place," she said, wincing as the words sounded sarcastic even to her own ears.

Pink colored Katherine's cheeks, and she pouted her rosebud lips.

"No need to poke fun at me," she said.

"I wasn't," Zera promised. "I really do like it. It's cozy."

"That's what I was going for." Katherine crossed the room and fell onto the couch, the crash landing sending pillows flying in every direction.

"What does your current husband think of it?" There were no signs of a man living there, but the question was more of a test than anything. Katherine kicked her feet in the air and stretched her arms overhead.

"I don't have one!"

"What?"

Zera would never count herself as a historian, but until relatively recently it seemed ill advised for a woman to live on her own.

"After our last meeting, I swore off men for a while." She sat up, her headband slipping and falling to the floor with the rough movements. "I'm a doctor now. Can you believe it?"

The hem of Katherine's dress rose, exposing her long legs, and Zera tried to look anywhere but at her. The room felt warm, so she crossed to the window and shoved it open, sticking her head out into the cool night air.

"Are you sick?" Katherine appeared next to her, resting a hand on her back.

"I'm fine, just got kinda hot." She put her head in her hands. "Those drinks are almost as strong as your coffee."

"Almost only counts in horseshoes and hand grenades."

"I don't think that's how the saying goes."

Drinking had been a mistake. It wasn't to blackout level, but she was definitely at a point that usually led to wrong decisions. Zera took one deep breath, and then another. She had to focus. If she didn't do her job, the program would get canceled. And if they canceled the program, she would never see Katherine again, not her honey brown eyes or her sharp jaw or those perfect lips—

Stop it. Focus.

Step one, sleep off this drink. Step two, get back on track with the mission. The mission the military assigned to her. The important mission given for the sake of humanity. *That* mission.

A quiet part of her reminded her that if she was lucky, she could also complete her mission to save Katherine too.

"What?" Katherine asked.

"Nothing," Zera said around the lump in her throat. Katherine was looking at her the same way she had in Central Park, and thanks to the alcohol Zera could now see the layer of affection there.

"Doesn't look like nothing," Katherine said. Her smile dropped slowly as she searched Zera's face.

Zera pushed away from the window and away from Katherine. If she put some space between them, maybe she could build a strong enough barrier to hide all her dismal thoughts. "It's just been a long few hours. The trips aren't exactly getting easier." It wasn't a complete lie. "And I wasn't expecting to show up in 1980 and get sloshed at an underground gay bar."

"Shh!" Katherine hissed, slamming the window shut.

"What? I thought you were fine with all that?" Zera asked, suddenly nervous. Was it all a ruse? Or had she looked too far into things again?

"I am, but not everyone is," Katherine said with a wide gesture toward the city. Her old accent was back. "A person's orientation is of no concern to me, but we can't jeopardize our safety for the sake of it."

"There she is." Zera laughed, now glad the drinks had let her fear drop. "I wondered where Miss Princess went."

Katherine's jaw dropped. "I am not *Miss Princess*."

"You totally are, but I wouldn't have it any other way."

Katherine crossed her arms. "I've half a mind to kick you out."

"Please don't, I don't want to sleep on a bench again." Zera thought they were still playing, but there was a slight needle of fear in the back of her mind. "It was so uncomfortable. And cold. You know I hate the cold."

Katherine tapped her cheek for a moment, making a big show of thinking. Finally, she heaved a dramatic sigh. "Very well, I suppose you can stay here." She glanced down at her watch, and her slender eyebrows rose. "We should probably go to bed. It's pretty late."

"Work in the morning?" Zera asked.

"Unfortunately. But no mind, we're young and able to recover. Come along, I'll let you borrow my toiletries and a towel. And pajamas."

It was then Zera realized how gross and sweaty she felt. A shower sounded amazing. Katherine went first, coming out in a loose silk robe with her hair wrapped in a towel. Remembering how Hank said how obvious she was, Zera kept her eyes on the floor and took her turn.

Top floor plumbing limited the shower's strength, but in the luke-warm dribble she scrubbed away the sweat and grime from the speakeasy, and some of the inebriation as well. She only thought about Katherine in the next room three times, max. The rest of the time she spent soaking in the water, even when it ran cold. Who knew a real shower could be such a treat?

Luckily Katherine favored pajamas a few sizes too big, otherwise Zera would have nothing to sleep in. The fabric—she didn't know if it was silk or something else—was softer than anything she'd worn in the past two decades. It spoke of luxury, which was wild to Zera.

When she returned to the living room, Katherine stood at the stove with an apron over her pajamas and a pie dish in front of her. With narrowed eyes and extreme care, she sliced into the pie, but instead of fruit or cream, meat and cheese filled it.

"What is this?" Zera asked as Katherine set a slice in front of her.

"Impossible cheeseburger pie. Genius, really."

Zera asked no more questions, instead digging in with gusto. A cheese-burger? Forget the satin and silk—*this* was true luxury. The salty meat and gooey cheese were so savory and delicious she wanted to cry. Not to mention the crust, which was some buttery biscuit situation. It was abso-lute heaven, and when she finished her piece, Katherine smiled and slid the pie dish over, allowing Zera to finish the rest.

"How many days until the next storm?" she asked once Zera had eaten her fill.

"The storm's on the twenty-eighth."

"Ah, so we have one more day of fun until we have to work."

"*You* have work in the morning. I get to lounge around all day and wait for you to get home."

"Right. And when is our first meeting?" Katherine asked. Lie after lie popped up in Zera's mind, each less plausible than the last.

"I can't tell you." It wasn't the truth or a lie. It was an escape route. "Mess up continuity, and all that."

"Ah, good point. I guess we haven't fixed things, hmm?" Her voice was soft and warm, and something about her posture looked weird. It took a second for Zera to realize she was relaxed.

"Not yet. And, um," she paused, floundering for the words. "I haven't found a way to help you yet. I'm sorry."

Katherine went from relaxed to deflated. "That's alright, I understand. It's not an easy thing I'm asking for."

"Still, I'm trying." She fumbled through her bag then, retrieving the butterfly syringe and the test tubes. "Before I forget, I need your blood."

"Oh, yeah. We forgot that last time. For what?"

"I wish I knew."

"Mission secrecy and plausible deniability?"

"Honestly, I'm not a scientist. I literally have no clue how Kissi's gonna use it."

Katherine let out a ladylike snort which quickly dissolved into giggles. A moment later, the giggles evolved into a full on belly laugh. She was so beautiful, and it made Zera mad. Why did she have to die? Why did everyone have to die?

"Very well then," Katherine said, taking the pie knife and holding the blade to her forearm. "How much do you need?"

"What? Holy fucking—no, I'm gonna use a needle, Jesus." Nausea hit, and she held onto a nearby chair while her brain recentered.

Katherine laughed again and returned the knife to its block. "It was a joke, Miss Zazzera." She crossed the room and took the bag from Zera, analyzing its contents. "This looks easier to use than what I have. Can I keep the extras?"

"Gods, does your immortality make you sober up quick too?" Now that she was close, Zera could see more of her silvery scars, different ones from their last meeting.

"I wish," Katherine said, examining the equipment. "But no—curiosity steadies my hands. Shall we give this a try?"

"What did I say about saying 'shall'?"

"I can't recall, I'm forgetful in my old age."

Zera let out a long breath and pinched the bridge of her nose. With her eyes closed, the room swayed underneath her feet. Drawing blood right now would be a terrible idea.

"We'll do it tomorrow." The longer she could avoid looking at that needle, the better. "Once we sober up a bit."

"Very well, tomorrow it is. Come, it's time for bed." Katherine turned on her heel and marched toward the door.

"I don't know if I have enough pillows." Zera admired the couch, wondering if she could fit.

"Miss Zazzera, I believe at this point we can share a bed. After all, you are technically my oldest friend." She leaned against the doorway to her room, wholly unbothered.

"You sure?" Why was she asking?

"You'll sleep better than on the couch. It's late, let's go."

Katherine didn't wait, instead crawling into the perfectly made bed and settling on one side. Zera stood at the door, trying to decide whether to follow her instructions or ignore them. But the bed looked nice, and she was tired.

Against her better judgment, she slipped into the other side, and rolled over to find Katherine facing her. The moonlight fell just right from the window, illuminating the edge of her cheekbones and the curve of her neck. Katherine scooted a little closer, until their knees were touching beneath the sheets and only a few inches separated their faces. She kept opening her mouth and closing it again, as if considering what she wanted to say. In the end, she said nothing, only reached out a hand to touch Zera's cheek.

Zera knew Katherine was about to kiss her. She could've stopped it. Instead, she froze and watched the decision arrive in her eyes. She stayed steady as Katherine shifted closer, just a bit.

The first kiss was soft, hesitant, timid. Emboldened by the contact, Katherine dove in, her kiss hot and fast and full of teeth. Trembling hands wandered over the angles of Zera's hips and ribs and into her hair. Zera gripped her waist and tried to keep up, which Katherine took as an invitation to move closer, rolling them so they rested chest to chest. It was fast, it was all too fast—

"Wait," Zera gasped, pulling away. She rested her forehead against Katherine's, both of them breathing too hard.

"You don't want to?" She looked vulnerable, she looked *hurt*, and Zera very nearly gave in to what her body wanted.

"Not like this," she whispered. "I want you, but not like this."

She didn't want to be a one night stand, or an experiment, or whatever else this might entail. Katherine was drunk and lonely and in pain, and sex was not going to fix that. She might have more life experience than Zera, but Zera knew the last part for a fact.

Katherine's eyes darted to her lips, as if she was contemplating an attempt to change her mind. If Zera was honest, one more kiss might undo her resolve completely. But Katherine moved off her, her eyes on the sheets.

"Very well. I'm sorry." Her words were cold and distant as she moved to the very edge of the bed, facing away. "Goodnight, Miss Zazzera."

Apologies wouldn't help, and neither would explanations, though Zera wanted to give her both. Instead she returned the sentiment, rolled over, and fell into a fitful sleep.

1980

Zera woke early the next morning to the sounds of Katherine trying her damnedest to sneak out.

It was clear this wasn't her first quick morning escape, but Zera chose not to comment on it. Instead, she sat up, the bed creaking loudly and making Katherine jump from where she was stuffing makeup into her purse and whirl around.

"Morning." Zera folded her legs. It was obvious Katherine hadn't anticipated getting caught, and it took a few seconds for her to reply.

"Good morning, Miss Zazzera," she said after clearing her throat. "I trust you slept well?"

She was back to her earlier accent, a surefire sign she was nervous. She probably avoided conflicts like this entirely with the certain set of skills she developed over the decades. Impressive, really.

"Slept okay," Zera said. "You?"

Katherine blinked, as if considering lying. "Not my finest night, but that happens from time to time."

Her makeup brushes clicked as she set them down on her vanity, and she moved the stool so she could sit in front of the mirror.

"Well," Zera said, trying to fill the silence, "at least the hangover is minimal." Her head only felt half full of cotton, which was impressive after the number of drinks the night before.

"That's good." Katherine kept her eyes on the mirror as she brushed on the powder with long, even strokes. Zera had expected awkwardness after the night before, but she certainly didn't anticipate the silent treatment. It was like their first meetings all over again, and it stung.

"Do you have work all day?" She may not have always known the right thing to say, but damn if she couldn't keep a conversation going long past its expiration.

The brush stopped, and Katherine placed it on the counter and looked at her through the mirror. "You don't have to do this, Miss Zazzera." Her voice sounded so damn formal it made Zera want to scream.

"Do what?" Playing dumb sometimes worked.

"I understand the position I put you in last night was inappropriate and rude." There was something around the edge of Katherine's tone now, but Zera couldn't tell if it was anger, embarrassment, or impatience. "I don't want you to feel you need to mollify me. I'm a grown woman, I can tend to my own wounds."

"But you don't have to," Zera said. "Look, Kat, we're still friends. I just didn't—"

"No need to explain. I understand." She started her makeup again, this time with broad, fast movements.

"I don't think you do. It's not that you—"

"Miss Zazzera, I can—"

"Stop interrupting me."

Katherine's movements didn't stop; in fact, she hurried the brushes until her mask was finished. "I have to go." She stood and made for the door with silent, pantyhose-covered steps.

"Wait, no." Zera scrambled out of bed, nearly tripping over the blankets. "Can't you be a little late?"

"I have patients waiting." Katherine didn't look at her, just walked to the door and slipped on her shoes. "I'll see you this evening."

"Kat—"

But she was gone.

The slam of the door lit a brief spark of anger in Zera's chest. For calling herself a grown woman, Katherine ran away from that conversation like an embarrassed teenager. And now Zera would have to wait the entire day to try again.

It wouldn't be a hard talk, it just needed to happen. Zera occupied her hours by snooping around the apartment, reading a book of poetry by Lisa Ben, and analyzing the instructions on the butterfly needle and test tubes. If Katherine let her get close enough to take her blood, she needed to be prepared, so hopefully she wouldn't pass out while performing the operation.

The pull settled in her stomach late in the afternoon, mixing well with her anxiety-induced nausea as she thought over and over what she could say to Katherine. A half hour before seven, she took the spare key she found in the back of a drawer and locked the apartment.

The clinic wasn't far away, but she was in an unfamiliar area *and* time, and she needed room for error. Women walked alone now, their heads high, a vision compared to the demure damsels from earlier decades. It was one thing to see the transitions in history books, another to see it in real life.

The clinic was small, tucked between an abandoned restaurant and a used book store. Professionals slipped out the front and dispersed quickly, walking away in pairs or threes. All except Katherine, who stayed behind to lock the door. She watched the others go, her lips parted and her shoulders tense until she spotted Zera.

Mask back on. "I was just coming to get you."

"Yeah, I decided to come to you first." Zera held out the spare key, and Katherine took it, her teeth grinding.

"You looked through my things."

"I was locked in your apartment all day. What did you expect?"

"That you wouldn't go through my things."

"Bold move, princess."

Katherine didn't smile, she just walked away. "Let's get this done."

"Stop trying to lead, you don't know where we're going."

Katherine stopped so quickly Zera nearly ran into her. "Where are we going, then?"

"Why are you being like this?"

"I'm simply trying to complete your mission for you, Miss Zazzera."

"You're simply being an asshole." Zera crossed her arms. "You're the one who kissed me, why are you acting like it's my fault?"

"Hush!" Katherine's cheeks turned red, even with her makeup, and she glanced around at the people on the street. No one paid them any mind. "Not here."

"I'm not moving until you chill out."

"I've never been *chill* a day in my life."

"Bullshit, I've seen the Woodstock picture."

"You've seen—" Katherine's jaw dropped, and her blush spread all the way to her neck and the tips of her ears.

"It's a cute picture."

"Miss Zazzera—"

"Loved the peace fingers."

"They're called peace *signs*. That was a different time."

Zera couldn't help it. She laughed. "You would be the resident expert."

Katherine maintained her chagrin for a few moments, but Zera could see the corners of her mouth quivering, her chest hiccuping with contained laughter. Threads of tension still stretched between them, but at least half of them snapped as she released her shoulders.

"You are—"

"Incorrigible. I know."

"Let's go, Miss Zazzera, before I get really pissed."

"Which way to that big fountain?"

"Buckingham? This way."

On the maps, it looked close, but between street traffic and pedestrians it took nearly half an hour to reach their destination. Blues and greens swirled in the sky as the aurora set in, and the people stopping to stare slowed them down further.

There were surprisingly few people at the fountain, and while Katherine paused to look at the sky, Zera went up to it and stuck her hand in, letting the cold water slap into her forearm.

"Stop it, Miss Zazzera, that water's disgusting."

Zera didn't stop. Big drops hit her hard enough for pain to tingle in her skin, but she kept her hand there anyway, soaking in this completely extravagant use of the stuff. Oh, to live in a world without water rationing.

"Miss Zazzera, aren't you supposed to be doing something?"

"Oh right, I almost forgot." Again. Zera removed her hand from the water and grabbed her scanner. Once it was on, the numbers climbed rapidly, the machine humming as it gathered and stored data. She returned it to her pocket and exchanged it for the needle and tube. "Okay, let's give this a shot."

Katherine turned her attention back. The sight of that infuriating blank face back in place made frustration curl in Zera's abdomen again, but she swallowed it down.

"I didn't think you'd still want to help me," Katherine murmured, interlacing her fingers in front of her.

"What? Why not?" The confession threw Zera, making it more difficult to handle the needle.

"After last night. After I...accosted you."

Zera lifted her brows. This was the most open and honest she'd seen Katherine. Sober, at least.

"No one accosted anyone last night," Zera said.

"But I...I didn't tell you the whole truth."

Zera thought about the truth she hid too. "We all have to protect ourselves sometimes. Now, roll up your sleeve."

Katherine followed her instructions, the pale skin of her forearm shining in the light of the storm. A long scar cut across the meat of her elbow, fading from pink to silver.

"What happened here?" Zera touched the scar with her thumb as she cradled Katherine's forearm. Her grip was likely too tight, but any looser and Katherine would feel her hand shaking.

"That's from Robert," she said lightly.

Zera froze with the alcohol swab over her elbow. "I'm sorry," she said, sanitizing the skin and avoiding her eyes.

"It's alright, his wounds were significantly worse."

"Still, I'm sorry."

"He had it coming."

Zera felt the corner of her mouth tremble as a song from a musical played in her head.

"Right, okay." Zera psyched herself up. The instructions were simple: apply the tourniquet, find a vein, slide the needle in at a slight angle. Hold the butterfly down against the arm while attaching the tube. Simple.

The tourniquet was easy enough, but as Zera stared at the mile long needle, bile rose in the back of her throat and her fingers tingled. The needle shook, even as she willed it not to, and she very nearly dropped it.

"Miss Zazzera?" Katherine asked. She sounded far away. Zera took a deep breath, and another, but it didn't impart any sense of calm.

"Sorry, I..." She covered the needle again and loosened the rubber band around Katherine's arm. "Gimme a second. I thought my issue was just when the needle was going into me."

"I can do it." Katherine held out her hand as Zera sat on the edge of the fountain, the cool water splashing onto her back.

"No, no I got it. I just need to breathe." The world was starting to buzz at the edges of her vision, and she gulped. It was fine—it was just a stupid blood draw, and it wasn't even on her. She needed to get it together.

"Give me the instructions." Katherine left no room for argument this time, snatching the papers from Zera's weak grip. As she read, she rested her other hand on Zera's back, the touch comforting and steady.

"I've never done it before. Kissi had me practice on a simulation before I left, but I guess it isn't the same as the real thing."

"A simulation?" Katherine asked, her eyes alight with a spark of curiosity. "Like practice models?"

"Yeah, but like a computer." It was a tedious conversation, but it was helping distract Zera from her fear.

Katherine furrowed her brows. "Computers? Wonderful. They must be massive to do that."

"Actually, they can fit in your pocket."

Katherine's jaw dropped. "What? Really?" Then she remembered she was supposed to be on ice. "I mean, sounds interesting. Hope I never see them." She returned to the instructions.

Zera wanted to call bullshit again, but held her tongue. "Okay," she said after a minute. "Let's try again."

"Very well." Katherine kept the instructions and held her arm out. They repeated the process from earlier, but once Zera had the needle in her hand, the wooziness returned, this time accompanied by a cold sweat.

"Hold on—"

"For heaven's sake."

With outrageous confidence, Katherine plucked the needle from Zera's shaking fingers and slid it into the swollen vein at her elbow. Zera nearly vomited at the sight and barely had the presence of mind to hand over the tubes when Katherine beckoned for them. Thank gods Katherine had it under control, because Zera needed to lie down for a moment and stare at the stars.

"I don't understand how you got those tattoos when you can't even look at a needle," Katherine said, unclicking one tube and snapping another into place.

"You can't see the needles on tattoo machines. At least I can't." Not to mention the reward of beautiful art versus the pain deep in her bones from shots. Tattoos never made it impossible to raise her arm for twenty-four hours.

"Well, here you go," Katherine said, followed by a click from the tube and another from the needle retracting. In the moonlight, her purple blood sparkled with reflections from the aurora. "That wasn't so bad."

"You must be a badass doctor."

"Helps that I can't get sick," she said, depositing the test tubes in their protective case and laying it on Zera's stomach. "But I believe my bedside manner leaves something to be desired."

"Doubtful."

Katherine let out a breath that could've been a laugh or a sound of frustration. Zera chose to be positive, staring at the colors of the sky as she recovered. A few minutes later, Katherine gave up and lay down beside her.

Zera broke the silence. "So, do you want to talk about last night?"

She felt Katherine flinch beside her. "I don't believe there's anything more to talk about."

"Look, Kat…" Zera sighed, the truth on the tip of her tongue. She could part with a piece of it. "It might be a really, really long time before I can see you again. I don't wanna leave things between us like this."

"Everything between us is fine."

"Wouldn't 'stellar' be a better word to use there?"

"Stellar, no. Legit, maybe."

"You're not helping your case here."

"Then what do you want me to say?" Katherine sat up and stared down at her, looking her full in the face for the first time that evening.

Zera sat up with her, ignoring the swimming in her vision as she did so. "Earlier, you said you lied. What did you lie about?"

This time, the sigh was definitely from frustration. "It doesn't matter."

"It does."

"Like you said, it will be a long time before we meet again," Katherine shrugged. "Perhaps, by then, I'll have an answer for you."

"Answer the damn question."

"I don't know," Katherine snapped. "I'm already an abomination, Miss Zazzera. I've committed atrocities I never thought possible. So excuse me if I don't want to consider something else I was told for over a century is wrong."

"It's not wrong." Even if things had changed and Katherine was no longer attracted to her, she needed to at least know that. "It's not. You're not an *abomination*, Katherine. You're human."

"Am I? I don't know anymore."

Zera opened her mouth, closed it, then opened it again. "You are. I know you are."

"Perhaps whatever tests you do on my blood can give us the final answer."

She was skirting the questions. It was infuriating, and Zera got tired of it.

"Why did you kiss me, Katherine?"

Katherine's gaze grew sharp. "I thought we covered this."

"No, we didn't." Zera knew she should back down, but it was too late now. "You could've kissed any of those girls you knew. Why did you kiss *me*?"

Katherine kept her eyes on the sky, watching the waves of the aurora bend and sway. It was hard for Zera to stay quiet and let her think, but if Katherine wanted Zera to break the silence, she'd be waiting a long time. Zera was done dancing around it all.

Finally, Katherine released a shuddering breath and looked back at Zera. A tug pulled at Zera's stomach, twisting it into knots.

"I kissed you because..." She paused, a crease forming between her brows. "Miss Zazzera, are you alright?"

"Huh? Yeah, I'm—"

The tug turned insistent, turning into a sharp stab of sickness in her gut. Stupidly, she thought it was a remnant from the night before, some delayed alcohol poisoning. But then the stab twisted, and her eyes widened.

"No, no no no—"

The world shifted, spun, and exploded into color, as if she'd been sucked straight into the sky and catapulted among the stars. Pain and dizziness washed over her as the lights threatened to blind her, the pressure of the river pushing all the air from her lungs. This was wrong, so wrong—she still had things to do, she and Katherine hadn't finished their conversation—

When she landed, it wasn't the usual kind of chaos in the room. Alarms sounded, lights flashed, and the distinct smell of something burning scorched the inside of Zera's throat. She tried to breathe and ended up coughing harshly as smoke filled her lungs.

"Zera!" Kissi's voice cut through the noise, and a second later, she grabbed Zera's arm, pulling her off the platform. "C'mon, you gotta get up."

"What happened?" The words came quiet and slurred, definitely not audible over the noise.

"Lieutenant Zazzera, come on." Phillips appeared on her other side and helped Kissi haul her to her feet. Zera's vision swam. She wanted desperately to be sick, but swallowed it down and let the two women drag her from the room.

Consciousness didn't completely stick, and Zera caught bits and flashes of hallways and lights as Kissi and Phillips took her away from the platform room. Heat built in the corridors, making it more difficult to stay awake. Finally, they landed in the medical bay—the normal one she'd use after digs.

"Kissi?" Zera asked as another nurse sank a needle into her arm. The sensation sent her over the edge and she finally vomited, blood appearing in the mess on the floor.

"Just breathe." Kissi rubbed her back.

"A tremor hit," Phillips said. "It hit the generator room, short circuiting the platform."

"What?" Zera heard the words, but she didn't like the sound of them. "What does that mean?"

"Unless we can fix the platform," Phillips said, "the program is canceled. Indefinitely."

2058

"THIS IS FUCKED UP."

Zera paced the narrow space of their bunk, every turn making her vision swim. Kissi sat at the desk, her conspiracy wall on display behind her. There were a few new pictures, but Katherine looked the same in every one.

"You're right. Again." Kissi said this more to her tablet than to Zera.

"How can they do this? I mean, they can't just cut a program like *this*," Zera said, gesturing widely in the direction of the platform. "I mean, fucking time travel? We're just gonna cancel fucking time travel?"

"That's the government for ya." Kissi's voice was flat at this point. They'd been over this same discussion enough times over the past week for her to grow bored with it, but that was probably because Zera had left out the most interesting bit.

"It can't be that hard to fix the machines. I've been stuck down learning machines. *Mechanics*. When I was a time traveler. What could possibly be a better investment?" Another turn, another wave of dizziness, and Zera crossed the room again.

"I don't know, probably your mechanic license. Then you could fix the machine," Kissi said for the fourth time. "Why does it matter? You're the one who's always saying we're supposed to follow orders."

"Yeah, I mean, when the orders...when they...make sense?"

Kissi raised her eyebrows. "This is probably the most level-headed order we've gotten since this whole thing started. What's really crawled up your ass?"

Zera sighed and stopped pacing, pinching the bridge of her nose. "Katherine kissed me."

"Katherine? I'm sorry"—Kissi smacked a turn of the century picture of Katherine, with a dress laced up to her chin and covering most every available portion of skin—"*this* Katherine? Kissed you?"

"Technically the 1980 version, but yes."

"Katherine kissed *you*?"

"Why do you have to sound so surprised by it?"

"It's not the *you* part, it's the *Katherine* part," Kissi said. "And that she initiated."

"Trust me, I was just as surprised as you." Zera resumed treading a line in the floor.

"Was it good?" Kissi leaned forward, her eyes alight with mischief like a preteen at a slumber party. Zera wished she had a portion of her giddiness, but unfortunately all she could muster was dread.

"Kind of?" she said, her voice jumping an octave. Speaking ill of Katherine wasn't her goal, but she couldn't lie to Kissi.

"Uh oh, what does 'kind of' mean? Did you not want her to?"

"You're enjoying this way too much."

"You've had a bit of a dry spell, and I'm aching for drama. Even my friends over in the kitchens have no new gossip for me."

After a groan, Zera said, "I mean, of course I wanted her to. Look how pretty she is. And she's smart, and captivating, but like...I mean, I don't think it was premeditated."

"Oof," Kissi said with an appreciative wince.

"Yeah. It was a whole ordeal. Less a profession of interest and more..."

"An experiment."

"I think so," Zera said. "We were talking the whole thing out when they pulled me."

"Oh," Kissi breathed. "Oh no."

"Oh, yes." Zera took another lap. "So what do we do with Katherine's blood now?"

"I don't know, I don't even know where they put it."

Zera gave her an unamused look. "Yeah? You didn't dig into the system to find where they cataloged all my stuff and sent it for decontam?"

"I would never," Kissi said, clutching imaginary pearls. "Unless, of course, you asked me to. Then I'd totally do it."

"If you get caught, just tell them I lost a personal effect and needed it back."

Kissi scoffed. "Please, I don't get caught."

"Right, right, sorry," Zera said. "So, we get Katherine's blood back, and then what?"

"We test it and see what we can do with it," Kissi replied.

"And how exactly are we going to test it?"

"That's your job to figure out. I just get all the materials," Kissi said.

Zera tapped at her chin. "I bet we could run it through the clinic tester, the one they use after digs. Could you figure out her anomalies and what they mean?"

"Without a control sample? No, but that doesn't mean I couldn't figure out something else."

"Would the data I brought back help any with that? Or, I dunno, the dirt on my boots?"

Kissi furrowed her brows and put the end of her stylus to her lips. "There's an idea. Really, a blood sample from someone else from her time would be best, but maybe there's physical stuff that could tell us something."

Zera groaned. "This plan sucks, doesn't it?"

"Yeah, but it's the only one we've got," Kissi said. "Unless you're willing to give up."

"No. Maybe? No." Zera shook her head roughly, even as her heart tripped at the thought. "But this is stupid, right? Stupid. Super stupid."

"Oh, the stupidest. I've only forgiven you because you were still doing your job when they pulled you," Kissi said. "But I mean, how good was that kiss?"

"Not good enough to risk it all, that's for sure," Zera said, a little too quickly.

"And yet, you're still thinking about it. Interesting."

"I said I'd help her out, and that's what I'm trying to do. Nothing more, really."

"Sure, if you say so." It didn't sound like Kissi believed her.

"Besides, it's not like we could do anything with it," Zera said.

"Not unless you learn how machines work and fix it."

"Which isn't happening."

"The learning? Or the fixing?"

Zera ground her teeth. "The fixing. I'll learn."

"So if we ran this sample, it would be for curiosity?" Kissi asked.

"Yeah, for science," Zera said. They were silent for a beat.

"Okay, so I'll get the sample, and it's your job to run it," Kissi said.

Zera flopped onto the bottom bunk and threw her arm over her eyes. "I've done way too much breaking and entering since starting this job."

"And while everything's running, you have to study for your mechanics test."

"But that sounds boring." Zera sat up and reached into her drawer, intent on digging more solder out of the pocket watch seam. However, the watch was nowhere to be found. In fact, neither was her knife or keycard. "What the...Has anyone been in here?"

"No, why?" Kissi turned and saw the open drawer. "Are you missing something?"

"A couple somethings, actually," Zera said.

"You're sure they were in there?"

The pocket watch, yes. The knife and the keycard were a little less certain.

"Yeah, I'm positive."

Kissi rolled her desk chair over to her own nightstand and threw open the drawer. After scanning the contents, she looked up at Zera and shrugged.

"I dunno, all my stuff is here," she said. "What are you missing?"

"My knife, keycard, and that pocket watch."

"Pocket watch? What pocket watch?"

"The one from the Pit."

"Oh, right," Kissi said, blinking and shaking her head as if knocking a piece back into place. "I guess I didn't realize you kept it."

Zera was about to say she hadn't hidden it, that it'd been in here the whole time, but discussing the origin of the object wouldn't help her current situation.

"Maybe I took it somewhere and forgot," she said, standing. "I'm gonna go check around and then case the testing unit."

There was no crowd in the hallways, and Zera was grateful it was mid-shift. The less prying eyes, the better.

Her first stop was the training room. Some sort of group workout was going on, and a couple of the soldiers glanced over at her. It wasn't illegal for her to be wandering around the base, but after years of rigid structure, it felt like it.

Once she found her locker, she keyed in the code and pried open the rusty door. Her training gear sat the way she left it, folded and stacked on the shelf. She took each piece and shook them out, as if her missing items would simply appear between the thin cotton layers, but all she found was dust and lint.

Zera refolded the clothes and packed her locker, speculating where to go next. Visiting medical wouldn't be a bad idea, then she could kill two birds with one stone. And if Martin happened to be there, all the better.

She didn't recognize the medic at the front desk, which made sense, seeing as her only previous visits were during the night shift. The day shift medic was tall, bearded, and well muscled, but he managed to soften the tough exterior with burgundy nail polish.

"What's up?" he asked as Zera arrived at the desk. Startling blue eyes looked out from under thick, dark eyebrows, and his name tag read Brooks. "Don't tell me it's that damn stomach bug going around."

"Huh? Oh, uh, no, thank the gods." But if she thought about that gin from a few nights ago she could definitely recall the symptoms. "I was in here a while ago, and somewhere between now and then I misplaced a couple things. Is there, like, a lost and found I could check? See if I forgot them here?"

"Yeah, for sure." He tapped his screen a few times, then asked, "Name and ID number?"

"Zazzera," she answered, spelling it for him afterwards and tacking her numbers on at the end. He keyed them in and read the screen at dazzling speed.

"It's been a long time since you were here last," Brooks said. "Guess the stuff wasn't that important, huh?"

"I got transferred to a different group for a while, so I didn't need it," Zera said. She took a careful glance toward the testing machine and found she couldn't quite see the entry port. Good to know. If she came back, the waiting medic wouldn't be able to see it either.

"I hate when they do that. Just when you get comfy, they send you to another spot." He stood and gestured for her to follow. "Come this way."

With a swipe of his keycard, he let her into the back room. It was more of a closet, with shelving all the way up the walls filled with supplies and junk. A door to the back, protected by another keycard reader, had various stickers announcing *Medical Personnel Only* and *Biohazard*.

"Here's the main lost and found bins." Brooks tapped his manicured nails against two big plastic bins. "Need help with the search?"

"Nah, I got it," Zera said. "I imagine you have more important stuff to do."

"The higher ups usually like it when I do my job, I guess," he said with a shrug. "Just clean up before you leave, okay? I don't really wanna deal with more mess than I have to."

"Yessir," Zera said. Brooks nodded and left, closing the door behind him.

The bins were stuffed with forgotten items, from single gloves to handhelds to the good luck trinkets a lot of diggers wore. One corner had a handful of pocketknives, all the same standard issue, but none had the *Z* she'd scratched into the handle during the academy. A few keycards littered the bottom, but none had her ID number.

"Shit."

The only other place she stored things was the locker in the hutch, but she hadn't been there since the night of her last dig. It was a long walk, but she was out of ideas and had time to kill, so she booked it across the bunker.

During day shift, the garage was buzzing as mechanics fixed the vehicles and other equipment, patching wear and tear from the unforgiving landscape and adding reinforcements to protect the riders from the heat. She kept her head down and slipped into the hallway leading to the hutch. Hopefully she wouldn't actually have to meet any of the mechanics, though the likelihood of her and Kissi fixing everything by Monday was unlikely.

Despite their reassignments, the lockers still had the names Kissinger,

Zazzera, and Liebowitz on their fronts. Either they never formed a new dig team to take over for them, or they anticipated their return. Both answers were equally unsettling. She would take the mechanic shop over the dig sites any day or night.

Once again, Zera keyed in her code and the locker popped open. A fresh uniform hung in the locker, the right-sized helmet and boots sitting on the top shelf. It felt like a relic from another life, one she barely remembered. Nope, being a mechanic would be much better than this.

Zera pushed the jumpsuit aside so she could see the bottom shelf. In the place where a water bulb usually sat, the pocket watch, keycard, and knife all waited for her. They were in a neat pile on the edge, placed there purposefully rather than thrown in a hurry. She'd used this locker to hide important things on a few occasions, but that was a long time ago as well. Had she done this in her sleep?

A tingle started between her shoulder blades, and Zera shot up, looking around for signs of a lurker. But the hutch was empty except for her, her paranoia, and maybe a few ghosts. She moved quickly, stuffing the watch deep into her pocket. The knife and keycard she kept readily available.

The feeling of being watched grew stronger, and Zera followed the instinct, leaving the hutch quickly. In the garage, the machine clatter felt louder, as if it was drawing attention to her rather than hiding her. She just needed to get out, as long as no one saw her—

"Zazzera!"

She stuttered to a stop. She didn't recognize the voice, but if they'd called her by her full name, it had to be someone important. At least the machines muted her curses as she turned around, fully expecting a reprimand. Instead, she found Byrd hobbling toward her, no crutches or cast in sight, but a black boot encasing his foot.

"Jesus, Odin, and Zeus, Byrd, you scared the living shit out of me," she said, putting a hand over her racing heart.

"Why? Oh, right, *Zera*, sorry." He laughed. "This sucks, right? About the program getting shut down?"

"Yeah, it does," Zera said. "Did they move you down here?"

He shook his head and tapped the heel of his boot on the concrete floor. "Until I'm out of this thing, I'm still on light duty. Inventory, mostly. You?"

"Been reassigned to mechanics," she said. "I was just grabbing something from my locker. It sucks, though. I was really making headway, and if I had you with me, we could have made a big difference."

"I appreciate the flattery, even if I'm not sure I agree," he said. "How crazy was it? Back then?"

"Oh, a shit storm." Zera laughed, remembering Mack's. "But super cool. Even made a friend."

"Just one? Guess they were getting pretty old, huh?"

"You have no idea," she said. "It was kinda nice though, having a buddy there to help out."

"What was his name?"

Zera narrowed her eyes. "What makes you think it was a man?"

Byrd opened his mouth, closed it, then laughed and shook his head. "I was wrong to assume...anything." He rubbed the back of his neck and looked anywhere but at her.

Zera fought the grin threatening to break her façade. "Makes an ass out of you and me. But *her* name is—was—Katherine."

"Katherine?" he asked, clarifying over the sound of the machines.

"Yeah," Zera said. "I feel bad, kinda left her high and dry since I can't go back."

"I'm sure she managed alright," he said. "But hey, I've got an in with one of the higher ups—worked with him back in the day—and he mentioned there wasn't much damage to the machines."

Zera paused. "Really?"

"Yeah, and they're still combing through the data, seeing if it's even worth it to fix them."

"Oh, damn." A plan formed, quick and dirty.

"That's what I said—where are you going?"

"I just remembered Kissi needed me for something!" she called over her shoulder.

She stuffed her hands into her pockets, making herself smaller to navigate the busy hangar. When her fingers hit the cool metal of the watch she nearly jumped out of her skin, completely forgetting the reason she was down there to begin with.

The earlier conversation returned to her. Why couldn't she fix the machine? It was something her instructor repeated a thousand times. Electricity was all about where the current flowed, and the pieces were there to connect them.

Zera kept her head down as she strode through the halls. If she acted like she was supposed to be in the restricted area, then no one would question her. It was an age old rule, which she followed faithfully as she weaved through various doorways until she reached the machine room.

A jagged crack ran along one side of the platform, but everything else seemed mostly intact. She went to the side with the crack and, after pulling out her pocket knife, removed the bolts and pulled off the protective casing. The jumble of parts and wires underneath scared her at first, but then she took a breath, calmed her mind, and really looked.

She didn't need to know what every piece did—she just needed to put them back together. Her eyes trailed the wires and circuits, and even with her minimally experienced eyes, she could find the interruptions. A couple more days of training, and she could probably patch it all together. That's all it would take.

To be sure, Zera removed the other covers and looked underneath. The platform was separated into six wedges, and each wedge matched the rest, connected at a few specific points. This was perfect, she had five other examples to follow. She could do this—she could *definitely* do this.

It was a long trek back to her quarters, and silence greeted her when she returned to her room, Kissi off on her extraction mission. Every picture of Katherine on the wall gave Zera the creeps, like the sensation of walking by a shrine in memoriam. She didn't want to think about Katherine's death. If she could find a way to go back, then she could find a way to undo the 2040 Storm. And if she could find a way to undo the effects of the Storm, then...

Then what? Katherine would still be gone, just like everyone else. They couldn't change the past, and Zera needed to stop acting like they could.

She hadn't looked closely before, but now she sat in Kissi's chair and really took notice of the photos. With no co-conspirator in sight, there wasn't much else to do.

There was a stiff one from the '30s, with a man that had to be Alfred. Another where she was just in the background with the bandana over her hair, eyes haunted by the pressure of the Depression. The next in her skirt suit, a staff picture from the clinic in Chicago. Another, later that year, with her in a white dress and holding onto Hank.

Sometime in the 1960s, Katherine became more outgoing. Kissi had a whole stack of pictures with Katherine's face circled in the crowds of rallies and protests against the Vietnam War. Hells, she was even at fucking *Woodstock* in 1969. She no longer looked like someone wishing for her end of days.

Fashions changed—hair got longer and skirts got shorter, and the pictures went from grainy to color to well defined. Over a hundred years of life in one organized wall.

A thought formed. Maybe Zera couldn't save Katherine from the Storm, but maybe she didn't have to live through the Storm at all.

Zera jumped as Kissi entered, closing the door behind her. A suspicious bulge in the cargo pocket of her fatigues told of her success.

"You got it?" Zera asked.

"Of course I did," Kissi said, pulling out the box. She nodded toward the wall. "Gazing longingly at your girlfriend?"

"She's not my girlfriend," Zera said. "We barely decided on friends. But that's not the point."

"Oh, you have a point?"

"Byrd said they rebuilt the machines."

"What?" Kissi dropped the sample onto the desk. "Already?"

"Apparently damage was minimal."

"Why haven't they said anything?" She took a seat on her bunk, eyes intense. "We could be up and running already."

"Funding got cut. But the machines...they still work."

Kissi paused. "I don't like the way you said that."

Zera changed tactics. "Do you know why I can travel?"

Kissi raised her eyebrows. "Excuse me?"

"No, I mean—" Zera took a breath. "Do you know the literal reason why I can go through the machine, but other people can't?"

"Oh, uh, something to do with that anomaly I found in your blood," Kissi said. "After the last time you went into the Pit."

"So if we test Katherine's blood, would you be able to tell if she had the same anomaly?"

Kissi blinked. "Okay, that's a bad idea."

"I'm just saying, if we test it—"

"We can't just bring her back here," Kissi said. "That would—I mean, an *uproar* would be the least of your worries. We're talking jail time at the very least."

"What other option do we have?" Zera threw her hands up. "You said it yourself, there's something different about her. I can't just let her die like everyone else."

"I'm all for bending rules, but this is playing God," Kissi said. "Why do we have to save Katherine and not everyone else? What about your mom, or my parents, or any of the other billions of people we lost that day?"

"I..." Zera fumbled for an answer, grasping at the ring hanging under her shirt. "I don't know. Because she was alive when she wasn't supposed to be, maybe? Or because of the way she looked at me back in Central Park?"

"For the record, I think you're right. I think before this is all over, Katherine's gonna help in some way or another," Kissi said. "But as your best friend, I'm telling you that trying to bring her back here is a bad idea."

Sometimes Zera hated how often Kissi was right. The weight of the situation sank her heart to somewhere amongst her intestines. If one more moving part joined in, it might break her.

Kissi tapped the box with Katherine's blood. "First thing, you need to run this sample before it goes bad. We don't know if or when you'll be able to get another one. After that...we can talk about options."

Zera nodded and grabbed the case. Nothing else would matter if they didn't have the data first. All the different avenues they might take, all the schemes they might come up with, none of them mattered until they ran Katherine's blood.

Planning ahead was a luxury in this world, and she needed to remember that.

2058

AFTER THREE WEEKS of sneaking around under the platform, Zera returned to her old bunk sweaty and covered in grease to find Kissi frowning at her screen.

"Did you get the results?" It was a daily question.

"Yes, I did." Not the usual daily answer. "I'm sorry, but beyond normal human stuff, there's no markers that match between your stuff and hers. I don't think she could survive a trip back here."

"Oh," Zera breathed. She'd been so confident before. If Katherine could live over a hundred years and still look a few days beyond thirty, then traveling through time should have been easy. "Is there...I mean, I didn't always have the markers. You said it yourself after that last dig, there were anomalies in my blood check."

"I have no idea what caused that though, and there's no way for me to recreate it. You're not thinking, Zera."

"Of course I'm not," Zera said, the Katherines from the wall continuing to stare at her. "Nothing about this situation makes sense. 2040 isn't the first storm, but Katherine is ground zero for it. Every storm before it, things are fine. But something happens with Katherine between 1980 and 2040, and we need to figure it out."

"Why?" Kissi said.

"What?"

"No, *why*."

"I heard—never mind," Zera said. "What do you mean 'why'?"

"Why is it our job to figure out whatever happened to Katherine?" Kissi clarified. "If you remember, our job is to find a way to save this shitty situation the 2040 Storm put us in."

"And to do that, we have to figure out what happened to Katherine," Zera said. "I have to get back to her. Based on how she reacted in 2040, I know for a fact we'll meet at least one more time." Unbidden, the vision of Katherine in Central Park returned to her, but this time she saw the joy in the smile. There was no way she'd look at her like that after the way they left things in 1980.

Kissi sighed. Though it wasn't an outright no, it sure felt like one. And if she didn't have Kissi on her side, there was no way in any hells she could go back again.

"I feel like you're not taking this seriously."

"I am! I am taking it seriously. I just..." There was no use lying anymore, to herself or to Kissi. "There's just something about her."

"Ew, that sounded way too sentimental." Kissi's lip curled, and she turned back to her laptop. Zera stepped over and draped her sweaty, greasy goodness over Kissi in a hug.

"Thank you, Kissi," she said. "For everything."

"Yeah, yeah," Kissi said, pushing her off. "I mean, I want to answer these questions just as much as you do. I've just got other priorities."

"That's fair." To seal the deal, Zera gave a soft punch to her friend's shoulder. Their plans hung suspended in the air, leaving Zera to wonder why she felt so strongly about returning to the past. It was easy to cite saving the world, or even going back to a time when she could walk outside without a suit.

But as she lay awake that night, turning over the different plans in her head and the silver watch in her hands, she wasn't thinking about science or air or sunshine. All she could think of was the smile on Katherine's face, the adoration in her eyes.

Zera hadn't slept by the time Kissi woke, the latter moving carefully around the tiny bunk in an effort to keep quiet. Little did she know, Zera was waiting for this moment.

"We're missing something," she said.

Kissi yelped and nearly lost her balance, grabbing onto the bed frame at the last moment. "What the hell?"

"Sorry, sorry, good morning." Zera rolled off the bunk and went to the wall, staring at the pictures. "We're missing something."

"Zera, come on," Kissi said, going back to her morning routine. "I'm late for my weekly brupper date with Keirnan."

Zera grimaced. "I hate that you guys call it that."

"What? My breakfast, his supper. It makes perfect sense."

"Anyway, I still think we're missing something."

"Well, when you figure it out, let me know." Kissi sat down and went through the process of donning her prosthesis, the movements quick and accurate. "Currently, our choices are to wait for the higher ups to reopen it, or break in and use the machines ourselves."

Zera spun to her. "You'd do that?"

"Absolutely not," Kissi snapped, then paused. "I mean, probably not. No. Maybe?"

"Maybe?" Zera raised her eyebrows. A thrill spilled through her veins, both from the idea and the thought of breaking so many rules. "Maybe? 'Cause I did it. I fixed it."

"You're sure?" Kissi had wide eyes, and her shoulders tensed.

"Completely. Did everything except turn it on. But it matches all the other wedges."

Kissi returned to her bunk and steepled her fingers, and waited an abnormally long time before speaking. "We would need an airtight plan."

"Oh my gods you're serious." Zera leaned forward, getting close.

"Of course I'm serious, weren't you serious?"

"Yes, I was! I just didn't think you would actually be serious."

"I mean, I'm your best wingman. I'll break a few rules to get you back to your girlfriend."

"I thought we were trying to save the world?" Zera said.

"One of us has to focus on that, since the other can't keep her hands off the locals."

Zera had already moved on. "If we turn the power on full blast, they'll definitely notice, especially if we let it run for an hour. So we probably can't keep the air conditioning on."

"If we don't turn it on, the machines will overheat in about ten minutes. They blow again, you might be stuck for good or get lost in between," Kissi said.

Zera resumed her pacing, but this time it was so her brain could move while it worked. "Okay, so maybe we turn it off in between when I leave and when I come back."

"That could work," Kissi said, tapping her chin, "but that means two power surges people could notice."

"Could you leave in between?"

"It means I'd have to find a way back in."

"Shit." Zera ran a hand through her too-long hair. The parts on top could even tangle now. "Can we shorten the window?"

"Shorten the...shorten the window." Kissi stared into the middle distance before returning to the present with a snap. "Yeah, I think I can hack the device in your arm and reset the return time to like, one minute after."

"Get in, get out. No one's any the wiser."

"Well, it'll be a little longer for you," she said. "But Zera, you have to–and I mean *have to*–find something big. Something that, if we get caught, it'll be worth it."

"I will." Even to her own ears, it didn't sound confident. She cleared her throat and tried again. "Katherine and I were right on the edge of something before I got pulled back."

"I don't wanna hear about your sexcapades," Kissi said, holding up a hand.

Zera rolled her eyes. "Not what I meant, and you know it."

"Still fun to mess with you," she said. "You've been flying blind this whole time, just going back and seeing what you can find. That data isn't worth shit and we know it."

"What are the odds of us finding a spare magnetometer in some forgotten storeroom?" Zera asked. "The one they sent me with looks for disturbances in the atmosphere, but obviously that isn't working."

"I'm not sure the magnetometer is our best bet. It just measures the movement of the fields around Earth, not what causes them."

"So when you say we need something big, you mean I have to find something in a way we never could before. Something all the way new."

"Exactly." Kissi let out a breath, her dark eyes gleaming with sympathy. "You know, no pressure."

"Fuck," Zera muttered, running her hand through her hair again and cursing when her fingers got caught in the tangles. "Fuck!"

"Look, if you get me one of those scanners they sent with you, and maybe I can hack it to do something...else." It was Kissi's turn not to sound confident, which didn't help Zera's sense of impending doom.

"But you just said it looks at the atmosphere when we need to go deeper."

"Maybe you can tie it to a fishing line and drop it?" A wince came with the suggestion. Zera's mind whirred as she fumbled for a solution, but it had been a long time since she needed to use her brain like this. It kind of hurt. After all, since finishing the academy, she was just a digger—

She was a *digger*.

"What about the poles?" she asked.

"The magnetic poles? I mean, that's kind of what the magnetometer is for—"

"No, I mean, what about the anchor poles? The ones that hold me up when I go down in the Pit."

Kissi stared. To anyone else her face might have looked blank, but Zera could see the gears turning in her big, beautiful brain.

"The poles. They have sensors to tell the pressure and how deep they are," she murmured, no longer talking to Zera. She moved to her desk, her *brupper* date long forgotten. "The software should be somewhere in the common domain. I had to monitor that thing the whole time you were down there. If I could find a way to make it send different signals—"

"It could read what was going on inside the Earth. Or the crust, at least. How thick is it again?" The last time Zera had thought about the Earth's crust was sometime around sophomore year, and she wasn't entirely sure she could name the thickness then.

"Approximately thirty-two kilometers," Kissi said absently, because *of course* she remembered. "But we shouldn't have to read all the way to the center. Any big fluxes would reverberate through the layers...I think."

"Who can we fact check it with?"

"Uh..." Kissi dragged out the word as she thought. "Wait. Lieb was in geo before he got moved to digging."

"Dude. He *was*." Back when they first started, he bragged about it all the time, saying something about his muscles being too big for him to stay an analyst. It usually ended with offers of arm wrestling matches. "What sector is he in now, do you know?"

"No, all contact got cut when we switched programs, and I haven't seen him since we got out." She tapped her laptop with a finger. "I can find him though."

"Isn't that, like, against the rules?" Zera asked.

Kissi looked at her. She looked back. Then they both dissolved into laughter.

"Rules, right. Gimme a minute." Whatever magic Kissi performed on the computer was completely lost on Zera, who waited patiently for an answer. After a few beats, Kissi let out a huff of triumph.

"Where's he at?"

"Still working nights," Kissi said. "They moved him to *Theta* team."

"You're shitting me." Zera looked over Kissi's shoulder. Sure enough, on the team's roster, Liebowitz now appeared under Theta. "Those bastards."

"I know. Bet he's losing his mind."

"When's their next dig?"

Kissi shuffled through some more documents. "Two nights from now. So we have until then to finalize a plan."

"Yeah, easy," Zera said. Kissi waved her off.

"Leave me alone now. I have to scrub the last hour from the records and I don't need you distracting me."

"Yes, ma'am," Zera said with a mock salute. She moved toward the door. "Hey Kissi?"

"Yeah?"

"Have you checked your blood?"

Kissi paused. "Maybe."

"And?"

Kissi took her time with a response. "I might have the same anomaly."

"What? That's awesome! You could come with me."

"Who will man the controls?"

"What could happen in the minute we're gone?" All of this would go so much smoother if Kissi was with her, especially if she was designing something brand new.

"Sure, I'll...I'll check it," she said.

"Good," Zera said. "Okay, well, I'll get out of your hair at least. Let you...scrape, or whatever the hell you're doing with that thing."

"Scrub. But close enough."

———————

Two nights later, walking through the halls right before shift change felt both eerily familiar and like a lucid dream. Zera's body felt fatigued, now accustomed to the new sleep schedule as if she hadn't spent years nocturnal. Adrenaline from her mission—she thought of everything as a mission these days—made her spine and fingers tingle, but she ignored them and followed the familiar path down to the hutches.

Back in the day she stopped at the Epsilon hutch, but tonight she went all the way down near the end. True to form, Lieb sat on the bench, clocked in thirty minutes before anyone else as he prepared his rescue gear. At the creak of the door, he looked up, his familiar annoyed expression making something in Zera's throat tighten.

"Zera?" When he saw her, the glare softened, and he even brought out an actual smile. "Hey, you're still alive."

"Barely," she said. He rose and crossed the small room, gathering her in a rough hug and making sure to ruffle her hair when he pulled away.

"What's this mop on your head?"

"Haven't had time to take care of it," she said. "So, you're going with Theta now?"

He rolled his eyes. "Don't remind me. These assholes don't know tit from tat and it's making me work extra."

"We always knew they sucked."

"Yeah, but now it's like, confirmed." The bench creaked as he sat, returning to his prep. He jerked his head toward the other side, inviting Zera to join.

"Not as fun as working with me and Kissi?"

"Of course not," he said. "Now, are you gonna cut the shit and tell me why you're here? Or do we need to keep on with this small talk?"

Zera smiled and clapped her hand on his shoulder. "Ah, Lieb, I missed you."

"Not enough to message in the past few months." He said it lightly, but his knuckles were white as he wound and bound a paracord.

"You're right, I'm sorry." She meant it. "We were told to go no contact. I was hoping they'd at least let you know we were okay, but..."

"Nope." He tied the cord with a knot and clapped carabiners onto it, the clacks loud in the small room. "Just said y'all got moved to another division and I was over here now."

"It's been a whole fucking mess, if I'm honest." Zera let out a long breath. "Hopefully I can tell you all about it someday. In like fifty years when the records get released."

"I'll hold you to that." He sounded hurt, but at least he wasn't angry. Zera didn't blame him; if she was in his shoes, she wouldn't be so forgiving. "Now, what do you need?"

"You kinda can't tell anyone about it," she said.

He raised his brows. "Going rogue?"

"Not gonna tell you."

"Ah, plausible deniability. What a heartless bitch."

"I know."

A sigh escaped him. "Alright, alright, cross my heart and hope you die, yada yada yada. What's up?"

"I don't think the phrase is 'hope you die'."

"Semantics. Get on with it, Beece will be here soon and he can't keep a secret to save his life." He drew circles with his finger, egging her on.

"Right," she said. "Okay, so the poles..."

Zera gave him the quick and dirty, and while she probably shared more information than necessary, she knew Lieb's word was good. He listened as he packed his gear, his eyes unfocused as he solved the problem.

"Hypothetically, it'll work." He zipped his bag. "I don't know if it'll give you the information you want, but it'll give you something different than above the surface."

"Awesome, that's what I need," she said, though relief didn't loosen the knot in her chest.

"Where do they have you digging? Sounds like it's way outside the red zone." He looked concerned, and Zera knew, given the opportunity, he would transfer to help.

"You could say that. Unfortunately, I'm kind of on my own with it. It's not near the same as the three of us together."

Lieb smiled, then reached over to squeeze her knee. "I know, it's easy to miss me. Maybe come around and say hey again. Preferably not after a few weeks of radio silence, though."

"If I make it through, you'll be the first to know," she said, smiling.

He scoffed. "Don't flatter me. Kissinger gets all the gossip first, I know that." He patted her leg. "Now go on. Beece will be here any second."

"Thank you, Lieb. Truly." He didn't respond, only grinned, and sent her on her way.

Zera spotted Beece at the end of the hall and ducked into an equipment closet until he passed by, the thunks and clicks of his digger suit sending shocks of memory through her. A few weeks felt like a lifetime. How did the decades feel to Katherine?

Step two: she needed to get the anchor and the return syringes.

When she checked her watch, she found the hour had betrayed her; she'd taken too much time talking to Lieb and would now be cutting it close to return to their side of the bunker and get into Dr. Doyle's office. That syringe was the only surefire way they'd get enough time.

Zera set the timer on her watch and strode double-time back. As predicted, darkness coated the medical hallway except for a single light in the doctors' lounge. Someone probably left the light on, but Zera paused against the wall before passing the door, making every effort to calm her breathing. Slowly, soundlessly, she inched down to a low squat and moved just enough to see into the room. People often looked head height, she learned long ago. Better to be lower.

Dr. Doyle sat at the table, his wheelchair turned almost completely away from her. Almost. He had his tablet propped on the table, displaying a wall of text so small Zera couldn't read it from her vantage point. If he turned his head just a few degrees to the right, he would see her walk by.

Shit. The room was supposed to be empty by now.

He shifted and muttered something to himself, flipping to the next page of his manuscript. While he seemed completely absorbed by his reading, Zera wasn't willing to risk everything on his focus.

She glanced back to where she'd come from; the longer she sat, the more likely someone would spot her. She was officially stuck between a rock and a hard place.

"Huh."

Zera nearly jumped out of her skin at Dr. Doyle's voice. But he hadn't noticed her, only found something particularly interesting in his reading. The fact he hadn't heard her gasp or the slam of her heart against her ribs was a good sign. He turned away from the door, reaching for his bag.

Without taking the time to second guess herself, Zera took one long step and shifted her weight onto that foot, staying low as she passed in front of the door. The movement took less than a breath, but she kept her eyes on the back of Dr. Doyle's head the entire time until the doorframe forced her to lose sight.

She pressed herself against the wall, silent. Her ears strained for any sounds of alarm, or confusion, or curiosity. All she heard was a soft whoosh from the cushion in his wheelchair as Dr. Doyle shifted, and his continued muttering as he tapped on the tablet screen.

Crisis averted.

The offices in this wing were older, and Zera thanked all the gods that Katherine taught her how to pick a lock. The door swung open just enough to allow her entry, and she squeezed in. Bubbling experiments and a weird lamp with a gloopy substance floating up and down in blobs gave her more than enough light to find the drawer the doctor had opened during her very first visit. It required another use of her lockpicking skills, and she needed a few attempts before it finally sprang open with a loud *thunk*.

Zera swallowed her surprise and sat completely still, waiting to hear boots on the concrete, or at the very least the wheels of Dr. Doyle's chair. Nothing. She let out a long breath, her head starting to buzz from the oxygen deprivation.

She was so very close. The container held five syringes, and for a moment she considered grabbing all five, but she decided that was too obvious. The drawer above held a different pile of syringes, unopened, and a few clear boxes with the chunky trackers needed for the long trips. She took one from the very back and slid everything into her pockets.

With careful hands she closed the drawer. There was no way to lock it again, so she had to hope Dr. Doyle wouldn't freak out the next time he accessed it. The office door she locked from the inside before squeezing out, mindful of the click as the door closed. The hallway in front of her was completely dark now, the lounge light off.

She made it. She actually fucking made it.

With supplies, a set date, a set plan, and altered poles ready to do their bidding, there was nothing left except to actually do the thing. Just break every rule in the book. Or rather, throw the rule book out the window and hope it was worth it.

It took another week to map the security route and shifts, comparing the written details Kissi had found to the men in action. Most of the time, no one occupied the hallway leading to the platform, but it was near a high traffic area. They would need to time their movements just right.

Child's play, Kissi called it. Zera thought they had very different childhoods.

At half-past eleven, they walked from their bunk to the storage room two hallways from their destination. The room itself was a catch-all closet, a common stop for everyone on this side of the door. Kissi grabbed a first aid kit and stuffed it in her pocket, while Zera took extra batteries for the poles. Electricity might have been commonplace by 1992, but the last thing she needed was incompatibility with an outlet to ruin her last chance.

The three big poles were less than subtle as they walked through the hallway, but people on this side of the bunker carried things weirder than digger poles all the time.

"Last chance," Kissi murmured, two turns away from their destination.

"You having second thoughts?" Zera asked.

"Not at all."

"Me neither. Let's go."

Kissi checked her watch and picked up the pace. There seemed to be more people than usual, but Zera figured she was just on alert due to the sensitivity of the mission. Her heart stuttered as nerves caught up with her, but overall she was not as scared as she thought she would be, or ought to be.

At the last turn, the flood of people parted, leaving their way free and clear. Kissi checked her watch, started a timer, and punched in the door code. It slid open with the familiar whoosh, but the usual blast of cold didn't hit.

Half the desks lay empty, their computers packed in boxes in the corner with identification numbers written in blocky handwriting. The tentacles of wires coming from the platform were smaller than before, missing the connections.

"We'll have to be quick," Kissi said. A whir kicked in below Zera's feet, the tower already combating the temperature. Kissi grabbed a handheld scanner and gestured to Zera. "Come here, let's reset your return time."

Zera held out her arm and Kissi held the scanner over it, looking at the time on the computer and typing in sixty seconds in the future. The countdown on Kissi's watch ticked down to three minutes as she did the same to her own arm, where she'd sliced a shallow cut and stuck the tracker in. A layer of gauze and tape kept it inside.

"Okay, go time," she said. Zera nodded, checked her inventory once more, and hopped onto the platform. A bead of sweat that had nothing to do with the heat trickled down her back. Kissi joined her, her hands clammy as Zera helped pull her up.

"Is it gonna hurt?" Kissi asked.

"Like hell," Zera replied.

Kissi's eyes grew wide and her jaw dropped. "Son of a—"

The river swept them up together.

DALLAS WAS the right kind of hot.

While the heat of summer verged on stifling, it brought with it the sense of school vacation and limitless possibilities. The river dropped Zera and Kissi in an alley, the shadow of the buildings protecting them from the blinding sun but not the loud rumble of cars.

1980 was livelier than her three previous trips, but 1992 brought patterns and colors Zera had previously only seen in photo albums. The smell of hairspray and polyester made a memory tingle at the edge of Zera's brain, something about the first and only time she met her grandmother. Slowly but surely, she recognized the world again.

Thank the gods Kissi sent them back in the early morning, as it took nearly five hours before she felt whole enough to walk again, even with the stinky dumpster nearby. Kissi let Zera rest her head on her leg as she reassembled, soaking up the sights and sounds and smells. A few people gave them odd looks as they passed, but no trouble.

"You good?" Zera asked, her voice raspy.

"Yeah. Feel kinda like I'm being held together with superglue right now, but I managed not to throw up," Kissi said. "You think you can get up?"

"Only one way to find out."

Once ambulatory, it was easy to stash the poles behind the dumpster and venture out. Better cars made for less foot traffic, so they didn't have to worry about pedestrians spotting them. They sported t-shirts and their formal trousers, and traded their boots for old-fashioned training shoes. For once, the military's obsession with tradition helped.

"Wow." Kissi tilted her face to the sun. Zera wanted to rush, but reminded herself of her own first visit. It was a big deal, and she needed to grant Kissi time to enjoy it.

There were many resources available thanks to the proximity in time, and for once Zera walked with confidence, turning toward the South-western Medical Research Building. Thanks to reverse image searches and lengthy staff records, she knew not only Katherine's last name now but also where she continued her medical practice. She also knew the reason Katherine was in Dallas—Roger Siftlin, former Arctic adventurer and current resident of a nearby psychiatric hospital.

She attributed the sizzle under her skin to the bright Texas sun. People around her fanned themselves with pamphlets and hats, but after eighteen years in a bunker this temperature wasn't enough for her to break a sweat.

"You got this part?" Kissi asked as they stood in front of the building. "Even if it's the '90s, I don't wanna risk causing some kind of uproar." She gestured to her skin that, while paler from years underground, was still a rich, dark brown.

"Yeah, for sure. You hang out and soak up nature." Zera gestured to a nearby bench. With a grin, Kissi saluted, and posted up under a tree, looking happier than Zera had seen in a long time.

Cool air hit her as she pushed the medical center door open, barely avoiding smacking into a reedy man in a lab coat. Most of the people in the lobby wore lab coats, and most of them were men, which made Zera's initial assessment of the space relatively easy. The only woman present—a secretary—sat behind a desk, answering the phone and smacking her gum. Her red lips matched her red dress and nails, and Zera bet her entire paycheck the shoes under the desk were red too.

"Thank you for calling the Southwestern Research Building, how can I—" The secretary spotted her, and her lips broke into a big smile. "I'm sorry, please hold. How're ya doin', sugar? What can I help you with?"

Zera hoped her surprise at the woman's sickly-sweet Southern accent didn't show on her face.

"Oh, um..." The woman's blue eyes pierced her, making her forget all the important things she'd come here to do. Finally, she remembered one. "I'm looking for a friend of mine, she works here."

"Okay, which department?" The woman—Tammy, if her name plate was to be believed—tilted her head slightly, never breaking eye contact. Zera felt like a lab specimen under a microscope.

"Cellular...shit—I mean, shoot!—cellular processes?" she squeaked. If she didn't know her current era, she might think Tammy a very lifelike robot, the way she held her gaze. Had she blinked? Zera didn't think so.

"Alright, and what's her name?" Tammy picked up a thick green binder, her blood-red nails contrasting with the cover.

"Katherine. Katherine McCall." At least she could say the name with confidence.

Tammy flipped open the binder and selected the correct tab. Names filled the entire paper, and she trailed her finger down until she found the one she wanted, giving it an extra tap. A second later, she was back on the phone and dialing an extension, making sure to give Zera a warm smile. Zera wanted to trust it.

The ancient phone was loud enough Zera could hear the rings, and counted them as they sounded. After eight, it went to the answering machine, but she couldn't hear that part. Tammy hung up before the message ended.

"Sorry, honey, she's not at her desk. She may be in her lab or out to lunch, Dr. McCall tends to wander a little bit," she said with an apologetic smile.

"Oh, uh, okay, that's okay," Zera stuttered. Just like Katherine to have an actual presence and trail to follow, but not be where she was supposed to be. "I'll just...wait for her outside."

"Come back in a couple hours and we can try again, hmm? Or call this number and I'll transfer you." She plucked a business card from a holder and slid it across the desk.

"Thanks—" Zera looked up from the card to find Tammy already back on the phone, Zera long forgotten.

She joined Kissi on the bench, enjoying the show of people walking around the medical center campus.

"No luck?" Kissi asked.

"Wasn't at her desk."

"Oh no, guess we have to wait here and do nothing, huh? How sad."

"Yeah, I can tell you're really broken up about it."

Zera hoped Katherine would leave through the front doors and not another secret exit, which was a bit more her style. She was surprised Katherine allowed such a thing as her name and picture on a staff registry, especially if someone was still trying to track her down and kill her. Or perhaps she'd taken care of the threat.

It was hard to be patient knowing she was in such close proximity to Katherine, and that Kissi was risking everything to be here with her. Not to mention, how she and Katherine had left things.

Her heart leapt into her throat. She'd never been good at those kinds of conversations, and considering Katherine had twelve years to decide what to say, she felt she was at an extreme disadvantage even with her favorite third wheel in the world. Would Kissi's presence help or hinder?

Zera rose and leaned against the tree behind the bench, the bark smooth and warm. In the shade, she could last for hours, running through every scenario for what Katherine might say when she found her after work. The conversation would start with an apology, of course, and an explanation for her abrupt departure. After that—

She didn't get to decide what she would say after that, because Katherine was weaving through the picnic tables out front and heading straight toward her.

Shit.

Zera straightened. Katherine could be heading to a car, or to meet someone, or just for a walk around campus. She might not have noticed her.

Except her honey eyes were trained right on her, and she sported a smug smile on her perfect lips. A breeze picked up her light brown curls, and the sun hit just right to show off her freckles.

That's when Zera knew she was a goner. If Katherine tried anything like she did back in 1980, she'd be physically, emotionally, *spiritually* incapable of saying no.

"Well, aren't you a sight for sore eyes." Katherine stopped in front of her, even more stunning up close. Gone were the corsets and the billowing skirts; instead, she wore a loose blue button-down tucked into maroon straight-legged jeans that hugged curves her previous dresses managed to hide. Two more rings adorned the collection on her fingers, which she clasped in front of her.

Zera realized she was staring.

"Hi," she said lamely, standing.

Katherine's smile grew wider. "Hi. You knew where to find me this time."

"Yeah, uh, the internet. It's a beautiful thing." Her mouth was so dry, and the Dallas humidity stole whatever moisture she had left.

"Ahem," Kissi said.

"Ah! Sorry. Kat, this is Kissi—Camila Kissinger, my best friend."

Katherine gave Kissi a brilliant smile and held out a hand for a normal shake, as opposed to knuckles first. "I've heard a lot about you," she said.

"Same," Kissi replied. "Whatever she said, it was a lie."

Katherine laughed. "Well, I'm sure whatever she told you about me was the truth."

Katherine gave Zera one of those conspiratory looks, like they were sharing an inside joke. It made her chest squeeze.

"I'm going to go get the poles," Kissi announced.

"Oh, I can help—"

"Please God, no." She gestured between the two of them. "Get your reunion out of the way so we can maybe get some work done."

Katherine laughed again, waving as Kissi turned on her heel and strode off, ignoring any of Zera's protests.

"Oh, I like her," Katherine said.

"She's alright," Zera replied. She cleared her throat, where her heart was suddenly lodged. "Look, about how we left things—"

"No, me first," Katherine said, reaching out to rest her hand on Zera's forearm. "I owe you an apology."

"Me? For what?"

"I was not in a good place last time we met." The words flowed so easily, like she practiced them a thousand times in the past twelve years. "It wasn't kind of me to take that out on you."

"I could've been gentler," Zera said.

"You did the right thing," Katherine said. "After the past few years, I understand why you said no."

"You're not an easy person to say no to, for the record," Zera said.

"Oh, I know," she said. "Nevertheless, I'm sorry."

"Yeah, yeah, apology accepted." Zera paused. "How did you know I was out here?"

"I was out having a smoke," Katherine said, nodding toward a corner where a circle of people in lab coats congregated, the air above them as hazy as a campfire.

Zera grimaced. "People still do that?"

Katherine laughed. "You know, they used to say cigarettes were good for you. Then, by the time they figured out otherwise, everyone was hooked."

"Aren't you a doctor still? Shouldn't you set a good example, even if they can't kill you?"

"I mostly work in research now. Turns out, you can help solve a few problems when you have more time than most."

"Look at you, making a difference." Zera tried to smile, but it fell flat. "As for your predicament...I wasn't able to figure anything out with your blood. I'm sorry."

Katherine shrugged. "I can't say I'm surprised. I've got access to a lot of technology and I can't figure it out either."

"To be fair, mine is a little more advanced."

"I do what I can with what I have," she said. "I've got another few hours before I can leave, but I can give you my keys and directions to the house."

A pain shot through Zera's chest. "You don't have to, not after—"

"I know how it looks when you leave on purpose, and I'm sure you'll tell me all about it tonight. Do you want to go to the house or not?"

"Depends who's waiting for me there," Zera said. "Any spouses? Or a hundred other women?"

"Nope, no one," she said with a laugh. "I've done very well financially, since I've had so many years to accrue interest. Have a nice little townhome all to myself." She dug into her purse and pulled out a ring of keys, taking a moment to unhook two and hand them over. "Here, for the car and the front door."

"Thank you, Kat." It all felt too easy, like most things with Katherine. "I appreciate it. Really."

Katherine waved the words away. "This is how it goes, right? You show up at random, I feed and clothe and house you, and we have a little bit of adventure."

"That's a good way to look at it."

"It's the only way I can keep myself from going crazy. Wait, this isn't the first time, is it?"

"No, it's not."

Katherine huffed. "I'll figure it out one of these days."

Zera hoped she didn't.

Once the poles rested in the back of Katherine's car instead of behind the dumpster, Zera and Kissi made the two-mile drive to her home. The house had a small footprint and two stories, the paneling on the outside painted a beautiful shade of blue already fading thanks to the aggressive Texas sun. Air conditioning greeted her when she unlocked the door, a marvelous invention.

In the quiet of the empty house, reality seeped back into Zera's consciousness. They were officially here against orders. Before, breaking protocol meant taking a few extra minutes on a dig, or leaving her fatigues on the floor instead of in the closet. Now, it was taking an unsanctioned visit back in time.

If she was going to go, might as well go all out.

She and Kissi raided the kitchen for lunch, the old-fashioned refrigerator and stove making her feel like she was on the set of one of those old sitcoms. Limited to mess hall food for the duration of her adulthood, she didn't know how to use the stove, but there were the right fixings to whip up a turkey sandwich, a dish definitely in her wheelhouse. The deli meats were practically a delicacy.

During past trips, this would be the time for her to sleep off the effects of the river, but the stress of the situation kept her wide awake, even if her vision and brain felt hazy. She thought the afternoon sun would be too strong, but upon stepping out—per Kissi's request—they found something great and wonderful, something she never thought she'd see again.

A swimming pool.

Abandoning all decorum, they stripped to their skivvies. With no hesitation, Zera launched herself from the edge, pulling her knees to her chest as gravity brought her back down. Kissi rapidly doffed her prosthesis, then slid in after her. The initial splash of cold water sent a shock through Zera and took the breath from her lungs, but she couldn't find it in herself to care as the sweet water covered her. Chlorine made her eyes sting as she opened them, the blurry ocean-blue world leaving her with long-lost memories and an ache in her throat.

When her lungs burned, she pushed to the surface, and the heat of the day kissed her cheeks once more. The muscles of her legs threatened to sink her until she remembered how to hold the residual air and float on her back. Her skin burned from the sun—she'd likely be as pink as a grapefruit later. It was definitely worth it.

"You two having fun?"

Zera sputtered and splashed as the muffled words reached her through the water. When she and the water calmed, she spotted Katherine standing by the edge, swimsuit on and a pile of towels next to her. Zera coughed out the last of the pool water and thanked the gods for both bikinis and Kissi's sharp mind.

"Sorry, we probably should've asked first. It's just been a long time since we've seen one of these." She treaded water, neither looking apologetic nor distracted by Katherine's long, tanned legs and low-cut swim top.

"Oh, don't worry about it, that's what it's here for." She dropped the towels to the side and jumped in after them, which was the most unexpected thing Zera had seen from her so far. What the hells happened in the past twelve years?

They spent the remaining daylight hours playing stupid children's pool games, Katherine humoring the fact that they hadn't seen a swimming pool in nearly two decades. It felt absolutely ridiculous but positively freeing, and for a couple of hours Zera forgot about the rules they were breaking, and the potential for trouble when they returned.

"Miss Zazzera, do you eat salmon?" Katherine climbed out of the pool and began toweling off.

"Yeah, I think so." Zera wasn't sure the last time she'd eaten salmon, but it sounded good in theory. She followed Katherine's lead, accepting a towel warmed by the sun.

"And you, Camila?" she asked.

Kissi swam to the edge and hoisted herself up, staying seated while she toweled off her top half and gently squeezed water from her locs.

"Sounds good to me. Would you mind if I showered real quick?"

"Of course, let me show you to it."

Kissi got up and dried off her lower half, accepting Katherine's hand as she left her prosthesis behind, gesturing for Zera to get it.

"I think I might have some crutches in a closet, if that would be easier for you," Katherine said.

"Thank you, that'd be great," Kissi said. As the door closed, Zera heard her ask, "You wouldn't happen to have some clarifying shampoo? Or maybe some apple cider vinegar and baking soda?"

Whether she had the items or not, Zera didn't know. She smiled after her friends, then finished drying and gathered their stuff to bring back inside. The inside was extra chilly now with her wet underclothes, a fact that she was all too aware of as Katherine came back in the room.

"I'm afraid I've only got one shower, so you'll have to wait."

"That's okay, I'm patient," Zera said, leaning against the counter. Katherine was still in her swimsuit, a gauzy white robe over it, and Zera was having a lot of trouble keeping her eyes on Katherine's face.

"Patient? Hmm, that makes one of us," Katherine said. "I already told the lab I wouldn't be in tomorrow, so we have plenty of time. I assume the storm is tomorrow?"

"Tomorrow morning. So, unfortunately, a short trip."

"Guess we better make the time count, then," Katherine said. She looked so intense it made Zera's breath catch. It also made her want to push Katherine against the counter and kiss her, this time for real.

Across the house, the shower cut off, the silence announcing Kissi's imminent arrival. Right, Kissi was there because they had a job to do. This wasn't a date, or a vacation, and Zera needed to remember.

But it was really, *really* difficult when Katherine was looking at her like that.

1992

"HOW CAN YOU HANDLE THIS HEAT?" Katherine asked.

"You consider this hot? This is *nice*."

Even with the evening sun beating down on them and their hubris, Zera and Kissi relished being outdoors, sporting tank tops and shorts and totally not burning to a crisp.

"I'm sweating," Katherine said, fanning herself with her hat.

"Air conditioning has made you soft." Zera pushed the tip of the pole into the ground and held it steady as the gears spiraled it deeper. Gone from its computer counterpart, it moved faster than safety standard speeds.

Kissi grinned. "Zera said you were a tough old bird."

"I didn't call you old!" Zera said quickly. "Or a bird, for that matter."

"I see how it is, Miss Zazzera," Katherine sighed. "I speak of you with fondness, and in return you insult me behind my back."

"Now, Kat, c'mon. You know I'd insult you to your face."

"Oh my God," Kissi muttered, not looking up from her handheld as she configured her home-brew program.

"You know, this would go a lot faster if you guys helped by starting the other ones." The pole shifted when it hit a rock, and Zera grunted as she corrected it. "Just saying. It's not my fault the storm happened during the day this time."

"I'm learning, hush," Katherine said from next to Kissi. Big sunglasses and a floppy hat made her look like some kind of bug as she analyzed the handheld control device for the poles.

"It's not gonna tell you anything, it's just there to collect data." A crunch and grind announced the pole's official placement. "Come on, hand me another one."

"I'm busy." Katherine said. Kissi gave her the handheld and pointed something out. Katherine's thumb moved awkwardly, not used to a touchscreen. "Plus, I like to watch you lift heavy things."

"Jesus Christ," Zera muttered. Dark lenses hid Katherine's eyes, but Zera could feel her gaze as she got the next pole and measured its proper position. "You talk to all the girls like that?"

"Oh, no, only you. I've been staying out of trouble the past few years, just so you know."

"You've been a good girl," Zera said, because joking was the only way to respond.

"I wouldn't go that far." Katherine paused her assessment of the device long enough to grin.

"Get a room," Kissi groaned.

Gears grinding covered the sound of Zera's snort, and she shook her head. "Would if I could," she said under her breath.

Bored with the device, Katherine wandered over and started analyzing the screen on the pole. An analog diagram kept track of the drilling depth, and Zera worked to keep her eyes on it and not on the nice deep V of Katherine's denim romper. Flirting was harmless while she worked, right?

Less than twenty-four hours, and she already had to remind herself of her purpose, despite the severity of the situation.

"So Camila rigged these to..." Katherine tapped the screens with confidence now, seeing how they communicated. If Zera did find a way to take her back to their time, she'd fit right in.

"They're gonna read what's going on below the surface. At least, that's how it was explained to me. I have a feeling there's a lot more scientific thought that went into it."

"Hmm, good move."

"Have you made any headway working at the lab?" Zera knew the answer, but asked to be polite, and to hear Katherine talk.

Katherine huffed. "No. Any abnormality I find in my system is something already found and categorized before. The answer's probably woven into my DNA at this point."

"You can't just check your genetics?"

"I didn't make it onto the Human Genome Project." Katherine helped with the last pole, even if it didn't need the strength of two people.

"You ever miss the clinic?"

"No. I liked helping people, but I've got to keep a low profile. The wolves are still hunting me, and I'm no closer to finding my enemy than twelve years ago."

"Uh," Zera stopped the drill. "Your name and picture are totally on the staff list at the lab."

"Just my name," Katherine corrected, but Zera noticed the way she straightened, and her grip on the pole. "They said it would be just my name."

"Kissi and I saw a picture," Zera said. "That's how I knew exactly where to find you."

"Shit." Katherine dropped her hands to her hips and started pacing. "Shit, shit, *shit*."

"Hey, it's okay," Zera said. She checked to make sure the pole wouldn't be damaged if she stopped partway, then followed Katherine. "We only found you because we have reverse image search. Whoever you think is following you doesn't have that, they just have...I don't know, a phone book?"

"Right, you're right." Katherine put her hands on her head then, taking in measured breaths. "You have better resources, that's why you could find me."

"Exactly."

She sighed, and the sigh turned into a groan. "I thought I had more time. *Shit*."

"Such foul language."

"Oh, hush," Katherine snapped. Zera held her hands up. Kissi watched them from afar, the handheld forgotten in her grasp.

"Sorry," Katherine said with a gentle touch to her arm. "You didn't deserve that. I apologize."

"It's okay, just remember I'm here to help you." Zera returned to the pole, to her mission, leaving Katherine to brood a few feet away. As Zera started drilling again, Katherine stood with her arms crossed, her face turned to the Dallas skyline. The drill bit into the earth and Zera was glad for the noise and the physical exertion needed to steady the thing; it gave her something to focus on besides her hurt feelings.

But soon the pole was in place, and she had nothing to distract her. Discomfort hung thick in the humid air, and Zera forced herself to unclench her jaw so she could speak.

"Okay, it's ready. You wanna see how this thing works?"

Katherine stiffened at the direct question, and despite the sunglasses and subtle movements, Zera saw her suspiciously wipe the area beneath her eyes. Her frustration dissipated.

"C'mon, Kat, it's not—"

"I'm fine," Katherine interrupted, and if Zera hadn't been so familiar with her formal voice, she might've missed the slight thickness to it. "Please, instruct me in this machinery."

"Do you always resort to that princess talk when you're mad?"

"No, Miss Zazzera, I reserve this specifically for you. Now show me this machine, please."

"Tell me what you're really thinking instead."

The lenses of Katherine's glasses hid her eyes and reflected a bug's eye view of Zera's face, but even so she could feel the force of her glare.

"I'd rather not."

"So you have to move, it's fine. I moved all the time as a kid. At least you get to see different parts of the country." Zera put her hands on her hips, which made her feel like her mom, who did the same thing when Zera tried to hold a pity party.

"At least I—?" Katherine turned so sharply it sent her hat flying off, and she didn't bother to retrieve it. Kissi silently followed the hat, a firm *oh shit* look on her face. A second later Katherine ripped the glasses from her face so Zera could see the full intensity in her eyes. "Do you think I do this for fun, Miss Zazzera? This may be some grand adventure for you, but this is my way of life. This is the way it's been for over a hundred years."

"Yeah, and—"

"Don't"—Katherine held up a hand—"interrupt me."

A defensive wave built in Zera's chest. It simmered behind her sternum and she let it steep like the toxic coffee Katherine brewed. With a sarcastic wave of her hand, she gestured for her to continue.

"Every eight to ten years, I have to uproot my entire life, leave behind everyone and everything, and go somewhere no one knows me—to start completely over," Katherine said. Her words were too clear and concise to be improvised; this had to be something she thought over and over, day after day. "I have to rebuild everything. I have no friends. No family. Everyone I love dies. And to top it all off, I have to watch for whoever might be chasing me.

"So no, this is not *fun*. I see the country because I'm forced to. You, Miss Zazzera, are the only constant I have in my long, painful life. The only thing I have to look forward to anymore."

Zera's breath caught. Katherine's words made sense, and the heat of chagrin burned her more than the summer sun ever could. Naivety and perspective combined to make her feel like a proper asshole.

Katherine was still tired of living, and Zera needed to stop expecting that to change.

"You're right. I'm sorry." She dropped her hands.

"Thank you," Katherine said. Her chest rose and fell as she breathed too fast. Those words had circled in her head for years, probably decades, and she'd finally gotten to let them out.

"If you want..." Zera struggled for something to say, for any way to make her feel better, "We can help you move?"

Katherine stared at her, the gentle breeze lifting her beautiful waves and making stray hairs stick to her lipstick. She didn't notice, or more likely, she didn't care.

Katherine shook her head and let out a croak of a laugh. "I guess that's the best you can offer in your situation. It's not like you can stay."

"No, I can't stay." Zera didn't think about how nice that sounded. "But you can rest easy knowing you'll see me again at some point in the future."

"What a treasure."

"I know. You're welcome. Now c'mon, let's do some good old-fashioned science."

"Ah, there's a joke in there somewhere, but I can't find it," Katherine said. Kissi chose that moment to return, and wordlessly handed Katherine her hat.

"Of course not, you're not funny," Zera replied. Out of the corner of her eye she saw Katherine's jaw drop and Kissi's eyes roll, and made an effort to keep her expression blank.

"I beg your pardon?" Katherine said darkly.

"You heard me."

Katherine took in a deep breath. "You are such a—a—"

"A what? C'mon, Kat, spit it out."

"You try shuffling through decades of insults just to find one scathing enough for your purposes," she huffed.

"Now you're just stalling."

"Oh, how I loathe you."

"You missed me."

"Okay, seriously?" Kissi cut in. "Is this what it's like? You two are a mess, shit."

She pulled out the handheld and tapped away, ignoring Katherine as she leaned against her shoulder to see the screen. Kissi grumbled to herself, the complaints too low for Zera to make out, but Katherine was clearly holding in a laugh.

"There. God, let's get this over with."

The handheld dinged, and the green lights on the tops of the poles turned on, barely visible in the bright sunlight. Light pulsed on the screen and Kissi tapped it before going through the settings as Lieb described. The mechanisms hummed as they collected readings from beneath the earth, going deeper than the days in the Pit.

"Is it collecting the data?" Katherine asked.

"I sure as hell hope so," Kissi replied.

"Yeah, 'cause if we don't get something good, this may be the last time you get to see me," Zera added.

Katherine scoffed. "Haven't had our first meeting yet, hot stuff. You can't scare me with that anymore."

Numbers flew across the screen, but Zera didn't pay attention to them. She watched the green bar at the top as it inched across, tracking their progress. If this worked, if she got the right kind of data, they might be able to get the program reopened.

Zera looked over to find Katherine scanning the numbers, rapt with attention. Her face was close enough to see the dusting of freckles across her nose, as well as a new scar at her temple. The one on her neck was now so faint she'd miss it if she didn't know where it was.

The bar reached the end, and a pretty graph popped up with different colored lines zig-zagging. It was as foreign as a hieroglyph to Zera, but Kissi's mouth fell open, and as Katherine analyzed it, her eyes went wide.

"It wasn't just solar flares," Kissi said as Katherine flipped the graph to the next part. Now every swipe seemed as easy as if she'd grown up with a touch screen. "We knew changes came from the relationship between the magnetic fields, but it's not just reacting to the flares. It's *responding*."

"Okay, great, and that means?" Their excitement was contagious, even if Zera wasn't completely sure what was going on. She did know Kissi and Katherine's sciencey friendship was pretty adorable, though.

"It means the sun isn't the only thing talking. The Earth is answering. It's putting everything in a state of flux."

"Oh shit. And if it fluctuates too far to one side?"

Katherine furrowed her brows. "Too far to one side is unlikely. The problems may lie in the higher amplitude." She began pacing, holding the tablet with one hand and gesturing with the other. "If there was a high amplitude response in a specific area, that could cause all sorts of changes."

"Like your kind of changes," Zera said. "So if we're in the right spot, we could change you back."

"I...I don't know."

This was a bad idea. Zera shouldn't have been thinking like this. If anything, she should be taking this information back to the bunker and seeing if people much smarter than her could figure out how to use it. She literally had an entire world to save.

"Do you have to leave right now? Since you have this information?"

Zera paused. No matter how long they stayed here, she would always return to one minute following her departure. In that case...

"No, I said we'd help you move. Can't go back till you do that."

"Moving? Oh, absolutely not," Kissi said. She gestured between the two of them. "I'm not lifting heavy things and then sitting in a car while you guys do whatever the hell this is."

"Oh, but Camila, the discussions we could have along the way," Katherine said.

"Katherine, you're beautiful, and the conversation would be brilliant I'm sure," Kissi said, "but this raises so many questions, and if I can't answer them in a timely manner, I may lose my mind. Plus I still remember how much moving sucks."

Katherine sighed. "You're not wrong."

"Wait, so you're gonna ditch us?" Zera asked.

"Absolutely I am," Kissi replied. "Help me get these poles, I'll take them back so you don't have to lug them along."

"But Kissi, the outside—"

"If I get this data back, we can make our outside liveable again," Kissi said. "Now, go get the poles."

Despite her inner conflict, Zera did as she was told, pulling the poles and gathering them into a nice stack. Even if she did want some alone time with Katherine, she didn't want Kissi to cut her trip short.

"You don't have to leave, I'll behave," Zera murmured as they checked the bindings.

"Oh, I'm not leaving because of you guys. I'm leaving 'cause this is the best chance we have to fix everything. Also, I hate packing." Kissi patted the poles. "Besides, technically we're getting back at the same time."

"Are you sure?"

"I'm positive." She straightened. "Katherine, it was an absolute pleasure to meet you."

"Likewise, Camila," Katherine said, enveloping her in a hug. Kissi returned it, then stepped back and produced the return syringe from her pocket.

"See you in a minute." She winked at Zera, then plunged it into her leg. Zera expected her to dissolve, or perhaps blink from existence, but instead her body seemed to fold in on itself like a force pulling it through a keyhole, with limbs and organs swirling and breaking to fit through.

Zera put a hand to her stomach. "That's what it looked like this whole time?"

Katherine nodded. "You get used to it after a while. C'mon, I want to get going before the traffic gets bad."

"You want—okay, yeah, sure, normal." Zera shook her head and followed Katherine back to the car. Somewhere in between Kissi's exit point and the vehicle, her shock waned, replaced with the steady nerves of a first date. Because helping her immortal friend pack and move was *totally* a normal first date.

Katherine was so efficient in her packing Zera barely had a chance to help. It would be impressive, if it wasn't a painful manifestation of her earlier words. Everything fit in a carpet bag and a suitcase, and most of it was clothing and shoes.

"What's this?" Zera asked, pointing to the wooden box from 1968. Katherine looked up from her writing desk, where she'd penned something regarding the deed to the house. The box rested next to her on the heavy wood.

"That's my keepsake box." She touched it reverently. "Every once in a while I find something worth taking with me, and it helps me remember."

"Remember what?" Zera asked.

"The good things," she said. "It's so easy to dwell on the negative, so sometimes I have to remind myself it hasn't all been bad."

Zera thought the conversation would end there, but Katherine undid the latch and opened the box. The scent of cedar filled the air, accompanied by a familiar perfume, but Zera couldn't place the memory. Trinkets filled the box; even if Katherine talked like the good things were few and far between, enough time had passed for her to amass quite the collection.

"This is pretty." Zera picked up a dried flower. Two glass panels pressed it flat, preserving the pink and purple petals. A piece of paper read *1956* in a perfect script.

"That's from the gardens back in Philadelphia," Katherine said.

"The one you took me to?"

"The very same," she said. "Even if we didn't have the most pleasant ending, I still like to remember that day."

"Me too. Remember that creepy dude in front of us in line?" Zera grinned, and Katherine let out a very ladylike snort.

"That pocketknife wasn't sharp enough for him to be mad about our shenanigans."

Zera ran her thumb over the smooth glass, tracing the vein of a flower petal. "It was a pretty good day, overall."

"I agree."

Zera poked through the contents, eventually finding a picture labeled *1958*. But instead of a photograph, it was an artistic rendering of Katherine in only an apron, a cupcake in one hand and a knife with frosting in the other, the sugary point on her tongue. The apron managed to defy gravity to hint at her shape underneath.

"Ma'am! What is this?"

"What—oh! Give that back!" Her hand shot out, but Zera was quicker, and she moved out of the way to keep admiring the picture.

"I mean, hot damn, Kat, you're an absolute bombshell."

"I am not!" Katherine nearly wrestled her for the picture, which was just fine with Zera, since she could hold her own now and Katherine was pressed against her.

"You're right, you're a fuckin' smoke show."

"Miss Zazzera!"

Zera held the picture just out of reach with one hand and crushed Katherine to her chest with the other, putting them face to face.

"Yes? You don't want me to think you're hot?"

Katherine's eyes very obviously flicked to her lips, then back up.

"Hmm. Perhaps you're right." She stopped fighting, but didn't step away. "I'm so used to keeping it a secret, I didn't think twice."

"Obviously you're not ashamed, otherwise you wouldn't have kept it. And you shouldn't be, it's gorgeous." Zera was laying it on thick now, but she didn't care. If anything, it was nice to speak the thoughts aloud.

Katherine smiled. "Thank you. It wasn't my best moment, but it was fun." She stepped away, her hands lingering on Zera's waist for just a moment. "You can keep it, if you want."

Zera felt like she hit the lottery. "Really? What about your good memories?"

"What's the point of the fun memories if you don't have someone to share them with?" She tried for a flirty grin, but Zera could see the remnants of her earlier pain there.

"Well, thank you. I'll cherish it forever." Heartache threatened to bubble up as Zera remembered 2040. Her only option was to choose hope —hope that she could somehow fix everything so Katherine didn't have to die.

Katherine closed the box with a soft thump. The cedar scent lingered for a breath until the ceiling fan dispersed it into the past.

"Come, it's time to go." Katherine scribbled one last signature, then slid the packet into a manila envelope and wrote an address in large letters across the front. A smaller envelope sat to the side, and she slipped it in as well. "Shall we?"

"We shall." Zera grabbed the bags, bumping into nearly every corner, wall, and door between the bedroom and the driveway. "Gods, you couldn't get the ones with wheels?"

"Carrying builds character."

"I've built plenty of character, thanks." Zera held out her hand for the keys to the bright red Mustang. "I'll drive the first part."

Katherine smiled and handed them over. "My knight in shining armor."

"You're so full of it. Get in the passenger's seat."

"So bossy." Katherine put her sunglasses on and slid into the car with all the glory of someone from a '90s sitcom.

"Buckle up for safety." Zera clicked her own seatbelt, but if she was honest, she didn't quite trust it.

"These weren't even present in the first cars," Katherine remarked.

"Gods you're old." Zera started the car and rolled the window down, welcoming the sweet breeze. The car was just modern enough for her to be familiar with it. "Where are we going?"

"Let's just continue south, I guess." Katherine waved in the direction of the highway, and Zera pulled out of the driveway. "It feels easier."

ONCE, in a movie, Zera remembered a man mentioning sunsets were the best in Texas. At the time, Texas was a weird, far-away place where people rode horses everywhere and talked with a drawl. Those ideas certainly weren't true, but the man might've been onto something when it came to the sunsets.

This sunset had the aid of an aurora, but even with the strange colors, the wide open space made it all bigger and brighter. When the sun was halfway past the horizon, Zera pulled the car over and got out, moving to sit on the side of the trunk.

"What are you doing? Are you okay?" Katherine asked. She glanced over Zera's body checking for injuries, but Zera grinned and nodded toward the spectacle.

"Just looked cool. Wanted to stop and watch it."

"Uh..." Katherine glanced between her and the sunset before leaning against the car. "Okay. I guess we can do that."

"Don't be too excited."

"It's a sunset," she said. "Just with different colors."

"You know how you got mad at me for not understanding how painful it is to move every few years?" Zera asked. She wasn't upset, at least not enough to look away from the sun. It burned her eyes a little, that was why they were watering. Definitely.

"Yes?" There was an undercurrent of suspicion in the single word.

"Apart from when I've come to see you, I haven't seen the sun in almost twenty years." The metal of the car was hot underneath her, and she shifted to collect the heat on a different part of her legs. "So when I see a pretty sunset, I gotta stop and watch it."

Katherine paused, blinked, took a breath. "Got it." She joined Zera on the trunk, sitting close enough for their thighs to touch. "It is kind of romantic, I suppose."

"You've been married a hundred times, you've probably watched a thousand sunsets with someone." Zera meant it as a joke, but it came out sounding jealous. Whether she was jealous of the sunsets or the partners, she wasn't sure.

"There's a distinct lack of romance in many of my marriages," Katherine murmured, leaning her head on Zera's shoulder. "At this point it's more of a convenience. I actually just ended a marriage a few months ago, and the quiet is starting to get to me. I'm glad you showed up when you did."

"Why not just live with someone you..." She didn't want to make insinuations about Katherine and her preferences. It could be that she flirted with Zera because their time together always had a finite end.

"Because I'm lonely, Miss Zazzera. One night stands can be nice when there's needs to be met, but in a life where I've seen so much change, it's good to have something constant to come home to. Does that make sense?"

"Don't know, I stopped listening after you admitted to one night stands," Zera said, earning a smack to her leg. "I'm kidding, I'm kidding. It does make sense. And even if you've seen a shit ton of cool stuff, I'm sorry that you've been alone for a lot of it."

Katherine shrugged, her shoulder rubbing against Zera's. "Tell me, do things get easier in the future?"

"In what ways?"

"For people...like us," Katherine said. "I already have to hide so much, I just—"

"It does." Zera took her hand and squeezed it. "It takes a while, and there's always a little trouble, but it gets easier. You're already doing it right, surrounding yourself with people who won't judge you."

"The sixties were good for that." Katherine laughed and snuggled into Zera's side, still holding her hand. "You would've loved it. You think the eighties were crazy? They were nothing."

"So that *was* you at Woodstock?" She knew the answer, but she wanted the admission.

"Yes! That poor farm, no one cleaned up their mess afterwards."

"I don't think anyone else there was as polite as you."

"You're probably right."

Zera tore her gaze from the multicolored horizon to look down. The sun sparkled in Katherine's eyes and painted her skin a warm gold. Without thinking, Zera leaned over and pressed a kiss to the top of her head. Katherine stiffened for a moment, then relaxed against her again, accepting the affection.

"You're one of a kind, I hope you know that," Zera whispered into her hair.

Katherine squeezed her hand again and let out a shaky sigh, but kept her eyes on the distance. "You're missing the sunset," she whispered.

"I can still see it." It strained her eyes to look so far to the side, but she managed. The sky was painted in reds and blues and oranges, with a bright white line between the sun and the dancing aurora. Over the barren flatlands, the colors stretched forever. Zera wished they could stay here, trapped in this little moment, for a long, long time.

They stayed on the trunk until the sun fully descended and the only light they had was the car and the aurora. Katherine hopped off, the crunch of the gravel blending with the crickets.

"We've still got a long way to go," she said, laying a hand on Zera's knee.

Zera chose to lie back against the trunk and soak in the pleasant warmth of the metal. "Or we could just stay here, spend a night under the stars."

"Staying on the side of the road isn't ideal," Katherine said. "And I'm too old to sleep in a car."

"You're too old for a lot of things." A ripple went through the aurora as the last of it faded, and a second later a warm breeze followed.

Katherine popped Zera's knee with her fingertips. "Respect your elders."

"Never," she said. "C'mon, just for a minute."

"We can't stay still for too long." Katherine pushed her hips between Zera's knees and reached to grab her upper arms. "Let's go."

"Or, consider this," Zera said, going full rag doll. "Let's stay."

"Miss Zazzera." Katherine pulled harder.

"Miss—what's your last name again?" She resisted more.

"McCall. Now, stop with this childishness." She pulled again.

"Ugh, okay, fine," Zera said, sitting up. "Ruin all my fun—"

Katherine was close. Very close. Much closer than Zera anticipated. Close enough that their noses brushed and Katherine's hair tickled her cheek and she could see the reflection of the stars in her eyes. Rough denim from Katherine's shorts scratched the inside of her thighs, especially when she shifted close enough for their chests to touch.

Zera swallowed. "This is a bad idea."

"Is it?" Katherine whispered.

"This could be the last time I see you." Lie.

"It's like you're trying to make my point for me."

This would hurt both of them, Zera thought. But as she looked between Katherine's tender gaze and her perfect lips, the gravity lessened. Last time they were in this position, Katherine made the first move, and was rough and anxious about it. This time she stood with cool confidence and waited for Zera to decide.

And really, was it even a decision at all?

Zera placed her hand against Katherine's cheek, running her thumb over her freckles and the thin scar under her eye before pushing her fingers into her soft hair. She leaned in a fraction to meet her lips with a tender kiss, pushing fully a moment later.

Katherine accepted her kiss readily, but there wasn't the same frenzy as back in her bedroom in 1980. She moved her lips against Zera's with purpose, neither hesitant nor rushed, a burn slowly building, and Zera did the best she could to keep up.

It had been a long time since she'd been kissed like this, with feeling, and the sensation was intoxicating. Katherine's hands settled on her hips and she drew her close with surprising strength, their bodies now flush. Heat that had nothing to do with their current location pooled behind

Zera's sternum, and she couldn't get close enough. Sharp hip bones dug into her thighs as she squeezed Katherine closer, locking her against her.

"You've been practicing," Zera muttered during a brief reprieve.

"A girl has needs," Katherine said, leaning to kiss her again.

Zera balked. "Is that all this is? Meeting a need?" She ignored the weird ache the words caused. "Just want to be sure we're on the same page about this."

"Well, that's entirely up to you, Miss Zazzera," she murmured against her lips.

"What if I never see you again?"

"Then we'll have a night to remember."

"And if I do?"

"Then we'll make more memories," she said with a smile.

Zera turned her head and exhaled sharply. "You've got an answer for everything, huh?"

"A hundred years of answers." Katherine nuzzled her neck, then placed a soft kiss just below her jaw. Shivers traveled down Zera's spine, and with them her resolve crumbled.

"Guess I'm out of arguments then," she said, and kissed her again.

Zera slid off the car, her body pressing against Katherine the entire way down. With one smooth move, she spun so Katherine was against the back door, her legs bracketing one of Zera's as she deepened the kiss further. Nighttime nature sounds orchestrated the soundtrack to their kisses, and the aurora created a psychedelic ambiance fitting for the nineties. Zera felt like she was trapped in a magic bubble where there were no worries, just her and Katherine.

She put her arm around Katherine's waist and pulled her close, raising her just enough to open the car door. She was very close to knocking her head against the frame as they clambered into the back seat, but Katherine's kisses and wandering hands made her forget the danger.

Once the door was shut, they had nothing but the sounds of their breaths and rustling clothes to accompany the kisses. Being shorter, it was easy for Zera to climb onto Katherine's lap, her knees on either side of her hips. It was already hot in the car, making the tiny hairs at the nape of Katherine's neck stick to her skin as condensation started on the windows.

"Still think this is a bad idea?" Katherine asked, pulling back just enough for them to make eye contact. With their position, they were now the same height.

"Yes." Zera dipped her head down and pressed her mouth to Katherine's neck, trailing kisses from her jaw until she found her pulse. It fluttered beneath her lips, a sign to continue. Katherine's hands slid over her legs and hips, and her fingers tightened when Zera kissed a particularly sensitive spot where her neck and shoulder met.

"For the record," Katherine said, her breath hitching as Zera lightly nipped her skin, "I think it's a good idea."

Zera paused and moved so she could look her in the eye. "You act like I've never been okay with a bad decision before."

"Well then..." She grinned. "Carry on."

Katherine's hands went to Zera's ribs, and she pulled her flush against her chest, the leather underneath squeaking and groaning. Zera's knees dug into the back of the seat. It hurt a little, but it was worth the pain to feel Katherine's heartbeat against her own and the warmth of her skin beneath her hands.

Their kisses were feverish now, and Zera moved just enough to snake her hands between them and give Katherine's chest a gentle squeeze. Katherine inhaled deeply, pushing further into Zera's hands, and then sighed into the kiss. Her denim romper would make things difficult, but Zera had dealt with worse before.

Pearl snaps were, quite possibly, the best thing to happen in the button world. The first one pried loose under gentle pressure, bringing her one step closer to freeing Katherine from all the offensive clothing. She slowly loosened the second, and the third, until her fingertips brushed the edge of the lacy number underneath. Katherine wriggled beneath her in an effort to hurry her movements, which was an entire sensation in itself. Of course, this did nothing except encourage Zera to take her sweet time.

But Katherine wasn't hesitant anymore. She waged her own form of warfare, her thumbs brushing beneath the hem of Zera's shorts toward her inner thighs with a teasing pressure that made it difficult to remember why she needed to go slow.

The last few buttons gave way, leaving the front of Katherine's romper open to her navel and allowing her to maneuver out of it. Her bra was definitely vintage, but lace was lace, and Zera always found lace sexy, especially when it strained with every breath Katherine took.

"Is this what passes for lingerie nowadays?" She dipped her fingers just under the edge of the cup, and goosebumps erupted across Katherine's chest.

"It's not my sexiest pair, but it'll do."

Zera raised her eyebrows. "'Pair'? You planned for this?"

"I hoped for this."

With renewed fervor, Zera kissed her again, gently touching Katherine around and over her bra without actually taking it off. Seemingly displeased with the imbalance, Katherine grabbed the hem of Zera's shirt and pulled it over her head. She discarded it into the front seat, then made quick work of the sports bra underneath.

There was a time in Zera's life when she might've felt uncomfortable being topless with a girl for the first time. Her athletic build left much to be desired in the cleavage department, which usually led to a few awkward laughs and ample distractions. But the way Katherine looked at her made all those insecurities fade.

"What's this?" Katherine asked, touching the ring on the chain around Zera's neck.

Since it was the ring a dying Katherine gave her fifty years from now, Zera didn't want to think about it. Was she wearing it now? "Another time," she said. She thought Katherine would fight it, but she only nodded. When Katherine leaned forward to taste the soft skin in front of her, Zera forgot the ring completely.

For a brief moment, she let herself soak in the sensations. It had been a long time since her last encounter of this nature, and her body shivered like it was her first time all over again, only now she didn't have questions every step of the way. It quickly became obvious Katherine had been practicing more than just her kissing in the past few years, and Zera was very, very glad for it.

"Okay, wait, my turn," she said, pulling away. Katherine's lips disengaged with a soft *pop* that sent a shudder through Zera's abdomen. She chose to ignore it, despite the way the warm air felt on her now wet skin, and slid her hands up Katherine's sides, and her ribs, and eventually to the back, her hands finding the clasp as she kissed her again.

A pull and a twist was all it took to unhook it, and just like that the lacy garment dropped and joined Zera's clothes somewhere in the realm of the front seat. Katherine sat naked to the waist except for a single diamond ring on a chain that lay in the valley of her chest, mirroring Zera's gold band. Zera made a mental note to ask about it later, because her attention was very much needed elsewhere.

"You remember shoving these in my face with that corset back in the day?" Zera's mouth had gone dry and she nearly choked on the words.

Katherine gave her an evil smirk. "Me? I would do no such thing."

"Perhaps not a thousand years ago, but definitely now." Zera moved her hands and teased the most sensitive areas with her thumbs.

Katherine arched into the touch and let out a low whine. "What did you say about it being your turn?" she reminded, licking her lips.

"Ah, right, my bad," Zera said, and dropped her head.

Zera was used to being quiet with her partners since the bunker had such thin walls, but Katherine had no such worries. Every kiss, every touch, earned a little sigh or gasp or hum of approval. Perhaps she just wanted to bolster Zera's confidence. Or perhaps she was just as happy to be here as Zera was.

It was probably the best bad idea she ever had, right up until red and blue lights flashed through the steamy windows.

"Oh shit." Zera pulled back quickly and looked to Katherine, whose startled expression matched her own. "How illegal is homosexuality nowadays?"

"Still pretty illegal," Katherine said.

The world stopped for a second. "Shit!"

Zera scrambled off Katherine's lap and dove into the front seat. The flashing lights made it extra difficult to locate her clothing and even more difficult to find the right way to put them on. Katherine abandoned her bra entirely and snapped up the front of her jumpsuit, giving her more time to fix her face. Her hair was an absolute mess and her red lipstick was smeared far beyond the bounds of her lips. Even in the dim light, Zera could see a faint trail down her neck where her kisses had dragged the pigment.

"You can go," Katherine said.

Zera stopped, losing precious seconds in her confusion. "What?"

"Don't you have the injection that takes you back? Go, so you don't get caught."

"Absolutely not, I'm not gonna leave you."

Katherine's eyes widened, her expression raw and vulnerable just long enough for Zera to see it.

"Well then," she said, wiggling back into the driver's seat. She popped open the glove compartment and whipped out a handkerchief. "We need to be quick about this."

"You just have those in there?" Zera asked.

"Of course." She threw the handkerchief at Zera's face. "Clean up. You have lipstick all over you."

"Speak for yourself."

They both scrubbed at the cherry red trails, but as easily as the makeup spread with their kisses, it was three times as hard to get off.

A knock sounded at the window. Zera jumped, but Katherine's hand dropped to the side of the seat, and Zera spotted the handle of a knife.

"Seriously?"

"Hush."

Katherine rolled down the window. The officer greeted them with a bright light straight to the face, blinding them. In the light, the lipstick stains were painfully obvious.

"Well hey there, little ladies. What're y'all doin' out this time of night?" The officer had a gruff voice and a heavy twang.

Zera fought a grimace, but Katherine put on a brilliantly fake smile. "Howdy there officer," she said in a profound drawl Zera had never heard before. "My friend and I stopped to look at the aurora, but we fell asleep. I'm afraid we're not as put together as usual." She had the perfect chagrined expression as she tucked her hair behind her ear.

The officer flashed the light from Katherine to Zera, once again burning her retinas. She put a hand up to protect her eyes, which probably didn't help her case.

"That true?" He leaned away from the car and turned his head, and the light moved just enough for Zera to see him spit tobacco onto the road.

"Yeah?" His questions made her defensive, but her answer delivered the light back to her face. After years in the military, she could tell which authority figures deserved respect, and this man did not. Katherine pinched her arm. "Ow! I mean, uh, yes, sir."

"Huh." He flicked the light back and forth between them. "I'll be honest, it rather seems we've caught you in a compromising position."

It was then Zera noticed the deputy behind him, a young buck who looked just as frightened as Zera felt.

"Sir, they said—"

"Shut it, Wallace."

"We were asleep, officer," Katherine said, with way more deference than Zera could ever muster. "Honest, that's all. We've been on the road for a while, just needed a break."

The officer tapped his thumb against his sidearm, leaned back, and spat again.

"Have you been drinking tonight?"

"No sir," Katherine said.

"Any other...substances?"

"No sir."

"Anything in the car I need to be worried about?"

From Zera's point of view, the knife handle was rather obvious.

"No sir," Katherine said.

Pause. Lean. Spit.

"Why don't you ladies step out of the car right quick?"

"Are we being arrested for something?" Zera asked.

"Anythin' goin' on I should arrest you for?"

"Just get out of the car," Katherine hissed. She used the sound of the door opening to cover the noise of the knife dropping beside the seat.

"Listen to your, uh, *friend* here."

Zera gritted her teeth and followed, wishing he would make up his mind whether to charge them with indecent acts or let them go.

The aurora had faded somewhat, and the deserted highway appeared eerie and haunted. Zera was acutely aware of how alone they were with these officers, and how they had guns ready and available. Her forehead tingled as if the weapon were already trained on her.

"You sure you two haven't been drinking?"

"Positive, sir." Katherine's voice had an edge to it now. The officer raised an eyebrow and opened the back door, sweeping the flashlight across it. Now that the light was no longer blinding her, Zera could see the wad of chewing tobacco stretching his cheek.

"Hmm, that's funny," he said, leaning into the car. "What's this then?"

In his hand he held a large metal flask. Barely enough liquid remained to make a sloshing noise when he shook it.

"That...isn't mine," Katherine said.

Zera, having just been very familiar with the back seat of the car, had to agree. "Is that yours by chance, officer?" she asked.

He glared, the wad of tobacco even more apparent as he spoke through gritted teeth. "How dare you make such a claim against an officer of the law." In his vexation, his drawl added so many extra syllables the words sounded foreign. He slipped the flask into his back pocket—it seemed to fit there rather easily, Zera thought—and brought out two pairs of hand-cuffs. "Hands on the car."

"But we didn't—"

"I said"—He was seething now—"hands on the fuckin' *car*."

"Officers, please, this is just a misunderstanding," Katherine said, looking between the two men. She held up her hands in a placating gesture and somehow managed to smile. "Surely we can have a civil discussion, or maybe come to another arrangement?"

"Empty promises," he growled, putting his hand on his holster. "Hands. On. The car."

"Officer Blythe—"

"Wallace. Hush."

Zera could see Katherine sizing the men up and determining her odds. Hells, she was willing to let the woman try, considering she was sure of her survival. But this version of Katherine was missing a few scars from the version she'd met in 2040, and she didn't want to encourage more.

"C'mon." She touched Katherine's elbow and saw the officer's eyes flick down, eyeing what he no doubt saw as a tender, loving caress rather than nonverbal encouragement to *shut up and listen to the man with the gun.*

With a sigh, Katherine turned and put her hands on the car, and Zera followed suit. The officer huffed a laugh and stepped behind Zera first. She expected him to take her wrists and pull them behind her, but instead she felt his hands on her waist.

"Gotta pat you down, make sure you're not carryin' any weapons." He was too close for comfort.

"I'm not—"

"Gotta check."

He slid his hands over the back pockets of her pants, then the front. He moved slowly down her legs, and then moved on to her back and her shoulders and her chest, lingering there much longer than necessary. Zera cringed, and when she glanced at Katherine, she saw murder in her eyes.

Verbal communication was off limits, but Zera shook her head just enough for her to see. Despite the dim light, she could see the muscles in Katherine's cheek as she clenched her jaw, the way her hands shook on the car frame. This entire situation was loathsome, but it was not worth a fight. Poor Deputy Wallace watched in abject horror as the search continued.

"Guess you're clean." Blythe laughed at his own joke. The clicks of the handcuffs echoed down the lonely road as he locked them on her. "Relatively speaking."

"Told you," Zera said, because she couldn't keep her mouth shut. Without warning, she was falling toward the car, and it was only after her head smacked the side that she felt the sting of a blow to her back.

"You son of a—" Katherine turned on him, and the officer drew his gun with deadly speed.

"Hands back on the car." Gone was the laughing and the jeering.

Zera's head spun and she slid down the side of the car, the gravel underneath rough as she landed on her ass. Through dizzy eyes she saw Katherine put her arms up and turn, her hands balled into fists against the roof. Still holding the gun, Blythe proceeded to search Katherine, his touches rougher and lasting a lot longer than when he "searched" Zera. If it weren't for the handcuffs and the concussion, Zera might have tackled the man straight to the ground.

It hurt, getting to her feet. She had to use her shoulders in ways they didn't want to go, which made the action even more awkward and painful.

Blythe turned the gun her way. "You stay right there."

Zera couldn't force any words out through her rage, angrier at herself for being so helpless than with him for being disgusting.

"It's fine," Katherine said. Unspoken, Zera heard, *I've been through worse.* The idea of other people treating her this way, in worse ways, fueled the fire further.

"Damn right it is." Blythe holstered his weapon and pressed Katherine into the car with his entire body, roughly bringing her arms around to handcuff her too.

"Get off her," Zera said, moving closer.

Blythe stepped too, his fist raised in preparation. "Take one more step, I dare you."

"Miss Zazzera," Katherine whispered. Zera's breaths came short, her pulse pounding in her ears. Never in her life had she wanted to hurt someone so badly.

"Get in the car before you really screw up," Blythe said. His fingers dug into their upper arms as he dragged them back to the squad car, not taking any care when he threw them in the back. Zera's shoulder stretched painfully with the rough landing and nearly popped out of its socket when Katherine knocked into her a breath later.

"No canoodling back there, alright?" He slammed the driver's door behind him and the squad car roared to life. Wallace trembled in the front seat, looking at them through the rearview mirror.

"Wacko?" Zera asked as they pulled into the station sometime later. Katherine kicked her ankle, and she ignored her. "This town's called wacko?"

"Waco." Blythe pronounced it like *way-co*, and added a layer of disdain. Zera wondered how many times he'd gotten that question. "It's called Waco, and its police department humbly welcomes you to jail."

1992

"OKAY, I'll admit, this wasn't our best move."

At least they no longer had to deal with handcuffs. Instead, Zera and Katherine sat on a cold concrete bench with a respectable distance between them. Another woman claimed the entire other bench, lying out on it. Soft snores sounded from under her jacket, which covered her head and shoulders. A whiff of alcohol spoke of her activities earlier in the night.

The last occupant of the holding cells sat curled in the corner next to the bars, gesturing with her hands and murmuring. Every time an officer walked by, they kicked the bars, scaring her. Each time, Zera wondered if she could get to the bars fast enough to grab them and slam their heads against them, the same way the arresting officer did to her. Based on Katherine's face, she'd made similar calculations.

"You still have an easy escape," Katherine pointed out.

"Nope, it's back in the car."

"Ah, so you truly are stuck with me."

"I could think of worse things." Zera grinned, proud of the blush on Katherine's cheeks. "Kissi is gonna pitch a fit when I get back. We always thought she would be the first to get me arrested."

"This is your first arrest? How cute." Katherine reached over to pinch Zera's cheek.

Zera swatted her hand away. "You forget, I've lived in a bunker most of my life. You learn really fast to follow the rules."

"Not *everyone* learns that, though."

"Oh, yeah, but they're much braver than me. Nowhere to run, nowhere to hide." She furrowed her brows. "I wonder if this'll be weird in the future when my fingerprints come up."

"Doesn't matter," Katherine said with a shrug. "It's been a couple of decades since I've been arrested, but I don't think they share information between counties."

"They don't? Huh. No wonder there were so many serial killers."

Katherine startled. "Do you still have serial killers?"

"You'll be fine," Zera said, perhaps with a touch too much confidence.

"And what makes you so sure?"

For once, she made the right decision to stay quiet.

"Ah, that infamous first meeting, huh?" Katherine sighed. "I assume we'll get there eventually. I should probably take it as a good sign, for now."

"Don't be too confident." Zera didn't mean to say it out loud, but there it was, on the bench between them. At Katherine's intense stare, she stammered for an explanation. "I mean, Dr. Phillips said we couldn't change things, but I'm not so sure. Every once in a while, when I go back, things are...off."

"Off," Katherine repeated. She licked her lips, then nodded. "Alright, I guess I'll stay careful."

"Good, 'cause I do wanna see you again. In the future." Zera put her hand on the bench between them, but didn't touch her.

"I'd like that too," Katherine said. Her hands remained in her lap, but she moved her leg just enough so the skin brushed against Zera's pinkie. "I'd prefer it sooner than every twelve years, though."

"Trust me, if I set the dates, they'd be much closer together." Zera laughed. "Budget constraints."

"Always a problem," Katherine said. "When's the next one?"

"2004, if I can get the program reopened."

"And if you can't?"

Zera hadn't thought that far ahead. The more time she spent with

Katherine, failure became less of an option. She needed to get Vylek to reopen the program, and then...

And then what? Watch Katherine die again?

The thought, previously uncomfortable, now opened a deep ache in her chest. It was painful for her to imagine life without Katherine in it. She was too vibrant to be snuffed out.

She needed a new plan. Fuck what Phillips said—there had to be a way to change things. Maybe she wasn't thinking big enough. Maybe, in her future, she could find a way to bring Katherine back with her, and when she was old and gray and Katherine was really ready to go, she could send her back to that fateful day in Central Park.

The argument sounded weak, even in her head.

"Miss Zazzera?"

"Huh?"

One corner of Katherine's perfect kissable lips lifted in an affectionate smile. "You were going to tell me the plan, if your mission doesn't pan out."

"Oh, right, well..." She rubbed her hands on her legs, her palms suddenly sweaty. "I'm not sure, if I'm honest. I guess this would be the last time I see you. Besides the first time."

Katherine curled her lips in and dropped her eyes. "Right, besides the first time."

"I don't want it to be the last time, though," Zera said. "I'll figure out a way."

"You could always stay."

A beautiful idea, but an impossible one.

"I...I have to get back to Kissi." It was a lame excuse, but the thought of abandoning her friend to come back and live in normal times hurt worse than the idea of leaving Katherine forever. "I can't just leave her there. She's the only reason I've made it through."

Katherine's lips parted, and her eyes had a glassy sheen, as if she were on the verge of tears. Instead, she fluttered her eyelashes and smiled again. "You're a good friend, Miss Zazzera. To everyone around you."

"I told you my friends call me Zera."

"Is that what we are? Friends?" Katherine tilted her head to the side.

Zera inhaled. "We're something, that's for sure."

"Something," Katherine echoed. "Well, as I told you, I will only call you by your given name, so if you don't like it, you can tell me your first name."

"Nice segue."

"The question has been on my mind for fifty years, Miss Zazzera. I never forget."

The walls of the cell felt a little closer than they were a few moments before. "Hmph. Guess you'll have to wait a little longer."

"Miss Zazzera it is then."

Zera chuckled and leaned her head against the cool concrete wall. At this point, she no longer cared if Katherine knew her first name—she just wanted something to hold onto, something that promised a *next time*. How could the universe turn her down when Katherine didn't even know her name?

"I've never been arrested," Zera said, checking to see if their fellow criminals were paying attention. They weren't. "But it was super weird not having the whole, *anything you say can and will be held against you in a court of law* thing."

"What?" Katherine said, sitting up straight.

"The Miranda Rights? They do it in all the crime shows. Probably hasn't been invented yet—"

"They've been invented."

"What?"

"Twenty-six years ago, that went into effect. It was a big thing, but I didn't think of it because—"

"Because you're too smart to get arrested, I know."

"Well, yes," she finished. "But if that douchebag didn't read us our rights—"

"Watch that filthy mouth of yours, Miss Katherine!"

"If he didn't read us our rights, they can't detain us!"

"Wait, for real?"

The jacket on the other bench moved.

"For real," a voice groaned from beneath the leather. The woman rolled onto her side, nearly falling off the bench, then promptly resumed snoring.

"Was she talking to us?" Zera whispered.

"If she was, she was right," Katherine whispered back. She stood up, stepped to the bars, and slapped them. "Hey! Hello! I wasn't given my rights! You have to let us go!"

"Bullshit!" someone called back. Zera joined her, banging the bars even louder.

"We weren't read our rights! Let us go!"

"You got your rights, don't try and pull one over on us," Blythe said. His deputy looked between them, face pale.

"You! You, sir. Deputy Wallace." Katherine softened her voice in a well-practiced fashion. "You were there. He didn't read us our rights, remember? He was too busy feeling us up and slamming my friend into the car."

"Uh, I don't—"

"Wallace, keep your mouth shut—"

"Deputy Wallace, please, you know we're being held here for no reason," Katherine said. Her eyes were wide, pleading, and she added a tremble to her lower lip. Zera thought that was a nice touch.

"Please, Deputy Wallace. We're just trying to get back on the road. We didn't do anything wrong, but he did—"

"You two lying whores—"

"What in the Sam Hill is going on here?" A skinny man with bowed legs stumbled out of an adjoining room. If they were to believe the badge on his unbuttoned shirt, he was the sheriff, but the shirt moved too much for Zera to read the nameplate.

"Nothing, Sheriff," Blythe said, but Wallace took one last look at Katherine's pathetic doe eyes and grew a spine.

"He didn't read them their rights, sir!" he squeaked. The room went silent.

"What?" the Sheriff said. Blythe's face turned red, then purple.

"Wallace, you son of a—"

"Blythe, I swear to all things holy," the Sheriff said, pinching the bridge of his nose. "One thing. You gotta do *one thing* when making an arrest nowadays."

"But I caught them—*you know.*" Blythe made some awkward gestures, apparently implying romance. It didn't work.

"My office. Now."

Blythe muttered a few choice words as he went into the back room. Zera held onto the elation, even as angry yells sounded through the door.

A minute later, Blythe stomped out of the office and the station, throwing a couple of derogatory names their way for good measure. It took every ounce of self control in Zera not to flip him off as he left, but luckily the woman in the corner did it for her, singing a song in another language. Zera didn't need to know the language to understand.

The Sheriff walked over, the leather soles of his boots echoing in the quiet station. Up close, she could see the name badge and smell the alcohol he'd been drinking in his office

"Thank you, Sheriff Banks," Katherine said in a saccharine tone.

He looked at her from under his eyebrows, unimpressed. "You can quit the act, miss." He thumbed through the keys on a carabiner hooked to his belt loop. "Wallace is the newbie around here, not me."

"Isn't an act, sir."

"If that were true, I'd eat my own hat." He found the key he was looking for and stuck it in the lock. The iron squealed as he opened it. "There ya go. Wallace'll take you back to your car."

"Well, thank you all the same," Zera said. "We still have a long way to drive tonight."

"Good luck. Don't speed, don't pick up hitchhikers, and if you see a woman in a white dress, just pass her on by."

"—Can you expand on that?" Zera asked, but Katherine took her elbow and dragged her toward the exit.

"No, I'm sure the Sheriff is a very busy man," she said, her voice tight in a way Zera had never heard before. "Deputy Wallace, shall we?"

"Oh, uh, yeah, let's go," Wallace stammered. Pink covered his pale cheeks and traveled to the tips of his ears.

"Excellent," she said, and led the way out.

"Thank you again—" Zera turned back to Sheriff Banks, but he was already back in his office, the door shut. He deserved either the nap or the drink he was about to have.

"Sorry, uh, we're not supposed to have passengers in the front seat," Wallace said when they got to the cruiser.

"It's alright, honey, as long as we're not in handcuffs again," Katherine said. Her smile completely disarmed the poor boy, who hurried to open the door for them.

"You're gonna kill the kid," Zera said once the door was closed. Wallace opened the front door and tried to get in, but bumped his head on the top of the car. "See?"

"Oh, it's fine. Right, Deputy Wallace?"

"Uh, yes?"

"Told you."

"Deputy Wallace, what's the deal about the woman in the white dress?"

"It's nothing," he said with a nervous laugh. "Just a story they tell to the rookies, try to freak us out."

"See? It's nothing," Katherine said.

"Is she supposed to be a ghost or something?" Zera asked.

"Yeah, but that's silly." His laugh wasn't convincing. "'Cause ghosts aren't real." He glanced at them in the rearview mirror. "Right?"

"Are you asking if we know for sure ghosts aren't real?" Zera asked. "Or just looking for us to agree?"

"Ghosts aren't real," Katherine said.

Zera looked to her, but her focus was on the land rolling by in the car window, the aurora painting it an alien greenish blue. "You said that a little too fast."

"Ghosts aren't real." This time she sent a glare in Zera's direction. "Stop scaring the poor boy."

"Why do I feel like *he's* not the scared one?" she teased.

"Miss Zazzera I swear—"

"Nothing to worry about, though," Wallace interrupted, his voice a few notes higher than before. "Even if ghosts are real, I've never seen her. Maybe *she's* afraid of *me*."

"That's the spirit, Deputy Wallace," Zera said. "Or, well, not the *actual* spirit but—"

"He gets it," Katherine snapped. Sometime during the conversation, she'd gone from joking to very serious, and Zera had missed it.

She pressed her lips together and nodded. "Right, sorry."

She chose to watch the landscape instead of facing her embarrassment. From the corner of her eye she could see Katherine facing her, but she couldn't be sure if her expression was apologetic or angry, and looking to confirm was far too great a risk.

Discomfort was the fourth passenger in the car for the rest of the ride, and Zera was glad to see the Mustang until she remembered it would be just her and Katherine in the cab with no Deputy Wallace to buffer between them.

He pulled alongside the red car. "There you go, ladies," he said, his voice cracking in the middle of the sentence. "Be safe out there, okay?"

"Thank you, Deputy." Katherine attempted to wrench the door open, but it stayed in place. "Um, Deputy Wallace, I believe we're locked in back here."

"Oh, right, sorry." He fumbled with the handle and nearly tripped over himself getting out. Katherine let go just in time for him to open the door way too hard. Zera wanted to make a joke about losing a hand if she wasn't careful, but it seemed the wrong moment. By the time Wallace freed Zera from the squad car, Katherine was already in the driver's seat.

"Thanks again, Deputy. We owe you," Zera said, her words punctuated by the closing of the car door. "Seriously."

"Oh, no problem, ma'am." He rubbed the back of his neck, and even in the low light of the night Zera could see the blush on his cheeks. Behind her, the car turned on. "Just doing my job."

"Well you're doing great," she said. There was a distinct possibility Katherine would leave her if she took any longer, so she went to the passenger side, making sure to walk in front of the car for maximum abandonment protection.

"Okay," Zera said as she collapsed into the passenger's seat. "Are you gonna tell me what that whole thing was about, or are you just gonna keep pouting?"

"I was planning on pouting for at least the first fifty miles," Katherine said. She pulled out, and they continued their trek south.

"If you don't tell me what bothered you, then I can't address it," Zera said. "That's how it works."

"It doesn't concern you."

"If it concerns you, then it concerns me."

"But it doesn't matter—"

"Yes it does!"

Katherine slammed on the brakes and they lurched to a stop. Thank the gods for seatbelts, otherwise Zera would've gone right into the dash.

"Look," Zera said before Katherine had time to make her defense. "I get it, you're not used to telling people the whole truth. But I'm literally the one person you don't have to lie to, and if you don't want to talk about something, just say that instead of shutting me down and copping an attitude."

Katherine stared hard and took a deep breath. Then she took another, and a third for good measure. "You're right. I'm sorry," she said softly. "I think sometimes I forget how to act human."

"You don't have to act human, you *are* human."

"I'm not sure sometimes," she said. She closed her eyes and resumed her deep breathing routine, and Zera reached out to take her hand. Katherine interlaced their fingers. "Freak. Abomination. Demon. Witch. I've been called a lot of things over the years."

"And you're also a beautiful, intelligent, resourceful smart ass. Don't forget those too," Zera said with a smile.

Katherine gave her a watery grin. "I'm focusing on the negative again, huh?"

"It's not your best habit."

"Thank you," she said. Zera's grin widened.

"So are you gonna tell me why ghosts freak you out so much?"

Katherine sighed and started to drive again. "Because I know so many people who've died, and most I don't want to see again."

"Oh. Is there anyone you'd *want* to talk to again?"

"A few," Katherine said. "My mother, for one. And my sisters."

The way she talked before, Zera expected her to say no one, and say it emphatically. But this answer came quickly.

"How many sisters did you have?"

"Four, and two brothers," she said. Zera choked, which made Katherine laugh. "It was a different time. The seven of us were the ones who lived."

"Jesus, Odin, and Zeus," Zera said. "I can't imagine having that many siblings, even before the Storm."

"Do you not have any?" Katherine's jaw dropped.

"Not a single one. Shocking, I know."

"As much of a handful as you are, I'm not surprised," Katherine said. "You must have run your mother ragged."

"Kind of." The lines of the road helped soothe her, despite the sadness of her memory. "I don't remember a whole lot. I was thirteen when the world went to shit, and she didn't make it long after."

"Oh, I'm sorry." Katherine sounded sincere, which was more than most people could manage. Sympathy was hard to come by in a world where everyone lost someone. "That's terrible."

"How old were you? The last time you saw your mom?" Zera asked, eager to shift attention back to Katherine. Surviving helped keep the emotions at bay for this long, she could beat them back for a little longer.

"Oh, well..." Katherine paused to think. "I believe I was technically thirty-eight. I went back home after"—she gestured at the sky—"but after a few years, I noticed everyone else was changing, and I wasn't."

"Did it hurt? When you...changed?" Zera asked.

"Not really," Katherine said. "Or rather, there was so much else going on at the time, I didn't notice anything else. We were at the Arctic Circle on an expedition, and there was an explosion. We were all either dead or injured, our priority was getting back home alive."

"You were just casually exploring the Arctic Circle. Okay, sure."

"It was my first husband's expedition," she said, her gaze somewhere in the distance. "He was beside himself with excitement. Got to handpick the team and everything, and since I was his wife...well, I wouldn't go so far as to say the men respected me, but they didn't harass me. I still remember the look on his face the first time we saw the lights."

"Sounds magical."

"I hated every second of it."

Zera snorted, but the laughter died in her throat when she saw Katherine's face.

"The whole thing was miserable," she explained, her voice thick. "But it was for him. I did it all for him, but the explosion was next to him, and he..." She angrily brushed one tear from her cheek. "We couldn't even carry his body back, it would've been too hard."

"I'm sorry, Kat."

Katherine swallowed and nodded. "Thank you. I'm sorry, I'm afraid I've completely derailed the conversation."

"That's okay. How many times have you been able to tell that story?"

"This was the second time," she said, and squeezed her hand. "Thank you for listening."

"Sure, no problem," Zera said, warmth blooming in her chest.

"Would you like to talk about your mother?" Katherine asked. "I'd love to hear about her."

"Maybe another time," Zera said. After Katherine's vulnerability, she needed to be strong, solid.

"I'll hold you to that."

"I bet you will," Zera said. They drove in silence for a while longer, then Katherine broke it.

"You have to leave soon, don't you?" It was phrased as a question, but didn't sound like one.

Zera sighed. "Technically, the sooner I leave, the sooner I get back to you."

"From your perspective, yes," Katherine said, and it was impressive how she managed not to sound bitter. "And that's assuming your trick with the sticks worked."

"True." Zera hadn't thought of that. "I'll at least stay until you find a new apartment. Then, once you're settled, I'll go."

Zera could feel her hand sweating, but she didn't want to let go of Katherine. Not yet.

Katherine pressed her lips together, then brought Zera's hand up to lay a kiss to the back of her palm. The tender gesture made her heart hurt. "It's okay, Miss Zazzera. I'll be alright. Besides, I know I see you at least one more time, right?"

"At least one more." The ache shifted from her heart to the back of her throat as she thought of that stupid first meeting. First for her, last for Katherine.

"I'll come back. No matter what, I'll come back. If they reopen the program, we'll have that, and if not, I'll convince Kissi to come with me and we'll join you here."

"Please, Miss Zazzera," she whispered. "Please don't make promises you can't keep."

"I..." Zera paused. "I'll do my best."

Katherine smiled weakly. "That's all I can ask."

There was nothing left to do but drive away into the night.

2058

Zera dry heaved and choked as she landed back on the platform. Kissi was right next to her, gasping. Moments later, the lights flashed off and darkness overtook them, and she felt Kissi's weirdly strong hands under her arms. The world spun as she heaved Zera to her feet.

"Get it together." Her voice sounded far away. Zera grabbed at whatever part of her friend she could and stumbled alongside her, the cords tangling around her feet and threatening to send them both to the ground. Kissi grunted as their combined weight shifted more to her prosthetic leg, and she sounded much closer when she said, "Get up, Zazzera!"

Kissi had recovered quickly, whereas Zera wasn't certain she was completely out of the river yet. But even if she couldn't see and could barely feel, she forced her feet underneath her and stood a little taller. It occurred to her there might be a reason they pumped her full of fluids and drugs after each return. Now, they had to make do with a little bit of water and a whole lot of spirit.

The hallway outside was cooler than the machine room, or perhaps the minimal airflow felt better to Zera's feverish mind. Kissi put a hand on her lower back and pushed, forcing her further upright, but Zera's vision kept swimming and her legs threatened to give out. They tried to take a turn and she nearly lost balance as Kissi stepped wrong on her prosthetic leg, the wall catching them. It didn't stop the loud bang from echoing down the empty hall.

"We gotta move faster," Kissi panted. Zera coughed, wanting to vomit. Standing straight wasn't an option, but she could make her feet shuffle a little quicker as long as she didn't have to watch where she was going. Kissi swore, struggling to keep herself vertical as well, the effects of the travel taking their toll on both of them.

Night shift sounds greeted them as they exited the special door. They were on the home stretch now; two turns and two doors, and they'd be safe in their room to suffer in peace.

"Zera? Kissinger? You okay?"

Shit. Byrd was the last person she expected to see at this moment. Would he recognize the signs of travel sickness? Besides Vylek or Phillips, he was the worst person they could have run into.

"We're fine," Kissi said. It was impressive how calm she sounded. "One of our friends tried to make a home brew and she's not taking well to it."

The thought of bathtub gin made Zera's stomach roll, and she swallowed against the bile rising in her throat.

"Seriously? Thought you could hold your drink a little better than that," Byrd teased.

"I wish," Zera groaned.

"I gotta pour her into bed." Kissi moved to step around him, but to Zera's horror, he came to her other side and put her arm around his shoulders, his arm sneaking around her waist.

"I'll help—"

"We're fine—"

"You're both struggling." He started walking, and Zera had no choice but to follow. "Don't worry, your secret's safe with me."

Zera didn't like the way he said that.

The memory of Katherine's car was still fresh—she could still feel her soft hair in her hands, still taste the chalk of her bright red lipstick. Byrd's hands suddenly felt too close and familiar, and she longed to pull away. But if she did that, she'd probably fall to the floor and pull Kissi down with her.

They reached the barracks door and Kissi scanned them in. So close now. Byrd moved with a purpose right to their door. Had he been to their room before? Zera couldn't remember.

"Thanks for your help, I got it from here," Kissi said. She didn't unlock the door yet.

"You sure? If she's on the top bunk—"

"I got it," Kissi said, and this time Zera felt the glare which accompanied her words, even as she swayed. Zera leaned her head against the door, the surface somewhat cooler than the air.

After an age, Byrd said, "Okay. Let me know if you need anything."

"We won't."

Byrd huffed, then Zera heard his footsteps recede. Kissi waited until they heard the barracks door close before unlocking theirs.

"Still don't like him?" Zera asked.

"Not even a little."

Climbing into the bunk was rough, but after two close calls, they finally managed. Zera sipped her water with forced restraint, knowing if she guzzled it the way she wanted she'd lose it all over the floor.

"The poles are still in the room. Don't let me forget," Kissi muttered from the bottom bunk.

Zera made no promises, and sank into sleep.

***

Kissi rebounded quickly, but without medical attention, it took Zera over a week to recover. She called out every morning, her new boss in mechanics insisting she visit the infirmary, especially after day three. Zera managed to talk her out of it every time, but she needed to get her shit together, and fast.

They decided Kissi would be the one to pass on the information. After all, it would be an analyst who'd make the discovery of this data, not the traveler, and Zera needed to stay as far away from the project as possible until they were in the clear. So, with her brain covered in fog, Zera went to work in the machine shop and counted the minutes.

"What's going on in that head of yours?" Byrd asked one day at lunch. Despite Kissi's wariness of the man, Zera couldn't afford to drop him yet.

If the project reopened and his ankle healed, he'd be one of few lifelines she had during her trips.

Besides Katherine, of course.

"Huh? Oh, nothing." She gestured to her head with her fork. "Just crickets and clouds up here."

"There's a few other things, I'm sure," he said.

She shook her head. "Not much." She couldn't admit her secret, and she definitely didn't want to risk mentioning the woman taking up most of her brain space. "What about you? Anything new in the mailman world?"

"Ugh, no, it's so boring." He stabbed his potato wedge. Always dramatic, Byrd was. "I thought I'd at least hear the bunker gossip, but no such luck."

"Maybe you still have to work your way up the ranks. They can't trust you yet, you gotta earn it. Took Kissi years to make her connections."

Byrd rolled his eyes. "C'mon, everyone trusts me."

Zera snorted. "No, they don't."

"What?"

Wrong thing to say. "Nothing," Zera said, shrugging.

"No, who doesn't trust me?" he persisted.

"I don't know." She *did* know.

"You can't just say people don't trust me and then hold out on me like that."

"I don't know anyone that doesn't trust you. I just assume there's no way *everyone* can trust you. I mean, I assume there's people who don't trust me either. It's human nature or whatever."

She held his stare and her breath, waiting for the response. Red creeped from underneath his collar, telling of...what, anger? Embarrassment? Zera wasn't sure she wanted to find out.

"You'd tell me, right?" he finally said, his voice a measure cooler. "If someone said something about me?"

"Of course, we're buddies." Probably overkill, but the words seemed to assuage him. "Even if you decided to chicken out on me with our previous collaboration."

"Trust me, I'd kill to do more work on that project," he said with a laugh. "Oh well, not in the cards."

Zera looked down at her plate. The potatoes and mushrooms didn't seem appetizing anymore, and her stomach rolled at the thought of forcing them down.

"I'm done, do you want this?" she asked, sliding her plate toward Byrd.

His eyes lit up. "Don't mind if I do." Without hesitation, he grabbed her plate and added the remnants of her meal to his. "You good?"

"Yeah, just..." She waved her hand in the general direction of her head again. "Plus I gotta get back. New command isn't happy about me missing so much time."

There were no messages from Kissi on her handheld, just like thirty minutes before. She'd submitted the new data three days prior, after spending enough time scrubbing and changing timestamps and other fancy computer things. Zera doubted any other analyst was as detailed or suspicious as Kissi, and would likely take the numbers at face value, but it wasn't a bad idea to keep it clean. Three days should be enough to reopen a project, Zera thought. Wrong.

It took six more days before Zera and Kissi woke to a knock on their door at an ungodly hour. Zera heard the loud clatter of Kissi's prosthetic as she accidentally knocked it over instead of grabbing it in the dark, and she clambered out of bed to save her the trip.

"Yes—Byrd?" Zera's brief stand at attention deflated as she saw him, and she collapsed against the door. "What the fuck are you doing here? It's fucking middle of the night—"

"Did you see?"

"Why are you awake?"

"Night shift—it doesn't matter. Did you *see*?"

"Obviously not. I was *sleeping*."

"No need to be in such a bad mood," Byrd said.

"If I wasn't so tired, I'd punch you in the throat," Zera replied. "Now why the fuck did you wake us up?"

"What's going—oh. You." Kissi joined them at the door, leaning opposite Zera. "What do you want?"

"You're both going to be very grateful here in a second." He pulled out his handheld. After scrolling, he held it up, the screen bright in their sleepy eyes.

"Jesus, Odin, and Zeus," Zera muttered. She squinted through the lights and tried to make out the words. A few lines in, and she was wide awake. "They're restarting it."

"They're restarting it."

"It worked," Kissi said, and at the odd look from Byrd, she added, "I found some anomalies from Zera's last trip. I'd hoped it would be enough, but..."

Not a lie, technically.

"Day after tomorrow, we go back," he said.

"'We'?" Zera's stomach flipped.

"Yeah, we! My ankle's healed, I'm cleared and ready to go."

"You were in a boot *literally* yesterday."

"I ditched it once I got the email. Who needs it when there's work to be done?" He had a massive grin on his face, too big for this time of night. "Maybe your friend is still alive. What was her name?"

Ice stabbed Zera in the chest. "Uh, Katie."

"Right, maybe she's still around to help." An exaggerated wink made her insides squeeze. "Anyway, just wanted to let you know. See you in the morning!"

He had a pronounced limp as he walked away, and Zera had the feeling he was not, in fact, cleared to return yet. If he was, how was she going to explain Katherine, explain everything they'd been through? She couldn't tell him about her condition, or about the others she was looking for. In fact, it was best he didn't meet Katherine at all, just in case they had more travels in the future. The past. Whatever.

But the thought of going back in time and not seeing Katherine made Zera's heart ache. There was no way she could travel to a time and place where Katherine was and not see her.

"Fuck," she said, closing the door.

Kissi sat down on the edge of her bed and exhaled. "Shit." She rubbed her temples. "It worked. It actually worked."

"You doubted?"

"Only a healthy amount!"

Zera grabbed her handheld and started pacing, Vylek's message open on her screen. It held even less information than the one Byrd received and demanded her return to Vylek's office two hours before him. In less than forty-eight hours, she'd be back in the river.

Unless the altered message was because she knew of their rogue outing.

"Can they tell?" she asked.

"Tell what? But probably," Kissi said.

"Can they tell I took another trip?"

"I scrubbed everything from the machine," she said. "But...I mean, I can't say for certain if there isn't something on you keeping track. Something I couldn't find."

"Cool. Awesome. Excellent." Zera paced faster.

"We knew this could happen." Kissi grabbed Zera's wrist as she paced by. "We agreed it was worth the risk."

"It was. It totally was." Her stomach churned, fueled by the unknown. "I just...I don't know. I thought we'd get away with it."

"If it makes you feel better, I don't think they'd wait two days to call us out on it. I think it'd be Vylek at our door instead of Byrd."

It didn't make Zera feel better, but she appreciated it nonetheless.

Kissi eventually fell back asleep, her soft snores steady in the quiet barracks. Zera lay awake, counting her breaths in an effort to distract herself and losing count every time. Saving the world was one thing, arguably the most important thing. But all she could think about was Katherine. Katherine, alone in that apartment. Katherine, kissing her in the back of the car.

Katherine, dying in her arms in Central Park.

Zera rolled to face the conspiracy wall. Darkness hid the details, but she could see the outlines of the papers, a few corners fluttering as the air vent caught them. How in every hell did she get herself into this mess? No, it wasn't a mess. At least, it shouldn't have been. Her job was simple: get information, save everything. She'd decided, on her own, with sound mind and body, to screw it all up by getting close to the only person in the world who could topple the entire operation.

And yet, even as she accepted her own failings where her duty was concerned, she couldn't muster enough guilt to feel bad about it. Spending the time with Katherine was something unforeseen, something exhilarating, something once-in-a-lifetime. Even if her mission failed, she wasn't sure she'd regret it.

She turned onto her stomach and flinched as her knuckles brushed against something cold and metallic. The pocket watch, which she thought was in her drawer, sat nestled between the mattress and the bed frame. Soldering still caked half the seam, but as she ran her nail along it, she found bits and pieces weakened. It was too dark to grab her knife, but it would give her something to do while she wasn't sleeping.

Hours later, Zera's fingers were tender and her nail beds bruised, but she'd gotten a solid chunk of the old and crumbling soldering out of the watch as the circadian lamp switched from dark to gray and finally to orange. After spending the past few months experiencing actual sunrises again, Zera found the lamp didn't quite do it justice, no matter how many LED colors were available.

"Still think we're screwed?" Kissi said from the bottom bunk.

"Completely," Zera replied.

"Don't make me be the optimistic one. I'm shit at it."

The frame shook as Kissi sat up. She was supposed to use crutches when not wearing her prosthesis, but she ignored that fact and hopped to her desk before Zera could yell at her. A glance over her shoulder said she knew Zera would be mad, and that was her goal.

"What could you possibly be analyzing this early?" Now that Kissi was awake and had pulled Zera out of the spiral of her thoughts, exhaustion from the long night sank in.

"Nothing," Kissi said in a tone laced with plausible deniability.

"Kissi…"

"Don't worry your pretty little head about it," she said. Her fingers flew over the keyboard at lightning speeds, the lines on the screen moving too fast for Zera to follow.

"Kissi."

"Yes?"

"Are you trying to hack Vylek's private files to see if we're in trouble?"

"…No."

"Kissi, we just gotta sweat it out."

"Do we though?"

"Weren't you the one who said they wouldn't wait two days to court martial us?"

"Well you're freaking out, which makes me freak out."

"We can't both freak out, that's explicitly my job."

"Not today!"

Zera vaulted off the top bunk and stumbled to the desk, slamming the laptop shut with more force than necessary.

Kissi jumped and scooted her chair back, glaring at her. "Don't break my shit."

"Sorry," Zera said.

Kissi stared longingly at the closed laptop. "I'll be honest, I wasn't sure it would work."

"Well, it did," Zera said, ignoring the sting of Kissi's confession. "So now we have to reap what we planted or whatever."

"Sowed."

"I can't sew."

"Get Katherine to teach you." Kissi paused. "What are you gonna do if they really send Byrd back with you?"

"I...don't know." Zera resumed her pacing from earlier that morning. "I mean, if I find Kat first, I can always tell her to act like we just met. Or, I can find a way to separate myself from Byrd. Can't be that hard. Or maybe you can 'accidentally' send me to the 'wrong' place a few...hundred...miles away from him."

"Or you could not see Katherine."

"Don't be ridiculous."

"Right, what was I thinking?" Kissi said, throwing her hands up. "Don't you remember the actual point of your mission?"

"I can do both," Zera said.

"Zazzera. We might actually be able to fix this!" Kissi said, gesturing wildly at the rest of the world. "I get it, you like her, but it's bigger than you now. Bigger than all of us."

Zera's blood turned to ice. The argument made sense, but she didn't want to admit it, didn't want to think about how this might truly be the last time she saw Katherine.

"You're right." The words hurt. "Sorry."

"Don't be sorry, just...remember the big picture."

"No, I owe you a thousand apologies," Zera said, shaking her head. "You've been doing all the real work with this. I've just been throwing shit around and seeing what sticks."

Kissi smiled. "You're forgiven. Again."

"Okay good."

"Assuming we're not gonna get kicked down to the lower levels tomorrow...if I happen to send you in at the wrong time, well, maybe I'm just a little rusty. From not handling the controls in so long." Her grin got bigger, and Zera felt affection burn in her chest.

"You're a god amongst mortals, you know that?"

"Of course, but it's always nice to be reminded."

Zera smiled. Dread still coiled in her gut like a sleeping snake, but now it was joined by a layer of cautious, optimistic anticipation.

Either everything would come together, or it would all fall apart.

———————

Zera wiped her sweaty palms on her pants and fought the urge to vomit. She and Kissi arrived at Vylek's office at their designated time and sat in the folding chairs in front of her desk, waiting for her to appear. The tapping of Zera's heel against the linoleum was a deep, steady drumbeat to the rhythm of impending doom, and Kissi tolerated it for a few minutes before slapping the side of her leg.

"Sorry," Zera grunted. She crossed her legs and jiggled her foot instead. It was equally annoying, but at least it was silent.

Footsteps sounded from the hallway outside, and with no preamble, the office door opened. Zera and Kissi shot to their feet when Vylek strode in, her glare sharp as thorns as she settled in the chair.

"At ease." Their asses hadn't even hit the chairs when she said, "Explain."

Zera swallowed her nausea. "Explain what, Colonel?"

Vylek tapped the screen of the tablet, then slid it across the desk toward Kissi to show her the data.

"Explain how we missed this the first time."

"I'm sorry?" Kissi asked.

Vylek smacked the desk. "How in the hell did you miss this the first time, Kissinger? We've lost weeks of progress here—"

"What? I didn't have time." The interruption flared Vylek's impatience to volcanic levels.

Zera's anger flared as well. "We were kind of busy with the quake breaking generators, how was she *supposed* to find this?"

Vylek completely ignored her. "We hired you because you're the best."

"You hired me because I'm a package deal with Zazzera. You only discovered I was the best afterwards. *Colonel.*"

"And I'll fire you if you keep talking to me in that tone."

"I...Sorry, Colonel." Kissi balled her fists and stared at her knees, anger radiating off her. "But now I know a more efficient way to gather and analyze the data when Lieutenant Zazzera gets it."

"You're assuming you're still working with Zazzera?"

Zera's jaw dropped, as did Kissi's, and Vylek gave them a smirk that bordered on evil. "Thin ice, ladies. Remember that," she said, pulling the tablet back to her. "Now, get back to work. Dismissed."

The chairs squealed loudly as they shoved them back. Kissi grimaced, but Zera ignored it, offering a less-than-regulation salute which Vylek returned with even less enthusiasm. They'd won, they'd actually *won*, and now she was going back to see Katherine.

And to get data to change their current situation.

"We did it." Kissi elbowed her after Vylek's door was closed.

"We did it," Zera agreed. "Just wish Byrd wasn't coming with me. Kind of had my whole system figured out now."

"Meaning you just wanna hang out with Katherine uninterrupted."

"That too."

They made it back to their room, and Kissi retrieved a folder from the depths of a desk drawer. With a grand flourish she pinned two more pictures to the poster: Zera and Katherine's mugshots.

"You just had those on deck?"

"I've been saving it as a surprise." Kissi grinned wide, proud of the addition to the wall. "Look how cute you are, my little criminal."

"It wasn't on purpose."

"The charges were indecent acts. Care to elaborate on that?"

"In my defense, I had a bad influence," Zera said. She climbed up and dug through her covers for a second before spotting the pocket watch on her table. She could've sworn she left it on her bed, but she grabbed it and started picking at the soldering again. "And by the time the officer made it to the car there was zero exposure."

"A car? Zera, have some standards. Please."

"What? The stars were bright and it was an open road. Very romantic."

"Stop there." Kissi opened her computer. "You have to, *have to*, do things right this time. Are you listening?"

"I'm listening, I'm just not great at remembering things. The whole time travel thing kind of addled my brain."

"Trust me, if I could go again for you, I would," Kissi said.

"Let's be honest, Kissi—if you went, you would've figured it all out in the hour and a half before the 2040 Storm."

"You're right—can you stop messing with that thing?"

"What?" Zera looked up from trying to pry the ancient watch open with her bare hands. "I'm close."

"You're annoying. Don't make me change your trip from 2004 to 2016."

"You wouldn't."

"Don't tempt me."

"I promised Katherine 2004."

"And we must always appease Katherine."

"Hey, I'm her longest running friend."

"You're my longest running friend too."

"And that's why I give you all the credit for saving the world," Zera said. "And 'cause it's true."

"We haven't saved it yet. And also I'm gonna be a former friend if you don't quit fucking with that stupid watch."

"You fix it then." Zera tossed it and Kissi plucked it out of the air. In half a second, she pried it open, but flinched and dropped it on the table.

"Ouch! Shit! It shocked me again."

"Probably the universe getting back at you for being better than me at *everything*," Zera said. But she hustled to the desk anyway. "What's inside?"

"I don't know." Kissi sucked the side of her finger where the watch had shocked her and leaned over. "The inscription is way faded."

Zera turned the watch around until the letters faced the right direction. The second half of the inscription was mostly gone, with just a *d* and a faded *e*, but the beginning read, *To my darling...*

"Aw, darling kept his watch for a million years," Zera said.

"Poor darling was also at the wrong place at the wrong time," Kissi said. "Now we've just gotta make sure you don't end up the same way."

2004

Z ERA LANDED to an explosion of color, but not from the river and not from a brain aneurysm.

Fireworks burst above, showering the street with purple, green, and gold. The evening sky held no sign of the aurora, though she could barely see it through the smoke and lights. Music—jazz music, but different from the stuff back in the '40s—made the windows of the storefront next to her shake, the rhythm nearly as fast as her heartbeat and the melody some joyous riot of sound. She glanced at the sign above her and found herself at the corner of Bienville Street and Bourbon Street.

She was in New Orleans. And it was Mardi Gras.

People lined the street, sitting on curbs and benches, so Zera didn't stick out sitting on the sidewalk as her brain and body knit itself back together. Maybe Dr. Doyle could engineer another injection so she recovered better upon landing, or at least didn't cough up blood.

If the newspapers in the stand next to her were right, she had ten days until the storm. Kissi had graciously given her ten wonderful days without Byrd, and she wanted to find Katherine.

New Orleans was a big city, and the crowd was a sea of bodies rather than a gathering of people, but Zera chose to have faith that at least one deity would pull through and lead her to Katherine. It worked during the previous trips—why should she doubt it now?

The source of the jazz music rounded the corner. A large float covered in flowers and paper and dazzling lights led the parade, a six-member band playing a jaunty tune at astounding volume. Zera didn't know the song, but that didn't stop her from swaying with the rest of the listeners and cheering as the float grew closer. She could see more people on the float now, holding onto poles and handrails and throwing strings of beads that sparkled in the flashing lights.

Zera stuck her arm up as they passed and gasped in glee as the people on the float and the balcony above rained beads down on them. She managed to snag a strand and put it around her neck before anyone could say otherwise.

Magical was the best way to describe it. The lights gave her a headache, the air was thick with body odor, oil, and spices, and she couldn't move without touching a random person. It was *amazing*.

Zera wished Kissi could be there. When she got back, she'd find a way to take her too. What they had in the bunker was nothing compared to this.

People danced and sang and screamed and stripped, and once Zera could stand, she went along for the ride. Taking drinks from strangers was ill advised, but she did it anyway, because if she was going to feel shitty she at least wanted the excuse of alcohol. She removed her jacket and tied it around her waist, letting the glitter and night air kiss her skin. It was back to a sickly pale after so many weeks without her trips, and she felt very much like a beacon the way the lights reflected.

The crowd filled in the street behind the float, marching in time down Bourbon. Where they were going, Zera had no clue, but she couldn't wait to find out.

Lights and colors and people blurred the further they went. Eventually, Zera found herself in a park with a circle of booths surrounding an open area. The large float carrying the band parked right in the middle, turning the space into a grandstand. They were playing a different song now, one that reminded Zera of the bar back in Chicago.

Something tugged at her stomach, either wishful thinking or a god of star-crossed lovers. Katherine was here, she knew it. But how to find her?

The grass in front of the makeshift stage transformed into a dance floor. Another float pulled up to the front, and a wave of dancers and ribbon twirlers spilled from it, further limiting Zera's sight.

"You okay there, *ma fille*?" A woman with beautiful tan skin painted purple, green, and gold stopped and placed a gentle hand on Zera's shoulder. Ribbons of the same colors were braided into her hair, and she wore a stunning sleeveless dress that covered her from throat to foot. She was so pretty Zera lost her words for a moment.

"My—my friend," she stammered. "I lost my friend."

"Well, we can't have that, hmm?" She didn't seem to shout, but Zera still heard her velvety voice over the music. The woman slid her hand down Zera's arm and took her hand, guiding her through the crowd as if she had a map, and Katherine was at the end. But the woman didn't lead her to Katherine; instead, she led her to the stage.

"Oh, no, that's not—"

"It's okay," she said. She put her hands under Zera's arms and lifted her, making the world spin and colors flash. If her ass didn't smack so hard onto the edge of the stage, she might have continued spinning all the way into outer space.

"Do you see her?" the beautiful woman asked. Zera scanned the sea of faces with dizzy eyes, the lights from the stage and the booths casting shadows at odd angles. She should be able to see her. Katherine should be right in front of her, they were *supposed* to be together that night, she just knew it—

"There you are."

Two hands landed on her knees, and Zera looked down to find the object of her search staring at her with a bright smile and glitter around her eyes.

"Told you I could find her," the woman said with a smile.

"Thank you, Marion," Katherine said, leaning over to give the woman a kiss on the cheek. For a brief moment Zera was conflicted over who she was more envious of.

Marion smiled again and waved, her long nails sparkling in the lights. Katherine's hands never left Zera's knees, her touch warm enough to make her legs sweat. Her hair was straightened to an inch of its life, but the humidity added a slight wave. True to fashion, she had on a denim miniskirt and a flowy halter shirt with a pattern as loud as the fireworks.

"Been waiting for you," Katherine said.

Zera's heart skipped. She wanted nothing more than to lean down and kiss her, but she had no clue what Katherine's current relationship status was. It had been twelve years since their last meeting. She could have found someone new, a partner she wanted to spend her life with. Zera couldn't make any assumptions.

"Sorry it took me so long," Zera said. She slid off the stage and landed on the soft grass. Even in her boots, Katherine was still a few inches taller in her tennis shoes. Dammit. "Got caught up."

"Is this a sanctioned visit?" Katherine asked.

"Yeah, yeah it is. You did it." Zera couldn't help but grin.

Katherine pulled her into a tight hug that smelled of humid skin and hairspray, and Zera breathed it in, wrapping her arms around Katherine's waist.

"We did it," Katherine said. She pulled back and took Zera's hands. "Now, let's go celebrate."

"I like the sound of that."

"Have you ever been to a Mardi Gras festival?"

Zera was hoping for a different way of celebrating, but a festival would have to do. "No, show me everything."

The first stop was a tiny booth with a long line. The name on the banner was so faded Zera couldn't read it, but the people behind the counter knew Katherine by name and by sight, giving her a warm greeting when she reached the front. She purchased two hot chocolates and a bag of some fried powdered sugar concoction, and Zera had to learn very quickly how to manage an open cup and a crowd of people. The fried beignets were heaven in a bag, and despite the residual nausea from her trip down the river, Zera ate nearly the entire thing.

"You're earlier than I expected. I don't feel the storm coming," Katherine said as they weaved through the crowd. She linked their elbows and held her close, making it easy to slip through people like water.

"I think Kissi might've helped us out a little bit," Zera said. "The next storm isn't for ten days."

Katherine stopped. "Ten days?"

"That's what I said."

"Well," she said with a smile, "guess for once we don't have to rush."

"I mean, I'm sure you'll find someplace for us to break into, or something for us to steal, or someone for us to cross—"

"Of course not, I would never encourage such behavior." Katherine's voice held a slight drawl after spending a few decades in the South, and Zera wasn't sure she liked the twang. The hoity-toity accent from way back would always be her favorite.

"Oh, no, never," she said with a smile.

"I've never done anything wrong in my life."

"Of course not."

"Not in a hundred years."

"Aren't you closer to two hundred now?"

"I'm barely past one-fifty. I'm still in the prime of my youth."

They passed booths with children playing games, and another spot where a lady in brilliant face paint sat and created art on chubby cherub cheeks. Katherine waved hello to half the people they passed, apparently back in her socialite element. Zera couldn't help but smile; this Katherine seemed more real, more true to herself, than all the other trips.

"I'll have to make plans for us," Katherine said, after another brief conversation with a couple whose names Zera forgot instantly. "I don't have work currently, which leaves us plenty of time. We can go to Gulf Shores or—did you ever get to go to Disney World?"

"Disney World? No," Zera said. The name tickled a memory in the back of her mind, but she couldn't draw up anything more than the bare essentials. "I never made it out of New York."

"Perhaps another road trip is in order then," she said. "Oh, there's so many things to do, so many things to see. The technological advancements have been insane the past few years, I can't wait to see where they go."

With a pang, Zera remembered 2040. "We can do whatever you want. I'm just along for the ride."

"As long as we're here next Tuesday, we'll be fine," Katherine said.

"What's next Tuesday?"

"A parade and a masquerade ball," Katherine squeezed her elbow tight. "You can be my date."

"Your date? Sure. A friend in from out of town, here to see the sights and sounds of Mardi Gras. I can see the excuses already."

Katherine gently touched the back of her hand. "With this group, there's no need for excuses."

"What?" Zera's mouth went dry, and she cleared her throat. "I mean... I'm not sure what I mean. Or what you mean."

"I mean," Katherine said, enunciating every word, "that I wish for you to be my *date* to the ball."

There was the accent Zera liked, the one that made her stomach flip. "You're serious?"

"Serious as a heart attack." Katherine's gaze bore into her, and Zera didn't—couldn't—look away. She straightened and, in order to hide her blush, bent at the waist into a deep bow.

"Why, 'twould be my honor to escort the princess to the ball," she said.

Katherine snorted and tugged her back up to standing. "Always so dramatic."

"I learned from the best."

"Oh, so you're going to start listening to me now?"

"Only when I agree with it," Zera said. "On another note, I don't have anything to wear to the ball. I mean, I don't have anything to wear, period, but especially not ball-style clothing."

"Don't worry, we can go shopping," Katherine said. "Plenty of time for all that. Maybe we'll get matching crowns."

"Oh, I'm not going *unless* we get matching crowns."

They got more food and played carnival games, and between the booths, the performers, and the sights and sounds of the festivities, Zera had to stop herself from gaping in awe half the time. This was what life used to be like, back before everything. This was what life *could* be like, if she would focus.

The chance for success was slim, and the chance for failure so high, that for a moment Zera thought about throwing it away for good. She could keep hopping back and forth in time, gathering data and filling out reports, or she could just stay here with Katherine and live out the next thirty-six years happy and safe.

Unless...

"How's your investigation going?" Zera asked as they sat on the edge of the sidewalk.

Katherine sighed. "Not great. I still can't find the last man, though I've been staying here with Christopher. He at least welcomed the sight of me."

"So still no clue who's hunting you?"

"It must be Theodore," she said. "After all, it's just me and Christopher now. Everyone else is gone. But we can't seem to find any sign of him."

"So he's hiding his tracks," Zera said. "Maybe I can help somehow, back in my time. Hells, I'll help you hunt now, if you want. Gotta find him sometime."

"No, I think it's high time for a break," Katherine said. "Besides, it's Mardi Gras. It's about having fun. Ash Wednesday, we'll start up again."

"Ash Wednesday? Since when are you Catholic?"

"Since 1994 when I moved here."

Zera furrowed her brows. "You only spent two years in Austin?"

"Yes, well, Benjamin and I had kind of a fling, and it didn't end great," Katherine said.

"So technically it could also be him?"

"No." She shook her head. "We saw his name in the Statesman obituaries last month. He's gone too."

"Oh, Kat, I'm sorry," Zera said, putting her arm around Katherine's waist. Katherine leaned into her side, and Zera rested her cheek against her shoulder.

"I'll be honest, it's been a while since I've felt this hopeless."

"Good thing I showed up when I did."

"Good thing indeed."

The sounds of the festival dimmed, and the night chill truly sat in, but Zera didn't move. If Katherine needed to spend her night grieving on a sidewalk, that was fine with her.

But apparently it wasn't fine with Katherine.

"Come on." She stood and took Zera's forearms, hauling her to her feet. "We're going home and planning our escapades for the next ten days."

Katherine held her elbow again as they navigated the streets, which were quickly filling with people dressed up, dressed down, and generally undressed. The fact that so many sequins existed in the world surprised Zera, even more so that they all seemed to be here in New Orleans on bodices and jackets, pants and hats, even massive crowns and wings. It was a sight to behold, but she could barely focus past the way Katherine leaned into her and held onto her arm, her perfectly manicured nails barely grazing her and sending shivers down her spine.

The apartment building was old and grand, standing a few blocks off the French quarter. More than likely it was haunted, which Zera decided to take as a quirk rather than something scary. Purple, green, and yellow flowers dotted every surface and handrail, with matching Christmas lights to add to the pizzazz. It reminded Zera of Christmas in New York, only more of a celebration than a status.

Katherine's apartment was small, with a basic living area and two bedrooms on either side. Mardi Gras costume pieces took over most of the couch, most of which would be quite the delight if Zera ever got to see them in action. Katherine removed her shoes and left them by the door, and Zera followed suit, admiring how they looked stationed next to each other.

"You're home early," a man said from the kitchenette. He eyed Zera with mistrust, but the severity was lost due to the fact he was scrambling eggs and wore a frilly apron over a well-cut green suit.

"I ran into a friend," Katherine said, tugging Zera's wrist. "This is Miss Zazzera. Miss Zazzera, my roommate Christopher."

Christopher. Zera remembered his name on the list of Katherine's companions, but couldn't remember his death date. Surely it was years from now, right?

Christopher broke his facade, and with all the joy in his Scottish accent said, "Ah, nice to finally meet you, Miss Zazzera. We weren't expecting you this early."

"My friend Kissi thought it would be a fun surprise," she said. "Can you feel it too? When the storms happen?"

"Didn't realize what it was until I talked to Katherine, but yes. We're wondering if it'll be compounded now that we're in such close vicinity."

"Guess that'll also tell us if Theodore is close by," Katherine said. "A barometer of sorts."

"Kissi didn't say anything different regarding this one, but that doesn't mean it won't work."

"Ah, something interesting. Finally." Christopher plated his eggs and dug into them despite their obvious heat. "It gets so dull after a century."

"That's why you need to explore more." Katherine went to the cabinet and pulled out two wineglasses, then busied herself with a bottle of red wine on the counter.

"I've heard there's great ghost tours down here," Zera said. "Ever been on one of those?"

"Absolutely not," Christopher said through a mouthful of eggs. "I've lived here forty years without seeing a ghost, and I'll go at least forty more, thank you."

"What about you, Kat?" she asked, the dirty glare response making her grin.

"You know how I feel about ghosts."

"Thought you'd get over that in the past twelve years."

"No one gets over a fear of ghosts," Christopher said. He finished his eggs and put the plate in the sink before peeling off the frilly apron. "You two have fun, I'm off to the parade."

"Are we not going with him?" Zera asked, hoping the answer was no.

"Gentlemen only, I'm afraid," Christopher said with a wink. He picked up a massive plague doctor mask which matched his suit perfectly. "Farewell!"

"So old-fashioned," Katherine muttered after the door closed. She offered a wineglass to Zera, then held hers aloft. "To old friends."

"And new experiences," Zera added. The glasses clinked and Katherine lifted one brow. "You know, Mardi Gras."

"Is that the only new experience you were hoping for?" The way Katherine sipped her wine could only be described as sensual, and Zera took a gulp herself to wet her mouth.

"I wasn't going to show up and assume you were still interested in finishing what we started in Texas," she said.

Katherine put her half-full wineglass on the counter and stepped close. Zera, emboldened by her gaze, stood her ground.

"Tell me, Miss Zazzera, is this the first time we meet?"

Zera licked her lips. "Not even close."

"Then I don't mind admitting that I've thought about that night in Texas every day for twelve years," she said, her voice low and husky. The scent of wine hung between them.

"Me too," Zera said with a smirk. "Though not for that long—"

Katherine interrupted her with a kiss, soft and tender, and it ignited something in Zera's chest. Zera put her glass down and responded in kind, putting her hands on Katherine's flushed cheeks. The kiss deepened, and she slid her hands into Katherine's hair, using the soft locks to hold her in place as she kissed her firmly, confidently. Their lips moved together with practiced ease, as if they'd been doing this for years, and it was more intoxicating than the wine.

"Your first name, Miss Zazzera," Katherine said. Her lipstick had slightly more staying power than the last time they did this, but was still smudged. Zera liked it. "Will you please tell me?"

"Right now? Why?" It felt like the question came from nowhere.

"So I know what to call out later," Katherine said.

Zera's breath left in a rush, as did all her jokes and arguments. "Noelle. My name's Noelle."

Katherine grinned a wolfish grin. "Noelle, I'd rather like to show you my bedroom."

Did she know what that old accent did to her? Zera nearly had to bite her lip at the way her body responded.

"Well, Katherine, I'd rather like that myself."

KATHERINE DIDN'T WAIT until they reached the bedroom before planting her lips on Zera's again. It was as if the night in her car had never been interrupted. Their kisses were fast and easy, tingling with newness while feeling as if they'd been kissing all their lives, current and past and future.

"Thought you said we didn't have to rush?" Zera said as Katherine dragged her into her bedroom and kicked the door shut behind them.

"Oh do hush," Katherine said, that stupid pompous voice sending a shiver down Zera's spine. Katherine tried to kiss her again, but now Zera was on a mission to tease.

"Oh pardon me, princess," she said against her lips. Katherine pulled back and gave her the haughtiest, angriest glare, which was possibly the hottest thing Zera had ever seen.

"If kissing your mouth doesn't keep you quiet, perhaps I should try other ideas." Katherine gave her one more kiss before leaning down to press her lips against Zera's neck, magically finding the tender spot just below her ear that made goosebumps race down her arms.

"You know, for being immortal, you're really impatient."

Katherine stopped again. "I have literally been waiting decades for this," she said, pleading. "Now please, Noelle, there will be plenty of time for teasing later."

The comment reminded Zera their time together was truly and utterly finite, and she needed to treat it as such. "Right, sorry," she said.

Katherine threaded her fingers through Zera's hair and kissed her again, this time slow and deep and burning. "Don't apologize. Just kiss me."

Zera moved with a purpose after that. She grabbed Katherine's hips and walked her step by step to the bed until the backs of her knees hit the edge. She sank down, allowing Zera to straddle her lap just like the back of the Mustang. Only this time, Zera didn't have to fight the buttons of a stupid denim jumpsuit—instead, she toyed with the edge of the halter top for half a breath before peeling it off.

A jazz band struck up a tune somewhere on the streets below, and while it wasn't the most romantic music, the energy matched the beating of Katherine's heart as Zera traced the edge of her white lace bra. Katherine inhaled as Zera slipped a finger under the band and followed it to the clasp at the back.

"Okay if I take this off?" she asked.

"Absolutely."

A twist and a pull, and the bra came apart, a soft sigh escaping Katherine's lips as she was freed from its prison. Fireworks started outside, the bright lights casting dappled shadows around the scars scattered across her chest. Some were old and smooth, faint silver lines holding a remnant of a memory. Others were still pink and raised, the skin healed but the wounds not forgotten. Zera wanted to ask, but that was a surefire way to kill the mood, so instead she kissed the scar below her collarbone, then the one on her sternum, and then she abandoned the scars in favor of paying delicate attention to the softest, most sensitive parts of her.

Katherine gasped and arched her back, and Zera responded with a soft nip that made Katherine jolt and squeeze her legs together. Distracted fingers attempted to pull at the hem of Zera's shirt, but she quickly shut that down.

"I can't leave things uneven," she said, and continued her ministrations on the other side. Katherine didn't object. Instead, she leaned her head back and relaxed into the sensations, which was a sign of encouragement if Zera ever saw one. She'd found at least one of Katherine's favorite places; she hoped one day she'd find them all.

She could feel the self-satisfied smile she gave as Katherine looked at her with flushed cheeks and red lips. Good, she hadn't lost her touch.

"Now might I remove this?" Katherine asked, grasping the hem of Zera's shirt.

"Why, please do, princess."

This time she didn't fight back when Katherine tore her shirt over her head, tossing it into some corner of the room. Her sports bra quickly followed—she really should've dressed better for this—and then Katherine's hands were roaming, unhindered, over the muscles of her back and chest and abdomen. Zera had never been shy about her body, but the utter scrutiny from the busty bombshell in front of her left her feeling a little self conscious.

"You're stunning," Katherine murmured, then pulled her in for another searing kiss, crushing Zera to her chest with surprising strength.

Emboldened by the compliment, Zera wedged her hands between them and made quick work of the buttons on the front of Katherine's skirt. When the last one gave way, Katherine shifted slightly to give her more space.

Zera hooked her finger over the waistband of her underwear. "Good with this?"

"Absolutely." More fireworks reflected in her eyes, which rolled and closed as Zera slipped her hand beneath the underwear and brushed her fingertips over her.

Oh no, she *definitely* hadn't lost her touch.

Katherine hummed in pleasure as Zera began slow, steady circles. She leaned her head against Zera's shoulder and spread her legs as far as their position would allow, her hands gripping Zera's thighs with each circle. Zera's own desire burned in her stomach, but Katherine had been waiting for this, waiting for *her*, and dammit, she wanted to see this woman, this endlessly strong and poised woman, become utterly undone.

An indignant squeak escaped when Zera drew back, but before Katherine could ask what she was doing or chastise her for stopping, Zera was off her lap and on her knees. She gripped Katherine's hips and pulled her to the edge of the bed, and with her help, removed the skirt and underwear in one go.

Surely it was a goddess sitting on the edge of the bed in front of her, not some woman Zera had met by happenstance over and over. She silently thanked every deity she ever prayed to for banding together and giving her this night.

"Holy shit," she breathed, running her hands over Katherine's thighs, her stomach, her chest. "I mean, Jesus, Odin, and Zeus, Kat—"

"Though you're on your knees, Noelle, this is not the time for prayers," Katherine gasped. Even in the low light of the room, her readiness was evident, and Zera was only too willing to oblige.

She wedged herself between Katherine's legs and pressed a kiss to the inside of her knee. "So you want this, yeah?"

"Please," Katherine said, and that was all the encouragement Zera needed.

She kissed her way up Katherine's thigh before landing in earnest at the apex, seeking out the spot she would most appreciate and paying special attention to it with her tongue. Katherine moaned and gripped Zera's head with her thighs, the fingers of one hand tangling in her short hair. With her ears blocked by luscious legs, Zera could no longer hear Katherine's responses, but instead felt them as they echoed through her bones.

For someone so good at hiding her emotions, the higher Katherine climbed, the less she concealed. Her breath came shorter and shorter, and her muscles twitched and held, coiling tighter and tighter. Tired of the near-silence, Zera pried Katherine's knees from their hold and pushed them as far apart as they would go. Now that she had a little more room to work, she raised one hand and took a tentative touch before easily, seamlessly slipping one, then two fingers inside.

"Oh, God, Noe—"

"No?" Zera asked, pulling back.

Katherine kept her hold on Zera's hair, almost desperate now. "No, I mean, yes, Noelle, please don't stop—"

"See, this is why I stopped using my first name—"

"*Miss Zazzera!*"

"Yes, ma'am," Zera said, and returned her mouth and her hand to their previous positions. Katherine whined and held her head with both hands, curses and praises falling from her rosebud lips as Zera did exactly as she asked. Zera felt the muscles clenching around her fingers, heard every gasp and moan and call of her name—every name Katherine knew—and continued without hesitation or remorse.

When she came, Katherine fell silent, her head back and her body seizing. Zera slowed, just slightly, to work her through it gently. But she did not stop as Katherine exhaled and relaxed, instead continuing her motions until she fell to pieces all over again. The fireworks kept on outside—or were they here, in this bedroom?

"Jesus." Katherine relaxed her hold on Zera's hair. Her scalp tingled with the release of pressure, and she might have lost a few hairs, but they were worthy casualties of the cause. She placed a wet, messy kiss to Katherine's inner thigh before standing and planting another one on her mouth. Katherine kissed her back, wrapping her arms around Zera's waist and pulling her back onto the bed.

"Worth the wait?" Zera murmured against her neck. She couldn't help but kiss the skin over another silvery scar.

"It's a good start," Katherine said. Her pulse still pounded in her neck and under her sternum, and her words sent a thrum of need through Zera's abdomen. Thousands of ideas ran through her head, and as she tried to prioritize them, Katherine pressed her lips to Zera's neck, right in that damned spot.

Words failed her, as they often did when pretty naked girls kissed her neck and ran their hands over her body. Katherine took in every inch with her fingertips, every rise and valley of muscle and bone. The touches were gentle and caressing, leaving fire in their wake. She unbuttoned Zera's pants and slid the zipper down, then pushed them past her hips. Zera wriggled out of them, the new sensation of skin on skin making her burn. The pants ended up on the floor, right where they belonged, and then she was completely undressed. There was nothing to hide.

Katherine's hands went to the back of her thighs, and she rolled them over so she could settle on top, Zera's legs around her waist. She moved in a slow rhythm with her hips, the motion and contact just enough to take the edge off of Zera's bone-deep need. If Katherine didn't pick up the pace, she was simply going to fall into the sun.

"Remember how impatient you were earlier?" Zera asked as Katherine sucked on her neck, probably leaving a godsdamned hickey like a teenager.

"Mhmm." She slipped a hand between them, so close to where Zera wanted and yet so far. "Is that what you want?"

"Please, yes," Zera groaned, then gasped as Katherine obliged and pushed a finger into her. Zera's legs fell further open, and Katherine began to move in and out at a steady pace, the heel of her hand occasionally pressing against the sensitive spot begging for more attention.

"Kat, please—"

Katherine stopped kissing her neck and moved to look her in the eye, though she never stopped her hand. Her long hair, loose and messy, cascaded around them like curtains hiding them from the rest of the world.

"Please what?" she asked. Her gaze was so intense it took Zera's breath away, but another nudge with her finger brought it back sharp.

"More, I need more," Zera said, because her brain wasn't working correctly, because Katherine's chest was in her face and her finger was inside her and—Zera moaned as she added another. "*Fuck.*"

"Is that what you meant?" She gave her a wide eyed, innocent look that made Zera grip her fingers for a moment. Then the evil smile arrived. "Or did you mean something else?"

"I like that but..." Zera reached up and ran her thumb over Katherine's lower lip. "I would really like your mouth too."

Katherine ran her free hand over Zera's cheek, their faces mere inches apart as she pressed the heel of her hand against her with steady, perfect pressure.

"Let me have this one first," she murmured, her voice so low it sent a zing through Zera's body. "I want to see your face when you come."

Zera lost all words as Katherine increased her pace, her fingers curved just right to hit something deep in Zera and make all her thoughts disappear.

"Oh gods, right there," Zera gasped as the wave built in her. "Please don't stop."

"I won't," Katherine promised. She bit her lip in an entirely too sexy way, her eyes never leaving Zera's as everything rose more and more until Zera came with a cry, the pleasure overwhelming. But Katherine didn't allow her to settle, instead rebuilding just as Zera had earlier.

"Still want my mouth?" she asked. Zera nodded emphatically. Katherine raised her brows, that devious smile still in place, and it took a moment for Zera to realize what she was waiting for.

"*Please.*"

"Well, since you asked so politely."

Katherine kissed her mouth, then her neck, then her sternum, all the way down. Zera moaned with relief, gripping the sheets tight in both hands as the initial sensations rocked through her. Some rather unladylike words spilled from her as well, but the impropriety only encouraged Katherine more as she sucked a little harder and moved her hand a little faster.

Katherine's other hand held her hip tight, keeping her still despite her instinct to rock against her face. She looked down and met Katherine's eyes, the sight so damn sexy that a shudder went through her and pushed her right over the edge.

She was pretty sure she called Katherine's name, or at least some variation of it, as her body tensed and flooded with release. Stars exploded—or perhaps it was just more fireworks—and Zera's voice jumped an octave as she sang Katherine's praises.

Her hips hurt from the position and her fingers ached from clenching the sheets, but Katherine refused to be outdone. She stopped moving her hand, but continued light flicks with the tip of her tongue. Zera fell silent as she came one last time, her head pressed into the mattress and her body shaking.

Zera's breathing echoed around the quiet bedroom, and the mattress squeaked as Katherine crawled up next to her. She pulled Zera to her and intertwined their legs, fitting them together like two halves of a whole. Under her ear, Katherine's heart beat slow and steady, and for a moment Zera didn't think about her mission, or Central Park.

"I've missed you," Katherine murmured into her hair. "I always miss you."

"I missed you too," Zera said. Once again, it was a few weeks for her, but over a decade for Katherine. And once again, Zera wondered if she needed to return to her time at all.

The celebration continued outside, and despite the window unit blowing cool air, the humidity kept their skin sticky. But the thought of untangling from Katherine was worse than the discomfort of their position.

Ten days. She had ten days until Byrd arrived. Ten days to enjoy with Katherine, with no threat of astronomical events ruining the moment. Ten days to figure out exactly what she was going to do.

The parade sounds began to fade, and Katherine grew still beside her save for the rise and fall of her chest as she breathed slow and deep. All the tension she normally carried was gone, and for the first time Zera saw her fully quiet and relaxed. She wanted to think the sex was only part of it.

The idea of leaving behind Kissi and Lieb and the rest of her friends back in the bunker had always seemed ridiculous, but the longer Zera stared at the smooth lines of Katherine's face, the more seriously she took the idea. After all, prior to the 2040 Storm, people left their homes all the time to be with a partner.

Call her old-fashioned.

Katherine mumbled in her sleep and rolled over, freeing up just enough of the sheet for Zera to tug it from beneath her and drape it over her. The way it fell looked too much like a funeral shroud, so Zera slipped beneath the sheet as well and scooted behind her, holding her close. There she could feel the warmth of Katherine's skin and the way her ribs expanded with each breath.

The 2040 Storm would take place in thirty-six years. She could get the data they needed, go back with Byrd, say her goodbyes, and then make up a bullshit excuse for why she needed to come back. She and Katherine could have a good thirty-six years together.

Something nagged at the back of her mind, something to do with the visit to Central Park. She didn't want to think about that day, not with Katherine here in her arms, but one of these days she'd have to. There was a hole in her plan—she just couldn't find it.

Katherine hummed again and found Zera's hand, pulling it into her chest. Now wasn't the time for plans, Zera thought, the day—and night—catching up to her.

She could figure it out in the morning, with Katherine's help.

2004

ZERA HAD HEARD a lot about Disney World from older people in the bunker, but they'd never mentioned how exhausting it was.

"I don't think I'll ever walk again," Zera said, collapsing onto Katherine's couch.

"Oh, you'll be fine," Katherine said. She dropped their bag of merchandise in her room, then went to the kitchen. "Do you want some coffee?"

"Who's making it?"

"Me, of course."

"Then absolutely not."

"Christopher says my coffee is fine." Katherine rummaged in the cupboards for a second, then filled the pot.

"That's 'cause Christopher is from the same ass-backwards time you are," Zera pointed out. "Or, he's too polite to lie to you."

"Both are viable options." The coffee machine buzzed and gurgled, reluctant to perform its job. "But you'll have to find a way to stomach it. You'll need the caffeine for tonight."

"Tonight? What? We're sitting here and watching TV tonight. I really wanna know the deal with *The Sopranos*." She tried to sit up, but deemed it too much effort and collapsed back on the couch.

"You'll have to wait until tomorrow." Katherine came back and playfully smacked her thigh. "Get up, we've got a lot of preparation for the parade."

"Parade?" Zera groaned.

"And the masquerade ball afterwards."

Though Zera's eyes were closed, she could hear the grin in Katherine's words. "Wait, you were serious about that?"

"I got you a dress and everything, you're going to be so fancy."

Warm hands gripped her wrists and pulled, but Zera remained adamantly on the couch. "I can't, Kat, I'm too tired."

"It's Fat Tuesday, Noe, you have to rally. It'll be worth it, I promise."

"I can't. Go on without me."

Katherine sighed and dropped her hands. Zera heard a rustle of clothing and cracked one eye open.

"I understand." Katherine sighed again for good measure. She'd removed her jacket and dropped it on the floor, walking backwards toward the bathroom. "I guess I'll just have to get ready all by my lonesome." Her shirt followed, and Zera's mouth went dry.

"You're doing this on purpose," she said.

"Of course I am," Katherine replied, peeling the short shorts off her long legs. "Is it working?"

Zera groaned and somehow found the energy to get off the couch. "Yeah. It is."

When the shower water ran cold, they returned to the real world. True to her word, Katherine gave Zera a plush terrycloth robe to match her own and sat her down at the edge of the bed, drying and styling her hair before getting the makeup out. Zera tried to sneak touches under the edges of Katherine's robe, but she was a woman on a mission and would not be distracted, unlike Zera.

The skin of her face felt heavy by the time Katherine finished. She directed Zera to the vanity mirror, pride aglow on her face.

"Holy shit," Zera said, in an expert analysis of the work. By day-to-day standards the green, gold, and purple wings adorning her face were ridiculous, but based on what she saw on her first day here, it was perfect. "You should get paid for this."

"I did for a while." She shrugged. "It got boring. Plus you have to talk to a lot of people, and that wears me out."

"You? The New York socialite?" Zera returned to the edge of the bed as Katherine sat at the vanity. In the mirror, she saw her face betray a touch of sadness, just for a moment.

"I haven't been a socialite in quite a long time," she said.

"It's hard, huh? To make friends." It was something she mentioned before, but Zera always forgot.

"Yes." Katherine picked up the brushes and began her work on her own face. "Here it's easier, but more often than not I just wonder what their obituaries will say someday."

Zera stood, wrapping her arms around Katherine's shoulders and leaning their heads together.

Katherine stiffened in the embrace, then relaxed into it. "You'll mess up your makeup."

"You'll fix it."

Zera held her for a few minutes, until her heart rate picked up and then returned to normal. The kiss she planted on her cheek left a purple lip mark, but when Katherine noticed it, she simply smiled.

"I think I'll leave it," she said. "Let all the other ladies know I'm spoken for, at least for tonight."

"Just tonight?" Zera asked. She didn't want to think about the fact she would have to leave at some point, or how it may be a long time before they saw each other again—if they ever saw each other, as they were now.

"Well, perhaps tomorrow too, if you're lucky."

"Maybe I should put a green one and a gold one on your cleavage, so I can make sure no one bothers you."

Katherine finished her lips and cheeks and hair while Zera lay on the bed and flipped through fashion magazines, pointing out the particularly modern and sophisticated choices for the women of 2004. They both laughed at the pictures, and they both ignored the weight of uncertainty between them. Now would be the time, Zera thought, to bring her in on the plan, to figure out how she could go back and save the people in her time, then return to Katherine.

Because, as Dr. Phillips loved to point out, Katherine was already dead.

"Don't look so glum," Katherine said as she opened the closet.

Hangers packed the small space, the wooden rod creaking ominously as she wrenched the clothes apart. On the floor, tucked amongst the skirts of her dresses, sat the old carpet bag from before.

"I don't look *glum*," Zera said, though she absolutely did. "I just don't want to wear a dress." A good enough excuse.

"You'll be fine." Katherine pulled out a sparkly monstrosity and laid it across the chair. With puffed sleeves and a short skirt in the front, Zera couldn't imagine herself in it, let alone going outside where people could see her.

"Hells no, Kat," she said.

"Oh, that's not yours." Katherine waved her off. Suddenly Zera liked the idea of the short skirt and low-cut bodice, if she wasn't the one to wear it. Katherine removed another hanger from the closet, this one sporting more subdued swirls of green and purple and gold. "This is yours."

"That's...a corset."

Katherine grinned wolfishly. "You are correct, my dear."

"You want me to wear a corset."

"That I do."

"Why?"

"Why not?"

Zera glared, mad she didn't have a comeback.

"Oh, c'mon," Katherine said, removing the corset from the hanger and holding it out. "They're much more comfortable—they don't even use whalebone for them anymore."

"I don't think I can fill it out," Zera said, eyeing the satin cups of the bustier.

"We won't know until we try." Katherine gave her the most pitiful look, with a pout and batting eyelashes and all. Damn her.

"Fine," Zera said as Katherine whooped in success. "But if it's terrible, I'm not wearing it."

"Oh, of course, I'd never ask such a thing." She sounded like she would, in fact, ask such a thing. "Go on, disrobe please."

Zera muttered a few choice words under her breath but did as she was told. She stood in nothing but her skivvies, trying her best to appear confident.

"Arms up," Katherine commanded. When Zera obliged, she reached around and wrapped the corset around her. The underlay was surprisingly silky, and the pokes and prods she expected never came.

It took a few seconds for Katherine to attach the closures in the front. The garment wasn't as tight as expected, the main discomfort coming from its strapless design. Perhaps she could get used to it, especially if it made Katherine look at her like *that*.

"Oh, it looks good already," she said, resting her hands on Zera's waist. "Now, make sure the girls are in place and we'll tighten it up."

"It's not tight yet?" Zera asked.

Katherine laughed. "No, now turn around."

"Isn't it good like this?"

"It'll shift around like this. So unless you're planning on flashing everyone at the party..."

"Will they give me beads?"

"No."

"Dammit. Okay fine."

She adjusted herself and turned around, holding her breath and waiting for the pain of crushed ribs or a cracked spine. One by one Katherine tightened the ribbon crosses at the back, cinching the corset tighter, but the fractures never came.

"There, done," Katherine said. "Must you be so dramatic about it?"

"That's it?" Zera found she could move a lot easier than she thought. She could even breathe. Katherine took her waist again and directed her in front of the mirror, showing her she not only had a waist, she had *cleavage*. "Holy shit."

"You're welcome." Katherine looked much too satisfied with herself, and went to retrieve her own corset. She donned it with practiced ease and presented the back to Zera. "Now, if you don't mind."

Despite performing this same ritual only a couple months prior, Zera was still too gentle with the ribbons, but at least she could admit it was due to the distraction of Katherine's body. She helped her into the sequined mess of a dress, then waited for the reveal of her own attire.

"Don't look so concerned." Katherine dug into the closet again and pulled out a purple paisley suit. On any other day, Zera would refuse to wear the outfit, but it was Mardi Gras and she was already wearing a corset. What was the addition of a full paisley outfit? It was cut for Katherine's height, but luckily her curves allowed enough room for Zera's more athletic build.

"So? What do you think?" Zera asked after she shrugged on the jacket. In Katherine's defense, the jacket-corset combo was surprisingly sexy and did wonders for Zera's confidence.

Katherine grinned and grasped the edges of the jacket. "Looks amazing," she said, pulling Zera in for a quick kiss to preserve the lipstick. "It'll look better on the bedroom floor later."

"Promises, promises," Zera said. For good measure, she said a few prayers both in thanks and in burning desire. Katherine handed her a mask and showed her how to tie it around her wrist, completing the look.

Now dressed to the nines, they left the apartment and followed the sounds of a band warming up. People in equally amazing outfits milled through the streets, squealing excited greetings to each other and sharing shots from flasks pulled from unlikely places. Katherine introduced her to a hundred different people and Zera remembered none of their names, only their brilliant clothes.

The organizer of their float gave Zera an odd look, but after a quick glance at her and Katherine's clasped hands she chose to ignore a stranger's presence. With a cymbal crash and four loud drum beats, the band struck up their song, and then they were on their way.

It had been a long time since Zera had seen a true parade, and she'd never participated in one, but it was easy enough to blend in. A tall woman with a sharp jaw and sharper eyeliner wings put a stack of beads around Zera's neck, with instructions to throw when the mood struck. Without letting go of Katherine's hand, Zera removed one string and looked to the crowd lining the streets.

Men, women, and even some children packed the sidewalk and the balconies above. Each restaurant they passed boasted its own soundtrack, but it couldn't compete with the brassy jazz band on the float. Zera tossed her first beads to a girl with wide eyes and a scared expression, the fingers of one hand toying with the hem of her shirt as if she were building the courage to take part in the time-honored tradition. A grateful expression followed, and Zera passed her by with a wink.

"You're such a softy. They should work for their prize," Katherine yelled over the music. A flick of her wrist sent a string of beads flying toward a man with his shirt up, his friends laughing around him.

"What can I say, I'm a giver," Zera replied, pressing a kiss to Katherine's neck. She bestowed the next round of beads to two children in overalls, perched on their parents' shoulders. They had more beads than anyone else on the street.

"That you are." Katherine leaned over and kissed her cheek. It was meant to be saucy, but Zera thought she heard a touch of sincerity.

The parade flashed by in swirls of color and music, showing her the streets of New Orleans at their very best. It seemed to last forever and no time at all; when they reached the end destination at a grand hotel, Zera felt like they'd just begun, though her tired throwing arm said otherwise. A shot of bourbon at the door helped immensely.

"Now it's time," Katherine said, unlacing her mask from her wrist. She artfully donned it, the swirls and sparkles giving her the glow of an ancient goddess. She helped Zera put hers on, and while she doubted it looked as good, it still gave her an unexpected burst of courage.

"Shall we?" Zera offered her hand, and Katherine took it. In the ballroom, the band played a jazzy cover of some old song Zera remembered from the radio during their road trip.

Katherine immediately pulled her to the dance floor, leading her through a waltz. It felt ridiculous, and probably looked even more so, but the smile on Katherine's face made it worth it.

"Remember New York?" Zera asked, holding her close.

"And Chicago," Katherine said. "Miss Zazzera, when it comes to you, I remember everything."

The band took a break a couple of hours in, giving them an excuse to go onto the balcony. The cool night air kissed away the heat on their skin, and under the stars and fireworks and emerging aurora, Zera kissed Katherine without guilt or remorse.

She owed Kissi *so much* when she got back.

"Having fun?" Katherine leaned into Zera's side, and for a moment Zera saw past the glitter and makeup to the woman she was back in 1980, when they kissed for the very first time.

"Too much fun," she said. This was it, the time to say she wanted to come back, to stay. "It'll be hard to go back."

Katherine's smile changed. "Yes, I admit I'll miss you when you're gone," she said. "When's the next time again?"

Byrd would come tomorrow, and Zera yearned to say she'd return the next day. But she wasn't in the business of making promises she couldn't keep.

"I'm not sure, honestly." She traced the line of Katherine's lip, wiping a smudge of lipstick away. "But soon. As soon as I can. Maybe I—"

"Smile!"

Zera and Katherine turned to find a short woman in a flowing green dress and locs down to her waist. Gold beads glittered and clicked as she adjusted the small, crystal blue camera in her hands. Without a second thought, Zera grabbed Katherine around her waist and crushed her to body, the alcohol in her system saying if she didn't hold on, she'd lose her forever. If she'd had to hold the fake smile for longer than a second, she might have broken down in tears.

"I'll have to hunt down a copy of that later," Katherine said. She leaned over and watched where the woman went back in the ballroom. "Actually, let me just—"

She stepped to the doorway and paused. At first, Zera thought she was scanning the ballroom for the photographer, but the woman was still very much in view, and Katherine held herself stiff as a board.

"Kat? You okay?" Zera put a hand on the small of her back. In the light, she could see Katherine's skin was deathly pale, her lips parted and trembling, as if a ghost danced in front of her. "Kat, what's wrong?"

"He...he's..."

"Who? Christopher? William?"

"Edward."

"Edward? Who the fuck is Edward?" And why was Katherine so afraid of him? Sobriety found her, and she palmed her ever-present pocket knife.

"My...my..."

Zera had never seen Katherine so unnerved, and it scared her. She followed Katherine's gaze and saw a man pulling a cheap purple mask over his eyes, his wolfish grin evident even from across the room.

"Katherine, what—"

"Edward was my first husband. We need to go *now*."

Katherine grabbed Zera's wrist and kicked off her heels, breaking into a run. For a woman in a corset and dress she was remarkably fast, and Zera was lucky to keep up with her. They discarded their masks as they ran back to Katherine's apartment, pushing and weaving through the crowds.

The walls of the stairwell thumped with music from outside, but Zera barely heard it over the sounds of their ragged breathing. On the landing, she spotted her apartment—and the slightly open door.

"No," Katherine breathed. She slid to a halt and barged in, Zera hot on her heels and confused as hell.

Christopher lay propped against the couch, a dark stain next to him. Katherine rushed over, staining her knees red in the pool of blood as she knelt at his side. Zera noticed the bottoms of her feet were also streaked red, chunks of asphalt and glass embedded in her soft skin.

"He's alive," she said, her hand on his neck. She pulled the pillow back from his chest to reveal a bright red stain on his shirt, a gurgle of blood bubbling from a massive wound.

"Shit!" Katherine returned the pillow, applying pressure to the hole.

Christopher grimaced and his eyes fluttered open, his face going a shade paler when he saw her. "Ed," he coughed out.

Katherine pressed the pillow harder against his chest. "Yes, darling, we saw him." She turned to Zera. "Call an ambulance."

"On it." Zera jumped up and went to the corded phone in the kitchen, grateful that emergency numbers never changed.

"You have to run," Christopher said. The emergency response picked up and Zera explained the situation, half listening to the responder as Christopher coughed again.

"I'm not leaving you like this," Katherine said as Zera returned to the living room.

"He's right," Zera said, joining them on the floor. She put her hand over Katherine's, holding the pillow. "If Edward is the one hunting you guys, he'll come back. He already knows where you live. He might be on his way back already."

Katherine looked from her to Christopher, her eyes shining. Zera's heart broke to see her own regret reflecting back at her.

"Go, Kat," she said. If all else failed, Zera could escape. Katherine didn't have that luxury, and Zera needed her to live. Time travel rules or not, Zera wouldn't take that risk.

Katherine took a breath and nodded, tears leaving trails through her Mardi Gras makeup.

Zera kept her hand on Christopher and met his scared gaze. "I got you," she said. Katherine went to her room and shuffled through the closet. It was too easy to picture her grabbing the stupid carpet bag from the floor and stuffing it with the contents of the top drawer.

"Hurts," he replied.

"I know, the ambulance will be here soon." If she listened hard enough, she could hear the sirens in the distance. How many blocks of partiers did they have to go through to get here?

Katherine whirled back into the room, now in a nondescript sweatshirt and jeans. The purple kiss marks stained her cheek and neck, dark like a bruise in the low light. She limped every step, but her physical pain was unmatched compared to the hurt on her face.

"I can't leave you like this, Christopher," she said.

"Edward's probably almost back here," Zera said, the words stinging on their way out. "We can't lose you, Kat."

"She's right." Christopher cleared his throat, and Zera put more pressure through the pillow when the color continued to drain from his face.

"I'm here, I'll take care of him," Zera said. "If that bastard makes it here before the paramedics, I'm ready for a fight."

"If Christopher must depend on your defense skills for safety then I'm afraid this might be our last meeting," Katherine said.

"Quit fucking around, Kat," Zera said. Pain lanced deep in her chest, close to where Christopher's injury was. Tears choked her words. "We're out of time. Go."

"But what about..."

"We'll see each other again." Zera used one hand to pull the chain from around her neck and stuffed the ring into Katherine's hand. "I promise."

Katherine's lip trembled, and Zera could see her searching for another excuse, another reason to stay just a breath longer. She shook her head, laid a blazing kiss on Zera's lips, then ran out the door. An ache spread behind Zera's sternum, and she channeled her attention toward Christopher.

"You're gonna be okay, Chris." She took his hand, and he squeezed back weakly.

"Not so sure about that, love," he replied. There was a gurgling with each breath he took now. "But I've lived long enough, I suppose."

"Don't talk like that," Zera said. "If you die, Kat's gonna kill me. So I need you to go ahead and survive this, okay?"

A half-hearted laugh escaped. "I'll do my best."

"Thank you."

The sirens were closer now, and the lights flashed through the windows. The seconds ticked by, thick and slow in the silence as Christopher struggled and Zera did anything she could to keep him awake. She strained to hear sounds of someone in the hallway, any sign Katherine's husband had returned to the scene of the crime, but it was quiet until the pounding of boots and the rattle of a gurney echoed from the stairs.

Paramedics arrived, and the whirlwind began. Zera shuffled back and gave them space, the movement reminding her she was still in her outfit from the party. As they worked, she retreated to Katherine's room and ripped off the suit and the corset, changing into a random sweatshirt and shorts before grabbing what clothes of hers she could see and stuffing them into a bag. Her hair was a mess and her face even worse, but she could still move.

"I'm going with you." She caught the group as they filed out of the room.

"You his wife?" the closest man asked.

"Yes." The lie was easy. Past the tubes and breathing bag, she could swear Christopher smiled. "Please, I don't want to leave him."

"Alright then, follow us."

It was slow going down the hallway, and as they navigated the stairs, Zera took one last look back at the apartment. A trail of blood led to the closed door, back to the place where she and Katherine spent the past few days living something close to normal. It felt like the end of something, and it left Zera unsettled.

Someone appeared at the other end of the hallway. He was dressed in a black suit and stood so still Zera had to blink a few times to make sure she wasn't imagining him. The same purple mask from the party shone in the lights, looking less like a cheap plastic imitation and something more sinister. His eyes were two dark spots beneath the mask, but Zera could tell he was staring right at her. At his sides, his hands clenched into fists, and he shifted ever so slightly. A silver pocket watch chain chimed with the movement, the warning bell.

Zera slipped her hand into her pocket and grabbed her knife, turning to face him. Behind her, the paramedics continued to ease the gurney and Christopher down the stairs, unaware of the threat down the hall. Edward would likely beat her in a fight, Katherine was right about that. But she could at least slow him down.

He stayed coiled like a snake, and Zera held her breath, her hands shaking in rage and fear and everything in between. *Come on, come on!* she egged him, the waiting game worse than whatever the fight might bring.

"Ma'am? Are you coming?" The paramedic sounded far away, and when Zera glanced around, she found them at the foot of the stairs.

"What?" She turned back to the hallway, but Edward was gone. Shit. "Uh, yeah, sorry. I'm coming."

Mardi Gras continued around them as the paramedics loaded Christopher into the ambulance. Zera kept her knife in her hand, her eyes scanning for any sign of a black suit or the mask. But they ushered her into the back and closed the door without any more interference from Edward. His prey incapacitated, he was gone.

And so was Katherine.

ASH WEDNESDAY DAWNED cold and cloudy, a day of remembrance and of loss.

With little sleep and Christopher's blood under her fingernails, Zera shuffled through the empty streets of New Orleans to the rendezvous point. Trash littered the place, and discarded beads added to the sparkles in front of her tired eyes. The fifteen-minute walk to New Orleans City Park might have lasted an hour for the work her tired legs produced.

She checked her watch: ten till nine, exactly when Kissi advised her to return. She had five minutes to compose herself before Byrd arrived.

Katherine was gone. Christopher was in critical condition. And Zera had to save the world like it hadn't crushed her in the past twenty-four hours.

Moisture seeped through her jeans and jacket when she sat on the grass to wait. She'd disposed of the blood-covered remnants of her borrowed clothes and donned her original outfit, glad she had pants to hide where her knees were still stained red. The cool, humid air hurt her face where she'd scrubbed her makeup away, but any further discomfort was a blip on her radar as Byrd materialized.

Light gathered and swirled in front of her, almost like rapids churning.

Disembodied hands and feet and elbows and organs appeared and disappeared, his body reorganizing a hundred horrific ways before solidifying and dropping him back to earth. The collecting poles landed next to him with a loud clatter. She'd seen it with Kissi back in 1992, but somehow it seemed so much worse this time.

Byrd rolled onto his hands and knees and vomited for an impressively long time. Zera grimaced and turned away until he finished with ragged gasps and a low moan.

"God, it's like it doesn't even bother you." His face was pale, but not as pale as Christopher's the night before.

"It gets easier." Especially when she had ten days to recover. "You okay?"

"Yeah." He coughed and wiped his mouth with his sleeve. Then, as if remembering where he was, he looked up at the sky and laughed. "Holy shit. It's like the first time all over again."

"That's something I'll never get used to." No matter how many mornings she woke up in Katherine's bed, she was always surprised to see the sun shining amicably outside her window, a friend instead of an enemy. She wondered if that would ever go away once she returned for good. "You ready to get started?"

"Get started? Hell no, Zera, we've got some exploring to do. Do you know how long it's been since I've been to New Orleans?"

"You've been here before?" She pushed herself up, then hauled Byrd to his feet. He grabbed the poles and stashed them in a thick copse of trees nearby.

"Once, a long time ago," he said. "C'mon, I'll show you the best breakfast spot."

"You sure you can manage to eat?"

"I'll find a way. Have you ever had a beignet?"

"Yeah—I mean, maybe. Not the real thing, probably." She needed to get her story straight and stick to it. "Not here, at least."

"Get ready. They're amazing."

Zera almost said she preferred the king cake they had a few nights prior to the beignets, but stopped herself just in time. Byrd walked with a purpose, renewed at the thought of fried dough, and Zera had no choice but to shove down her sadness and follow.

A few early risers stumbled down the streets now, and a solid half of the cafe booths held at least one patron with plates of food and large cups of coffee. Byrd was easily the most conscious person there despite having the longest commute, and cheerfully ordered his breakfast.

"Man, never thought I'd be here again," he said, settling into a wire chair outside.

"When were you here?" It was only polite to ask, though Zera found herself uninterested in the answer. It got Byrd talking though, which meant she didn't have to force conversation through the lingering hurt. Was Christopher okay? How was she going to get back to the hospital without making Byrd suspicious?

"What about your friend?" The question broke her spell.

She choked on her coffee. "What?"

"The friend you ran into a couple times. Katherine? Is she still alive? She's gotta be ancient by now, right?"

"Oh, uh, I don't know." Navigating this question was more difficult.

"You didn't look her up before we came?"

Right, because they came together.

"No, it, uh, slipped my mind." She scrambled for an excuse. "Between Vylek's email and the meeting and everything, Kissi and I didn't have time to look. Plus, I figured I'd mind the rules now that you're here."

"That's a shame," Byrd said. "I was hoping to meet her."

"Why?" Zera asked, defensive over Katherine and their time together.

Byrd shrugged and took a sip of coffee. "I don't know, it's probably rare to meet someone cool with time travelers." He adopted what he probably thought was a charming smile. "Bet I could get her to help us more than you could."

If only he knew the ways she could convince Katherine. "I think you underestimate the bonds forged between women."

"Maybe." He didn't sound like he agreed. He downed his coffee in one go, and Zera forced hers down as well, finding it weaker than she wanted. "C'mon, I wanna see the city before we have to go work. What time does the storm start again?"

"Half past four, or somewhere around there." She checked her watch. Over seven hours of suffering with Byrd, not knowing what was going on with Christopher—or Katherine.

"Plenty of time," Byrd said with a clap, and he started off again.

Zera followed him like a zombie through World War II museums and tourist shops. Every so often she spotted the tower of the hospital in the distance, and her thoughts drifted back to the night before. With a chill she realized Edward might still be in New Orleans, searching for Katherine. Would he also search for her?

Adrenaline spiked at the thought, and for the rest of their walking tour she kept her head on a swivel and her hand on her pocket knife, waiting to see that cold, dead stare through the crowd. It would be hard to recognize him without the mask and the suit, but she could place those eyes anywhere.

"Are you sure you're okay?" Byrd asked. He was reading a plaque in yet another World War II museum, the picture above it displaying a group of soldiers staring at the camera with gaunt eyes and baggy uniforms.

"This one just got to me, I don't know why." She shook her head. "I'm sure I'll perk up here in a little bit."

Byrd grinned. "I'll make sure of it. Still plenty of fun to see."

He led her through the rest of the museum, spouting random facts to supplement the displays Zera paid no attention to. All the while she kept looking around and startling at the slightest movement out of place. Any shadow could be Edward, any object a knife ready to cut.

Byrd no doubt thought his enthusiasm would spread to Zera, but it only grated on her as the hours passed. Even when they stopped for lunch, he kept talking with food in his mouth. She remembered finding him funny, even charming at one point, but her grief and fatigue compounded her annoyance and she wanted nothing more than to retreat to Katherine's apartment to cry and sleep.

"Alright, I guess we can go do some work or something," Byrd said as the clock ticked past four.

Zera sighed, the pressure in her chest releasing a touch. "Was the trip everything you hoped for?" she asked. With the end in sight, it was easier to be polite.

He shrugged. "I guess so. I just wish I could stay longer, you know? You've had so many opportunities to see the world again."

"I mean, it wasn't all fun, and it wasn't that many days." This trip was, but he didn't need to know that. "I did almost get stuck in a burning building. And I did get arrested. And I had to stumble around hoping I found something that would help the whole situation back in 2058."

"Blah, blah, blah, excuses," Byrd said. "I know you were just partying it up, that's why it took so long. And now that I finally get to go, it's all business."

"I hardly think today was 'all business,'" she said with a dry laugh. "I think we did everything New Orleans has to offer besides the ghost tours."

"Ah, shit, you're right." They entered the park again and made their way to the center. It was close to empty, which could either help or hinder them. "Think they'll get mad if we stay the night? It's not like it matters what time we leave if we get back at the same point."

Zera didn't like that idea. If she was going to stay the night, it wouldn't be with Byrd, it would be crying in Katherine's apartment—alone, like an adult.

"And where are we gonna stay, hmm? You got money for two hotel rooms?" she asked.

"I could get some."

"From where? Actually, where did you get the money for today?" If she hadn't had Katherine, she wouldn't have survived all the days she spent back in time. Military credits didn't transfer here—they didn't even exist yet.

"Oh, I've got skills you know nothing about." He probably meant for it to sound flirtatious, but Zera grimaced. "Besides, we're adults. We could share a room."

"Absolutely not," she said quickly.

Byrd rolled his eyes. "Don't make it weird, Zera," he said, retrieving the poles from their hiding place. He handed one to her, then set his up and messed with the screen. "It would just be to save money. But hey, if you wanna be prudish, that's fine too."

"I wouldn't say I'm prudish." It wasn't an insult, but she was tired and combative. "I just don't think my girlfriend would like it." Technically, Katherine was not her girlfriend, but the excuse was good enough.

Byrd's eyebrows flew toward his hairline. "Girlfriend, huh? Do tell."

"No thanks."

"Oh, come on, you can't just drop a bomb like that and then back away."

"That's literally what you're supposed to do with bombs."

"You're evading the question."

"You don't know her."

"Not Kissinger then," he said. A moment later, the pole started digging, the sound giving Zera enough time to collect her thoughts. She was far enough away by the time it finished to warrant raised voices for conversation. "Who is it then?" Byrd called.

"Remember where we are," she called back. While New Orleans seemed an accepting city, it was still 2004, and Zera was not willing to risk another arrest. He was far enough away that she didn't hear his response, but she did see him roll his eyes.

The whir of the pole drowned her thoughts for a moment, the reprieve welcome. Stressing about Katherine, Christopher, Byrd, *and* the mission was taking its toll, and she was counting down the minutes until it was over. Byrd, apparently accepting defeat in the conversation, took the last pole to its measure point and dug it in.

At thirty-two minutes past four, the sky shifted. If Zera were an everyday citizen, she wouldn't have noticed. But she knew how to look for these events now and felt the roll in her stomach that accompanied it, the lingering nausea raising its head.

"Whoa, feels weird." Byrd met her in the middle and handed over the tablet. "You feel that?"

"I think that's your imagination," Zera said. There was no way he could feel it on his second trip; she hadn't until her...third? Fourth? She couldn't keep track now.

Byrd put his hands on his hips and looked up at the sky. "Crazy," he muttered. "So this finds all the anomalies or whatever?"

"I'm not sure, if I'm honest." She tapped the screen and initiated the program. "I just know it gets the data that can help reverse the effects of the Storm."

"Just casually saving everyone, it's fine," he said. "I'm definitely gonna hold this over everyone for the rest of my life."

"You're that asshole on the group project, huh?" Zera's eyes stayed on the screen, watching the numbers flood in.

Byrd laughed. "I'm just efficient like that."

"Typical," The numbers kept running, and the timer in the corner counted down five minutes.

"So about this girlfriend..." he continued.

"Nope."

"No one's around, and I'm bored."

"You can't sit still and shut up for five minutes?"

"Tell me."

Zera closed her eyes and took a deep breath. "You don't even know her."

"It's a small bunker, I know everyone."

"No you don't, she's on the civilian side."

"Fine. How did you meet her then?"

"Just happened to cross paths." Close enough.

"Ah, fate then."

"Luck at best." And perhaps a few deities—Zera was never quite sure.

"And you two are...serious?" The way he wiggled his eyebrows implied a second meaning.

"We're not having this conversation."

"I'm just talking shop!"

"I'm not 'talking shop' with you."

"Why not?"

"'Cause talking to women about women never goes the way you think it will," she said. "You wanna learn something, do your research like the rest of us."

"Oh, I can assure you, every partner I've had didn't harbor any complaints—"

"And we're done!" The timer dinged and the numbers stopped. They were ready to leave. "Let's pack up and head back."

"I still say we should stay the night."

"I feel like shit, Byrd. I'm going back." She wanted to check on Christopher one more time, but she couldn't with Byrd around.

An idea formed.

"Ugh, fine." Byrd stomped to the far pole, and once again the grinds and whirs sounded as they removed the poles from the ground. Zera took care to keep her face neutral, though her heart was ready to leap from her chest. It was such a simple answer—why didn't she think of it earlier?

"Okay, got everything?" she asked. It was a stupid question—she could see all their materials right there—but it kept Byrd's focus on their stuff rather than her face.

"I think so." He pulled the return syringe from his pocket, and she did the same. "We really just slam this into our leg?"

"Yep. And don't think about the needle." A cold patch appeared in between her shoulder blades at the thought of the sharp point, but she turned her thoughts to the situation at hand.

"Okay. You first," Byrd said.

Zera balked. "What? Why?"

"I wanna see how it looks," he said eagerly.

She narrowed her eyes. "You just wanna stay behind and paint the town red tonight."

"You're right, grandma," he said. "With no judgment from you."

"Byrd, just—" Zera groaned. He was going to ruin all her plans. She marched over and grabbed his wrist. He was stronger than her, certainly. The way his forearm muscles bulged under her fingers meant she couldn't pry the injector from him. But it gave her a nice target for the syringe she held.

"What the—"

As expected, Byrd dropped his anchor syringe when she sank her own into the meat of his forearm. She dropped his arm and swiped the unspent one from the grass, light gathering next to her.

"Zera you bi—"

Byrd was gone before he could finish the word.

"Thank you," she said, stuffing the return syringe back in her pocket.

It was easier to breathe on her walk back to the hospital. Katherine was gone, she knew, but it was still dangerous. As soon as she checked on Christopher, she would go.

The lobby of the hospital was much more welcoming than the emergency room the night before, though the woman sitting at the desk looked no less fed up than her counterpart. She looked at Zera over the silver frames of her glasses, her mouth puckered as she took in her unruly hair and disheveled clothes.

"And what can we help you with, miss?" Oftentimes the women of the South sounded sickly sweet, but there was a fermented edge to her tone.

"I'm hoping you can direct me to my husband," Zera said.

The lie was apparently the proper password, and the woman brightened. "Well then, why didn't you say so? Do you know what unit he's in?"

"The ICU, I think." Zera tapped her fingers against the countertop and sent a casual glance over her shoulder. The syringe sat heavy in her pocket, ready for a quick getaway.

"The ICU? Oh, I'm so sorry, dear." She pointed to the elevators. "Second floor, turn right and it'll be at the end of the hall."

"Thank you." Zera didn't wait for the response, instead moving to catch one of the elevators before it closed. It felt wrong to take it up only one floor—and her companion in the lift seemed to feel the same—but she didn't have time to care. Her heart pounded as she exited and walked at a controlled pace toward the sounds of whirring and beeping machines in the ICU.

The nearest nurse looked up as Zera entered, her large eyes even bigger behind her thick glasses. "Hi, looking for someone?" she asked.

"Yes, my husband Christopher? He came in late last night with a knife wound." She wasn't certain of the injury, but the paramedics were confident enough in the ambulance ride.

The nurse's face fell. "Oh, honey, they didn't call you? I'm so sorry," she said softly, putting her arm around Zera's shoulders. "Let me get the doctor for you."

"No, no, just show me where he is." Zera wriggled from her grasp and strode down the hallway, looking through the open doors in search of a familiar face.

"Miss, please—" The nurse jogged after her and took her arm. "Please, let me grab the doctor."

"I just need to see him, where is he?"

Zera stopped and looked at the nurse, waiting for an answer. The nurse swallowed and opened her mouth, but no sounds emerged.

Tears bristled behind Zera's eyes. "What happened to him? Please."

The nurse nodded. "He passed a few hours ago. I'm so sorry, honey."

Passed.

Zera couldn't breathe. She'd told Katherine she would look out for Christopher, that he would be okay. Logically she knew it wasn't her fault —the injury was bad, and she did everything she could. But the thought of telling Katherine that one of the last people in this world who understood her was gone made bile rise in the back of her throat.

"Miss? Are you okay? Do you want—I can take you downstairs so you can say goodbye. And we can arrange for him to go to—" The nurse reached for her again.

Zera stepped back. "I'll...say my goodbyes in a minute." She turned quickly on her heel and walked out of the ICU. The nurse called after her, but Zera moved faster, spotting the sign for the stairs and pushing through the door. She was halfway down before she heard the door open behind her, but the nurse couldn't catch up to her.

Once out of the hospital and away from prying eyes, Zera retrieved the syringe from her pocket. Byrd's name was printed on the side, reminding her of her treachery. She would have to make it worth it. Katherine was gone, Christopher was dead, and Edward was alive, hunting. She sank the needle into her thigh and waited for the river to claim her.

There was only one answer. She had to find Edward first.

2058

NEVER BEFORE DID Zera think winning would feel like drowning.

"It's all done, Lieutenant," Vylek said. The lines around her face were soft, and her shoulders seemed looser than usual. Though her hands sat intertwined on the desk, the knuckles were her normal skin tone rather than bleached white with tension.

"The mission?" she asked. Kissi, from the chair to her side, placed a hand on her leg.

"The *whole* mission." Vylek sounded happy, maybe even proud. "The data you and Lieutenant Byrd brought back from New Orleans was enough for the brains downstairs to figure out a plan."

"What?" It was supposed to be a good thing. Zera was supposed to be happy. Why did it fill her stomach with lead? "What about the other trips?"

Vylek leaned back in her chair and held her hands up. "You don't have to take any more trips. We can move forward now and reverse what happened."

Zera straightened. "How can they be sure we got enough data? There's still another storm in 2016, and in 2028. Things might change—"

"What confidence interval did they use for the calculations?" Kissi interrupted, squeezing Zera's leg hard. "We only used the below-ground sensors once. There's no way we have enough data to create a counter-measure."

Vylek shrugged. "That's outside my wheelhouse, Lieutenant. But, as a thank you for your hard work, I did secure you positions in the new project. And, got you a promotion. You're both captains now, effective immediately."

"What?"

Kissi squeezed her leg again. "I think Zazzera meant what are our new positions as captains?"

Vylek raised an eyebrow, her expression mildly threatening, but Zera didn't heed the warning. Everything Vylek said passed through a buzz of panic.

"Kissinger, you'll be helping with the experimentation, of course," Vylek said, starting with the obvious. "Zazzera, thanks to that month you spent with the mechanics, you'll be manufacturing the stuff to test."

Manufacturing.

She'd gone from sweating at a dig site to sweating in a machine shop, and would leave Katherine wondering until the end of time.

No, not the end. Just until 2040.

"What will happen to the equipment?" she asked.

Vylek blinked. "It served its purpose, so it'll be broken down and used in other areas."

"You invented time travel and you're just going to disassemble it?" One more go, that's all Zera needed. Then she could dig the tracker out of her side, find Katherine, and carry on.

Vylek leaned forward again, this time with some of her old anger. "That technology could be dangerous in the wrong hands. What do you suggest we do with it, hmm? Send everyone back to the time they prefer and hope they survive the trip? Go back and kill people who caused prob-lems? You're thinking small, Zazzera. We can't change anything. This was never about going back—it was always about going forward."

Forward, but to what?

Zera dropped her gaze. Vylek was right—this was bigger than her and Katherine. They were supposed to make this world better for everyone, *right now*, and this was the way to do it.

But the reason didn't ease her pain any less.

"You'll report to your new assignments on Monday. Good job, you two, and thank you again."

"What about Byrd?" Zera hadn't seen him since she returned, and was actively avoiding him.

"Byrd's still in the hospital wing. He didn't recover as easily as you," Vylek said. "But I'm sure he'll still be around. He always manages to put his nose where it doesn't belong."

"Sounds about right," Kissi said. She stood and dragged Zera to her feet. "Thank you, ma'am. Will that be all?"

"Dismissed," Vylek said.

And just like that, Zera's life was over.

"C'mon, Zera." Kissi grabbed Zera's elbow and led her out of the room. When the door closed behind them, Zera could breathe a little easier and walk on her own accord, which she did at mach speed back to their room.

"This is bullshit!" she yelled before the door closed all the way. The conspiracy wall fluttered as she paced by it, hands in her hair. "We were supposed to go two more times, I told Katherine—"

"Cut it out," Kissi interrupted, "and think for a second. Not about Katherine, but about everything."

Zera whirled around to find Kissi glaring. "What are you talking about?"

"We saved the *fucking* world, Zazzera," Kissi said. "And you're freaking out 'cause you won't get to hang out with some girl again."

"I'm freaking out because without Katherine, we wouldn't have gotten all this information. And we're just leaving her to die." It was, at least, partly the truth.

"She did help, but you only care because you've got feelings for her," Kissi said. She raised her hands up before Zera could reply. "No, don't deny it. You need to be honest with yourself."

Zera's cheeks burned, both with anger and chagrin. "Okay, fine, you're right. I only care about going back because I like her. Happy?"

"Yes, because now we can move past it."

"Move past—"

"It's bigger than us, Zera. Vylek got us promotions. Working down in the science levels will give us bigger rooms and more money. It'll be better."

"You know what would also be better? Going back in time and staying there."

Kissi jerked back as if struck. "You can't be serious."

"I'm one hundred percent serious." Zera stepped closer. "Think about it. We go back to 2004. We have a solid thirty-six years before the 2040 Storm occurs. That's thirty-six beautiful years of sunshine, and space, and real food and real people. We wouldn't have to maintain our commission."

"We also have to deal with all the shit from those years." Kissi gestured to her face, highlighting her dark skin. "Or did you forget how things could go for me? Or you, for that matter, since you wanna be out with your girlfriend."

"Katherine's got that stuff figured out." It was an assumption, and Zera hoped it wouldn't come back to bite her in the ass. "She's a hundred and fifty years old, she knows how to find and build a safe space."

Kissi let out a long breath and pinched the bridge of her nose. "It doesn't matter. We don't have access to any of that stuff anymore. You heard Vylek, they're going to break it down."

"We can find more serum and stuff. I broke into Doyle's office once, I bet I can do it again." She resumed pacing. "Think about it. We can get an apartment, get normal jobs, have normal friends—"

"And just leave everyone else here?" Kissi asked. "Lieb and Martin and everyone we've shared space with for the past eighteen years?"

"You heard Vylek, they've got stuff in the works now. They'll rebuild or whatever."

"So why not stay and see it through?"

"Because I don't want to do grunt work in a basement for the rest of my life!" Zera snapped. "It took them eighteen years to find a fix—how long will it take to implement it? Five? Ten? Fifteen? What if something goes awry and they have to reopen the project or figure out something else?"

"And staying here with me during all that would be so bad?"

"Kissi you're literally the only reason I came back," Zera said. "Can you honestly tell me you wanna sit behind a computer forever?"

A muscle in Kissi's jaw flexed. "I wouldn't mind it, actually. I'm good at my job, and I like it."

"But you could do something else where you didn't have to live underground."

"And just abandon everything here?"

Zera took one breath, then another. "Kissi, I know it's scary, but it's... this isn't much of a life, what we've got here. Not when we could have something better. Sure, maybe you get to spend the next twenty years fixing everything. Or maybe a quake hits tomorrow and turns this whole place to rubble."

Kissi paused at that. "You just want to get back to your girlfriend," she said after a moment.

"Yeah, but I wanna bring you with me."

Kissi stared at her, and Zera could tell she was going through each argument and thinking of the pros and cons. Zera was extra glad she took her back to 1992, where she could see exactly what they missed by living in this hole in the ground. She wanted to get back to Katherine, yes, but she also didn't want Kissi stuck here. Her job was fun now, but there were so many unknowns, a hundred risks waiting in the dark. Better to face them in the sunshine.

Finally, Kissi groaned and collapsed at her desk. "Zazzera if you get my hopes up just to crush them I'm gonna be so pissed."

"Well earned."

"And this isn't me agreeing. This is just me assessing options."

"Of course."

"I'll still send you back, even if I have to stay here."

"I—wait, what?"

Kissi turned. "That's what you want, right? To go back regardless?"

Zera knew what the correct answer was, but she still hesitated. "No, I want to stay with you. If you don't go, I won't go."

"Bullshit." Kissi gave her a sad smile. "But I appreciate it nonetheless."

"Just...think about it. Sleep on it. We don't have to make any long term decisions right now."

"I'll think about it." Kissi sighed. "Now, are you gonna tell me about all the extra time I gave you?"

"Will it convince you to come back with me?"

"Worth a shot."

Zera told her everything, from New Orleans to Disney World to Katherine's dead husband showing up at the Mardi Gras Ball.

"Hold up, stop," Kissi said, raising a hand. "Did I hear that correctly?"

"Yes, dead husband is actually living husband and is the one hunting down Katherine and her friends," Zera said. "Now you see why I'm a little eager to get back to her."

"Shit." Kissi rubbed her hands together. Then she drew the word out. "*Shit.*"

"Yeah. Problem is, he wore a mask the whole time, so I have no clue what his face looks like."

"But you have a name now." Kissi turned back to her computer and opened the intranet archive.

"I have a first name," Zera reminded her.

Kissi waved her off. "You said Katherine noticed she changed after an Arctic expedition in 1884?" Kissi asked, already typing in the search bar.

"Yeah. So it was Katherine, and Edward"—She spat the name out—"then also Christopher, and William, and..." She squeezed her eyes shut and wracked her brain. "Shit, every name sounds correct. But I know Christopher and William for sure, as well as Katherine and Edward."

"Easy," Kissi said. "There were a ton of Arctic expeditions in the late 1800s and early 1900s, but with all those names and a specific year..." She typed it all in and pressed enter. The results page was short and included two scanned photos with edges chewed by time. Zera recognized the photo of those who returned, but another showed an entire crew.

Zera moved closer and rested her chin on Kissi's shoulder. The photo was grainy, with vaguely human-shaped blobs positioned in a line, their faces washed out and clothing dark. If it weren't for the bun on top of Katherine's head, Zera might not have recognized her at all.

The caption named William and Christopher and all their companions, but spots blotted out most of the names, including Edward and Katherine's. Zera huffed, which made Kissi flinch.

"Stop breathing on me."

"Stop getting in the way of my breath."

"I'm trying to help you here."

"Oh, right, sorry." Zera gave her space.

"I can enlarge this photo and try to do an image search," Kissi said, circling a face that might be Edward's. "But the quality's pretty low, I doubt we'll get anything."

Zera snapped her fingers. "Wait. At the Mardi Gras Ball, there were a bunch of people taking pictures. Maybe some of them made it into the archive."

"It's a possibility," Kissi said. She refined the search to the group Katherine was a part of in New Orleans, and for Mardi Gras in 2004. There were more results this time, one of which was an entire folder of photos.

"Jackpot." Zera clapped her hands. Kissi opened the file, and both their jaws slowly dropped as hundreds of pictures unwound.

"Holy shit."

"Dammit."

The photos numbered eight hundred and forty-two in total, with zero identifying captions.

"Well," Kissi said. "If you can find me some coffee and some snacks, I'll get started."

"No, this is my problem," Zera said. "You've already done more than enough. I can do the search."

Kissi looked like she wanted to protest, but in the end, she nodded and pushed back from the computer. "Fine. But I'm getting you coffee and snacks."

"My card's in the drawer."

The door shut and left Zera in silence. There were so many things she needed to do, so many plans to make. Would she say goodbye to Lieb? To Martin? To any other friends she made here?

As if he knew her thoughts, Byrd sent a message, asking how she was and if she heard the news. Zera left the message unread—she'd message him later, once she'd scanned through all the pictures waiting for her.

Zera cleared and organized the things on the desk, giving her mind extra space for her search. There were so many pages of little details they found over the course of this investigation, so many things that would've been lost to history. The list of death dates popped up, and just to punish herself, Zera looked at Christopher's.

Weirdly, Christopher's death date was listed in 2004, but it was a few weeks after Mardi Gras. Had something changed? Or did they just write down the wrong date in the records?

There was no way to know at this point. With a sigh, Zera clicked on the first photo and slowly scanned the faces, looking for a man with a dark mask and a pocket watch.

Kissi came back sometime later with the promised refreshments, and by that point Zera was knee deep in the pictures and had three unread messages from Byrd. A jolt went through her at every dark suit, which was a pain considering her own suit that night was a deep plum. It was hard not to stop and save all the pictures with her and Katherine, even ones where they were simply dancing in the background. They even had the one from the balcony, and the sight of their smiles made Zera's heart ache.

Sitting at the desk also made her back and neck ache, but she continued on, even when the circadian lights dimmed and Kissi crawled into her bunk. She continued even though her eyes felt like sandpaper and fatigue weighed down her limbs. For someone who traveled through time, she never seemed to have enough of it.

It was well past the witching hour when Zera spotted a black suit among the flood of color in the ballroom. Her heart beat faster, and her head swam from the potent mixture of exhaustion and adrenaline as she flipped through each picture carefully.

He was in the background as she and Katherine danced, leaning against the wall.

He appeared a few feet over in the next picture, trying to catch Katherine's eye.

In the next photo, she and Katherine were gone, having their romantic moment on the balcony. Step by step, she watched Edward move through the crowd to the center of the ballroom, in a direct line of sight from the doors. Any second now, Katherine would go back inside and see his face.

He stopped.

The mask lifted.

Zera jumped back from the desk, the chair clattering to the ground and waking Kissi.

"The fuck—"

"It's—he's—"

"You found him?"

Kissi rolled out of bed and righted the chair before using it as a crutch to get to the desk. The light of the screen blinded her, and Zera held her breath as Kissi squinted and rubbed her eyes to adjust to the glare. She saw the moment Kissi found his face.

"That's him?"

"Yes."

"You're sure?"

"Positive."

Zera moved closer to look at the screen again, hoping it was a trick of the light, or that her eyes had simply given up on her. But there, in a perfectly crisp picture, with his black suit and dark eyes that Zera was so sure she'd recognize, stood Katherine's husband Edward.

Edward Byrd.

2058

STEALTH NO LONGER MATTERED.

Though she had seen neither hide nor hair of Byrd since their return, Zera looked over her shoulder every few seconds, as if he was going to appear out of nowhere.

"There's no time to get a serum," Kissi said. "I'll send you on and come later."

"No, he was acting super weird in New Orleans," Zera said as they ran through the halls. "He's gonna put two and two together, probably sooner rather than later."

People passing gave them weird looks, and they nearly ran over more than a few, but they didn't stop. At this point, it was literally life or death.

"I told you there was something off about him!" Kissi said.

"Can we revisit this later? I promise, you can yell at me all you want in 2004."

"I'll remember that."

Dr. Doyle startled as they bulldozed into his office. "What the fuck—"

"Sorry Doc, but we need serum," Kissi said.

"The project's been canceled—"

"No time to explain!" Zera leaned out the door and checked for Byrd.

Still no sign of him, which was more worrisome than encouraging. "But we need the serum, right now."

"Surely there's something—"

"I'm sorry," Kissi said, ripping open the drawer. The case sat in its depths, and Kissi grabbed it.

"You can't—"

"We have to!"

Zera heard him calling after them, tossing out threats about *trouble* and *court martial*. But Zera knew a court martial was the least of their worries; after decades of killing, Byrd could make them disappear.

Two more turns, and they'd be in the clear. But as they entered the final hallway, a group of men entered at the opposite end, Byrd at the very front. He grinned, bordering on maniacal.

"There you are. I was wondering why you weren't replying to me."

"Run!"

Zera dragged Kissi down the hall and they managed to slip into the platform room and close the door just before Byrd and his group met them. Fists slammed against the door, but Kissi rigged it to stay locked.

"Here you go." Zera uncapped one of the serums and stabbed it into Kissi's leg as she bent over a computer screen.

"2004 for a land date?"

"Yeah, do it," Zera said. "I don't care where, just not New Orleans."

"Got it."

Zera took the second syringe and, without thinking too hard, slammed it into her thigh. Her adrenaline drowned out the pain from the needle, but not the warmth of the serum. She jumped onto the platform and found her spot.

"Ready?"

"It's throwing an error at me," Kissi said. "It wants a return time."

"Just set it, and we'll dig the tethers out when we get there."

Heavier things hit the door now, but Kissi's override held true. Zera didn't know how long it would stay locked, only that she wanted them both to be gone when it failed.

"Ugh, fine, okay." Kissi typed a few more things, then left the desk and joined Zera up on the platform. "You're sure this'll work?"

"You're the analyst, not me!" Zera looked around as the machine hummed and the temperature climbed. "Why isn't it working?"

"It takes sixty seconds to send two people," Kissi explained.

"Sixty—"

The door groaned, and the sounds of scraping crowbars sounded over the grind of the machine.

"There's no way to speed it up?"

"Not that I know of!"

Zera glanced at her watch. They had forty-five long seconds left.

"Listen, Zera, if something goes wrong—"

"Don't talk like that," Zera said. "We don't need any bad energy right now."

"Just wanna say I'm glad we lived through the apocalypse together."

Zera looked over, then took Kissi's hand. "Me too. I'll see you on the other side."

The scraping intensified, and light spilled through the crack in the door. Zera squeezed Kissi's hand tighter, the countdown continuing in her head. They didn't need the door to last forever, just seventeen more seconds.

More light came through as the gap widened, but the machine was picking up now. Zera felt the tingle as it resonated with whatever crap she injected into herself each trip, the pull of the river starting low in her gut. Beside her, Kissi breathed fast and shallow, trying to stay brave.

"Stop right there!" the military policeman said as he continued to wrench the door. Zera took a breath and prepared herself to throw back something snarky, but the words died in her throat. Because behind him stood Byrd, with that dark stare.

Those were the eyes she recognized.

"I knew it was you." His voice carried over the machine.

Five more seconds.

With a few inches of space, Byrd shoved the military policeman aside.

Four seconds.

He forced himself through the door, the narrow space ripping his fatigues.

Three.

He went to the computer. Kissi shouted and tried to move, but Zera held her fast.

Two.

Surely it would take longer than a second to cancel—there had to be passcodes or protocol or something.

One.

Byrd looked up and smiled.

The machine didn't stop. In fact, it continued its pull. But the last thing Zera saw before the river claimed them was the mad grin that said someway, somehow, Byrd had won.

2040

THEY LANDED with a loud thud and a sense of foreboding.

"Holy—" Kissi leaned over and vomited. Zera crawled over and did her best to hold her locs back. When she finished, she rolled onto her back and looked up at the pristine blue sky. Zera knew that wonder, that awe, of seeing the sun again. While Kissi recovered, Zera lifted her shirt, found the bump in her side that signified the tracker, and sliced her skin open before she could think too much about it.

The implant was shallow, but the wound still bled, and a web of scar tissue pulled her entire side as she ripped the tender threads holding it in place. A slow trickle of blood painted her skin and soaked the waistband of her pants, but with one last grunt, Zera removed the tracker completely and tossed it in the grass.

"Sorry about this."

Kissi lay on the grass, breathing, and didn't fight as Zera sliced into the meat of her arm. Luckily, since her tracker placement was shallow and applied by amateurs, it came out much easier than Zera's. She barely had time to yelp at the knife digging into her flesh.

Zera looked around. They were in the middle of a park, the trees and grass and path familiar. But this wasn't New Orleans, where they'd gathered data.

A chill settled in Zera's stomach.

"Where are we?" Kissi righted herself and wiped her mouth with the back of her hand.

"Central Park," Zera said.

"Back in 2004?"

The trees were too tall, the trails too organized. In the distance, they could hear the cacophony of the city.

"No." A construction zone sat a few yards away, the weak tape and orange barrels marking off the section. "No, I think we're—shit!"

She grabbed Kissi by the elbow and dragged her behind a bush. The world spun as they rolled into place. Gods, she was going to have to relive this day all over again, with the same outcome.

"What the hell, Zera?"

"Shh!"

Sure enough, a few minutes later she saw herself—a past version of herself, fresh on her first time travel mission—running toward the construction zone. Past Zera stopped, and current Zera's stomach boiled. She remembered this moment, trying to decide whether to focus on the task at hand or go find her mother.

In a few minutes, she'd meet Katherine in the clearing, and hold her as she died.

Dr. Phillips said nothing could change. But maybe she was wrong.

"Let's go," Zera said, once her past self was gone.

"Where are we—oh, no, is this—?"

"Yes. Maybe we can save her after all."

"She'll still die in the Storm. We all will."

Zera took the long way around, begging her adrenaline to sharpen her senses and purge the travel sickness as she limped toward the opposite edge of the clearing. If she and Katherine met on the north side, then the shooter—Byrd, it *had* to be Byrd—would be south of them. She pulled her knife from her pocket and flipped it open. *This* was why he'd wanted to separate during the first trip; somehow, he knew Katherine would be there, and he was ready to enact his revenge.

The thick grass hid the sounds of their careful steps, Kissi following right behind her despite having very little idea of what was going on.

Zera was literally taking a knife to a gun fight, but what choice did she have?

They rounded the southern edge of the clearing, and sure enough, there was Byrd, hiding behind a tree. But this wasn't the Byrd she knew, with a crew cut and fatigues. This was Edward, dressed in civilian clothes, his blond hair long enough for the light breeze to pick it up. Something about his appearance tickled her memory, and she remembered with a jolt the man in 1968, running in front of a blue car.

Now, he held a revolver at his side. With his other hand, he withdrew a familiar-looking pocket watch and idly checked the time. They were standing at the epicenter, where the Storm first hit. Where, in the future, a massive pit waited for Zera to find that very same watch.

She readied her knife and took one step, then another. A few more, and she would be close enough to stab him, and Katherine could spend her last few moments in joy instead of pain.

A shot rang out. *Her* shot. The warning shot she'd given Katherine, before she knew what she would mean to her.

Zera hit the deck, pulling Kissi down with her.

If Edward noticed Kissi's squawk, he didn't show it. Granted, he was probably distracted by Past Zera's stray bullet tearing through his shoulder. He fell with a groan, and it almost sounded more frustrated than pained. His back was to them, the gray of his t-shirt quickly staining red. She remembered seeing the scar of that shot on their very first day in the program. Everything was adding up.

"Shit," he said.

This would be the right moment, Zera thought. Just sneak up behind him and stab him. That would show Dr. Phillips—no future version of Byrd could shoot Katherine if Zera killed him right now.

Two more shots rang out. She was already too late.

Movement across the clearing caught her eye. The Byrd she came with on her first trip stalked across the park, tucking his pistol into the back of his pants. She couldn't win this fight, and couldn't risk him seeing her. But she could find Katherine and let her die with someone who knew her, who cared about her, rather than a stranger.

"Go," Kissi whispered, pushing Zera toward her past self. "I'll take care of him."

Zera hesitated. She would have remembered seeing herself in the past.

"I won't make it," she said. They couldn't change anything. How often had Dr. Phillips stressed that?

"Not with that attitude." Kissi had a point.

Zera stayed low as she tore around the clearing. Katherine was on the ground now, and Past Zera held her and looked to Past Byrd for help. Now she realized the look in Katherine's eyes wasn't fear of death, or even the pain. It was the horror of seeing Byrd again, knowing he caught her. His face changed, and Zera no longer saw him as she knew him. How could she ever have believed he wanted to help?

She held her breath as they talked. Any second now, he would move away. She'd have mere moments before the Storm occurred, just long enough to see Katherine once more.

Past Byrd stalked off in the direction of his previous self—Edward—and for a split second, rage and protectiveness swelled behind Zera's sternum. She could sprint, tackle him, kill him in sweet revenge for Katherine. But when she looked at Katherine, she saw the minutes ticking away. Without a backward glance, she ran to her.

There was more blood than she remembered. Katherine's shirt and jeans and honey-colored braid were soaked and stained red. Past Zera lifted her head and startled when she met her own eyes.

"Don't freak out," Zera said, which was by far the worst thing to tell herself at that moment. She went to Katherine, ignoring the pressure pushing her away from her past self like the same side of two magnets.

"What the hell is going on?" Past Zera asked.

Present Zera ignored her. "I couldn't let you go, not like this," she said, taking Katherine's hands. "Not with someone who doesn't know you."

"Yet," Katherine said with a bloody smile. "Doesn't know me *yet*."

The pressure increased, and heat pushed from behind her.

"Can you feel it?" Katherine asked.

Zera did.

The Storm was starting.

Zera looked into her own eyes and saw the fear and the confusion. They weren't supposed to be able to change anything.

But what if she could?

Her past self took one step back, and with one grand motion of stupidity, her present self reached out and grabbed her wrist.

"Wait—"

The Storm hit. But this time, it was different.

Instead of an overwhelming wave pushing them into a fiery abyss, time stopped. Zera's stomach flew to her throat as the world dropped a few feet and landed in a hazy twilight. The colors of the aurora and the river mixed and mingled in the sky, waves pushing and swirling together like the surface of a bubble. Occasionally the colors rippled as if some great predator lurked above, biding its time until it dove and swallowed her whole.

Past Zera's eyes were still wide, but her face appeared frozen, lips parting around an unasked question. On the ground, Katherine gazed at Present Zera with the same affection as that very first meeting, her hand on Zera's wrist. Zera pulled away from both of them, and both their arms remained outstretched, Katherine's fingers folded as if she continued to hold her.

The sound of boots crunching in grass alerted her to a new presence. Past Byrd—the version she'd come here with on that first trip—stalked toward them.

Zera's heart stopped. He'd gone after Edward, and so had Kissi. Where was she? Had he done something to her?

"How could I not realize it was you?" Past Byrd's eyes blazed in the light of the sky. "All those years ago in New Orleans. I should've trusted my instinct when I saw you in the bunker."

"So what are you gonna do?" Zera asked. "Kill me now?"

"You? No, not you." He sneered. "You were simply a means to an end."

He walked toward her, but his attention was no longer on her. Katherine lay beside her, breathing and bleeding in slow motion, taking a hundred years to blink. The bubble must've sent everything into a stasis, giving Zera the one thing she needed more than anything: time.

She stood and squared herself to Past Byrd, knife at her side. "I won't let you kill her."

"She left me. They all left me." Past Byrd raised his pistol. "Do you know what it's like to lie in the snow and wait for death to come while the universe tears you apart?"

"Cold, I'd imagine—"

The pistol fired and Zera instinctively shut her eyes, waiting for the sensation of a bullet tearing through her flesh. But it never came. She opened one eye, then both. In the dim twilight, it was hard to spot the bullet at first. It moved faster than Katherine's eyelids, but not by much, crawling in the air toward her. Past Byrd stopped and watched its progression, and when it came within arm's reach, Zera simply reached out and pushed it to the side.

"The old-fashioned way, then."

Past Byrd broke into a sprint, barreling toward her like a ram. Zera knew she was no match for him at that speed, but she didn't have to stop him—she just had to keep him away from Katherine.

In their sparring, he used his height to his advantage, and this time Zera used it to hers. She ran forward, lower than him, easily ducking under his reaching arms to slam her shoulder into his abdomen. Their momentum shifted and she wrapped her arms and legs around him, sending them both tumbling to the ground. She used the inertia to continue their roll and move them as far away from Katherine as possible.

"Dammit!" Past Byrd stopped their roll and kicked her away. Thanks to their close proximity the blow didn't hurt like it should, but Zera felt a rib bend under the pressure.

Past Byrd scrambled to his feet. Zera pushed herself to her knees and dove, grabbing his ankles and sending him to the ground once more. "I won't let you kill her!"

He flipped onto his back and lifted his leg again, but Zera was ready this time. She shifted, and his foot flew past her, giving her the perfect opportunity to reach out and punch him in the crotch.

She'd never beat him in a fight before, but that was only because she'd been playing fair.

Past Byrd howled. Zera thought she'd won until his face shifted to one of white-hot rage. This time, he tackled her hard enough to slam her head into the ground. In between the stars she saw him raise a fist, and she couldn't put her hands up fast enough to block the blow to her temple.

For a brief moment, Zera thought her head had exploded, her brains all over the ground. Then her vision cleared. Something shined in the grass.

Her knife.

Past Byrd stood, stooped over from the pain in his groin. As he took a step toward Katherine, Zera reached out and grabbed the knife by the blade. Her vision swam and her stomach threatened to empty itself, but she swallowed the discomfort, took a steadying breath, and charged.

Her target was his back, in the soft space between his ribs and his hips. She missed, unable to keep her feet underneath her, but with a satisfying *thump* the blade sank into the back of his thigh.

Past Byrd shouted and pulled the knife from his leg. He turned, spotted her, lunged. Zera dodged just enough to avoid the killing blow, earning a slash to her ribs instead of a stab to her heart. Past Byrd tried again, and this time her forearms got the gash. If she wasn't careful, she'd die from a thousand cuts.

Vertigo made her stumble. Past Byrd, not anticipating the sudden movement, missed his target by a wide margin. Zera clamped onto his arm with both hands and twisted. His shoulder joint ripped apart with a deep pop and a squelch.

Good thing Past Byrd was busy screaming, because between the noise and the dizziness, Zera succumbed to the nausea rolling through her stomach. She had very little to give, but she left it all in the grass.

"I swear to God," Past Byrd growled, stalking toward her. He was limping from the stab wound, and his arm hung at a terrible angle, but he didn't slow.

There, on the ground between them, was her knife.

Past Byrd had a longer reach, but Zera was faster, and she launched herself onto the knife and covered it with her body. A boot connected with her ribs, but she didn't move. There were a few more cuts on her hand by the time she found the handle. She ignored them.

A wild swing with the knife connected with Past Byrd's standing leg. He dropped, and Zera climbed over him, slashing wildly. He struggled beneath her, but she sank her knees into his forearms.

"You lost, Byrd."

He stopped struggling, though his labored breathing continued.

Zera gritted her teeth. "This is for Katherine."

She raised her knife up, but as she did, Past Byrd went still. Oddly still, as if he were already dead.

Or, as if he were going into the same stasis as Katherine and Past Zera.

The blue-green sky reflected on the whites of his eyes, his gaze somewhere Zera couldn't see. She turned quickly to Katherine, her hand still in the process of falling from where Zera had dropped it. Alive then, at least for now.

Light sputtered in the middle of the field, arms and legs and organs flying in and out of the hole ripping through time and space. Byrd—the most current version, the one she thought she'd escaped on the platform—was here.

Zera should've felt fear, or maybe anger. But she was tired and beaten and didn't know how she was going to rally for another fight, especially against a fresh opponent.

She looked at Katherine again.

It was time to find her strength.

Ignoring the pain lancing through her body, Zera pushed herself up and limped toward the newest Byrd.

He spotted her, and once again sent her that same old glare. "How could I not—"

"Realize it was me?" Zera interrupted. "Yeah, yeah, yeah, we already had this conversation."

"Oh, we did, hmm?" He looked so smug Zera had to resist rolling her eyes. "You don't know the half of it, Zazzera."

"Your friends and your wife left you to freeze to death, so you've been hunting Katherine and the rest of them. I've got the gist," Zera said, gesturing her knife in a circle. The movement stretched the cut across her forearm and made it sting anew.

"You won't stop me from killing her this time," Byrd said, pulling out the same damn pistol.

Zera stopped and put her arms out. "Oh no, please no, not the gun." It wasn't a given the bullet would do the same thing twice, but she was willing to bet her life on it.

Byrd pulled the trigger, and once again the bullet fired in slow motion. His eyes grew wide as he tracked the progress and completely missed Zera picking up steam.

"The—"

"Old-fashioned way, I know!"

Zera slammed her shoulder into him, ignoring the blossom of pain through her neck and head. If she lived through this, she would have one hell of a concussion. Her first fight was all fear and instinct, but now she knew she could beat him if she was smart enough and held onto her weapon.

Unfortunately, Byrd the Third brought a knife with him this time and unsheathed it with a maniacal grin. Zera wondered how many people he'd killed, and how easily they'd gone.

Well, she wouldn't go down without a fight. Or two.

Between her concussion and his still-healing ankle, the fight was unsteady. Byrd was still the superior fighter, but she knew his tricks now, where he would feint and where he would strike. He was angry enough for his slashes to be fast, but his injured ankle made his strikes miss their mark. It was good for Zera, because she could dodge with only a few more cuts to add to the collection.

Her endurance waned. Her head throbbed, her stomach rolled, and every muscle screamed. Byrd pushed and herded her, and she didn't realize what he was doing until they were close to his past self, her past self, and Katherine.

"Ha!" Byrd leaped toward Katherine, but Zera grabbed his shirt and flung him back. Her knife, once again, went tumbling away, but her past self had a gun, which would make a fine blunt object.

Byrd rose, and Zera scrambled up just enough to send her boot into his chest. He flailed back, and she took the opportunity to jump for the gun in her past self's hand.

The world shifted, exploded, and dropped once again.

2004

ZERA'S HEAD SWAM, the stars in her eyes bigger and brighter than ever before.

No, they weren't stars. They were fireworks.

The sky continued to boil in greens and purples and blues, but closer to earth, fireworks sparkled halfway through their burn, each flicker lasting well over a minute as time stretched and pulled and folded. At the edge of their quiet bubble, Kissi stood in mid-strike, the oldest Edward Byrd clutching his shoulder and unaware of the danger behind him.

"Where the hell are we?" Byrd gasped. He still wasn't taking the travel well, which Zera needed to use to her advantage. With all her injuries, her own travel sickness was negligible.

"New Orleans," Zera said. Behind her, Katherine lay nearly motionless, and Zera's past self stayed bent over her. Past Byrd remained frozen on the ground next to her current adversary.

"How the fuck did you do that?" he asked.

"Hell if I know. Doesn't really change anything, does it?"

Outside their bubble, shadows moved and paced. In the distance, she spotted the ghost of a float looming over everyone.

"Huh," Byrd said, his eyes flicking between Zera and the two women behind her. It seemed like making contact with her old self sent them back to a prior storm, but everything stayed slow, lethargic, crawling through time.

"It's not too late." Maybe, after all this, Zera could reason with him. "You grabbed an anchor syringe, right? Just head back and leave us here. We'll die in 2040 anyway."

Byrd leaned to one side, taking the pressure off his injured ankle. Though his grip relaxed, he still held his knife. "Could you let go, Zera? After a hundred and seventy years, could you just cut your losses?"

"You've killed everyone else—"

"Everyone except the one person who matters," he said through gritted teeth. "We took a vow: *till death do us part*. And she decided to tap out early."

"She didn't know—"

"This has nothing to do with you. You helped me get back here, which is all I needed. And now, you wanna stand in my way? Face it, Zera. You can't beat me."

"I did earlier." She jerked her thumb at Past Byrd, still lying on the ground. "So much for telegraphing my moves, huh? You're not gonna get me this time."

"Always so damn quippy." His gaze slid from her and landed on Katherine and Past Zera. "But maybe you aren't the one I have to kill."

His meaning hit her brain a second after he moved. He wasn't aiming for her anymore, but her inanimate past self, locked in the time loop. There wasn't time to stand, and she had no knife to throw, so Zera instead rolled into his knees as he tried to run past.

They hit the ground in a tangle of limbs. She grasped any bit of him she could, tearing him away from her past self. A stray elbow caught her in the nose and his shirt slipped from her fingers. In a last ditch effort, she clamped her legs around his ankle. It was the weak one, and he fell with a disproportionate cry of pain.

Hot blood trickled down her chin. Half-blind, she grabbed the waistband of his pants and hauled him backward with a roll, away from her helpless past self. Debris from the parade crunched beneath them as they wrestled, the cool concrete grating on every cut and bruise. Byrd landed facedown on the pavement, and Zera saw the hilt of a knife in his boot.

She grabbed it and clambered over him, making sure to send her knee into the middle of his back.

If he wanted to kill her past self, she'd kill his first. And if she killed the past version of him, the present version would no longer exist to menace her.

Byrd caught onto her plan and grabbed at her legs as she crawled toward his past body. She reached for it, but his hands closed around her ankles, holding fast no matter how she kicked and twisted. He pulled, the asphalt biting into her as Past Byrd moved further and further away.

His nails dug into her arms as he flipped her onto her back. He cocked his arm back with record speed, and she barely managed to move her head out of the way as he punched. The crack of his fingers echoed loudly in her ears, only drowned out by his screech of pain. He leaned back, holding his injured hand, and Zera took her opportunity to grab his shirt, pull him forward, then flip him over her head with a shove from her legs.

Byrd landed on his past self. Time once again took a bite.

1992

Time chewed them up and spat them back out.

Zera coughed, and her empty stomach heaved. It was one thing to take a single trip through the river, but she'd never taken so many in such a short time. She thought she was tougher than Byrd, but considering it took a few minutes before she knew for sure her arms and legs were still attached, perhaps she could be a little more humble.

Through the swirl of the time pocket, she could see the skyline and the car headlights moving so slow they appeared stationary. Dry grass crunched beneath her as she rolled to her side and saw one of the holes in the ground from her trip to Dallas. A small but notable difference from before her arrival.

So, things *could* change.

"Jesus, Odin, and Zeus," she muttered, heaving herself to her feet. Darkness sat at the corners of her vision, the rest of the world blurry as she swayed. Might as well be on a boat for how much the world rocked. Byrd lay gasping on the dirt, pale and gleaming in sweat. Even with her current struggles, she could see his knuckles swelling from their meeting with the concrete.

"That was all you," she said.

He didn't move, barely even breathed. His knife sat half buried in the grass between them, the handle pointing toward her and the blade submerged. Perhaps he didn't see it. Perhaps she hadn't lost her chance.

A crack from behind her stole her attention. Turning her head quickly was a mistake, and when her eyes caught up and settled, she spotted her past self and Katherine. Katherine's arm was nearly on the ground now, her eyes closed. Strange blue lightning crackled across the side of the bubble again, turning both Past Zera and Katherine ghastly shades of white.

"No, no, no." Zera scrambled over to them and knelt by Katherine's side. It was impossible to tell if she was still breathing, and Zera was afraid to touch her, lest they get sent to some other random time. "Kat? Kat, c'mon now."

She held her breath and scanned Katherine's body for any sign of life. Behind her, Byrd groaned, and when she glanced over, he had one leg bent up. Zera cursed herself for not acting sooner. Taking care of Katherine was important, but to do that she needed to keep her head on straight and take any opportunity given to her.

Standing was torture. Her muscles and joints screamed at every movement, and her head swam as blood failed to fight gravity back to her brain. If she focused just enough, she could still see him.

"I'm gonna enjoy killing you," Byrd gasped. He'd only managed to rise to one knee, but his ragged breathing was starting to even out. If she didn't act now, she'd be a goner.

With three short steps, she reached the knife. She picked it up and half ran, half fell toward Byrd's face. His head stayed half bowed, eyes downcast. It was the best shot she would get.

She swung the knife at his throat. His hand shot up and blocked it before she could make contact.

"Nope, still telegraphing your moves."

Zera slammed her left fist into his face.

Byrd's head snapped back, blood spurting from his nose. Pain wracked Zera's hand and she could feel the joints swelling, but the satisfaction kept her from completely giving in. She wrenched her wrist from his grasp and leapt toward his past body, still frozen in stasis.

Byrd righted himself as she lifted the knife over the body. He was too far to grab her this time, unable to stop her from driving the blade home.

But he was well within reach of his past self.

As Zera drove the knife down, Byrd grabbed his past self's leg.

"Fu—"

The river reclaimed them.

Everything was warm and light. A breeze flitted over Zera's face, soothing her hot cheeks. Was this heaven? It felt like it. Was she dead? At this point, she wouldn't even be mad.

"You can't give up yet."

She looked up to see Kissi sitting next to her.

Zera squeezed her eyes shut. When she opened them, Kissi was still present.

"Is this real?" Zera asked.

"You tell me." It was a terribly Kissi-like thing to say.

"Fuck."

Zera took a moment to soak in this peace, then accepted her lot and willed herself to wake up.

She was back in that damn parking lot in Chicago. Garbage and city stench wafted around her, the hot asphalt aerosolizing it. To her left, Byrd sprawled across the hood of a silver car. His past self lay twisted on the ground next to him.

Where was Kissi? Where was Katherine?

It was getting more and more difficult to stand, but Zera forced herself up and took a few stumbling steps toward Katherine's last known location. Leather boots stuck out from behind a truck; Zera hoped she'd landed softly. On the opposite side, Kissi moved in slow motion, only a few inches past where she was last time Zera checked.

Byrd coughed and retched, his vomit landing on his past self. Gross.

"Stop doing that!" Zera snapped.

"You started it!" he shot back.

Each transition cost more and more. Zera's hands shook, and it felt like ants crawled through the vessels of her extremities. Her legs gave out and she landed hard on her knees, the concrete biting through a tear in her pants. How many trips did Martin say she could survive?

"You can't win this, Zera," Byrd said. Blood dripped from his nose at a steady pace, both from Zera's hit and from the time travel.

"Remember that time you called me a stubborn ass?" she said. "Still applies."

"That was just empty flirting."

"There were a lot of empty conversations with you, but I think that one might have been pretty truthful."

Zera pushed back up. The handle of the knife was slick in her hand, and she took a second to wipe it on her pants. She didn't know if it was blood or sweat, and she didn't care to look and find out.

"Are you done stalling now?" she asked. She had little in her tank to pay the toll for the time travel, but she had more than him. Byrd's skin somehow paled further, the green light making the blue of his veins more prominent. Maybe she couldn't beat him, but she could outlast him.

"What's the rush? We have all the time we need," he said. "All the time in the world."

"Not all of us."

She meant herself, but his eyes darted to Katherine. The grin that spread across his face made Zera's blood boil so furiously she was afraid her head might explode.

"You're right," he said. "Not all of us."

He moved first, stumbling a few steps before his strides evened out. Zera responded too slowly, her feet dragging through mud. Fear struck her as he approached her past self and Katherine, both in nearly the same position as when they started this dance. He was too fast, too close. She wouldn't be able to catch him in time.

Byrd jumped over Katherine and tackled Zera's past self.

Pain bloomed in her chest, a dull ache of a still-healing injury. Zera gasped and laid a hand on her sternum, her stomach rolling as she felt ridges on the bone that weren't there previously.

It was definitive proof. Dr. Phillips was wrong. They *could* change things.

Zera took a breath. Byrd had no weapons—instead, his hands wrapped around Past Zera's neck. How long would it take to suffocate someone stuck in a time pocket? Zera didn't want to find out. And she didn't want to wait for him to think about breaking her neck.

And so, to beat him at his own game, she ran—despite the pain in her chest—and grabbed onto her past self's hand. She braced for impact, and through the rushing in her ears and the scream of the river she heard Byrd howl with rage and pain and everything in between.

ZERA HAD the distinct sensation her unconsciousness lasted a lot longer this time around, and she wasn't even compensated with a lovely dream. Her only consolation was Byrd's unconscious form when she woke up.

Flowers surrounded them. Even beyond the wall of their little time pocket, the shadow blooms waved in the slight breeze of Philadelphia. It smelled exactly like Zera remembered it, though now the sweetness of the botanical gardens nauseated her.

Her gun lay on the ground, discarded after Byrd's tackle.

It took a few tries to grab hold of the barrel, but despite her blurred double vision, Zera managed.

Byrd was awake now, dry heaving on hands and knees. For once, a stationary target.

She took one big step and swung. The gun fell from her hand as it struck his skull with a sharp crack. Both of them fell to the ground, dazed, but Zera got up faster.

"You don't wanna do this," Byrd slurred.

Zera flipped the knife handle to a different grip and limped toward the inert form on the ground. "You're right," she said. She'd never killed anybody before. In fact, she'd spent her whole life trying to help people survive. "But I'll get over it."

"Killing someone changes you!"

"Clearly!" She knew he was stalling, but her footsteps never faltered. Killing him now meant saving Katherine, possibly saving everyone. Already she stalled the 2040 Storm—could she stop it completely?

She stood over Past Byrd's body. In her periphery, Byrd rolled onto his hands and knees again. It was time; the fight had gone on long enough. She raised the knife.

"I'll kill her too."

Zera stopped. Byrd was still on his knees, but he was next to Katherine now, his hands over her. Katherine's hand moved, just barely, as if she were trying to reach up and stop him.

"Don't." Zera meant it as a threat, but it came out as a plea.

"I'm closer to her than you are to me," he said. "One move, and I snap her neck."

Tears pricked the back of Zera's eyes. She was tired, so tired of fighting him, of doing everything she could only to have Katherine torn from her anyway. Perhaps that was how it was supposed to be: sacrificing someone dear to save the world. Fate had her losing from the start.

She was not ashamed to cry. It hurt to have all the dreams, all the might-have-beens, ripped away after all she'd been through. Katherine, her beautiful Katherine, who was so strong and had saved herself over and over for decades, now at the mercy of her hunter.

"I'm sorry," she whispered, and picked up the knife again.

Byrd grabbed Katherine's head, but instead of snapping her neck, he threw them into chaos once more.

1884

ZERA DROPPED INTO SNOW.

The time pocket did nothing to protect her from the biting cold. Though it slowed the wind to a manageable level, every step sent icy projectiles into her skin as she waded through the drift. It was too dark, and the snow was too thick; she couldn't find any version of Byrd, or herself, or Kissi. Most importantly, she couldn't find Katherine.

She trudged through the snow in what she hoped was the right direction. As she neared the end of the time bubble, her heart climbed into her throat. Two depressions in the snow appeared, and Zera rushed as fast as she could in the knee-high piles. Sure enough, she found her past self and Katherine, unmoving for all intents and purposes. Snowflakes caught on their skin and hair one at a time, the bubble continuing to slow everything down. They were right at the edge, so close to being thrown out. What would happen if they went past the boundaries?

She collapsed, the cold sucking all her energy from her. This close to the perimeter, she could see every swirl and sparkle of color, as if the bubble was made of aurora and starlight. Without thinking, Zera reached up, aiming to touch the wall. Luckily, she was distracted by movement just past her hand. Outside the bubble, seven dark shapes trudged through the snow. Time had thrown them back to 1884 it seemed, and these people had to be the explorers. Who else could it be? Her heart ached as she realized one shape was a young Katherine, believing herself newly widowed, with no idea the length of life ahead of her. Behind her, a dying Edward plotted his revenge.

"This is where it all started," Zera murmured.

She snapped her head toward movement in the snow. Byrd stood, stumbled, and fell into the powder again. The part of him she could see struggling over the snow looked haggard and sick. If she was honest, she wasn't sure she could stand much longer either.

She scanned the area, ignoring Byrd as he continued to fight his way to his feet. At the complete opposite side of the bubble, she spotted two shapes interrupting the light of the aurora. Those had to be Kissi and Edward, the very first version, the one who started it all. In a normal environment, it would be easy to get to him. But in this snow, Zera thought she might die before she made it.

That left Past Byrd, the one who shot Katherine. The one who had been there at the epicenter when the last Storm hit.

It hurt to curl her fingers around the knife handle, but her arms felt steady. With the landmarks, she knew exactly where she would find Past Byrd. In the back of her mind, she wondered if she would lose Katherine anyway, if killing Past Byrd would set off a chain of events destroying everything she'd worked for. After all, if Dr. Phillips' rules were wrong, then this unprecedented change was truly the worst kind of experiment.

In killing Past Byrd, would she doom Katherine? Herself? The entire world? Or would she save it?

There was only one way to find out.

As if he read her thoughts, Byrd—the most current version—forced himself up and barreled toward her. She tried to dodge, but the snow weighed her down, and she went tumbling down just as he reached her. It was a mad scramble from there, and too late Zera realized her escape cut a clear path for Byrd to follow. His hands grasped her shirt and he pulled her down, drowning them both in cold.

"Fuck off!" Zera did her best to kick and slash, but she was quickly losing feeling in her hands and feet. How long did it take for frostbite to set in? She didn't want to know.

Byrd had no reply for her besides a rasping growl as he climbed over her and grabbed her knife hand. Zera tried to wrestle it from his grasp, but he was stronger, and soon he had her hand flipped so the blade pointed toward her own gut. She struggled more, fighting back, watching as the tip of the blade inched closer and closer. But his fingers were just as frozen, and he lost his grip with one hand.

Zera took the opening and grabbed her own wrist as he struggled to regain his hold. As he pawed at her weapon, a jagged slash appeared across his palm. He howled and let go as blood splattered across Zera's hand and forearm, making her hold on the knife even more tenuous.

With Byrd distracted, she was able to slam her knee into his midsection. She missed the most sensitive part of him, but his air left him in a rush and he seized. It was easy to topple him over, despite her numb limbs and slick fingers. Once she scrambled to her feet, she kicked him in the stomach again. Trying to kill him was too much of a risk, as evidenced by her close call moments ago. Her best bet was Past Byrd, lying in a quickly disappearing hole in the snow fifteen feet away.

Adrenaline fueled Zera as she waded toward him, swinging her arms back so Byrd had to fight through at least *some* snow as he followed. Past Byrd was ten feet away now. Five.

"No!"

Zera fell into the opening around Past Byrd and straddled his frozen body. Fifteen feet back, Byrd leaned on one knee, his skin pale and green in the light of the aurora.

"Don't do it," he said. "We don't know what could happen."

"You're bullshitting me," Zera replied, denying she'd had the same thought.

"You can't save them. It's too late." He gestured at the shadows beyond the boundary, at his future victims fighting their way back home.

"I couldn't save them, you're right." Zera flipped her knife so her grip was solid. "But I can still save Katherine."

"No!"

Byrd's voice came too late, and the wind carried it far away. Zera's muscle and skin and bones ached as she raised the knife and plunged it into Past Byrd's chest. The tip of the blade slipped off his ribs but found the space between and sunk to the hilt, her aim true enough.

Byrd screamed, the sound as short and bright as a firework as he faded from existence.

The world exploded again, this time in reds and yellows and fiery oranges, but Zera felt no heat, nor cold, nor anything really. Not even victory.

Either unconsciousness or the river swallowed her whole; all she knew was she could finally rest.

2040

ZERA TRIED TO MOVE, but her entire body hurt. It was reminiscent of her first return back to 2058, only somehow so much worse.

So, she was probably alive then. Surely Heaven or Hades or Valhalla wouldn't have so much incessant beeping.

She squeezed her eyes shut for a second, preparing herself. If she saw herself back in the bunker, she would probably cry. The thought alone cost more energy than she had available.

Resigning herself to her fate, she opened one eye. She was in a hospital bed, but she'd guessed that from the beginning. The room was big, at least compared to the spot she frequented in the bunker. Large windows let sunshine in—a sun that wasn't burning the entire world to a crisp.

"Holy shit," she breathed. "Holy *shit*."

Then, she laughed.

It hurt a lot. The healing fracture in her sternum reminded her of the fight, and her throat was still raw from the cold exposure, but the incredulity dulled the pain. Pain meds also helped, she was sure. She was here, she was alive, and the world hadn't collapsed into fire and ash.

"Are you okay?"

A nurse popped into her room. She wore blue scrubs and had her straight, blonde hair pulled into a ponytail in a way that definitely wasn't bunker regulation.

Zera swallowed her laughter and nodded. "Great, I'm fucking great," she said.

The nurse sighed. "Excellent. Well, my name is Elizabeth, I'm your nurse. Can you tell me your full name?"

"Noelle. Noelle Zazzera."

The nurse wrote *Noelle* on the dry erase board next to the door. "And do you know where you are, Noelle?"

Zera looked out the window again. Familiar buildings stretched above busy roads and foot traffic congested the sidewalk. It had been over eighteen years, but she'd still recognize home anywhere.

"New York City," she said. Tears formed, and she couldn't blink them away.

"That's right," Elizabeth went on, politely ignoring the emotion. "And do you know today's date?"

Zera inhaled. "September 26, 2040?"

"Close," she said with a sad smile. "That's when we found you. It's the twenty-eighth now."

Zera put her hand over her mouth as the tears increased. The Storm hadn't passed—it had never happened. She'd done it. After everything, she'd done it.

"The..." She took a deep breath, steadied herself. "The women with me. Are they okay?"

Elizabeth's brows furrowed. "Yes, they're both here, and they're okay. Are they your friends?"

Zera thought of Kissi, who'd been with her through the worst of the world, and Katherine, who'd opened life back up for her again. "Yes, my best friends," she said.

"And the man. Is he the one who attacked you?"

Zera's blood went cold. "Yeah, he is. Did he...is he alive?"

"No, he was gone by the time paramedics got to you." Elizabeth pulled a phone from one of her many pockets and texted someone. "Police want some answers, though. Would you be up to speaking to an officer and giving a statement?"

"What?" Zera asked. "I mean...Why?"

"I've been told it's protocol," she said. "I'm afraid I don't have any more information than that. But can I tell the officers you're awake and have them come down after you eat?"

"Can I see my friends?"

A muscle above Elizabeth's left eye twitched. "Yes, I can take you to your friends. But I really need an answer on the police thing."

"Oh, right, sorry." Zera shook her head to clear the cobwebs. Mistake. "Yeah, absolutely, I'll answer whatever questions they've got first."

Saying she wanted to move and actually moving were two very different concepts. Pain shot through every part of her. More lacerations covered her arms and legs than she originally estimated, but most of them were covered. Only a few required stitches, but those hurt like a bitch every time she stretched them.

After a brief conversation with police—yes, that man attacked them, no, she didn't know him, yes, all the injuries were from him—Elizabeth procured a wheelchair and helped Zera into it. After a fight spanning over a century and six different climates, Zera's body was confused, tired, and beat up. But the idea of seeing Kissi and Katherine kept her going.

The nurse took her down the hall, but gave no indication to whom they were seeing first. Zera held her breath when she stopped and knocked at the door.

"Hey, you have a visitor," Elizabeth said softly. "Up for it?"

At the affirmative, Zera pushed her wheelchair into the room. Kissi sat in a recliner next to her bed, a newspaper open on the tray table.

"Hey there sunshine," she said with a smile. "Guess you finally decided to wake up, huh?"

"A girl needed a break," Zera replied. Elizabeth helped park the chair next to Kissi, then left with a conspiratorial wink.

"You holding up okay? They wouldn't tell me much, something about privacy laws," Kissi said. "I guess bunker life meant I got a little more information."

"Not always through the proper channels," Zera said. "But yeah, I'm okay. Sore, beat up, for sure. But I think I'll live."

"What happened after it all went dark?"

Zera could tell Kissi had been waiting eagerly to ask this, and so recounted the entire fight as best she could, with every version of Byrd and every year they landed in. When she finished, Kissi smiled widely.

"Perfect. Do you want to hear my hypothesis?"

Zera paused, and Kissi laughed at her expression.

"What?" Kissi said. "I've been awake for two days while you were wasting time sleeping. I think I figured it out, and you just gave me the last piece."

Zera took a deep breath and gathered herself.

"Lay it on me."

Kissi flipped the newspaper around until she found enough blank space. With a pencil, she wrote K, Z, B, another K, and E, all in relative proximity.

"After he shot Katherine, Byrd came back over to where I was. It was so gross, the way he was gloating and shit. And since he already lived through this moment, he knew exactly where and when all these players would be in this spot." She tapped for emphasis.

Zera thought back weeks prior, to an odd conversation in a hallway. "I should've seen it. He was always so desperate to go back."

"Told you he was a weirdo. Even went to give himself a congratulatory handshake. But based on what happened every time you made contact with your past self..."

Realization dawned. "Byrd—our Byrd—set it all off," Zera said.

"Exactly." Kissi said. "I've been watching a lot of movies. I think the term *paradox* best describes what happened. Basically, a closed loop went out of control."

The information swirled in Zera's mind, and slowly the picture formed. "Like when two mirrors face each other, and it looks infinite."

"Yep. And the space-time continuum didn't like it. But since you *also* made a paradox happen, it kept the first-trip Byrd from making contact with his even-further-past self."

"And if he never made that contact with his past self?" Now Zera was smiling too.

"Then there was nothing to cause the Storm in the first place."

Kissi looked supremely satisfied with herself, and Zera had to agree. The elation she should've felt back in 2058 hit then. They'd fixed it all, and could now live a normal life, in a normal world. No more digging, or bunkers, or time traveling.

"But wait," Zera said. "If the Storm never happened, then how come we're all still here?"

Kissi chewed her pencil. "That one I can't quite figure out. It might be that we splintered away from a different timeline, and with no tether, can't go back. Or maybe it's just the space-time continuum giving us a win, since we fixed everything."

It was surreal, if Zera was honest. Their relationship was the same way it had always been, but now they weren't together by forced proximity in the bunker. If they wanted, they could part ways and never speak again.

Kissi grabbed Zera's hand, as if hearing her thoughts. No, they weren't separating anytime soon.

Elizabeth came in some time later with water and pudding, the most luxurious thing Zera had eaten in ages. If the nurse thought their exaggerated enjoyment of the snack was over the top, she didn't show it. Instead, she left and returned with another cup just as they finished their first.

"How about your other friend? Do you want to see her?"

Zera's breath caught and she glanced at Kissi, who nodded.

"Yes, please." She unlocked the wheels of her wheelchair. "I'll be back."

"I'll be here," Kissi promised.

Zera never felt her heart beat so hard as that trip down the hallway. Katherine was on a different floor, so she got to stay anxious for the ride three levels up to another hallway that looked the exact same, but green instead of blue. The few open doors she passed housed people with stacks of machines and ventilators, and she worried what state Katherine was in if this was her floor.

The nurse repeated the same process at the room door and received the same answer. Zera found herself awkwardly running her hands through her hair and discovering it a greasy, tangled mess. She wished she'd showered before leaving her room.

While Katherine did have a bunch of machines connected to her, she was alive, conscious, and breathing of her own accord. Bandages poked out the neckline of her hospital gown and formed bumps underneath it, marking the spots of her bullet wounds. There were bags under her eyes and her skin was pale, but it only made those honey eyes stand out more as she took Zera in.

"Miss Zazzera." Her voice was soft, but whether it was from pain or affection, Zera couldn't tell. "You've finally deemed me important enough for a visit, hmm?"

"Sorry, slept through my alarm," she said. Her pulse was so erratic, like she was a teenager again, as if she hadn't seen this woman naked a few days prior—in her view, at least.

"Well, better late than never, I suppose," Katherine said. Her mouth curled into a rueful smile, and she laid a hand on her bed. "Come here. I'm a bit tied down at the moment."

Elizabeth moved her closer, then made a graceful exit. Zera took Katherine's hand and smiled at how warm it was.

"You alright, Kat?" she asked.

"I believe I am, Noe," she said. "Thank you. For saving me."

Zera sighed. "You have no idea."

"Tell me then."

"You'll think I'm crazy."

"I've met you every twelve years since 1944. I believe we're past the point of crazy."

Zera took her hand and told her the whole story. It hurt her throat and her heart to think about it, but Katherine was one of two people in the entire world she could tell. And after all that time running from Byrd, Katherine deserved to know.

"Really?" she asked when Zera was finished. "That was the day the world burned?"

"It was supposed to be." Zera shrugged. "But uh, I guess we fixed it."

Katherine smiled. "I knew we would."

"And you? How do you feel?"

Katherine frowned. "Perhaps this is the drugs talking, but I feel different. Life feels more real, somehow."

"It's 'cause I'm here."

"You're not wrong." Katherine rubbed her thumb over Zera's knuckles. "I was scared I'd never see you again after you didn't show up in 2016. And again in 2028."

"It was touch and go there for a minute." Tears threatened again, and Katherine's eyes were glassy as well.

"Is that really how we first met? The very first time?"

Zera nodded. "Yeah. The first time I saw you, I watched you die." She paused, took a breath. "And after every mission, they kept reminding me that everyone I saw, everyone I met, was already dead. They told me I couldn't change the past, that I could only change the future."

"Well, they were wrong," Katherine said. "Only you would be stubborn enough to find that out."

"I don't know about stubborn," Zera said. "Desperate, maybe. Hopelessly..." She swallowed the feelings down. There was too much going on, too much that had happened in the past two days.

Katherine nodded, as though she too were holding back words they weren't ready to say.

"Thank you, for saving me in every which way," Katherine said.

"I couldn't have done it without your help." Zera took a shaky breath and wiped her tears. "You were as much a part of this as me and Kissi."

"Camila is a hell of a woman, that's for sure," Katherine said.

"Just promise you two won't gang up on me now."

"I shan't make a promise I can't keep."

Zera smiled, then looked down at their joined hands. "So you wanna try this? You and me? In a more...long-term way?"

"You're staying?" She sounded so hopeful it made Zera's chest ache for a reason besides injury.

"I'm staying. Can I stay with you?"

"Ah, darling, I've been waiting a century for you to ask me that," Katherine said.

Protocols and pain be damned, Zera pushed to her feet and pivoted to Katherine's bed. It was more of a crash landing than a smooth transition and ended with harsh winces from both of them, but then the giddiness of the day took over. Now, with no fear of being ripped away by a time travel machine, Zera leaned forward and pressed her lips to Katherine's. It was a gentle kiss, tender, like she was the most precious thing to her. Which, in the current state of the world, she was.

The machine measuring Katherine's heart rate beeped as it raised too much, and Zera gave her a self-satisfied smirk.

"I've still got it, hmm? Even after all these years?"

"Something tells me you'll have it for a long, long time Miss Zazzera," Katherine said.

The nurse came back multiple times to retrieve Zera, but they managed to talk a few more minutes out of her until it was time for shift change. The night nurse was not near as lenient, and marched Zera back to her room a few moments after clocking in. At least now Zera knew where Katherine was, and she was okay.

Everything, in fact, was okay.

———⟨○⟩———

It took a full week before the hospital released them. Kissi technically got out first, and after Zera delivered keys and directions, she spent what Zera imagined was an awkward few days living in Katherine's house by herself until the other two could join her.

Living in this world was so surreal to Zera that she forgot about simple things, like clothes and rent and work. Before, permanence didn't exist in her vocabulary, and she spent the hospital days sitting in Katherine's room and making plans. At first, her nurse was very upset about her wandering off, but once they figured out where she was going, the lectures were shorter, though just as often. Usually she could talk them into letting her stay, especially once Katherine flashed the ring Zera gave her in 2004, the one that would eventually be given back to Zera. It wasn't a real engagement ring, but it was some sort of promise that they would define later.

Once discharged from the hospital they took the subway to the Upper West Side. If Zera squinted, she could picture New York as it was back in 1944, when they first met for real. Most of the buildings were different, and the people were certainly different, but she could see the bones of the past, lingering like ghosts at every street corner.

The brownstone, however, was the same, at least on the outside.

"Holy shit, you got it back?"

"Bought it about ten years ago," Katherine said, unlocking the front door. "Felt right, to be back where it all started. For me, at least."

Flippers had renovated the inside over the years, but the layout was the same. The decorations, previously plain and proper, were now bright and colorful. Pictures adorned the walls, and Zera smiled as she spotted the one of them on the balcony from thirty-six years prior.

"How did you find this?"

"The internet is a beautiful thing," Katherine said.

Kissi came down the stairs, each one creaking in a different tone. She rubbed her eyes and yawned despite the late morning hour.

"Glad you two decided to show up, I was getting bored," she said. "Did you bring breakfast?"

"Feeling great, thanks. And Katherine's wounds are healing nicely." Zera said. "How are you?"

"Yeah, yeah, I'm fine." Kissi waved her off. "But to heal you need food, and I'm sorry Katherine, but a lot of your fresh stuff went bad."

"So inconvenient, getting shot on grocery day," Katherine said, shaking her head. She produced a phone from her pocket and started tapping away. "I'll get some essentials delivered. In the meantime, would you like some coffee?"

"Sure," Kissi said, at the same time Zera said, "Absolutely not."

Kissi gave her an odd look, but Katherine burst into laughter, holding her hands to her chest to stop the pain from her injury. "I've gotten better, I promise!"

"I sincerely doubt that. Trust me, Kissi, you don't want Katherine's coffee unless you have a death wish. Or, conversely, if you wanna be awake for three days straight."

"Oh, posh," Katherine said, going to the counter and pointing to a machine. "Look. Prepackaged coffee pods and an automatic machine. Even I can't mess it up, though I must confess even the bold setting is a little weak."

"Of course you think that." Zera slid into a chair at the dining table, not unlike all those years ago.

"So," Katherine said, bringing the coffee over. "What will you do now? I don't suppose you want to re-enlist, though I can help with that if you need it."

Zera looked at Kissi.

"College would be cool," Kissi said. "Kind of left all my qualifications back in 2058."

"Oh, those can be fabricated easily," Katherine said. She looked to Zera. "And you?"

"Uh, not sure," Zera said. "Never really had career goals before."

Katherine smiled. "Well, now you've got the time. Do you want to find your parents?"

Kissi and Zera both fell silent. Zera had thought about it a time or two while waiting in the hospital, how amazing it would be to see her mom again. But how could she explain everything, or expect her to welcome her grown daughter into her life when she had the younger version right there with her?

"Eventually," Zera said. "Once we get everything figured out."

"I agree," Kissi said. Zera wondered if she had the same concerns, or had thought of more things to worry about.

"Sounds like a plan," Katherine said. "A nice, long-term plan."

They spent the day taking it easy, and when night came, Kissi went to the guest room. Zera, not wanting to presume anything, made for the other guest room, but Katherine took her by the hand and asked her to stay. As they curled up together in the large bed, Zera made an effort to commit the moment to memory. This house, the woman next to her, the clean air and the open space—this was her life now. After everything, she was exactly where she wanted to be.

The full moon was bright, bright enough to speak over the lights of the city and demand attention. Her adventure had started with the full moon trying to burn her, but now it smiled upon Zera, and kept her company as she drifted into a cool, dreamless sleep, watching over her like a great celestial guardian. Zera thanked every god listening she could see it again in all its beauty.

And maybe the moon was a little grateful too.

2058

THE AFTERNOON SUN shone red and gold, but the breeze was cool as the first winds of fall graced the paths of Central Park.

"Noe, we're going to be late to meet Camila and Ezra," Katherine said, though she allowed Zera to drag her through the park. The light made the silver in her hair sparkle; her gray streaks were a badge of honor now, and Zera never wanted her to color them.

"We'll be fine. Kissi and Lieb know we're always thirty minutes late."

"*You* are always thirty minutes late. I was punctual until I married you."

"Well babe, you've had eighteen years to change me and yet we keep getting more and more tardy."

"There is no 'we' here."

"Of course there is."

They took a turn and Zera slowed, checking her memory. They hadn't been there since the fateful day, though the memories revisited them on their worst nights. There was more overgrowth in the clearing than before, but Zera easily stamped down the grass and laid down the picnic blanket and basket, an old-fashioned one like Katherine had a century ago.

"What's with the dramatics?" Katherine asked as she lowered herself to the ground.

Zera held up a finger and dug into the basket, producing champagne and glasses. "Because, my dear, today is our anniversary."

"Our anniversary is in June."

"Not our wedding anniversary," Zera said, pouring the champagne. "Not even our first date, or the first time we—"

"I get it, I get it."

"I was going to say 'kissed.'"

"Lies." Katherine accepted her glass. The sun melted away the laugh lines around her eyes. "So tell me then, which anniversary is today?"

"The anniversary of the first day we ever met," Zera said, tapping her glass against Katherine's. "According to my calendar, at least."

Katherine smiled. "You really remember the day?"

"It's not every day you time travel for the first time and meet the woman of your dreams. You're one in a trillion, Kat. Thank you for sticking with me all this time, and for sharing this life with me."

Katherine's eyes watered, and she leaned over to kiss her. When she pulled back, she laid her hand on Zera's cheek and caressed it with her thumb, those honey eyes gazing with all the adoration Zera missed the very first time she saw her.

"You are the single greatest thing to happen to me in my entire life," Katherine murmured.

"That's a long time," Zera said, because she had to ruin the moment just a little bit. "Are you sure?"

"Positive."

They kissed again and enjoyed the champagne and strawberries while the sun slowly set. They'd made many good memories, and were now rewriting a few of the bad ones.

Life, as they lived it, was good.

ACKNOWLEDGMENTS

To be honest, I can't believe we're here. Writing books has always been a dream of mine, ever since I was little and stapling together memo pad pages with stories about horses. And now, here she is, the fruit of all my labor. And honestly, it's everything I hoped for.

A special memoriam to my best friend Liz, who helped me learn how to take my writing seriously, and whom I spent years texting back and forth constantly, discussing our characters in AUs. Dude, you would've loved this.

To my husband Drew, who encouraged me and supported me in every way while writing this book. Thank you for asking questions, for closing the office door when the dogs got too rowdy, and for painting the best miniatures of Katherine and Zera. Without your love, I would never have been brave enough to do this.

To my sister in law Sarah, who always encourages me to be my most authentic self, and who screamed every chance possible about my cover art.

To Lauren and Ana, who sat up with me until 3am starting at a yarn wall figuring out all these timey wimey details. We don't need to admit how long those sticky notes stayed on the wall.

To my CP group who helped me in every step of the way. Thank you to KC Woodruff, PC Nottingham, Jaci M. Lunera, NC Scrimgeour (thank you for your brilliant editing!), Tiffany O'Haro, Matt Woodruff, Alex Bree, Alice Ayers, Loren Huxley, Maia Maile, and AJ Braun. Y'all are the reason this is an actual book instead of a hot mess, and I couldn't do it without you.

To my other friends Shouka Rohanizadeh, CJ Pearce, and Marina, who read earlier drafts and helped me iron out all the details. Y'all's hype and encouragement kept me going, and helped me believe that more people would like this book than just me.

To all my coworkers, who encouraged me to be brave and chase my passions outside of PT, even if bisexual sci-fi romance isn't what you're into.

To my therapist, who somehow tricked me into having enough self confidence to pursue this, and who helped me accept my most authentic self. You're super rude and I'm so lucky to have you.

To Jenifer Prince, the best and most encouraging cover artist in the business. Thank you for your patience and also for being the best.

To Tumblr user writing-prompt-s, who posted "A friendship between a time traveler and an immortal. Wherever the time traveler ends up, the immortal is there to catch him up to speed" back in 2017. They'll probably never read this, but thank you anyway.

And to you, dear reader. Thank you for getting this far, and for giving this indie author a chance. I hope you enjoyed the ride!

REVIEWS

If you enjoyed this book (or if you didn't), I would be forever grateful if you could leave a review on Storygraph, Goodreads, or Amazon! Besides shouting from the rooftops, this is the best and easiest way to help indie authors such as myself.

Thank you so much for reading!

ABOUT THE AUTHOR

Nico Vincenty is a science fiction and fantasy author from Texas. When she's not hanging out with her husband and dogs, she enjoys baking, playing Gaelic football, and spending countless hours with Link and Zelda in any iteration.

To keep up to date with Nico, feel free to follow her on social media, or sign up for her newsletter via her website.

For more information, visit https://nicovincenty.com or scan the QR code below.

Printed in the USA
CPSIA information can be obtained
at www.ICGtesting.com
CBHW021535230424
7406CB00004B/32